Thomas Fitch, Anna M Fitch

Better Days

Thomas Fitch, Anna M Fitch

Better Days

ISBN/EAN: 9783743373440

Manufactured in Europe, USA, Canada, Australia, Japa

Cover: Foto ©Andreas Hilbeck / pixelio.de

Manufactured and distributed by brebook publishing software (www.brebook.com)

Thomas Fitch, Anna M Fitch

Better Days

OR,

A Millionaire of To-morrow.

BY

THOMAS FITCH AND ANNA M. FITCH.

"Philosophy consists not
In airy schemes, or idle speculations;
The rule and conduct of all social life
Is her great province. Not in lonely cells
Obscure she lurks, but holds her heavenly light
To Senates and to Kings, to guide their counsels,
And teach them to reform and bless mankind."

SAN FRANCISCO, CAL.:
BETTER DAYS PUBLISHING CO.
1891.

TO THE

Eight Thousand Millionaires of America

THIS BOOK IS DEDICATED.

IF, THROUGH A PERUSAL OF ITS CONTENTS, ONE AMONG
THEM ALL SHALL BE LED TO SO DISPOSE OF A POR-
TION OF HIS FORTUNE AS TO HELP THE WAGE-
WORKERS OF OUR LAND TO HELP THEM-
SELVES, THEN THESE PAGES WILL
NOT HAVE BEEN WRIT-
TEN IN VAIN.

CHAPTER I.

"The earth trembled underneath their feet."

"CHICAGO," said Professor John Thornton, "Chicago, my dear doctor, is the typical American city. New York and San Francisco may be classed as metropolitan. Philadelphia, St. Louis, and New Orleans are local to their surroundings; Boston is—Boston, but Chicago is *sui generis*. Notwithstanding its large permanent foreign population, and the presence of the throngs of strangers attracted by the Columbian Exposition, Chicago remains intensely and distinctively an American city."

"I quite believe you, professor," said Dr. Eustace. "Certainly in all the world elsewhere there is no race track for locomotives, no place where iron horses are speeded, and purses of gold and diamond badges awarded to the winners."

"It is an innovation certainly, doctor, but just such an one as might have been expected in Chicago. The people of this city have not yet passed the *noblesse oblige* period. You know that in all large cities there is liable to come a time when the citizens divide into separate communities, usually with separate interests, and without any general public spirit. In New York, for instance, Madison Square takes no pride in the East River bridge; Avenue A does not care whether

the Grant monument shall ever be completed, and the
Statue of Liberty on Bedloe's Island is as strange to
many a resident of Harlem as if she were planted on
the banks of the Neva. But the people of Chicago,
though locally divided into Northsiders, and South-
siders, and Westsiders, are joined in interest for Chicago against the world. Any project that promises
glory or profit for the Lake City will cause her citizens
to open their pocket books. These Illinois Don
Quixotes never tire of sounding the praises of their
Dulcinea, and are ever ready to break a lance in her
honor."

"Is not this race," said Dr. Eustace, "under the
auspices of the National Exposition?"

"Not at all," replied the professor. "As I am informed, a party of speculators leased a thousand acres
of land here, ten miles from the city limits. They
have, as you see, inclosed it and provided it with the
usual buildings, including seats for one hundred thousand spectators. The race course is circular in form,
four miles in length, and seven railroad tracks are
laid around it. The officers of the leading railroad
corporations of the country readily consented to send
locomotives and engineers here to compete for the
prizes offered, and—you witness the result. This is
the third day of the races, and still the interest seems
undiminished."

It was late in the month of July, 1892, and although
the World's Exposition was not yet formally opened,
tens of thousands of strangers thronged the hotels of
Chicago and added to the gayety of her streets. The
great attraction of the day was the locomotive railroad

race, and about twenty acres of people, representing all nations, filled the benches and spread over the outer circle of the great four-mile track.

Seven of the largest locomotives in America, selected or constructed for this race, were steaming up and down the tracks, waiting for the signal to range themselves under a white cable, which was stretched diagonally across the race course at such an ang'e as to equalize the difference of length of inner and outer tracks. Each locomotive was draped with its distinguishing colors, worn also by its attendant engineer and fireman. The favorite engine in the pool rooms was the Chauncey M. Depew, entered by the New York Central Railroad Company.

The furnishings of this engine were of polished silver, with draperies of blue silk, and the engineer and fireman wore shirts and caps of the same color.

The engine which most attracted the admiration of the throng was the Collis P. Huntington, entered by the Southern Pacific Company. All the furnishings as well as the wheels of this locomotive were gilded and burnished for the occasion. The attendants wore shirts and caps of crimson, and the drapery consisted of ropes of crimson roses, the freshness of which, while coiled around smoke stack and boiler, was accounted for by the fact that they were cut from asbestos cloth made and tinted for the purpose.

The directors of the railroad corporations centering in Chicago had readily extended aid and co-operation to the company organized in that city for the construction and conduct of a locomotive race track, for it was conceded that no more instructive school for engineers and firemen could have been devised, and that there was no better field in which to make experiments in machinery, tests of fuel consumption, and economical creation and application of dynamic force.   Almost every railroad company in the United States and Canada entered one or more locomotives for the races, which were advertised for the last week of July, 1892, and, notwithstanding the large sums offered for premiums, and the great expense of building and maintaining the race course, the enterprise proved exceedingly profitable to its projectors.

Among the one hundred and fifty thousand spectators of the contest was Professor John Thornton, of Boston, who, ten years before, had been the hard-working principal of the Denver public schools, but who, through the death of an uncle, inherited a fortune of five millions of dollars, and was now one of the solid men and social magnates of the Hub.

During the years of poverty and struggle which antedated Professor Thornton's introduction to the ranks of wealth, he had grown to regard very rich men with aversion and contempt.   He was fond of quoting the aphorism that the Lord expressed his opinion of money by the kind of men he bestowed it upon, and he was stout in the belief that any man who, in this world of human misery, could make and keep five millions of dollars, was too selfish, if not too dishonest, for an associate.   He did not carry his opinions so far as to refuse the estate which fell to him, but he was exceedingly generous with his income, and he never ceased to criticise the millionaires.

Professor Thornton was generally regarded by his

friends as a Crœsus with the instincts of a Bohemian, a sort of gilded *sans-culotte*, with very radical opinions and a very conservative bank account.

The professor was accompanied to the race course by his family physician and old friend, Dr. Eustace. This gentleman, unlike the professor, was optimistic in his views of life. Pessimism, according to his belief, might be sometimes necessary for ballast, but as a rule he preferred to throw the sand and rocks overboard, and load up with the silks and spices of Cathay.

"What a country!" ejaculated the doctor, as, amid the cheers of the multitude, one of the locomotives dashed up the track to try her speed.

"It is a great country," said Professor Thornton, "but will its peace and prosperity endure?"

"Why not?" sententiously interposed Doctor Eustace.

"Are we," replied the professor, "so much wiser than the people of the republics which once encircled the Mediterranean, that we can afford to disregard the lesson imparted by their history?"

"Do you pretend to compare the ancient civilizations with ours?" queried the doctor.

"It may not be gainsaid," rejoined Thornton, "that our civilization is superior to that of the ancients in control and utilization of the forces of nature, and it is also true that in the relations of the individual to his government the former has gained in freedom and in security of personal rights. But otherwise we seem to be traveling the same round of national life from infancy to decay, which marked the course of Assyria, of Egypt, of Greece, and of Rome."

"But conditions were different with them," remonstrated the doctor. "Rome, even when a republic, was such only in name. There was never any basis of universal suffrage. The government of Rome was always a military despotism, and her prætorian guard sold the imperial purple, and rich men bought it, and she fell because of her corruption."

"And we have legislators and bosses who sell offices, and ambitious incapables who buy them," answered the professor. "And we are having now the same vast accumulations of fortune in individual hands that have ever proven the forerunners of national destruction elsewhere. Wealth, corruption, weakness, decay, the mob, and the despot have been the six stages of national life with other republics, and I doubt whether by harnessing steam and electricity to our chariot we shall do more than expedite the journey."

"Professor, you should go out as a missionary to millionaires," interposed the doctor, "and preach to them the doctrines of nationalism."

"Doctor, you are satirical," replied the professor, "but I am not so sure that events are not fast making missionaries of some such doctrine. Certainly the pressing problem of the hour is that of dealing wisely and justly with the new and unparalleled conditions which vast wealth has created throughout the world, and especially in these United States."

"We shall prove equal to the problem," said the doctor cheerfully. "A people who, North and South, were adequate to the achievements and sacrifices of our Civil War, will never allow their government to be overturned by a mob, or their politics to be always ruled by a few thousand wealth owners. And then the personnels of the pauper and the capitalist are ever changing. We have no law of entail by which the founder of a fortune can perpetuate it in his descendants. The vices and the brainlessness of the sons of rich men will come to our aid, and in the third or fourth generation the boatman's oar and the peddler's pack will be resumed. Let the millionaires add to their millions without molestation, say I. They cannot take their gold away with them. It must remain here, where it will again be distributed."

"Doctor," said the professor solemnly.

"Now, John," interrupted the doctor, laying his hand familiarly on his friend's shoulder, "possibly the country may be going to ruin, but we shall have time to see the race out. They are bringing the locomotives in line ready to start. If they should come out close together at the end, how are they going to tell which wins?"

"The judge of this race, doctor," explained the professor, "is electrical and automatic and cannot make a mistake. As soon as the engines are arranged in line for starting, a wire will be stretched across the track behind them. This wire will connect with a registering apparatus, dial, and clock in front of the grand stand, and each track is numbered. At the signal bell for starting, the clockwork will be put in motion. The first locomotive that crosses this wire will, in the act of crossing, telegraph the number of its track, close the circuit, and stop the clock, thus registering the number of minutes, seconds, and quarter seconds consumed in the run."

"How clever!" said the doctor. "Well, there sounds the signal bell—they are off!"

With a shrill shriek of challenge from their throats of steel, like unleashed hounds the giants bounded away, gaining speed as they ran. In thirty-eight seconds they rounded the curve by the half-mile post without much change in their relative positions   The next mile was made in fifty-five seconds, with the Chauncey M. Depew, which had the inside track, fifty yards ahead of the Collis P. Huntington, and the others all the way from fifty to one hundred yards behind.   At the third mile post the Huntington and the Depew rounded the curve almost side by side, with trails of fire streaming from their smoke stacks, and mingling in a luminous cloud, which hovered above their distanced competitors.

Then, with thunderous leaps and bounds, they came down the home stretch, the one a streak of blue and silver, the other a streak of gold and crimson, and the roar of the multitude fairly drowned the shrieking of the whistles as engineer James Flanagan, of the South-ern Pacific Company—his crimson cap gone, his black hair streaming in the wind, and his red flannel shirt open at the breast and almost blown from his massive white shoulders—rode across the signal wire five feet ahead of his competitor, winning the first prize of $10,000 for his company and the diamond badge for himself, making the run of four miles in three minutes nine and one-quarter seconds, or at a rate of over eighty miles an hour.

"It was nothing, sor," said Flanagan to the vice president of the Southern Pacific Company, who climbed upon the cab of the locomotive to shake hands with his engineer . "If it wasn't for the time lost in getting under way I'd engage to sind the Collis P. around the four-mile track in two minutes and a half. Sure, the machine was never built that could catch her on a straight run. She's a dandy and a darlin' and a glory to old California," and he patted the throttle valve affectionately.

"Flanagan," said Vice President Crocker, "the owners of this race track have made one mistake They give the diamond badge, worth $1,000, to the engineer, and the purse of $10,000 to the company. Suppose we trade and let the company take the badge and you take the purse."

"Oh, more power to you, Misther Crocker," said the delighted engineer. "It's thrade I will, and may you live until I offer to thrade back, and whin you die may you go straight up, wid never a hot box to delay you on your run to glory. I'll give twinty-five hundred dollars of the money to Dan Nilson, that shoveled the coals unther the boiler, like the good man he is, and wid the balance I'll buy a chicken ranch in Alameda that will be the makin' of Missis Flanagan and the kids."

On the bench behind the professor and the doctor two men were seated engaged in earnest conversation.

"I am not asserting," said one, "that the ore is so very rich. It will average fifteen per cent in copper carbonates, and that is good enough for anybody. But I do say that the lode is an immense one."

"How long do you suppose it would last, Bob, with a dozen forty-ton furnaces at work on it?"

"Last? why, if you had Niagara for a water-power, and the State of Colorado for a dumping-ground, and hades for a smelting furnace, you couldn't work that ledge out in a million years."

"Well, Bob," laughed the other man, "I will go and look at your mine. Can you start to-night?"

"Your time is mine," was the response.

"Very good; shall we go by the Iron Mountain route, or by Kansas City?"

"I will have to go by some other route than either," was the reply. "I cannot cross the State of Missouri; I am honorably dead there."

"Honorably dead?"

"Yes, sir. It was this way: I lived at Atchison for a while when I was a young fellow, and Abe Simmons and me were always at outs about something, and at last we quarreled in dead earnest about a girl, and he sent me a challenge to fight a duel. I always held that dueling was a fool way to settle things, but I wasn't going to take water for no Missourian, and so I placed myself in the hands of my second, as they call it among the chivs.

"Well, Abe's second and my second were good friends of both of us, and they were in for a sort of a lark, and they fixed it up to paint two life-sized pictures, one of Abe and one of me, on the door of an old stable, and we was each to fire at the picture of the other at the word. They had three doctors to examine the wounds on the paintings, and if they decided that the wound was mortal, then the fellow whose picture was killed had to consider himself honorably dead, and was to leave Missouri and never return. If the wound was not mortal, he had to lay up and keep his bed for such time as the doctors agreed would be necessary.

"Well, sir, they made a circus of us, that's a fact. We both signed a paper agreeing on honor to carry out the arrangement, and we went out one broiling afternoon in August in pursuit of each other's gore. The boys had passed the word, and we played to a bigger audience than was ever at a Democratic barbecue. I was the best shot, but I was getting ashamed of the whole business, and I fired in a hurry, and only plugged Abe's picture through its gambrel joint. He took a dead sight and shot my picture plumb through the heart. I wanted three days to settle my business, but the doctors decided that the weather was so hot I wouldn't keep more than twelve hours, and accordingly I lit out for Pike's Peak—as it was then called—the next morning, and I have never touched the soil of Missouri since."

"How about Abe?"

"The doctors agreed that he had to go on crutches or three months, and the boys laughed at him—so I heard—so much that at the end of the second week he limped out to his father's ranch, and stayed there until his time was up, when he went to St. Louis."

"And the girl?"

"Well, of course I was a corpse, and she had no use for me, and Abe had, before the duel, invited her to a dance, and, naturally, being a cripple, he couldn't go, and she allowed that she would neither go to a dance or tie herself for life to a man with a lame leg, and she married another fellow altogether. But you see I cannot honorably go into Missouri unless I can travel on a corpse ticket."

"Well, Bob, your remains shall not violate your pledge. We will keep out of Missouri this trip."

"All right, Mr. Morning."

The professor turned at the sound of the name, and, looking his neighbor in the face, exclaimed:—

"David Morning, have you altogether forgotten an old friend? True, it is nearly ten years since I saw you last, in Denver, but surely I have not changed so very much since then?"

"Forgotten you, Professor Thornton?" replied the party addressed, as he shook hands warmly, "forgotten you? no, indeed. I do not need to ask if you are well—and your wife and daughter? Are they both with you?"

"Both are in Boston, and well, thank you. Do you remain long in Chicago?"

"I leave to-night for the West. Pray convey to your family my remembrances and regards.'

"I will not fail to do so."

"The crowd seems to be going, professor; I suppose we must say good-by."

"Good-by, then, and a pleasant journey to you."

CHAPTER II.

"The light that shone when hope was born."

In the early dawn of an August day in the year of grace eighteen hundred and ninety-two, David Morning stepped through the French window of his bedroom out upon the broad and sheltered piazza of the railroad station hotel at Tucson, Arizona.

A mass of straight brown hair crowned rather than shaded a broad, high brow, over the surface of which thought and time had indented a few lines which gave strength and meaning to the face. Eyes of sea gray hue, as candid and as translucent as the deeps which they resembled, were divided by a nose somewhat too thick at the base for perfect features but running to an aquiline point, with the thin and flexible nostrils of the racer. A short upper lip was covered with a luxuriant chestnut brown mustache, shading a chin which, though long and resolute and firmly upheld against the upper lip, was yet divided by a deep dimple which quivered with sensitiveness. A thick-set but graceful and erect figure, clothed in a suit of dark blue flannel, completed the *tout ensemble* of the subject of our sketch, who, with thirty-two years of human experience behind him, had stepped five hours before from the West-bound Pullman sleeper.

David Morning—the only child of a Connecticut

father and a Knickerbocker mother—was born and passed the days of his boyhood in the city of New York, where he was a pupil of the public schools, and where he was making preparation for entering upon a course at Yale, when, at sixteen years of age, the sudden death of his father, followed within a fortnight by that of his mother, compelled him to surrender his studies and seek a means of livelihood.

A distant relative offered him a place as clerk in a general merchandise store in Southern Colorado, whither the lad journeyed. For two years he faithfully served his employer. Always of an exploring and adventurous disposition, he had, while "geologizing"—as he called it—in the neighboring hills, in company with a prospector who had taken a fancy to "the kid," discovered a quartz lode, which his companion located on joint account, David being under age. This location was soon afterwards sold to an Eastern company for the sum of $20,000, of which the lad received one-half. Declining several friendly offers to invest the money in promising mines, he wisely determined to return East and resume the studies which had been interrupted by the death of his parents; but, guided by his Colorado experience, and having a strong inclination for the vocation of a mining engineer, he determined to study in special lines which were outside of the usual collegiate course. He had not deemed it necessary to leave his own country to obtain the necessary instruction, and, four years later, he found himself with $5,000 left of his capital, with no knowledge of the Greek alphabet and but small acquaintance with Latin, yet able to speak and write fluently French, Spanish, and German, and possessed of a good knowledge of geology, metallurgy, chemistry, and both civil and mechanical engineering, and with a cultivated as well as a natural taste for politico-economic science.

At twenty-two years of age, having completed his studies, David Morning located in Denver, adopted the profession of a civil and mining engineer, and promptly proceeded to fall in love with the only daughter of Professor John Thornton, the principal of the Denver public schools.

Ellen Thornton at seventeen gave abundant promise of the splendid womanhood that was to follow. Above the middle height, slender in form, and graceful in carriage, with a broad, low brow crowned with silky, lustrous, dark hair, and eyes of chestnut brown, that, in moments of inspiration, grew radiant as stars, she captivated the young engineer and was readily captivated by him in turn. An engagement of marriage followed, to be fulfilled as soon as the clientage of Morning should be sufficient to warrant the union.

But business comes slowly to young men of two and twenty, and Ellen's mother grew impatient of the fetters which she deemed kept her charming daughter from more advantageous arrangements. Ellen was proud-spirited and ambitious, and, although she was earnest and conscientious, she was not so stable of purpose as to be unaffected by the arguments and appeals of her mother. At times she was sure that she loved David Morning, and at other times she was not so sure that her love was of that enduring and devoted character which a wife should feel for her husband.

Her reading had created in her mind a conception of an ideal passion which she could not feel had as yet come into her life. She believed that her affianced had undeveloped powers that would some day bring him fame and fortune, and again she was not so sure that he possessed the tact and persistence to utilize his powers to the best advantage. This doubt would not have deterred her from fulfilling her engagement of marriage if she had been entirely certain of her love for him. But she was divided by doubts as to whether the affection she felt was really the ideal and exalted passion of her dreams, or only a strong desire for a companionship which she found to be exceedingly pleasant.

She was not quite certain in all things of her affianced, not quite certain of herself, not quite certain of anything, and one day, yielding to an irresistible impulse of doubt and hesitancy, she asked to be released from her engagement.

Morning was amazed, indignant, and almost heartbroken at her request. Had he been of riper age and experience he would have known how to allow for the doubts and self-questionings of a young girl in her first love affair, but he was as unsophisticated as she, and more secure in his own possession of himself. Frank and proud, he took her at the word, which she regretted almost as soon as it was uttered. He neither sued nor remonstrated, but with only a "God bless you" and a "good-by," and without even a request for a parting kiss, which, if given, might have opened the way to a better understanding, he hurriedly left the house.

The next day he was on his way to Leadville, in fulfillment of a professional engagement, and when he returned two weeks later he found that his former affianced had accompanied her parents to Boston, where Professor Thornton had been suddenly called by the death of a relative, to whose large fortune he succeeded.

Our hero did not despair, and, having no natural inclination for dissipation, did not make his rejection an excuse and an opportunity for self-indulgence. He was of an intense and earnest nature, and he was really in love with the girl who had discarded him, but life was not dead of duty or achievement to him because of her loss, which he looked upon as final, for her newly-acquired position as a wealthy heiress made it impossible to his self-respect to seek a reconciliation. He applied himself with assiduity and industry to his profession, and soon became an exceedingly skillful and reliable mining expert.

Ability to comprehend the story written upon the rocks cannot always be gained by study or experience. At last it is a "faculty," rather than the result of reading or training. Fire and flood, oxygen and electricity, the tempests of the air and the volcanic throbbings of the earth, have been busy for ages with the quartz lode, and have left their marks upon it. It is possible sometimes to decipher these hieroglyphics so as to answer with a degree of accuracy the ever-recurring question, "Will it pay to work?" Yet such possibility cannot be reduced to a science. Professors of geology and metallurgy are often wrong in their conclusions, and even old prospectors are frequently at fault.

Go across a piece of marsh land on a spring morning accompanied by a bull-dog and a Gordon setter. The former will flush no snipe save those he may fairly run over as he trots along. But the fine nose of the dog with the silky auburn coat will catch the scent of the wary bird, and follow it here and there around tufts of marsh grass and across strips of meadow, until the sagacious canine shall be seen outlined against earth and sky. It is difficult to be certain of anything in this world of human deceptions, but one may be absolutely sure under such circumstances that the dog will not lie, and that he cannot be mistaken. There is a snipe within a few yards of that dog in the direction in which his nose is pointed. If the sportsman fails to secure the bird, the fault will be with his aim or his fowling-piece—the dog has done his part.

Some men—even among experienced miners—have the bull-dog's obtuseness, and some have an eye for quartz equal to the nose of a pointer for snipe. David Morning was of this latter class, and to the thorough training which he had received during his four years' studies he speedily added that practical knowledge of the rocks which, guided by natural aptitudes and intuitions, will enable the wooer of the hills to gain their golden favors. His honesty, good judgment, and fidelity caused his services to be eagerly sought by the mining companies, which—after the Leadville discoveries—abounded in Colorado, and at the date at which our narrative opens he had acquired a fortune of about $300,000, which was invested mainly in mortgages upon business property in Denver. But he made no attempt at further attendance on Cupid's court, and, indeed, gave but little attention to society.

Yet, while the physical Ellen Thornton thus passed out of the young man's life, there came into his soul instead an ideal, whose influence was ever an inspiration to higher thinking, purer life, gentler judgments, and loftier deeds. Well has the poet said, "'Tis better to have loved and lost than never to have loved at all." No man can be possessed by love for a good woman without being thereby moved upward on all the lines of existence. Damps cannot dim the diamond; its facets and angles of fire will never permit the fog to abide with them. From the hour that his heart is touched with the electric passion, the lover is in harmony with all delights.

The waters tinkle and the lark sings for him with sweeter notes, while the sunlight is more radiant, and the hills are robed with a softer purple. The woman who has evoked the one passion of a man's life may become as dead to him as the occupant of an Etruscan tomb, but the love itself will abide with him to enrich his life, and journey with him into the other country.

David Morning found in books the most pleasant and absorbing companionship, and those who gained admittance to his library were surprised to learn that there was a dreamy, speculative, poetical side to the busy, practical mining engineer. All the great authors on mental, moral, and political economy were well-thumbed comrades, and the covers of the leading English and German poets and essayists were free from dust. Especially was he a close and interested student of social science, and he had his theories concerning changes of various natures in society and governments which might ameliorate the condition and elevate the lives and purposes of mankind.

In religion Morning was neither an accepter nor an agnostic. His reading taught him that all religions inculcate the righteousness of truth, honesty, and unselfishness, and that any form of faith in the hereafter is better for the world than no faith at all. The Persian who bowed devoutly to the highest material sign of Deity, the sun, was thereby filled with a spirit which made him readier to relieve the misery of his brother. The Egyptian who brought tribute to the priests of Isis and Osiris, was the better for his self-denial. The Greek who believed in Minerva was a closer student. Odin's followers scorned a lie. Confucius taught love of home and kindred. Mahomet prescribed temperance, and the pure and gentle faith of Buddha in its benefactions to the human race has been exceeded only by the benign power of the religion of Jesus.

Skeptics strengthen their scoffings by recounting the wars and cruelties—in bygone centuries—of zealots insane with fervor. But these are only spots upon the sun. The rusty thumbscrews of the Inquisition, and the ashes of the fires amid which Servetus perished—fires unkindled and dead for three hundred years—may be forgotten when one considers the hospitals, and schools, and houses of shelter which now link their shadows across continents.

A few days before, while attending the locomotive races in Chicago, Morning had met an old mining friend, at whose earnest insistence he had been induced to visit and examine, with a view of purchasing, a large and promising ledge of copper in the Santa

Catalina Mountains.   It was the pursuit of this purpose that had brought him to Tucson.

From his seat on the hotel piazza David Morning gazed into the little triangular garden beneath, with its splashing fountain guarded by fragrant honey locust trees, its close-knit, dark green lawn of Australian grass, and its collection of weird and ugly cacti, transplanted from their native sand for the edification of passing tourists.

Then, raising his eyes, he beheld the ancient adobe pueblo, with a few belated saloon lights blinking through the murk, which was now slowly changing into ashen dawn.   In the east a pencil line of light was beginning to glow, and to the northward the blackish purple of the Santa Catalina Range upreared itself against the night sky.

In yonder mountains, as tenantless, as forbidding, as inaccessible, and almost as unexplored as when they were first upheaved from the tortured breast of chaos, there reposed the golden power which, in the hands of David Morning, was to change the economic and social relations of mankind, and, possibly, the governments, the boundaries, and the history of nations.

Nothing of these ripening purposes of Omniscience were then revealed to the soul of our hero; none of them even rested in his dreams.   Yet the nations, weary of centuries of error, centuries of wrong, centuries of toil and tears and martyrdom, were waiting, even as he was waiting before commencing his work, for the light which every moment grew brighter in its scarlet beauty against the eastern horizon—the light which was to guide humanity to its destiny of better days.

"The storm is abroad in the mountains."

THE Santa Catalina Mountains, although commonly designated as a part of the Sierra Madres, are, in truth, a small, isolated range, towering to a height of seven or eight thousand feet above the surrounding plains. They are steep, rugged, and practically inaccessible, except at the eastern end, where they may be entered through a long, narrow, crooked canyon, which runs from the plain or mesa to within a short distance of the summit. This canyon widens at intervals into small valleys, few of which exceed a dozen acres in extent, and through it the Rillito, a mountain stream, carrying, ordinarily, about five hundred miner's inches of water, tumbles and splashes. Along and above the bed of this stream, at a height of fifty feet or more, in order to avoid the freshets created by the summer rains, runs a very primitive wagon road, which was constructed for the purpose of allowing supplies to be transported to the miners, who, during the era of high prices for copper, were engaged in taking ore from the carbonate lodes which exist in abundance in a range of hills half way to the summit and ten miles from the mouth of the canyon.

The lower hills of the Santa Catalinas are covered

with a scant growth of mesquite and palo verde, along the Rillito there is a fringe of willows and cottonwoods, and near the summit is a large body of pine timber, but its practical inaccessibility and distance from any available market have protected it from the woodman's ax. The absence of any extent of agricultural or grazing land in the Santa Catalinas has proven a bar to their occupation by settlers, and their isolation, rugged nature, and unpromising geological formation, have deterred prospectors from thoroughly exploring them. Such searchers for treasure as visited them always returned with a verdict of "no good," until a *quasi* understanding was reached by the miners and prospectors of Arizona that it was useless to waste time looking for gold or silver in their fastnesses.

Above the copper belt no prospector was ever able to find trace or color of any metal, and the low price of copper and the high charges for railroad freight which prevailed in 1883 and succeeding years, caused abandonment of the rude workings for that metal, and at the date of the opening of our narrative it might have been truly said that the entire Santa Catalina Range was without an occupant.

At the western and southern end of the range its summit and rim consist of a huge basaltic formation, towering perpendicularly one thousand feet, upon the apex of which probably no human footstep was ever placed, for its character excluded all probability of quartz being found there, even by the Arizona prospector, who will climb to any place that can be reached by a goat or an eagle, if so be silver and not scenery entice him.

In the spring of 1892 Robert Steel, who, in years gone, had acted as superintendent of a copper company operating in the Santa Catalinas, and was familiar with the ground, had been inspired by a considerable advance in the price of copper to visit the scene of his former labors and relocate the abandoned claims. It was at his solicitation and representations that David Morning, who had known him well in Colorado, was induced to take a trip to Arizona to examine the properties.

Robert Steel was designated by those who knew him best as "a true fissure vein." With hair that was unmistakably red, and eyes that were blue as the sky, with the upper part of his face covered with tan and freckles, and the lower part disguised by a heavy brick-red beard, his personal appearance was not entirely prepossessing to the casual observer. But under the husk of roughness was a heart both tender and true, a loyalty that would never tire, a thorough knowledge of his business as a miner, and a tried and dauntless courage that, in the performance of duty, would, to quote the vernacular of the Arizonian, "have fought a rattlesnake, and given the snake the first bite."

He carried his forty years with the vigor of a boy, and his occasional impecuniosity, which he accounted for incorrectly by saying that he "had been agin faro," was in fact the result of continued investments in giving an education to his two young brothers, and furnishing a comfortable home and support for his parents and sisters in Wisconsin.

There are many Robert Steels to be found among

the prospectors of the far West. They are the brightest, bravest, most generous, enterprising, and energetic men on earth. They are the Knights Paladin, who challenge the brute forces of nature to combat, the soldiers who, inspired by the *aura sacra fames*, face the storm and the savage, the desert and disease. They crawl like huge flies upon the bald skulls of lofty mountains; they plod across alkaline deserts, which pulse with deluding mirages under the throbbing light; they smite with pick and hammer the adamantine portals of the earth's treasure chambers, and at their "open sesame" the doors roll back and reveal their stores of wealth.

They are readier with rifle or revolver than with scriptural quotation, and readier yet with "coin sack" at the call of distress, and they are not always unaccustomed to the usages of polite society, though they scorn other than their occasional exercise. Under the gray shirts may be found sometimes graduates from Yale, and sometimes fugitives from Texas, but always hearts that pulse to the appeals of friendship or the cries of distress, even "as deeps answer to the moon."

Among these pioneers no one man assumes to be better than another, and no man concedes his inferiority to anybody. In the last forty years they have carried the civilization, the progress, and the power of the nineteenth century to countries which were beforetime unexplored. In their efforts some have found fortune and some have found unmarked graves upon the hillside. Some with whitened locks but spirits yet aflame continue the search for wealth, and some, wearied of the search, patiently await the summons to cross the ridge. Wherever they roam, and whether they spin the woof of rainbows upon this or upon the other side, they will be happy, for they will be busy and hopeful, and labor and hope carry their heaven with them evermore.

Two days after the arrival of David Morning at Tucson he left for the Santa Catalinas. The party consisted of Morning and Steel and two miners who were employed for the expedition. A wagon drawn by four serviceable mules was loaded with tools, tents, camp equipages, saddles and bridles, provisions, and grain for the animals sufficient for a week's use. Late in the afternoon of the second day the site of the copper locations was reached, and a camp made upon the mesa a few hundred feet from and above the bed of the stream.

A cursory examination of the copper locations made before nightfall satisfied Morning that before he could form any judgment upon which he would be willing to act in making a purchase, it would be necessary to clean out one of the old shafts, which had, since the mines were abandoned, been partially filled with loose rock and earth. This work it was estimated could be performed by Robert Steel and his two miners in about three days, and while it was being done Morning proposed to explore, or at least visit, the source of the stream, near the summit of the range ten miles away. Assuring Steel that he was an old mountaineer, and that no apprehensions need be felt for his safety if he did not return until the end of two or three days, Morning saddled one animal, and, loading another with blankets, camp equipage, a pick, a fowling-piece, and three days' provisions, he departed next morning, after an early breakfast, for the trip up the cañon.

Above the old copper camp the wagon road came to an end, and only a rough trail running along and often in the creek took its place. Following the trail, Morning proceeded, driving his pack mule ahead, until, at a point about six miles from where he had left his companions, further progress with animals was found to be impossible.

One hundred feet above the bed of the stream, which here emerged with a rush from a narrow gorge, was a plateau of probably ten acres in extent, on which were a number of large oak trees, and the ground of which was at this season covered with a heavy growth of alfilaria, or native clover. Here Morning unloaded and tethered his mules, and made for himself a temporary camp under a huge live oak tree.

After eating his luncheon, he buckled a pistol about his waist, that he might not be altogether unprepared for a possible deer, and, using a pole-pick for a walking staff, he climbed out of the cañon and commenced the ascent of the mountain to the southward. It appeared to be about a thousand feet in height, and upon its summit towered, one thousand feet higher, the basaltic wall which Morning recognized as that which was visible from Tucson, and which formed the southern and western rim of the Santa Catalina Mountains. His purpose was to reach at least the base of this wall, and ascertain if there were any means of ascending it to its summit, from which it might be possible to obtain an extended view of the country.

After half an hour's hard climbing, our adventurer gained this wall and found along its base a natural road, with an ascent of probably three hundred feet to the mile. Slowly plodding his way among the loose rock and débris, which had, during many ages, scaled and fallen from the basalt, he soon reached an opening about sixty feet in width.

Supposing that this might be a cañon or gorge that would furnish a means of ascending the wall, he turned into it.   In a little more than a quarter of a mile it came to an abrupt termination.   It was a *cul de sac*, a rift in the wall made in some convulsion of nature. It ascended very slightly, being almost level, and at both sides and at the end the basalt towered for a thousand feet sheer to the summit, without leaving a break upon which even a bird could set its foot. It was now midday, but the rays of the sun did not penetrate to the bottom of this rift, and the atmosphere and light were those of an autumn twilight.

After ascertaining the nature and extent of the gorge, Morning turned, and, plodding through the sand and loose rock to its entrance, resumed his journey along the base of the great wall. The ascent of the little ridge or natural road grew steeper and steeper, until at length the top was reached, and our explorer stood upon the summit of the great basaltic formation, a mile in width and ten miles in length, which forms the southwestern rim or table of the Santa Catalinas. From near the outer edge spread as grand a prospect as was ever vouschafed to the eye of mortal.   Tucson, seven thousand feet below and fifteen miles away, seemed almost at the foot of the mountain. To the southeast stretched a narrow, winding ribbon of green, the homes of the Mexicans, who, with their ancestors, have for more than two centuries occupied the valley of the Santa Cruz. Farther yet to the southward the lofty Huachucas towered. Northward a higher peak of the Catalinas cut off the view, but to the southwest broad mesas and billowy hills stretched for more than a hundred and fifty miles, until at the horizon the eye rested upon the blue of the Gulf of California, penciled against an ashen strip of sky.

As Morning gazed in awe and delight, there appeared in the sky, scudding from the south, flecks of cloud, chasing each other like gulls upon an ocean, and remembering that this was the rainy season, and feeling rather than knowing that a storm was about to gather, Morning retraced his steps. He had proceeded on his return to a point about five hundred yards above the mouth of the rift which he had visited on his upward journey, when the rapidly-darkening clouds and big plashes of rain drops warned him that one of the showers customary in that section in August was about to fall.

Such storms are usually of brief duration, but are liable to be exceedingly violent, the water often descending literally in sheets. It would have been impossible for Morning to reach the camp where he had left the animals in time to avoid the storm, and a hollow in the basalt wall—a hollow which almost amounted to a cave—offering just here a complete shelter from the rain, which was approaching from the south, over the top of the wall, he sought the opening, and was soon seated upon a convenient rock, while his vision swept the slope to the cañon a mile below, and thence followed the meanderings of the Rillito until it vanished from sight.

And the clouds grew and darkened. Like black battalions of Afrites summoned by the "thunder drum of heaven," they trooped from distant mountains and nearer plains to gather upon the summit of the Catalinas. The south wind—now risen to a gale—swooped up the fogs from the distant gulf, and hurried them upon its mighty pinions, shrieking with delight at the burden it bore up to the summit of the basalt, above which it massed them.

Then the demons of the upper ether reached their electric-tipped fingers into the dense black watery masses, and whirled them into a denser circle, whirled them into an hour glass, whose tip was in the heavens and whose base was carried by the giant force thus generated slowly along and just above the top of the great wall.

Whirled in a demon waltz to the music of the shaking crags, yet touching not those peaks, for to touch them would have been destruction, the circling ocean in the air sailed, roaring and shrieking, to the eastward, growing denser and more powerful, and black with the blackness of the nethermost pit, as it journeyed on. At last it reached the blind cañon so lately visited by our explorer. The air—imprisoned between the earth and the clouds—rushed with a tortured yell down the rift in the mountain. The wall of water sank as its support tumbled from beneath it; its base touched

the ragged rocky edges of the cleft; the compactness
of the fluid mass was broken, and the forces fled and
left to its fate the watery monster they had engendered.

Then, with a roar louder than a thousand peals of
thunder, with throbs and gaspings like the death
rattle of a giant, the waterspout burst, and its vast
volume descended into the gorge, down which it
seethed with the power of a cataclysm.

Out of the mouth of the *cul de sac* a torrent issued,
or rather a wall of water hundreds of feet in height.
Down the mountain side it sped, tearing a channel
deep and wide, and crumbling into a thousand cata-
racts of foam, which spread and submerged the slope.
A deep depression or basin on the side of the mountain just southward of the bed of the Rillito deflected
the torrent for a few hundred yards, and it rushed into
this basin and filled it, and, leaving a small lake as a
souvenir of its visit, went roaring down the cañon,
which it entered again about a quarter of a mile below
the spot where Morning had tethered his mules.

Not more than fifteen minutes had elapsed since the
bursting of the waterspout when the storm was over,
the sun was shining, the water had departed down the
cañon, and our awe-stricken witness to this mighty
sport of elemental forces started to retrace his steps.
He had witnessed the deflection of the water wall, and
knew that his animals were safe, and he also knew that
no harm would come to his companions down the
cañon, for their camp was hundreds of feet above the
bed of the ravine.

A few minutes' walk brought Morning to the mouth
of the gorge which he had visited an hour or more

before.   From it a small stream of water—the remains
of the waterspout—was yet running, and, being curious
to observe the effects produced upon the spot which
first received the fury of the waters, he descended into
the channel which had been torn by the torrent, and
again entered the rift.

The tremendous force of the vast body of water
precipitated into the gorge had excavated and swept
through its opening the fallen and decomposed rock
and sand and bowlders which had been accumulating
for centuries.   The channel rent by the waters as they
emerged was quite twenty feet in depth and sixty feet
in width, and Morning found that the floor of the box
cañon had been torn away to a similar depth.

The waterspout had accomplished in one minute a
work that would have required the industrious labor
of one thousand men for a month.   The gorge was
swept clean to the bed rock, which showed blue limestone, and in the center of this limestone bed there
now stood erect, to a height of twelve feet, a ledge of
white and rose-colored quartz of regular and unbroken
formation, forty feet in width, running from near the
entrance of the rift to the end of it, where it disappeared under the basalt wall.

The experienced eye of Morning taught him at a
glance that this was a true fissure vein of quartz, and a
brief examination of some pieces which he knocked
off with his pole-pick convinced him that it was rich
in gold.   But for the waterspout which had swept away
the sand, gravel, and loose rocks which ages of disin-
tegration of the face of the wall had deposited over
this lode, its existence must ever have remained un-

discovered, for there were no exterior evidences of the existence of quartz, to tempt a prospector to sink a shaft.

The primal instinct of the miner is to locate his "find," and Morning proceeded forthwith to acquire title to "the unoccupied mineral lands of the United States" so marvelously brought to light. His note-book furnished paper for location notices, and an hour's work enabled him to build location monuments of loose stone, in which his notices were deposited.

It was now more than two hours since the water-spout had expended its force. Morning conjectured that Steel and his miners, after the flood had passed them, would probably set out in search of him, and he did not wish his location to be discovered until he should have perfected it by recording at Tucson, and possibly not then. But he knew that it would require at least three hours for the men at the copper-camp to reach him, and, though the light in the cañon was beginning to grow dim, he determined not to leave there without further examination of the ledge.

Accordingly, he walked around it and climbed over it. From its summit and its sides at twenty different places he broke off specimens, which he deposited in his pockets until they were full to bursting. It was beginning to grow dark when he emerged from the rift and started along the base of the basalt. He had not proceeded a hundred yards from the mouth of the rift, when he beheld three figures a quarter of a mile distant, rapidly picking their way along the channel which had been worn by the torrent in its descent of the mountain.

Five minutes more in the gorge and his secret would have been discovered.

He shouted to his friends, who responded to his hail, and in a few minutes they met and descended the mountain together to the plateau under the trees, where the tethered animals, surfeited with alfilirea, were whinnying loudly for human companionship.

It was too late to attempt to return to the copper-camp that night, and, indeed, daylight was needed for the journey, for the trail had been in many places washed away by the flood.

After a supper, which made havoc with the three days' rations, a large fire was built, more for cheerfulness than for warmth, blankets were divided, and all retired.

Morning slept less soundly than his fellows, for his quick and accurate brain was filled with an idea of the colossal fortune and the mighty trust that the events of that day had placed in his hands.

CHAPTER IV

"Gold is the strength of the world."

Morning concluded it would be unwise to make another trip to his location, lest suspicion might be excited and discovery follow, so, breaking camp early the next day, he returned with his comrades to the copper-lodes, which they reached before noon.

Work was resumed by Steel and his two miners in clearing the old shaft, and Morning, taking a fowling-piece, avowed his purpose to look for quail down the ravine. Having reached a point where he felt secluded from observation, he began a critical examination of the quartz specimens, which until now he had not dared to withdraw from his pockets.

As with his microscope he scrutinized piece after piece, he grew pale with excitement and astonishment. With the habit of a mining expert, he had sampled the ledge as for an average, and the average value of the twenty different specimens of quartz, taken from twenty different localities, enabled him to determine the true value of the property with great accuracy. He discovered that the amount of gold in each one of the twenty specimens would not vary materially from the amount of gold in proportion to the quartz in each and all of the others. In other words, the entire body of quartz was uniformly impregnated with gold, and, therefore, of uniform richness and value.

(39)

There was no better judge of quartz in all Colorado than David Morning. He had been accustomed, after careful inspection, to estimate within ten or twenty per cent of the value per ton of free milling gold quartz, and his accuracy had often been the subject of amicable wagers among his friends. He was able in this instance to say that each one of the ore specimens carried not less than five hundred ounces of gold to the ton of quartz, or that the entire lode would yield, under the stamps, an average of $10,000 per ton.

This was marvelous! unprecedented! phenomenal! No such deposit for richness and extent had ever been found in the history of the world.

Ten thousand dollars in gold, distributed through two thousand pounds of quartz, may not make much of a showing in the quartz, for in bulk there is fifty times as much quartz as gold; but one hundred tons of such quartz would yield a million dollars, and the ledge uncovered by the waterspout was forty feet in width and thirteen hundred and sixty feet in length to where it ran under the basalt wall. It cropped twelve feet above the ground, and extended to unknown depths below the surface. Thirteen feet of rock in place will weigh a ton. In that rift in the mountain there was now in sight above the surface, all ready to be broken down and sent to the stamps, six hundred and fifty thousand cubic feet, or fifty thousand tons, of quartz, containing gold of the value of $500,000,000.

What was to be done with the vast amount of gold which might be extracted from the Morning mine? How was it to be placed in circulation without unsettling values, reducing the worth of all bonds, inaugurating wild speculation, and revolutionizing the commerce and the finances of the world?

Would not the nations, so soon as they should be made aware of the existence of this deposit, hasten to demonetize gold, make of it a commodity, change the world's standard money to silver exclusively, and so lessen the value of the Morning mine to a comparatively small amount?

Under the plea that increased production of silver necessitated a change in relative values, that metal was demonetized in 1873 in Europe and in the United States, and its value reduced one-third. Might not gold now be similarly dealt with, and, with such a vast deposit known to be in existence, be diminished by demonetization to the value of silver or less?

The entire production of gold in the world for the last forty years, or since the California and Australia mines began to yield, had been but $5,000,000,000, and as much might be extracted from the first one hundred and twenty feet in depth of the Morning mine. All the gold money of the world was but $7,600,000,000, or less than might be excavated from the first two hundred feet in depth of this marvelous deposit. The total money of the world—gold, silver, and paper—was but $11,500,000,000, and a similar sum might be extracted from the first three hundred feet in depth of the mine.

If the ledge extended downward a thousand feet, it contained as much gold as three times the sum total of all the gold, silver, and paper currency of the world, and its value was equal to the value, in the year eighteen hundred and ninety, of one-half of all the real and personal property in the United States.

How much of this gold could be added to the circulation of the world with safety? and how could the existence of the vast quantity held in reserve be kept secret?

His studies in political economy had taught David Morning that gold, like water, if fed to the land in proper proportions, would stimulate its fertility and add to its power of beneficent production, but if precipitated in an unregulated and mighty torrent, would, like the waterspout, prove a destructive power.

Knowledge of the existence of the gold, if generally diffused, would be nearly as injurious to the world as to extract it and place it in the channels of finance. Yet how could the secret be kept? The ledge as it stood could not be worked without half a hundred men knowing its extent and value. No guards or bonds of secrecy would be adequate. The birds of the air would carry the tale. Even now a vagrant prospector or wandering mountain tourist might reveal the secret to the world.

Not in any spirit of self-seeking did David Morning ask himself these questions. All his personal wants, and tastes, and aspirations might be gratified with a few millions, which could easily be mined and invested before knowledge of his discovery could destroy or lessen the value of gold. But the purpose now beginning to take possession of him was to use, not merely millions, but tens and hundreds and thousands of millions, to bring peace, and progress, and prosperity to the nations, to ameliorate the conditions under which humanity suffers, to raise the fallen, to aid the struggling, to curb the power of oppressors, to remedy public and private wrongs, to solve social problems, to uplift humanity, and comfort the bodies and souls of men. To accomplish this work it was necessary that he should have vast sums at his command, and it was also necessary that his possession of vaster reserves should not be known.

The discoveries in California and Australia by which in ten years fourteen hundred millions of gold dollars were added to the world's stock of the precious metals was a beneficent discovery. It lifted half the weight from the shoulders of every debtor; it made possible the payment of every farm mortgage; it delivered manhood from the evil embrace of Apathy, and wedded him to fair young Hope; it invigorated commerce, it inspired enterprise, it led the armies of peace to the conquest of forest and prairie; it caused furnaces to flame and spindles to hum; it brought plenty and progress to a people.

But this addition to the gold money of civilization was gradually made, and the product of forty years of all the gold mines in the world was not equal to the sum which in less than four years might be taken from the Morning mine.

If, as a consequence of Morning's find, gold should not be demonetized, if it should be permitted to remain as a measurer of all values, and the extent of the deposit should be made known to the world, the inevitable result would be to quadruple the prices of land, labor, and goods, and to reduce to one-fourth of their present proportions the value to the creditor of all existing indebtedness. The farmer whose land was worth $10,000 would find it worth $40,000, and

the man who had loaned $5,000 upon it would find
his loan worth but $1,250 practically, because the pur-
chasing power of his $5,000 would be reduced to one-
fourth of its present capacity.

All government bonds of the nations, all county,
city, and railroad bonds, and all the mortgages and
promissory notes and book accounts in the world,
would, if all of Morning's gold should be poured at
once into circulation, without preparation or warning,
be reduced at one blow to one-fourth of their present
value, and all the owners of land, and implements,
and horses, and cattle, and merchandise would find
their value at once increased fourfold. The laborer
who had only his hands or his brains would remain
unaffected. His wages would be quadrupled, and so
would the cost of his living.

Knowledge of the extent of the Morning mine
would immediately enrich the debtors and ruin the
creditors of the world, unless the governments of earth
should demonetize gold, deny it access to the mints,
refuse to coin it, and so degrade it to a commodity.

An illustration in a small way of the operations of
this immutable law of finance may be found in the
history of San Francisco. The foundations of some
of the great fortunes of that city may be traced to the
days of the Civil War, when San Francisco wholesale
merchants paid their Eastern creditors in legal tender
currency, the while they diligently fostered a public
sentiment which made it discreditable to the honesty
and ruinous to the credit of any California retailer
who should attempt to pay his debt to them in
the despised greenbacks. The interior storekeeper

glowed with pride when Ephraim Smooth & Company gathered in his golden twenties, and commended his honesty for "paying his debts like a man, in gold, and not availing himself of the dishonest legal tender law." But Smooth & Company paid their New York creditors in greenbacks, and pocketed the difference.

Inflation of the currency, or an increase of the money of a nation, if it can be gradually made, need not prove disastrous to the creditors, and must prove a benefaction to the debtors of the world. The relation of wages to the cost of living, whether the volume of money in a country be contracted or inflated, practically remains the same. It may be claimed that the workman who receives an increase of wages, and whose cost of living is correspondingly increased, is no better off at the end of the year, yet economy brings to him larger apparent accumulations, and he is thereby encouraged to practice frugality.

The American mechanic who wandered to the Canary Islands, where he received $400 a day in the local currency for his wages, was enabled to save $100 a day by denying himself brandy and tobacco, and but for this dazzling inducement he might have surrendered to temptations that would have made him a proper subject for the ministrations of the W. C. T. U.

But though an inflation of values which should be beneficent might follow the discovery and working of the Morning mine, clearly the first thing for the discoverer to do was to take effectual measures to conceal from human knowledge the extent of his discovery.

David Morning remained for some time in deep

thought, and then, rising from his seat upon a bowlder behind the manzanita bushes, he tore into fragments the paper upon which he had been making calculations, and, excavating with his foot a hole in the sand, he dropped into it and covered the specimens of gold quartz which he had taken from the ledge, and, retracing his steps, was soon at the copper-camp, where, in answer to the queries of his companions, he replied truthfully that during his absence he had not seen a single quail.

Two days elapsed, and, the shaft having been cleaned out and the copper lode thoroughly exposed, Morning took samples of it, and also of croppings of the other lodes included in the ground located by Steel, and the party broke camp and started for Tucson, where they arrived early in the afternoon of the second day.

Making an appointment with Steel for that evening, Morning deposited his copper samples with an assayer, and, walking to the Court House, he filed the notice of location of the Morning mine with the county recorder. Two hours later he had the report of the assayer upon the copper samples, showing an average of twelve per cent of carbonate copper in the ore. This was not so rich as had been predicted by Steel, but was of sufficient value to warrant the purchase of the copper prospects at the low price which had been fixed upon them, provided that arrangements could be made for economically working them, and Morning had already formulated in his own mind a plan of action by which the working of the copper lodes could be made to advance his project of working the gold lode so as to conceal the extent of its yield.

Morning calculated that the amount of money needed for labor, supplies, machinery, and buildings, to work the mines in accordance with his plans, would be about $300,000, and his first thought was to obtain this money by breaking down, and shipping to reduction works in California or Colorado, about thirty tons of the quartz before he should commence the work which he projected for the concealment of the ledge.

With his own hands he could mine and sack such an amount of ore in a fortnight, and with the aid of half a dozen pack animals, managed by himself, transport it a mile or two from the rift, where it might be thrown into the channel cut by the waterspout, and, with a blast or two, be covered with rocks and dirt until teams should be brought from Tucson for it.

With this idea uppermost, he sought the freight agent of the railroad company of Tucson.

Then he came in contact with the system in vogue on the Pacific Coast—and possibly elsewhere—that of a one-sided railroad partnership with the producer, on the basis that the producer furnish all the capital and suffer all the losses, the railroad company providing neither capital, experience, nor services, but taking the lion's share of the profits.

"What," said Morning, "will your freight charges be for three car loads of ore to Pueblo or San Francisco?"

"What kind of ore?"

"Gold-bearing quartz in sacks."

"What does your ore assay?" inquired the agent.

"What has that got to do with it?" questioned Morning sharply.

"Everything," answered the official. We charge in car-load lots $12 per ton to San Francisco, or $24 per ton to Pueblo, and $2.00 per ton in addition for each $100 per ton of the assay value of the ore."

"Very well," said Morning, "I believe I will ship thirty tons to San Francisco."

"Have you it here?" said the agent.

"It will not be ready for some weeks yet," replied Morning.

"You did not mention its value," said the agent.

"I will state its value at $100 per ton," said Morning.

"All right," said the agent, " we will take it at that, subject, of course. to assay according to our rules by the assayer of the company at your expense."

"Well, I don't know that I care to trouble the assayer of your company," replied Morning. "In fact, the ore is a good deal richer than $100 per ton. But I will ship it at that valuation, and release the company from all liability for loss or damage beyond that. In brief, I will take all the chances, and if the ore shall be lost, or stolen, or tumbled off a bridge, or overturned into a river, the company will only account to me for it at $100 per ton. I suppose that will be satisfactory?"

The agent shook his head.

"It looks as if it ought to be satisfactory," said he, "but my orders are imperative. The ore must be assayed, and you will have to pay two per cent of its value."

"But this," replied Morning, with some heat, "is unreasonable and outrageous. If the tax of two per cent is to be regarded in the light of a charge for insurance, I am sure there is not a marine or fire insurance company in the world that would charge one-fourth of one per cent for such a risk."

"Company's orders," said the agent.

"Suppose you wire headquarters at my cost, and say that David Morning wishes to ship thirty tons of gold-bearing quartz from Tucson to San Francisco, at a valuation of $100 per ton. Say that he will prepay the freight, and load and unload the cars himself if permitted. Say that he does not wish the railroad company to take any of the risks of mining, transporting, or reducing the ore, nor to share any of the profits of the business. Say that he will release the company from all liability even for gross negligence or theft, beyond $100 per ton. Say that he does not wish to acquaint the company's assayer or the company's freight agent with the value of the ore, or permit either of them to form any accurate judgment for speculative or other purposes as to the value of the mine from which the ore was taken. Say that he wishes the privilege of conducting his own business in his own way. Say that if the railroad company will kindly fix a rate at which it will consent to carry the freight he offers, without sticking its meddlesome, corporate nose into his business, he will then consider whether he will pay that rate or refrain from shipping the ore at all."

"Mr. Morning," said the agent, "if I were to send such a telegram as that, it would cost me my place, and, indeed, my orders are not to communicate remonstrances made by shippers at the company's rules, except by mail. Of course you can send any message you like over your own name to the head office, but

4

I can inform you now that they will only refer you to me for an answer, and I can only refer to my general instructions, and there the matter will end."

"Well, replied Morning, "I will ship the ore by ox teams or not ship it at all before I will submit to the injustice of your general instructions. I suppose I am without remedy in the premises?"

"You might build another road, Mr. Morning," said the agent, with a slight tinge of sarcasm in his voice.

Morning answered slowly, as he turned away:—

"I may conclude to do so, or to buy up this road, and if I do I will run it on business principles that shall give the shipper some little chance."

"When will that halcyon hour for the public arrive, Mr. Morning?"

"By and by," rejoined our hero, "and then you may look for better days."

CHAPTER V.

"The rich man's joys increase the poor's decay.

"FORTY-FIVE years ago, doctor," said Professor John Thornton to his friend, Dr. Eustace, "do you remember that, as barefooted boys, we fished for pickerel together in this very pond, and from this very spot?"

"And caught more fish with our bamboo poles and angleworm bait than we appear likely to capture to-day with this fancy tackle," remarked the doctor.

"Everything about this lovely little lake seems unchanged," resumed the professor, "but elsewhere the great world has indeed rolled on. Then there were less than one hundred millionaires in this republic—now, doctor, there are more than eight thousand."

"And then," said the doctor, "we came here in a rickety old stage wagon, and we were ten hours in making the same journey which to-day we achieved in an hour while seated in a parlor car. Then the telegraph was in its infancy, the electric light was unknown, the great manufacturing cities were unconstructed, the petroleum of Pennsylvania and the gold of California and Australia were undiscovered, the great Western railroad lines were unbuilt, and the web of complex industries with which the land is now laced was unspun. The victim of a raging tooth or a crushed limb was compelled to suffer without relief from chloroform or ether, and it was a crime punishable with social ostracism to question the righteousness of human slavery, the curative virtues of calomel, or the beneficence of infant damnation. I never could think, John, that the good old times, whose loss you are always bemoaning, were nearly so comfortable times to live in as those amid which we now dwell."

"Dr. Eustace," said the professor, "you attach undue importance to a few physical comforts and conveniences. If our fathers lacked the advantages of our later civilization, they were also without its vices. In the good old times which you deride, wrecking railroads, stealing railroads, and watering stocks were unknown. Senatorships and subsidies were not procured by bribery; the legislator who sold his vote made arrangements to leave the country, and bank burglars and bank defaulters kept, in the public estimation, the lock step of fellow-criminals."

"And what, in your opinion was the cause of our descent from this high estate of public virtue and whale-oil lamps?"

"The main cause, Dr., of the corruption of the human race everywhere,—gold. It was the gold of California that revolutionized the finances, the business methods, and the morals of the nation. After the year 1849 the advance of values, the aggregation of wealth, the increase of population, and the magical growth of the West, made additional facilities for inland travel and transportation a necessity. This necessity caused the rapid construction of new lines of railroad. The differences and difficulties of local management suggested the advantages of consolidation—and then the reign of the centripetal forces commenced."

"But all the millionaires of the country are not railroad men, John."

"Concentration of capital began with them, doctor, and their example was soon followed by others. The Civil War broke down local prejudices, made East and West homogeneous, introduced communities to each other on the battle-field, obliterated State lines, and made individual effort in business, in finance, in manufactures, and even in politics, less advantageous to the individual than participation in aggregated effort, where his gains were increased, though his personality was submerged."

"I have always thought that our civil war was a moral education to this people and to the world," remarked the doctor.

"War was an educator," conceded the professor, "yet the tree of knowledge with its crimson leaves yielded evil fruit as well as good. The moral nature of the American people has, I fear, reacted from the tension of generous and patriotic sacrifice which war evolved. Some of the very men who helped to strike shackles from black slaves have been busy ever since forging other shackles for white slaves, and in twenty-five years from the days when we freely paid lives and treasure to preserve the existence of the nation, and free it from the wrong of slavery and the rule of a slave-holding oligarchy, we have passed under the sway of other despots, more selfish, more sordid, more relentless, and more rapacious of dominion. The duskbrowed tyrant of Egypt has been overthrown, but in his place Plutus reigns."

"I grant you," interposed Dr. Eustace, "that the wealth owners are the rulers of our later civilization, but, so far as I have observed, instead of endeavoring to curb or overthrow them, we are all doing our best to join their ranks and participate in their power. You appear to be the only living millionaire who declaims against his class. I know of no other man who is brave enough to defy the power of money, great enough to ignore it, or strong enough to resist its influence, and I dare say you would change your views if you were to lose your millions. We all defer to the plutocrats. The Spanish nobleman who, for his ancestor's services, was permitted to remain with his head covered in the presence of his sovereign, would have been sure to take off his hat if he had entered the office of the president of a country bank, with a view of negotiating a small loan on doubtful security. There was a great truth inadvertently given to the world in the programme of a Fourth of July procession, wherein it was announced that the line would end with bankers in carriages, followed by citizens on foot."

"This subservience to King Gold, and pursuit of his favors, must cease, Dr. Eustace, or this republic will be lost. The people must be taught to assume a more independent and manly attitude toward the owners of money."

"Ah, John, money is so necessary, and it is so hard to turn one's back upon it! This way lies comfort, ease, luxury—that way deprivation and sacrifice. This way 'the primrose path of dalliance trends'—

that way 'the steep and thorny road.' This way the wife and children beckon and sue for safety and peace —that way only rocks, and bruises, and hunger, and loneliness summon. What wonder that the Christ, voicing the cry of the human to the infinite Father, placed as the central thought of the Lord's prayer the words, 'Lead us not into temptation'! But, John, honestly now, do you think the eight thousand millionaires you rave about are such an utterly bad lot as you make them out to be?"

"Individually I dare say they are good husbands, fathers, and neighbors," replied the professor, "but they conceal their selfishnnss and rapacity, and exercise their despotism from behind the shields of corporations which they create and govern, and tyranny is none the less tyranny because it is decreed not by kings, but by entities which fear neither the assassination of man nor the judgment of God."

"Professor, pardon me, but you generalize a good deal, and I fear somewhat loosely. It would make a difference to me, in my feelings, at least, whether I was knocked down by a ruffian, or by an electrical machine."

" Doctor, your simile was not considered as carefully as are your prescriptions. If the machine be guided by the ruffian, what matters it whether you be struck by his hand, or with an electric current directed by his hand? If our great newspapers, which are influential, which claim to be independent, and which ought to be free, are restrained from publishing articles advocating postal telegraphy, or criticising the management of a news corporation, what matters it that the freedom of the press is choked by a board of directors rather than a government censor? If the citizen dare not give voice to his views on public affairs, what matters it whether his utterances be choked by the knuckles of a king, or the polite menaces of an employer? If the voter cast his ballot against his own convictions, and in accordance with the will of another, what matters it whether he be coerced by a soldier with a musket or a station agent with a freight bill? If the settler lose his land, what matter whether the despoiler be a personal bandit armed with a rifle, or a corporate robber equipped with a land-office decision? If capital exempt itself from taxation, and place the burden of sustaining government upon the broad back of labor, will it alleviate the pain of the load to know that it is not the law of feudal vassalage but of modern politics which accomplishes the exaction?

"Hallo! I have a bite! Ah! ha! my boy, your eagerness to swallow that minnow has brought you to grief!"

And the speaker lifted a twenty-ounce pickerel from the placid waters of Nine Mile Pond, and deposited it, struggling and shining, upon the green turf at his feet.

"Well, John," inquired the doctor, "what are you going to do about it all?"

"We will have him split down the back and broiled for luncheon," replied the professor absently.

"Broil who?" queried the doctor, "Jay Gould?"

"Eh? No; the pickerel I mean, though I am not sure that similar treatment might not be accorded to Gould, with advantage to the country."

"You ask," continued the professor, "what shall be done about it all? The wealth owners themselves should be able to see that existing conditions must sooner or later find cessation either in relief or in revolution. Monopolies in transportation, intelligence, land, light, fuel, water, and food—all concealed in the impersonality of private corporations—now sit like vampires upon the body of American labor, and suck its life blood, and they have grown so bold and so rapacious that they even neglect to fan their victims to continued slumber."

"Why, John, you seem to have an attack of anti-corporation rabies. You talk like a sand-lot politician who is trying to sell out to a railroad company. What is the matter with you? What have these much berated entities done?" said the doctor.

"Done?" replied Professor Thornton. "What have they not done? They have torn the bandages from the eyes of American justice and fastened false weights upon her scales. They have turned our legislative halls into shambles where men are bought and honor is butchered. They have written the word 'lie' across the Declaration of our fathers. They have struck the genius of American liberty in her fair mouth, until, with face suffused with the blushes and bedewed with the hot tears of shame, she turns piteously to her children to hide if they cannot defend her."

"John Thornton," ejaculated the doctor, "your remarks would be admirable in substance and style for an address before some gathering of work shirkers, organized to procure lessened hours of labor and larger schooners of beer, but to me you are talking what our transatlantic cousins call 'beastly rot.' I deny that a majority, or even any considerable number, of the capitalists of this country are dishonest, or unpatriotic, or indifferent to the rights and needs of their fellow-men."

"I have not said that they were, doctor," replied the professor. "Indeed, if such were the case, we might cry in despair, 'God save the commonwealth!' for only Omniscience could work its salvation. What I claim is that it is full time for the conscientious millionaires who love their country and their kind, to seriously consider a situation the perils of which they are every day augmenting by their indifference."

"What perils do you mean, professor? How, for instance, would anybody be hurt or periled if I were to become a millionaire?"

"A great fortune is a great power, doctor, and not every man is fit to be intrusted with great power. To-day no second-class power in Europe can negotiate a treaty or make even a defensive war without the consent of the Rothschilds, while in America the owner of fifty millions is more powerful than the president of the United States, and the owner of ten millions more influential than the governor of a State.

"And so he ought to be," interposed the doctor. "The man who can by fair means make $10,000,000 is more useful to the community in which he lives than a dozen governors of States."

"But look at the danger to the people, doctor, of these great fortunes. There are ten men in the United States whose aggregate wealth amounts to $500,000,-

ooo, and who represent, and control, and wield the influence of property amounting to $3,000,000,000. If these men should choose to settle their rivalries and combine their interests and efforts, they could about fix the prices of every acre of land, every barrel of flour, every ton of coal, and every day's wages of labor between Bangor and San Francisco. They could name every senator, governor, judge, congressman, and legislator in twenty States. They could rule a greater empire than any possessed by crowned kings. They could promulgate ukases more absolute, more despotic, and more certain of being enforced, than any which ever went forth from St. Petersburg to carry desolation to a race. They could say to the laborer in the grain-fields, 'Henceforth you shall be reduced to the condition of your brother in England or Scotland, and eat meat but once a week.' They could say to the toiler in the humming factory or over the red forge, 'Henceforth you must toil twelve hours in each twenty-four.' They could say to every wage-worker in the land, 'Henceforth we will take all the results of your labor, and give you only the slave's share—existence and subsistence.'"

"All you need, Professor John Thornton," said Dr. Eustace, "is a long beard, a woman with green goggles and a tamborine, a fat boy with a snare drum, and a pair of bellows in your chest, to be a Salvation Army seeking recruits for the church of Anarch. You know just as well as I do that you are talking nonsense, and that the capitalists of our country would be neither so inhuman nor so unwise as to push their power as you indicate."

"Maybe not, doctor, maybe not, but their ability to so use their power if they choose is a menace to a free people, and a standing inducement to disorder, and unless the plutocrats cease their aggressions the people may invoke the motto, '*Salva republica suprema lex*,' and tax all great fortunes out of existence."

"What aggressions do you refer to, professor? For the life of me I cannot see that this country or this people have any just cause of complaint. The census returns of 1890 show that in the preceding ten years there was added to our national wealth, values amounting to nearly $20,000,000,000."

"The census returns tell only a part of the story, doctor. The cottages of the land will tell you that while as a nation we may have grown of late years very rich and prosperous, yet among the individuals composing the nation its wealth is possessed and its prosperity enjoyed within a very narrow circle. The value of all the property in the United States in the year 1890 was $66,000,000,000. Do you know that $40,000,000,000, or sixty per cent of the wealth of America, is owned by less than forty thousand people? Do you know that in the last twenty years the laborers of the United States have added to the general wealth of the nation, values amounting to $30,000,-000,000?"

"Well, what is there to complain of in that fact?" questioned the doctor.

"The complaint is that the money has not been divided among the ten million workers who earned it. The complaint is that it has not furnished each of ten million households with a $3,000-shield against the assaults of poverty. The complaint is that as fast as created it has been seized by the centripetal tendency which now dominates our civilization and hurried into the strong boxes of ten thousand Past-Masters of the art of accumulating the earnings of other people."

"The complete answer, professor, to your diatribe is that the accumulations of which you speak are not the earnings of other people. The greater portion of this wealth has been developed from the bounty of nature in ways which could not have been pursued without large combinations of capital."

"That is a mere assumption, doctor."

"Not at all, professor. The money taken from gold, silver, copper, lead, iron, and coal mines, has come from the treasure vaults of nature, and has not been filched from the earnings of anybody."

"Mining is the one exception to the rule, doctor."

"I beg your pardon, professor, but it is not. Another avenue to wealth has been the organization and reorganization of great industries on unwasteful. and remunerative principles. For instance, the beef and pork packing establishments of the West supply the retail butchers of the land with meat at a less price than is paid for the live cattle."

"Where, then, doctor, do these philanthropists of whom you speak make their money?"

"They make it, professor, by scientific utilization of the hoofs and horns, bones and blood, which in small butcher shops are necessarily wasted."

"You believe, then, in the rightfulness of monopolies and trusts, do you, doctor?"

"John, there are no monopolies. No restrictions are placed by law on any man who chooses to embark in any reputable business. As for the much-abused 'trusts,' they have all resulted in higher wages and more constant employment to the workman, and lower prices and better goods to the consumer. I suppose you will not claim that the capitalists alone are responsible for all the crime and pauperism of the land?"

"No," replied the professor, "for the ignorant and vicious poor play into the hands of the selfish and vicious rich, and between the two the honest and industrious body of the people is being ground as between the upper and nether millstone. Indeed, I do not know which is the greater curse to the country, the stock thieves, whose dens are under the shadow of Trinity Church spire, and who combine to corrupt courts, juries, and legislators, or the dynamiters and anarchists who would involve the innocent and the guilty in one common wreck of social order. I hope I am no senseless alarmist, Dr. Eustace, but I am sure we must have relief, or there will be national ruin."

"From what source, professor, do you expect relief to come?" inquired the doctor.

"Frankly, I don't know," was the reply.

"Maybe your next National Convention will relieve the situation," insinuated the doctor, slyly.

"I am sure that relief will not come," said the professor, "from existing political parties, whose orators grow earnest and belligerent over the ghosts of dead issues, and travel around and around over the same path, like an old horse on an arrastra, forever going somewhere and never getting anywhere, neither knowing or caring whether he is grinding pay rock or waste rock, conscious only of the whip of his driver, and hopeful only of his allowance of barley.''

"Why, John, I thought you were a devoted partisan," said the doctor.

"Did you?" was the retort. "Well, you were mistaken. What can be hoped from political parties when legislators who are not free from suspicion of venality are voted for and elected year after year, because Grant captured Vicksburg, or Lincoln issued a proclamation of emancipation, or Stonewall Jackson was killed more than twenty-five years ago? Must the people forever submit to the rule of brawlers, and vote sellers, and trust betrayers, because such men hurrah for some flag which other men once carried into battle? Must the masses lie down in the path of Juggernaut and invite him to crush them, because the evil-visaged god parades his devotion to party issues which were long ago remitted to the limbo of things lost on earth?''

"The people will right all the evils of which you complain, professor, so soon as they see that it is to their interest to do so."

"How can they doubt that it is their interest to right them? It is they who suffer both in purse and pride for every unjust exaction and every dishonest evasion. The poorest do not escape the consequences; it all comes out of their toil in the end. It depletes their pockets in a hundred unobserved ways. They pay for it in enhanced taxation of their homes, in the fuel which cooks their food, in a greater cost of the necessaries of life, in a higher rent, in the nails which hold their houses together, and in the increased cost of the blows of the hammer which drives them. I do not need to tell you, doctor, that labor must bear the burdens of the State. Labor at last pays all and capital pays nothing—all burdens of government, all expenses of courts and juries, and prisons and police, all cost of armies and navies. The diamonds which glitter upon the shirt front of the purchased legislator, the wine which hisses down the throat of the lobbyist, the steel doors and locks which guard watered stock and stolen bonds, the very powder and bullets which shoot out the life of maddened and insurgent labor, are all paid for out of the toil of the laborer.''

''While there is much truth in what you say, professor,'' observed the doctor, ''yet where is the immediate necessity for you to work yourself into such a state of mind about it?''

''Your remark, doctor, is a representative one,'' replied Professor Thornton, ''and the general indifference which it expresses is the most discouraging feature of the existing situation. Like the villagers who cultivate their vineyards at the base of Vesuvius, we heed not the rumblings of the volcano. Like the citizens long resident in Cologne, we scent the tainted air without discomfort. We cry with the French king, 'After us the deluge,' and we seem to care very little what may happen so long as it shall not happen to us.''

''There is the mate to your pickerel,'' said the doctor, as he landed a fish upon the grass at his feet. ''Two of the millionaires of Nine Mile Pond have succumbed to their own greed and the patience and cunning of intelligent labor."

"Many of our millionaires," resumed the professor, not to be driven from his theme, "and some of the most active and powerful of them all, are as selfish, as rapacious, as arrogant, as ignorant, as corrupt, and as despotic as Russian Boyars or Turkish Bashans. At the same time they are unaware of their danger, are utterly obtuse to their social and moral responsibilities, and conceited with the invulnerable conceit of self-made men. They do not seem to recognize that they are unprotected by an army, or a strong government, or spies, or the machinery of despotism, or any traditions or practices of rule, and they appear to take no thought of the infinite possibilities of disaster which line the path of every to-morrow."

"You really fear, then, the fulfillment of Macauley's prophecy, professor?"

"What thoughtful man does not? There is in every large city of our land a multitude unindustrious, unfrugal of life, uncurbed of spirit, undisciplined, uneducated, fretful of small gains, accustomed to freedom of speech and action, jealous of anything which looks like oppression or class rule, unaccustomed to restrictions of any kind, irrreligious, materialistic, discontented, idle, envious, and often drunken."

"In brief, a powder magazine," said the doctor. "Great cities have always presented the same problem to rulers, yet civilization lives, nevertheless."

"Because," rejoined the professor, "in monarchial Europe the magazine is guarded by trained armies

5

and watchful sentinels, while in our country it is left open and unguarded, and anarchists with lighted torches pass to and fro. In Europe the train of government is built of carefully-selected materials, it is officered by experienced engineers, and at every station the testing hammer rings against the wheels. Here we put in any piece of crystallized iron for wheel or axle, and give the control of the engine to any loud-voiced braggart who can climb into the cab, or any ambitious dotard who chooses to hire the tricksters of the caucus to hoist him there. Then we throw the brakes off, the throttle-valves open, and go screaming down the grade."

"And how do you propose, John, to avoid a smash-up?" queried the doctor.

"We shall have passed the danger point," replied the professor, "and entered upon an era of safer and better life for the republic, only when the great millionaires of America shall elect to consider themselves not merely as conquerers on the field of finance, entitled to the spoils of victory, but as trustees for humanity, as suns whose mission it is to draw the waters of affluence from overflowing lake and stream, not to hold those waters above the earth forever, but to distribute them in bounteous and fertilizing showers."

"And do you suppose, John Thornton, that the people would either appreciate or respond to such seraphic unselfishness on the part of your regenerated and beatified millionaires?"

"Dr. Eustace, let me tell you that when the great, industrious, intelligent, patriotic body of workers shall be made to feel that there is no necessary conflict between labor and capital,—when they shall be made to know that any considerable number of our millionaires are seeking further wealth not merely to add to their personal luxury and power, but in order that labor may be helped in turn to higher planes of life, when it can be said truthfully—

> "'Then none was for a party,
>   Then all were for the State ;
> Then the great man helped the poor
>   And the poor man loved the great'—

In that day professional labor agitators will lose their vocations, the workingman who never works will be without influence among his fellows, and the brotherhoods of beer and brawling which infest the purlieus of our larger cities, and clamor for bread or blood—meaning always somebody else's bread or somebody else's blood—will find occasion to disband. I do not despair of relief, I know that it must come. Whether it shall come through 'a preserving or a destroying revolution,' whether it shall come in wrath or in peace, is a question which the capitalists of this country must answer and answer speedily."

"John, you dear old dreamer," said the doctor, "I know of one millionaire whose gold has not corroded his humanity. I hope there are many such, but I fear that if the world looks to its wealth owners to lead it in a crusade of unselfishness, it will wait a long, long time. But I do not diagnose the disease as you do. You resemble a boy who has stubbed his toe. To him there is no world and hardly any boy outside of that sore toe. Yet if the cure be left to nature, in time the pain will abate and the toe recover. I do not believe that any law framed by man can make a pound of flour out of half a pound of wheat, or that any scheme of government can equalize the inevitable inequalities of human life."

"Then you do not believe in the wisdom and beneficence of compelling the rapacious rich to aid the deserving poor?"

"No; I believe in the wisdom and beneficence of exact justice. I believe that the skillful and rapid bricklayer is entitled to higher wages and greater opportunities of employment than his stupid and slothful associate, and that to deny the former his rightful advantage is an outrage upon justice, whether such outrage be perpetrated by an employer or a trades union. I believe that every man is fairly entitled to all the fruits of his labor, his skill, his good judgment, and his good luck. The pickerel at your feet came by chance to your hook and not mine, and therefore it is your fish and not my fish."

"But by the law of nature, doctor, there is no difference between a beggar and a king."

"There is where you are wrong, professor. The law of nature is a universal statute of equality of opportunity and inequality of result, and man distorts her purposes and violates her statutes when he places an unearned crown on the head of a king, or an unearned crust in the mouth of a beggar."

"Do you think, then, that man has no excuse for his shortcomings, doctor?"

"He has many. He is controlled by the occult power of race transmissions, by laws which he did not help to make, by customs which he did not help to form, by organizations and environments beyond his power to change or combat. But because of these he should have no license to plunder his wealthier neighbor, for, in this republic, it is within the power of the people to change laws, and alter customs, and secure to every man the result of his own toil and skill—and that is all any man is entitled to."

"But the wealth owners, doctor, have monopolized nearly all the resources of nature."

"Nonsense. There is not a hungry idler in the purlieus of New York City but might catch fish enough at the nearest wharf to keep him from starvation, or find within a day's walk a piece of land he could cultivate on 'shares.' The resources of nature are inexhaustible. If every adult male in the land were to build for himself a marble palace, there would be no perceptible diminution in nature's supply of marble. If every farmer were to devote his energies and his acres to the production of wheat, until enough wheat should have been harvested to feed the world for five years, yet the capacity of soil and sun, water and air to produce more wheat would be neither exhausted nor impaired. For thousands of years the men of every civilization have been hewing forests, and smelting iron, yet the forests which are untouched and the mines which are unopened are practically limitless."

"Doctor, a man cannot stir the earth without a spade, or cut down a tree without an ax, or mine iron ore without a pick, and the owners of the spades, and picks, and axes, exact from the laborer an undue share of his labor for their use."

"Who is to determine whether the share exacted be an undue one? My own opinion is that the laborer's share of results has grown larger, and the capitalist's share smaller, during the last twenty years. At least, the rate of interest on money is not much more than half what it was before the war. But whether this be so or not it is not nature's fault. Nature is not only implacably just, she is impartially generous. No suitor is denied the chance to gain her favors, and none is refused any favor he may have earned. There are floods and tornadoes, frosts and fevers, burning suns and chilling winds. Yet these, as well as the fruitage and the harvests, are the offspring of inexorable law, and science now interprets the law. It warns us of cyclones ten thousand miles away; it predicts the date of arrival, speed, and duration of hurricanes; it brings the ladybug from Australia to combat and destroy the scalebug in California; it promises to conquer drought by exploding dynamite bombs in the air or by chemical production of rain; it restrains floods by diverting rivers; it destroys malarial germs by planting groves of eucalyptus; it analyzes soils; it selects seeds; it fertilizes with electric wires, and it ploughs and plants and harvests fields with iron-limbed and steam-lunged servants. A hundred years ago one man with spade and sickle slowly wrested from the earth the sustenance for his little household, with only sufficient surplus to scantily compensate the weaver, who, with hand loom, constructed a few yards of cloth between daylight and dark. Now a girl guides the spindles and shuttles and makes thousands of yards of cloth in a day, and the labor of one man industriously applied to so much land as he can advantageously cultivate with the aid of improved machinery, will in one year produce one thousand bushels of wheat, or their equivalent in agricultural products—enough to feed fifty men for a year.''

"I grant you, doctor, that the production of wealth has greatly increased. The problem of the hour is how to provide for a more equal and just distribution of it."

"John, the solution of the problem is not difficult. Allow every man to have that which he earns, and compel every man to earn that which he has. Accord every man the opportunity to work or starve, with the assurance that for his work he will receive full value, and for his idleness a hunger that no public or private charity will alleviate. Hard labor and hard fare for the criminal, generous diet and tender care for the sick, an ax or a pump handle for the tramp, and allow no healthy man to eat his supper until he has earned it. Consider sporadic and indiscriminate charity as great an evil as injustice. Accord every man his dollar and demand from every man your dollar, and give and exact shilling for shilling. Emulate and copy the inexorable justice of nature."

"Doctor," said the professor, "I am silenced but not convinced. The sun is getting too high for further fishing. Come, let us go to luncheon."

CHAPTER VI.

"No man can tell what he does not know."

"Bob," said Morning, "as they lighted their cigars, and seated themselves after supper upon the piazza of the railroad hotel at Tucson, "the copper assays are not up to your expectations, still I am inclined to buy the property if I can arrange to employ men at rates that will enable me to work it. What are miners' wages hereabouts?"

"Three dollars and a half a day for ten hours," replied Steel.

"And how much for unskilled laborers for road building, wheeling, and aboveground work?" said Morning.

"Two dollars and a half; but for work of that kind you can get Chinamen at $1.50 a day, Mexicans at $1.25, and Papago Indians for $1.00, if you wish to employ them, though I reckon you would have trouble about getting white men to work with either."

"I don't wish to cut wages on miners, Bob, for they earn all they get, but if I buy that property, there will be a lot of road building, and grading for furnace sites, and wheeling, and other work of the same nature, and unless such work can be done cheaply, it will not pay to hire miners for underground work, or, indeed, to work the copper mines at all. I shall want

(72)

these unskilled laborers for only a short time, and I have especial reasons for not hiring either white men or Mexicans, neither do I care to employ Chinamen if I can avoid it. Could I, think you, obtain enough Indians for this preliminary work?"

"Plenty of them at the San Xavier reservation, nine miles from here. I patter their lingo a little and can get you a gang if you want them."

"I may want to drill and blast down a lot of basalt rock to build the foundations of furnaces and ballast the road with," said Morning. "Will they do that kind of work?"

"Yes, until it comes to firing the blasts. You will need a white man for that. You will also need a white man for blacksmith work—sharpening picks and drills. The Indians cannot work at a forge, and they are nervous about 'big shoots,' as they call them."

"Bob, if I take those copper prospects of you at your price, will you hire a gang of Papagoes for me, and take them up there and work them for two or three months under my direction, you and I sharpening the tools and preparing and firing the blasts, I paying you say $10 a day for your services?"

"Well, Mr. Morning, I don't quite like such a job as that, but I am anxious to sell those copper prospects, and I will do it. But if you are going to hire Indian labor, I advise you to do first all the work that you intend to do with it. I mean, it will be best to get through with the Papagoes before you take any white men in there, or else there may be a row, and the white men will drive away the Indians."

"All right, Bob, I will take your advice. You may

consider the trade made. I will take your deed for the copper locations and give you a check to-morrow for $10,000 on the First National Bank at Denver, or I will arrange to get you the coin from the bank here if you desire it."

"Your check is good enough for me, Mr. Morning."

"Very well. Then you can go to the San Xavier reservation early in the morning and make a bargain with the Papagoes for three months. Obtain forty good men and agree to furnish them with rations and pay them $1.25 a day. They have ponies, I suppose, and can take their squaws along if they choose. It will make them more contented to stay. You might contract with them also to furnish enough cattle to supply themselves with fresh meat. They can drive them along, and there is now plenty of grass in the ra-vines. Don't let them come to Tuscon, for I don't wish the people here to know what I am doing. The Indians can strike across from San Xavier by Fort Lowell and meet us, or wait for us at the mouth of the Rillito. You can return here as soon as you start them, and we will buy teams and load them with sup-plies, and drive them out ourselves. We will do all the blacksmith work and blasting ourselves. And, Bob, keep your own counsel strictly about everything. I have reasons for secrecy which I will explain to you later."

"All right, Mr. Morning. I don't clearly see what you are driving at. It's a queer way to open a cop-per mine, but you are the captain, and I've known you a long time, and whatever you say goes with Bob Steel."

It was three o'clock the next afternoon before Steel returned from San Xavier. He was well known to the Papagoes, having often purchased grain and animals from them for mining companies with which he had been connected as superintendent. His mission was successful, and Manuel Pacheco, a leader among the Indians, had agreed to have the necessary force at the place designated on the third "sun up."

Tuscon, although not a mining town, is a commercial center for a dozen mining camps, and there was nothing in the outfitting of a party of miners calculated to attract especial notice. Two wagons and twelve mules were purchased, with all needed supplies, and Morning and Steel drove away to their destination, where they met the Indians and proceeded to the old copper-camp. After supper Morning opened the conversation which he had determined to have with Steel.

"Bob," said he, "to tell the truth, I do not intend to work this copper property at present, though I shall need it by and by for a purpose I will not now explain. I bought it mainly because I knew you intended to sell it to somebody, and I wished to keep others away from this vicinity. I have another use for the powder and the Indians, and, if you will accept the offer I am about to make, I have another service for you. I selected you because I know you are as true and as bright as your name. If you will work with me and for me in this cañon as I require, I will give you a salary of $1,000 a month for three years, and at the end of that time I will pay you—don't think I am crazy—I will pay you $1,000,000. What do you say to my proposition?"

"You take away my breath," rejoined Steel. "If I did not know you so well, I should say that you had been boozing on mescal, or were otherwise off your nut. But you don't talk usually without meaning what you say, and I reckon you are in earnest. But there is nothing that I can do to earn $1,000,000, or $1,000 a month either."

"Oh, yes, there is," said Morning, "as you will agree when you know all, or at least all that I intend to tell you! Listen: When I was up the cañon while we were here last week, I discovered and located a rich gold quartz lode that was uncovered by the waterspout. It is very rich and extensive—indeed, there are many millions in sight in the croppings. It was through my coming here to look at your copper lodes that I was led to its discovery, and in a certain way I consider you have a right to some profit from it, and I can well afford to give you a million dollars for your services and your silence, or several millions, if you want that much. The ledge is so rich that the first thing to do is to conceal it. No person but myself knows its extent or value, and I shall not disclose these even to you. When I commence working it and turning out bullion, people will be curious, and they will badger you to tell them all about. The elder Rothschild is credited with the aphorism that no man can tell what he does not know, and if you really don't know the extent of the Morning mine, it will be a good deal easier for you to baffle the curious. I propose that you shall not look at the ledge or go into the box cañon where it is. Will you agree to that?"

"Oh, I am agreeable!" said Steel. "I appreciate your reasons, and, anyway, it's none of my business."

Morning then explained to Steel the situation of the cañon where he had found the lode, and the manner of its discovery, but was silent as to its dimensions or the quantity of gold contained in the rock. He informed him as to his plan of operations, which was to pack all the supplies and tools on the backs of the animals as far up the cañon as it was possible thus to go, and there make a permanent camp. The Indians were then to carry the tools, powder, and a supply of provisions upon their backs up to the summit of the basalt wall near the rift, where another camp would be made.

Two Indians were to be left at the copper-camp, with directions if anyone appeared there to run up the cañon and inform Steel or Morning. Two Indians were to be placed in charge of the permanent camp and the animals, four Indians were to carry water in kegs to the top of the wall for the use of the main party there, two Indians to procure firewood and prepare food and attend to the camp at the summit, and thirty Indians to work at drilling holes in the basalt at the summit on both sides of the rift, and at a distance of about ten feet from the edge of it.

The squaws were to be suffered to make such disposition of their time as their social and domestic duties and inclinations might suggest. Steel and Morning would keep the drills sharpened at the portable forge, which, with a supply of charcoal, would be transported to the summit camp, and as often as the drill holes were ready they would place and explode the blasts.

It was intended thus to throw rocks from the summit down into the gorge, and this was to be repeated until its bottom should be covered to a depth of many feet, and all signs of the existence of the quartz lode obliterated. From the height of one thousand feet the lode could not be seen at all, unless one were to crawl to and look over the edge of the precipice, and then its nature could not—except by an experienced miner or geologist—be discerned from that of the neighboring rock. The Indians below would not be apt to disobey orders, leave their posts, and go into the cañon amid tumbling rocks, and the general stolidity and lack of interest of the Papagoes would lead them to attribute the entire work to the eccentricity of their white employer.

The plan formed by Morning was carried into effect. Drills of different length had been provided, and the work was systematized. At six o'clock each morning the Indians commenced work; from eleven to twelve they were allowed for dinner and rest. At five o'clock drilling was suspended, and the work of preparing the blasts was performed. The Indians then retired to a distance, and Morning and Steel would explode the blasts.

At the end of two months' hard labor the rift was filled with rock and débris to a depth of thirty feet, and the lode completely covered from view. Morning then made a relocation of the mine on the basalt wall above and on the mountain side below. He located extensions, side locations, and tunnel locations in every direction for a mile or more, so as to completely appropriate all approaches to the original location, and prevent others from obtaining any vantage-ground from which drifts might be run under his property. He also located the necessary mill sites, the waters of Rillito Creek, and the timber upon the mountains.

The plateau where he had tethered his horses on his first visit was, with the available adjacent slopes, chosen as a site for buildings he intended to have constructed for the use of the miners and their families, and a rock and earth dam was built in the Rillito several hundred feet above, from whence the water should be piped to the buildings. The Indians were then set to work constructing a wagon road to the mouth of the Rillito.

The work being completed, the entire party now journeyed to Tucson, and the Indians were paid off and returned to the reservation, where they doubtless regaled their tribe with an account of the work they had performed at the instance of the white lunatic who had paid them over four thousand "pesos" in silver to tumble rock into a hole. Yet it is doubtful if such information ever extended beyond members of their tribe, for, on parting with them, Morning presented each worker with a high silk hat, and each squaw with red calico for a gown, and Bob Steel made a speech to them in the Papago tongue, and asked them to agree not to tell the Indian agent, or any white man, where they had been working or what doing, beyond the statement that they had been "building wagon road." The Indians—naturally secretive—readily gave the required promise.

Having recorded his new location notices, Morning telegraphed to San Francisco for a portable sawmill. He loaded the wagons with a fresh supply of provis-

ions and tools and sent them with a gang of wood-
choppers in charge of Steel to the upper camp on the
Rillito, with directions to get out logs and haul them
to the site of the proposed sawmill.

While awaiting the arrival of the sawmill, Morning
visited the neighboring mining camps of Tombstone,
Globe, and Bisbee, and selected with great care—
after watching them at work and informing himself
as to their habits and antecedents—one hundred miners, to whom he agreed to give a steady job for several
years, working in eight-hour shifts, at $4.00 per day.
He preferred and obtained married men, each man
being promised a comfortable cabin, with transportation for his family and effects from Tucson.

In ten days the portable sawmill arrived, and with
it and a full outfit of building material, tools, and
pipe, Morning, accompanied by a gang of carpenters,
was again *en route* for the mine.

It was busy times at Waterspout, for such was the
name given to the new camp, for the next six weeks.
By that time the sawmill and shingle machine had
turned out sufficient material, and with the carpenters
and a number of the wood-choppers who were drafted
for the purpose, eighty comfortable board houses had
been constructed, with large buildings for shops and
offices, and a suitable edifice for a schoolhouse.
Water was piped to the little plaza about which the
buildings were gathered, and all was ready for the
miners.

The sawmill was now set to work getting out timbers for a mill, and for timbering tunnels. The men
were all alive with curiosity to know where was the

mine for the working of which all these preparations were made, but both Morning and Steel were reticent, and those who were too pressing in their inquiries were quietly given to understand that a continuation of questioning might cause their services to be dispensed with.

All being ready, the teams were sent to Tucson at the appointed time and returned with the miners and their household effects, a number of wagons chartered for the purpose bringing the women and children. Twenty or more adventurers on horseback and in wagons accompanied the party, as by this time curiosity was all ablaze at the proceedings of Morning, whose location notices had been read by hundreds, and been made the subject of frequent comment in the Tucson papers.

Numerous prospecting parties were dispatched to the Santa Catalinas during the next few months, and their members climbed all over the mountains, examined Morning's location monuments, and returned to Tucson with the report that the Colorado man was clean crazy, that there was not a sign of quartz, or any place where quartz could exist, and that Morning's friends—if he had any—would do well to appoint a guardian for him.

The plan of production upon which Morning had settled was to extract sufficient gold to gradually substitute that metal for paper, or to make it instead of bonds or credits the basis for paper money in all the civilized world, and to increase the circulation of all countries to the volume *per capita* of the country having the largest amount.

6

He learned from the statistics with which he had supplied himself that the money circulation of France, the most prosperous and the most commercially active nation in Europe, was $42.15 *per capita*, of the United States $24.10, of Great Britain $20.40, of Italy $16.31, of Spain $14.44, and of Germany, $14.23. In the Asiatic, semi-Asiatic and South American countries the money circulation was still less, being but $5.20 *per capita* in Russia, $3.18 in Turkey, $4.02 in British India, $4.90 in Mexico, $4.29 in Peru, $1.79 in Central America, and $1.29 in Venezuela.

Morning noticed that the greater the money circulation of a country, the greater the civilization, prosperity, and refinement of the people; and metallic money, or paper currency calling for metallic money, being the best money, it would be sure wherever obtainable to drive out all other currency. He proposed, therefore, to increase, as rapidly as was possible, the metallic money of the United States and Europe to the standard *per capita* of France, beginning with the United States, following with England, and then proceeding to the Continent.

The process of accomplishing this was to be exceedingly simple. He would ship gold bars to the mints of the country whose currency he proposed to increase, and ask that they be coined into the money of the country. The coin received he proposed to deposit in the banks of that country for investment or use therein.

The one danger against which he had to provide was demonetization of gold by the nations. He could only effectually guard against this by withholding all knowledge of the extent of his mine until he should have accumulated a vast deposit of gold bars—say $2,000,000,000 worth—and then deposit these for coinage suddenly and simultaneously at the mints of the world before any law could be enacted depriving gold of its quality as a money metal. Yet it would take several years for the mints to coin so large a sum, and in the meantime gold might be demonetized. In order for Morning to place his gold beyond the reach of such legislation, it was essential to have it coined, or put in form of money having a legal tender value. A slight change in the currency and coinage laws would effect this. In the United States it might be accomplished by an act of Congress requiring the government to receive gold bars, and to issue legal tender gold notes thereon, without actually coining the gold at all. The mints of the United States, working to their full capacity on gold alone, could not turn out more than $50,000,000 in coin per month, while a government printing press could issue $500,-000,000 in a day.

Morning concluded that one of his earliest duties would be to visit Washington while Congress was in session, and promote the necessary legislation.

Of the gold which he produced he could ship to the mints openly about one bar in twenty-five. The other twenty-four bars he could keep at the mine until he could build a smelting furnace and manufacture pigs of copper, which should be hollow, and in which gold bars should be concealed, and thus shipped to financial centers, where they could be stored ready for any occasion.

Morning estimated that the production of $100,-000,000 per month would require the activity of two hundred stamps, and that with the aid of improved machinery he could reach the ledge and commence the production of gold in about three months. He had now expended for labor, machinery, and supplies about $25,000, and as much more would be required to meet the labor expenses of the next sixty days, while the quartz mills he proposed erecting would require nearly $200,000 more.   As the business methods of the railroad company prevented him from keeping his secret, and at the same time realizing any money by shipping ore, he determined to obtain the necessary funds by a sale of his mortage securities, and, leaving Robert Steel in charge of the work, David Morning departed for Denver.

CHAPTER VII.

" Sick to the soul."

On his return to Denver, Morning found no difficulty in speedily closing up his business and convert-
ing his mortgages into money.   In about ten days he
was ready to depart for San Francisco, where he
intended purchasing the necessary machinery for five
mills of forty stamps each.   His sole remaining business in Denver was the execution and delivery to the
purchaser of a conveyance of some city property
which he had sold.

While breakfasting at the Windsor that morning,
his appetite was not increased by reading from the
Associated Press telegrams the following:—

"MARRIAGE IN HIGH LIFE.

"BOSTON, February 13, 1893.
"There was celebrated this morning at the residence
of the bride's father, Professor John Thornton, in
Roxbury, the nuptials of one of Boston's greatest
heiresses and acknowledged belles, the beautiful and
accomplished Miss Ellen Thornton, to the Baron Von
Eulaw.   The happy couple will sail on the *Servia*
to-morrow, and will proceed directly to Berlin.   It is
intimated that our fair countrywoman may be restored
to us after a season by the appointment of the Baron
Von Eulaw as envoy at Washington from the German
Empire."

Forgotten?   Ah, no! there are experiences in life

that may never be forgotten. Time rolls by, and against the door of the mausoleum where we buried our dead out of sight the years have piled events and emotions and distractions, and the passion which we once thought immortal becomes now an episode, and by and by a dream, and at last a vague and shadowy remembrance, and one day some new and mighty fact stalks forward, and sweeps away all obstructions, and the doors of the tomb are reopened, and the dead of our heart come forth, bringing to us sometimes the joys of life's morning, and sometimes the bitterness of a new death.

David Morning walked from the hotel to his office without noticing many of the friendly greetings bestowed upon him, for his thoughts were busy with the past, and there was a dull, dead pain tugging at his heart strings.

The notary who had taken Morning's acknowledgment to the deed whose delivery would complete his business in Denver, brought the instrument to Morning's office, and, not finding him in, slipped the paper in the top of a desk with a circular cover. This desk was one of Morning's first possessions in the way of office furniture, and, finding it convenient and commodious, he had caused it to accompany every change of quarters which his increasing business had from time to time rendered necessary.

Entering his office, Morning hurriedly threw back the cover of the desk, not noticing the deed in the top of it until it was too late to prevent the paper from being carried by the revolving cover into the interior of the desk, where it could only be reached by removing a portion of the back. The services of a mechanic from a neighboring furniture store were procured, the back of the desk was removed, and Morning recovered the deed.

He also recovered another paper. It was an unopened letter addressed to himself, which had doubtless reached its resting-place in the old desk through the same process as that which carried the deed there. The envelope was covered with dust; it was postmarked "Boston, Mass., February, 1883"—ten years before—and the superscription was in the handwriting of Ellen Thornton, now the Baroness Von Eulaw.

Dispatching the recovered deed to its destination, Morning closed the door of his private office, and, with breath coming thick and fast, proceeded to open and peruse the missive. It read as follows:—

ROXBURY, Mass., Feb. 13, 1883.

MY DEAR MR. MORNING: This letter may bring you a moment of surprise; if it be not a surprise mixed with chagrin, I am less justly repaid than perhaps I deserve for that which may seem my instability of purpose. But I have heard you say that you scarcely knew which was the weaker, the man who changed his mind too often or who never changed it at all, and in this recollection I find refuge.

With men as intuitive as yourself, explanations are almost superfluous. Nevertheless, you will bear with me while I pass under review a few of the causes which have led to this action.

After the change in my father's fortunes and our subsequent removal to Boston, life began to open up new possibilities, and what with the increased demands upon my time, and the many beguilements of flattering tongues, together with—let me confess it— an unresting desire to forget the act of folly which had shut out every ray of sunshine from my heart, as I found too late, I at length fixed my footing to the artificial conditions of the situation, and for a brief time flattered myself that you were forgotten.

My letter, if written at all, ought to stop here. But thus much I have learned—that passion tinctured with sorrow is the greatest of egotists, and that the feeling that brooks no measure of repression or discouragement inspires a degree of courage little short of defiance. Thus stimulated, I feel a growing joy in being able to surmount artificial restraint and to address you as I know you would wish an honest girl who loves you with her whole heart, should speak.

What will you think of me? Will you call me fickle and unworthy? unwomanly? In a word, will you misunderstand me? How could I know till my eyes were opened that there was but one sun? that the whole world to me was adjusted to your simple, noble qualities? How could I know that the music of the spheres meant the remembered tones of your voice, that your face should haunt alike every scene of splendor and every secret shadow, or that I would give my patrimony to be able to pass my fingers through your brown locks for ever so brief a moment?

What am I writing? I dare not read it. How confident I feel, how transported with the thought that you may in remembering me forget my much-repented dictum, or at least relegate it to the Quixotic realm to which it belongs.

As I near the close of my letter, I am possessed with a new fear. Shall I dare send it? What if you shall have discovered new powers in yourself, new persons out in the broad world, which shall make you glad of your escape? It is so long since I have heard of you, and life is so full of new things, I forget that you too have quite the right to change your mind. If this be your condition, do not, I beg of you, write me. I could not bear the humiliation as your great heart bore yours. Consign my letter, then, to the great silence, and only remember me as ever and always your sincere friend, ELLEN.

What was his colossal fortune to David Morning now? Out of the past came this message of life and love; of a love gone forever, and a life which now seemed barren of purpose and hope.

What is time but a name? The intervening years shriveled into nothingness, and he was again bathing in the light which shone from the eyes of the woman he loved, the one woman on earth or in heaven for him, yesterday and to-day and forever. Again he walked with her under the whispering foliage along the brow of the hill which crowns the Queen City of the plains, and watched the burning sunsets illumine the lavender mountains and change the clouds into embers of glory. Again he sat beside her, reading some tender or beautiful or stirring passage from poet or essayist. Again, at the good-night going, he felt her dainty kiss, thrilling his soul to ecstasy.

And she was lost to him now, lost through his pride, lost through his vanity, lost through such dense and inexcusable stupidity as never before possessed or afflicted a man. He had taken her girlish doubts as final. He had thought to exhibit his manly pride—which was, after all, only conceit of self—as an offset to her presuming to question the possibility of her being possessed by a great love for him. Coward that he was to surrender this glorious creature without an effort. Dolt that he was to so mistake her maidenly hesitancy.

And she—dear heart—had loved him after all. She had condescended to summon him, and he had never received the message. What had she thought of his failure to respond? What must she have thought of him, save that he was a cruel, conceited creature unworthy of her love? What humiliation his unexplained silence must for a time have brought to her gentle spirit! What wreck and misery had not this miscarriage of her missive brought to his life!

If he could have identified the clerk or postman whose carelessness had misplaced her letter, he would have beaten him in his fury, and he wished for an ax that he might hew and batter to splinters the inanimate desk whose machinery had been instrumental in wrecking two lives.

Were they hopelessly wrecked? He caught his breath at the thought. He at least was free, and whatever else might come never would he be otherwise. Never should wile of woman enchant him, never should desire for home and love and perpetuation of race and name beguile him. He would walk lonely to the gates of the eternal morning, and wait for her beyond the portal, and carry her soul upon the pinions of his immortal love to the uttermost confines of ether, where no entrapments or environments of earth could follow or molest them, and in the glow of the astral light he would claim her as his own, and give himself to her forever and ever.

Ellen's letter released the passion which had been locked for ten years in the silent chambers of David Morning's soul, and it possessed the man, and mastered him with throes of bitter agony and throbs of ecstatic delight. His cheeks were wet with the tears of disappointment, and again to the very center of him he laughed with joy as he covered the letter with kisses.

"She loved me, my darling, my own, she loved me!" he cried. "Maybe she loves me yet!" and again his heart beat wildly. "For ten years she remained unmated. But yesterday she married this German nobleman, this Baron Von Eulaw. Surely love could not have moved her to the union. Surely with her nature she could not have forgotten her first love. She was outraged and humiliated and incensed at the silence and seeming indifference of the man she really loved, and so she married, for reasons common enough in society."

Was this tie irrevocable? Could it not be severed? Might it not be possible that happiness should yet be in store on this earth for his darling and himself? He was now in possession of the lever that moves the world. Should he not use this power for her and for himself, as well as for the benefit of mankind?

Who was this German baron that he should stand against him? There were hundreds of barons, but only one owner of the Morning mine. He would

use millions piled upon millions to bring his Ellen to
his arms.

Napoleon divorced Josephine and married Maria
Louisa.   Cæsar put away one wife and married
another.   David placed Uriah in the front of the battle.   Many kings had used their power to readjust to
their liking their own domestic relations and those of
their subjects.

He was a mightier king than Darius.   He ruled
greater armies than any ever commanded by Bona-
parte.   Not the Kaiser or the Romanoff upon their
imperial thrones could exercise so great a power as
David Morning.

He would bid his golden armies serve their master.
Walpole had truthfully said that "every man has his
price," and the Baron Von Eulaw probably had his.
How many millions would this titled Dutchman take
for his wife? ten? fifty? a hundred? a thousand?—
he should have them multiplied again and again.

Morning smiled grimly at the grotesque fancy.
Von Eulaw aspired to the American embassy.   May-
hap he was not covetous but ambitious.   Very well,
he would ask the Hohenzollern to name his figures
for offices and ribbons and rank to be accorded to the
baron in exchange for a surrender of his American
wife.   He would pay off the national debt of Germany if necessary.   Or he would buy the baron a
kingdom.   There were always thrones for sale for
cash or approved credit in the Danubian country.
That of Servia was just now in the market, and even
that of Spain or Portugal might be purchased.

Maybe the baron loved his wife.   How could he

help loving her? Curse him, what right had he to love her? What if Morning emulated the example of the Psalmist and caused the Baroness Von Eulaw to be made a widow? Money would accomplish this, and none be the wiser.

None? Ah, what of the God that rules worlds and directs the eternities, the God that was in and a part of David Morning, the God that punishes and pities, the God that smote David, that struck down Cæsar, that gave Napoleon to an exile's death, and Henry Tudor to centuries of infamy?

If Morning gained his Ellen's arms through wrong to another, through wrong to his own imperial and impartial conscience, there would be bitterness in her kisses, and misery in his soul; they would go maimed and chained to the gates of death, and in the other land they should meet not again.

And, inch by inch and minute by minute, Ohromades and Ahriman fought for the soul of David Morning. The ebon-plumed spirit of darkness and the silver-armored essence of light battled along the lines of heaven and hell, and the light triumphed, and darkness was hurled from the battlements, and peace and strength came to the aching soul.

He would wait. He would not even jeopardize her peace by righting himself in her esteem. He would offer no explanation. He would wait, wait for the decree of the Father, wait for the hour of meeting in honor. If it came on earth, well; if it came only through the help of death, still well, for "life is short but love immortal." In the other land there would be readjustments, and each soul not mated truly here would find its true mate there, in a mating that should be prevented by no power, and limited by no death, but should endure so long as the planets circle in their orbits.

How did he know this? Not through any evidence presented to the material senses, nor through any logic of the schools. It is the spiritual sense of man that perceives his spiritual life. No priest can give him his intuitions, no scoffer can take them from him, and the querulous questionings of science are but as the babblings of infancy in the august presence of the soul.

And for full five minutes David Morning sat with his face between his hands, then rose and went forth a conqueror.

CHAPTER VIII.

BEFORE leaving Colorado Morning employed a force of skilled workmen, necessary for the successful conduct of both quartz mills and copper-smelting furnaces. It was his design to make Waterspout a little world in itself, the members of which should consent to remain in the cañon for three years, communicating with the world outside only by mail. To this end physicians, school-teachers, and a clergyman were secured, and a library, musical instruments, and theatrical scenery purchased, with the confident expectation that local histrionic talent would be developed; for where is the American community of five hundred souls which does not contain the material both for Hamlet and burnt-cork opera?

From Denver Morning proceeded directly to San Francisco, where the leading iron works were soon busy constructing quartz-crushing machinery. By the 15th of April everything was on the ground, and in one month thereafter the stamps were ready to drop. This result was achieved by working nights by electric light, the Rillito furnishing power for the dynamos.

In ordering the mining work Morning had arranged for a double-track tunnel, which would reach the lode at a depth of about one hundred and fifty feet from the surface, and there was now a broad, well-ventilated and well-lighted underground road to and along the entire length of the quartz lode, at a point five feet from it. From this tunnel Morning could cause to be run as many crosscuts into the lode as he desired, and thus control the amount of quartz extracted, and keep within his exclusive knowledge the true dimensions of the mineral deposit.

Conjecture was rife, and the general opinion questioned the sanity of a man who made such costly and elaborate preparations for extracting and reducing quartz in a place where no quartz or sign or promise of quartz was visible. But Superintendent Robert Steel kept his own counsel, the wages of the men were paid promptly, all bills were cashed on presentation, and the prevailing sentiment was voiced by big Jim Stebbins, the boss of shift No. 3, who interrupted and terminated a discussion among his men as to Morning's movements by saying:—

"Dave Morning is no mining shark or stock-board stiff. His money is clean money; he dug it out of the ground; and if he chooses to buck it off agin a syenite dike, a payin' you fellers $4.00 for eight hours' work, which is a sight more than some of you is worth, why, I reckon it's nobody's business but his own. It's only five minutes to shift time; put out your pipes, and get a move on you."

The mills were built on the side of the mountain below the tunnel, and were inclosed—as was the entrance to the tunnel—with a high fence, within which none were permitted except workmen on duty.

A light narrow-gauge road was built from the mill

yard at Waterspout down the cañon, past the copper smelters, to the mouth of the Rillito. The wagon road was destroyed, and the stream dammed in several places, so that the only means of reaching Waterspout was by rail; and, without a pass from Superintendent Steel, no person was permitted to ride on the cars. Tourists, prospectors, and seekers for information who should overcome these difficulties, and walk, climb, or swim to Waterspout, would need to carry also their own provisions and bedding, for they would find neither shelter, food, nor welcome, and could not gain access to mine or mill.

These discouragements stained the reputation of Morning for hospitality, but they helped to keep his secret, and proved effective against everybody except a special reporter of a San Francisco journal, who, disguised as a Papago Indian, journeyed to Waterspout, and remained there several days. He might have made a longer stay, but a Papago squaw, hearing of his presence, sought him with a view to connubial felicity. The reporter would have faced death for his journal, but he drew the line at matrimony and fled. He did not gain access to mine or mill while there, but he picked up considerable information, the publication of which might have proved damaging to Morning's plans.

It happened that the sagacious manager of the great daily, before ordering publication, frankly communicated with Morning—who happened to be in San Francisco—and, being persuaded by that gentleman that the public interest would be subserved by silence concerning the great gold mine in the Santa Catalinas, the notes of the reporter were not sent to the composing room.

At last all was in readiness. The men whose duties ended with the construction of mills, furnaces, railroad, and buildings, were sent with the teams to Tucson and paid off. All idle, dissatisfied, and unsatisfactory men were discharged, and their places supplied with others. The best mining and milling machinery obtainable was in place and ready to run. Supplies of all kinds, sufficient for months, were in the storehouses, five crosscuts, twenty feet apart, had been run to within one foot of the ledge, and the doors of the treasure caverns were ready to open, when the owner of the mine directed that all the men assemble on the little plaza at Waterspout in front of the company's offices.

"My friends," said David Morning, "I have called you together that we may have a more perfect understanding before entering upon the most important part of the labor that lies before us. You have doubtless felt surprised at the extent of the work which has been done in this cañon without there being any ore, or indications of ore, in sight. But your surprise will change to astonishment when you know, as you soon must know, how extensive and rich a body of gold quartz is here. It has been and still is my desire to withhold from the world any knowledge, or, at least, any accurate knowledge, of the amount of gold that will be produced. I conclude that the best method for securing secrecy is to make it in the interest of all concerned to keep the secret, and I desire to say now that each one of you, whether miner, millman, mechanic, laborer, teacher, clerk, clergyman, or physician, every man who

is or who may be on the pay-rolls, who shall faithfully
discharge the duties for which he was employed, and
shall remain in such employment for one year, without in the meantime leaving this cañon, and who shall
not by letter, or otherwise, communicate any information concerning the working or yield of the mine, will
be presented by me at the end of the year with the
sum of $5,000 in addition to his pay. Those who re-
main until the end of the second year will receive a
further present of $10,000, and those who remain un-
til the end of the third year will receive a still further
present of $15,000. Those who choose to go, or who
may be compelled to leave here because of either mis-
conduct or misfortune, will receive nothing but their
pay. Should any die, the present for that year will,
at the expiration of the year, be paid to his family—
if here. If strangers visit this cañon, I shall expect
you not to entertain them or converse with them.
Those of you who correspond with friends will please
say nothing whatever as to any facts concerning this
property, or any opinions you may have about it or
about me. It is only with your co-operation and good
faith that the secrets of this mine can be kept. Any one
of you may, to a certain extent, betray those secrets.
Should he do so, he will not only defeat my plans but
deprive himself of the fortune which I expect to pay
each of you as the price of three years of work and
reticence.''

The proposition of Morning was agreed to with
unanimity, and with an enthusiasm and gratitude
which can be comprehended when it is understood
that even the sum of $5,000 represented to the most

industrious and frugal workman the savings of from five to twenty years.

Three days afterwards the crosscuts were in ore, cars loaded with the yellow-seamed quartz began to discharge into the chutes and feeders, and the music of two hundred stamps resounded in the Santa Catalinas.

Morning's estimate of the value of the ore, which he made from the specimens taken by him at the time of the discovery, proved singularly accurate. The quartz contained $10,000 in gold per ton, of which amount ninety-five per cent was saved in the mill. The reduction power was two tons to each stamp per *diem*, and the yield of the mine was quite $4,000,000, or eight tons of gold, each day. The necessity of resting one day in seven was observed at Waterspout, both as a sanitary measure and because of the suggestions of the race germs that Morning had received from his Connecticut ancestors.

The disposition of the gold bars produced was made in accordance with Morning's plans previously made. Each day the product of the copper furnaces, cast in hollow moulds, was brought upon the railroad to the lower part of the mill yard, where were situated the gold-melting furnaces. Under the personal supervision of Steel, assisted by a few men specially selected for the work, a gold bar was placed inside each copper mould, the slight spaces filled with dry sand, a half inch of dry sand placed upon the end of the gold bar, and the mould then filled with melted copper.

When completed there was to all appearance a pig

of black copper or copper matte worth commercially $18 or $20. In truth there was a gold bar worth $40,000, which a few minutes' work with a cold chisel would release.

The gold bars intended for open shipment were cast one-half the size of those intended for imprisonment in the copper pigs. Of these small bars Morning had eight prepared each day, making the ostensible yield of the mill and mine $160,000 per day, or about $4,000,000 per month. Of the large bars he had eighty prepared each day, which were shipped as copper pigs. Their real value was about $4,000,000 per *diem*, or $100,000,000 per month. These were allowed to accumulate in the warehouse at Rillito Station until Morning should procure suitable places for their deposit in Eastern cities.

On the 1st of August, 1893, everything had been running smoothly for several weeks, and gold shipments amounting to millions had been made. Morning concluded that the running of the mill and mine no longer required his personal attention, while his projects demanded his presence at the great financial centers. Robert Steel was in full possession of the plans of his friend and employer, who, leaving everything in his charge, bade good-by to all and departed for Tucson to take the train for the East.

CHAPTER IX.

"And then hid the key in a bundle of letters."

From the Baroness Von Eulaw to Mrs. Peyces Thornton.

BERLIN, March 18, 1893.

MY DEAR MOTHER: Really I hardly feel equal to a detailed description of our trip over the ocean. Why is it that I remember only the painful things about our journey? Surely there were pleasant people, cultivated men and graceful women, such as one always meets in these days of free interchange between different nations. But I have observed that some temperaments catch first and make most visible the shadows upon the landscape. Much as I love the hues and tints of the changeful waters, I seem to remember only the rolling ship, and between me and the thought of the blue skies and the splendid sunsets which I would have carried away as a treasured memory, comes some trifling but harassing recollection. So narrow and individual is the composing-stone upon which our impressions are made up.

I assume, dear mother, that you remember our serious conversation that last night before my marriage, as, sitting upon my couch and looking into my sleepy eyes, you half chided me for that which you called—for want of a better term—indifference.

(102)

Pardon me, 'tis a word with a sex. A woman may love, she may hate, she may dissemble, but, pose as she will, there is no profile in her passion. I do not deny I am going to school to my own heart. I am honestly endeavoring to follow your advice. I am learning to love. Let me say in the beginning it is a mistake to believe that men love deeply. If ever they do, the object of their passion is themselves. Is this a sound foundation to build domestic faith upon? However, as I have said, I shall try very earnestly to do my part.

The baron told me this morning that as Americans were a nation of plebeians, I would naturally suffer many disabilities even as the Baroness Von Eulaw, to which I replied rather hotly that honor and courage required no purple swaddlings to hide their proportions, and that we Americans sprang full created from the brain of regenerate thought, whereupon his manly fist gathered muscle for a moment, then as speedily relaxed, and he only slammed the door of his dressing-room between us. Believe me, my dear mother, I was very sorry for the scene, and I have no excuse to offer save the gaping wound to my patriotism, which I find much more sensitive over here than at home.

We have constant engagements, and I feel a little worn, though otherwise quite well. Can you pardon a letter wholly devoted to myself? and in return will you not tell me all about yourself, dear papa, and everybody you know?

Always faithfully your own,   ELLEN.

From Mrs. Perces Thornton to the Baroness Von Eulaw.

ROXBURY, Mass., April 2, 1893.

MY DEAR DAUGHTER: I have your first letter written from Berlin, but how sad! That dreadful sea must have made you bilious. It has always just such an effect on your father; he sees the whole earth through smoked glasses.

But I can only imagine you as in a constant succession of raptures. Such a marriage for an American girl! A baron with such deportment, and such a delightful accent! I have no doubt, too, he is much richer than he represented. I assure you, the young ladies of Boston's high circles have turned all hues of the rainbow with envy, and you ought to find great pleasure in that recollection alone. Besides, such opportunities as you are having to meet crowned heads, and feel yourself as one among the titled people of Europe! What elevation! What distinction! You must not forget to make the most copious notes, so that you will be able to impress your superiority upon the world of society when you return.

Really, you should be, as I know you are, very happy. Of course "scenes" are unpleasant to one like yourself, not foreign bred. But I am told that such experiences are the real thing with nobility, especially if there is an American wife. And it is reasonable to suppose that high blood should feel intolerant toward all forms of assertiveness on the part of women, especially American women.

Therefore, be a little discreet, my dear, and remember what an English woman said to you, that it is not good form to be either clever or artistic, and above all patriotic.

You speak of shadows in your life. It was only the other day I read from one of your own books on the Newtonian theory of color, that dark objects were such as absorbed the light and reflected only somber tints, and I am sure it is so with your life; it is holding the light within itself.

I will not write more to-day, for your correspondence will be large, and time precious with you. How radiant you must look with your graceful gowns and your classic face; almost equal to a born princess! Believe me, my dear child, I am very proud of your noble marriage and of your dutiful conduct in making such an one largely, let me confess, to please me. And of all things, do not trouble yourself too much about the love business—that will all come about in good time, and if it does not—well, I can only say you will have a majority with you.

Greet your noble husband with the pride and joy that I feel in him, and present your loving father, who so seldom writes. Send fresh photos of your dear self, the baroness, and the baron, and do not permit them to exaggerate his nose, which is quite full enough at best, though a true sign of the blood.

Your devoted mother,

PERCES THORNTON.

From the Baroness Von Eulaw to Mrs. Perces Thornton.

BERLIN, April 20, 1893.

MY DEAR MOTHER: So far from the monopolizing

effect of minor matters of which I complained in my last, I seem to be losing my individuality altogether. Have you ever possessed your mind of one subject or object to the absolute exclusion of even yourself? What an unpleasant condition of mind it is! The baron I find to be a man most peculiarly constituted. The somewhat dominant manner which you suppose to be foreign breeding, as you expressed it, seems to have developed into an engrossing self-consequence, which appears to draw its vitality, if I may be pardoned for saying so, largely from his new marital connection.

For instance, at the opening of the season we attended the Emperor's Easter ball. According to our customs, after concluding the first dance with the baron, I accepted a waltz with an English nobleman, whom I had met on some previous occasion. We were resting for a moment after a round of the spacious ballroom when I felt my arm seized from behind, and with a muttered oath the baron commanded my instant release and return home.

What should I have done? Disregard him and precipitate a scandal? Impossible. I made excuse in some hypothetical disarrangement of my dress and retired. I am only able to write because it is my left arm which suffered the accident. The subsequent explanations of the baron were, of course, frivolous, but I was too relieved by any form of apology to add words, which, without reference to their significance, always irritate him. I mention this little incident in order to show you how it is that my visible life is subordinated, albeit my spirit is in no way depressed though severely harassed.

As I write I am doubtful if I ought to speak of these things at all. I do not ask myself what is due to my rank here, for that was conferred by him, but is it womanly to stand before the world an intelligent and willing indorser of his character and conduct, having given my public vows for better or worse, and then, cowering behind his faults, denounce such acts as only, at worst, affect me? Indeed, I must exercise more courage and less candor. One thing is certain, I am constantly looking for the better traits in his nature, and am making every effort to call them forth. Thus I escape self-reproach at least. But I am self-abashed at my attitude, for I abhor dissembling. The baron loves to taunt me with this trait, which he calls rudeness, and declares it to be the result of my " Yankee training." I only smile at this, for, as I have said, he cannot brook discussion.

But, my dear mamma, enough of this, for you will think my marriage a failure, and contribute my experiences to the building up of Mona Caird's theories. By the way, how shocked I felt at reading them, although I now divine some meanings that I had overlooked! But never can I tolerate the thought that there are not people—ideal, if you please—whose marriages might be too sublimated for earthly contract, and are, therefore—according to the proverb—made in heaven. Dear mother, pardon me, there is something wanting in your letters. You promised me to mention everybody we ever knew, or something to that effect. I am absolutely famishing for news of our old friends. By the way, how peculiar it is, I seem to remember with singular pertinacity the people we knew before we came to Boston, and dear, beautiful Denver is ever before my eyes. Please remember everything, and above all your affectionate

ELLEN.

From the Baroness Von Eulaw to Miss Fanny Fielding, Denver, Colorado.

BERLIN, May 1, 1893.

MY DEAR OLD SCHOOLMATE: Your kind letter makes me homesick. Can you imagine a homesick bride? Even before fruitage appears from the orange bloom, dismated for the decking of my nuptial robes, or even the fragrance departed from the yellowing buds on the garniture laid away to rest and rust, I am sitting with an unwilling face to the open door of the future, and groping with a blind but eager hand among the rustling leaves of a near past, for some familiar touch or sound to summon back the half-tasted joys which I so ruthlessly flung away.

You ask me for some advice concerning marriage, illumined, as you tersely put it, by experience. My sweet friend, what a useless task you impose upon me. Whenever was woman directed by the experiences of others, however wise or however bitter such experiences may have been? Always some suggestion or exception to change the verdict. "Mine has black eyes, yours has blue, which makes all the difference." Or, "one is fat, the other lean." Or, "this one walks, the other rides"—so infinite the variety of excuses, so single the faith of woman.

What else, then, shall we call marriage but destiny? The heart knows its wants and we know its plaintive cry, as a mother knows the wail of her famishing babe; yet for some frivolous fancy or conceit, some wound to our vanity, some plethoric ambition, or some glittering paste or bauble, we stifle the natural cry of the human heart, and wait for the mystic note upon which is to be constructed the music of our future. Alas! in the metaphor you understand so well, we too often touch only the diminished seventh, and the sure, complete, resolving chord is never sounded.

Somewhat, too, our institutions of marriage are at fault, or at least the laws and customs which control them. With a nation of men, free, rational, and liberal, we have a nation of women enslaved, dishonest, and miserable, and it is among her noblest and most common phases of fate that she goes mutely to her grave, a victim of such weak social prejudices as have grown to be even a subject of satire among Europeans.

Conscientiousness is a boasted virtue among Boston people of certain high cult, yet how many of her beautiful women go to the altar with a lie upon their maidenly lips? Why?—For the reason that there is some man whom she loves and dares not declare it. For the reason that society sets a seal upon her lips and turns her life into a drain-channel for misbegotten vows. For the reason that she cannot break the frost-bound usages of cowardly error with one stroke of her puny fist, and openly propose to join fortunes with the man after her own heart and her own high convictions. And so she rakes over the cold, unfruitful soil in her own soul, and plants the germ of a falsehood or a folly, and waits for the accident of some quickening power, in slavish and unheroic patience.

Witness the result: Some masculine hand, more or less clumsy or more or less cunning, little matter if it bring a wedding ring, sheds ephemeral warmth upon the unsanctified ground, and the victim starts upon her lonely, loveless journey toward race building and sacrifice.

As I indicated, dear Fanny, I have not drawn for my picture largely upon individual experiences, neither are my opinions stimulated by any observations taken from this side the water. Indeed, I even prefer, of kindred evils, the insipid method which leaves the marriage question in the hands of the parents. But let me leave this for subsequent discussion, for my letter is already too long, and I have not gossiped at all, and I remember, dear girl, how you do love innocent gossip.

Write to me often and I will fill my letters with the sweetest of nothings if you will. Love and adieu and think of me as your devoted friend,   ELLEN.

From the Baroness Von Eulaw to Mrs. Perces Thornton.

BERLIN, May 10, 1893.

DEAREST MOTHER: "Let fate do her worst, there are moments of joy," and such moments I owe to my fondness for music. What would have been all these dreary weeks and months of shallow acting, if the depths of my soul had not been stirred by the genius of that creative force which, mocking at our own crude disguises, rehabilitates pain with the fair seeming of pleasure, which relegates near sorrows to the realms of tradition, and illusionises common care?

Art, in any form, I conceive to be the benefactor

of the human race. If truth, shorn of its infinitude of possibilities, constitutes the religion of the civilized world, if the *deux et machina*, as Æschylus somewhere has it, unlyrical and unleavened by beauty of device, by rhetoric or action and climax, be persuasive and instructive and inspiring, then how ineffably shall truth have gained by the development of its powers through visible forms of dramatic conceit, through association with the elements of art, through characterization, through skillful adaptation, through harmonized mediæ of appeal to the sense or the sentiment, the sympathies or the imagination?

I am reminded here of an incident which occurred in our box at the Grand Opera House, during a late performance of Die Meistersinger, which resulted—as is not unusual in these days—unpleasantly. My husband, as you may remember, affects music solely for the paraphernalia of the stage, for the glitter and show of boxes and stalls, for the exposed shoulders of the diamonded dames of fashion, for the numbers of men with eyeglasses and uniforms—anything, in fact, but the music, which rather bores him.

Therefore it is I apprehend that he discusses music so incomprehensibly—to say the least—I would not say irrationally. Somewhere during the development of the plot I was struck with the similarity of the dramatic motive with that of the Greek tragedies, especially the choral odes, where occurs the element of transition which some scholars call the evolutionary or perhaps the re-incarnating period of the ancient drama. This similarity—in some ways identical—I inadvertently alluded to in a more or less critical review of the opera and its construction, which I ventured between acts, in the presence of a party of Americans who were our guests for the occasion.

Suddenly as thought, the baron's face was aflame. But "what it were unwise to do 'twere weaker to regret," and I prepared to defend my position as best became me. " You call my divine countryman a plagiarist," he hissed between his teeth. Our male guest glowered, and the ladies with heightened color looked at the orchestra.

"I beg your pardon, sir," said I, with an assumed smile, "I did not say so, though I admit that my suggestion was unfortunate in its inference."

The baron sprang to his feet and stood over me, his arms akimbo and the well-known look of suppressed rage upon his face.

" You called my divine countryman a plagiarist," he repeated, gazing out over the audience, and feeling for my slippered foot with his heel, which he settled firmly upon my silken-clad instep. The hurt made me wince, but I could not remove my foot from the vise. Then, in order to mollify his temper, which I had grown to know too well how to deal with, I added laughingly, though half wild with pain as he deadened his weight upon my poor instep:—

"If your countryman were amenable to the charge of plagiarism, so also is our Shakespeare, for in the comedy of Trinummus, Megaronides says, 'The evil that we know is best. To venture on an untried ill,' etc., and Shakespeare, two thousand years later, said, 'Rather bear the ills we have than fly to others that we know not of.'"

"You call my divine countryman a plagiarist," half-childishly, half-insanely repeated my noble lord, grinding my foot beneath his heel. A cry of pain escaped me, which a timely crash of cymbals in the orchestra had the effect to drown.

"Well, what of it?" blurted the American, throwing his full weight, as if by accident, against the baron's shoulder, and then turning to me with an apology resumed his place. Now while I never take refuge in my sex for at least a verbal retaliation of the wrongs I receive from my husband, it goes without saying that the man who visits brutality in any form upon a woman is a coward. But I had never seen the baron insulted, and was therefore wholly unprepared for the profuseness with which he apologized to our guests, and the blandness with which he offered his hand as he bade them good-night. But the most humiliating part of this humiliating affair was the fact that I was forced to repeat an apology fashioned by himself, the entire length of our journey home, even until the carriage stopped at the door.

It is not clear to me, my dear mother, that I am justified in rehearsing to you, or to anyone, details of my life, which may seem trivial, but for which I am able to offer no other excuse than your own solicitous insistence. I am always promising myself that every next letter shall be dictated in more cheerful spirit. Till then adieu. Present me with kindest love and beg papa to write me. I do so long for a sight of his letters. Love to those who love me.

As ever, devotedly yours,   ELLEN.

8

*From the Baroness Von Eulaw to Mrs. Perces Thorn-
ton.*

BERLIN, June 21, 1893.

MY DEAREST MOTHER: How shall we account for our various moods? Yesterday I was miserable; to-day I am joyful; to-morrow I may be hopeful or heart-broken, according as—oh! I forgot to say I am all alone; the baron has gone to St. Petersburg. I am supposed to have accompanied him, and so nobody comes. But I am not lonely; now that I am left to myself I see how beautiful is the world about me.

This morning I looked from my windows upon the river. The sharp lights I had watched so often swiftly changing to shadows, the warring glances suggestive only of inner strife, with all its complexity of passion, were lost in the soft peaceful flow of the waters as they hurried on to the ultimate sea. And I thought how much of this mood is due to fancy, that untenable, mercurial, and sublimated quality of the mind, half trickery, half truth, and altogether elusive as vapor. But how profligate of that precious sense of pleasure so steadily withheld from my heart these later months! Too precious, indeed, for the operations and experiments of the mental laboratory to which I seemingly so recklessly submitted it, and so I dismissed analysis and clung to my fancies, which at least made me happy in the present.

After my breakfast I prepared myself for a walk, with only my little fox-terrier for a companion. Poor little Boston, how grateful he seemed! I could see him laugh with joy as his little brown lips quivered with flexible feeling. Notwithstanding his many years, he could scarcely find footing for his bounding steps for looking back at me to search my laughing eyes. You remember who gave me my terrier, away out in Denver? how he was brought to me in two strong, guardful arms, a little loose-skinned, wise-eyed puppy, so quiet and serenely happy in the warm embrace— where was I? oh, yes! talking about Boston—so we pulled some roses, Boston and I. But never looked roses so red, or green so tender or so vivid, and I longed to find the secret of their voluptuous bloom and half-suffocating fragrance, but that I guessed all was again fancy; only an easy, translatable pinch of dust and a resolvable stain; a simple stroke of creative power and a dash of ether—only a rose.

How easy seem the processes of nature with harmonized material for working out the thought! Nature never experiments; gravitation is her law, deflection is anarchy, and defiance a destroyer. Love, I deem, is only obedience to this law. Obscure as are its operations and subtle as its teachings are, any smallest portion of scholarship, leveled at the finding out, divested of preconceived ideas and personal bearings, but persistently and conscientiously agitated by scientific and organized effort, might revolutionize a world of error, and establish a sure basis for sentiment and social reform.

For I believe that unhappy marriages are a direct result of ignorance. Passions called by various names go to make up the system. Sordidness, vanity, interdependence, weak abeyance to custom, contribute to the sum of human misery. But ignorance is the basis of the organized error. For what manner of

men or women would deliberately entail upon themselves the shackled conditions of a loveless marriage,
which has no alternative but subordination or rebellion? For only in love—another name for harmony—
may be found that unity which leaves no room for sacrifice or misconceit.

But, dearest mother, what can you think of my letters? I began to tell you of my one happy day and
have spread my speculations over the whole human
race. I started to take you for a promenade along
Unter den Linden, and to rest by the cool fountain
in the Lustgarten, and have ended with a few feeble
remarks upon the possible sources of sentiment and
sorrow.

But Boston is waiting for his dinner, for he dines
with me to-night. What a jolly day we've had, eh,
Boston? and we will sleep and dream of you, dear
mamma, and many more, for none but bidden guests
must fill my room to-night. By the way, I do wonder if
the poor, weak brain of my little terrier is in any degree susceptible of being stirred by memories of his
old friends? In any event, I envy him, for he is not
amenable to the necessities of a false life, "a liar of
unspoken lies."

Dear mamma, a sweet good-night. I am sending
you a few pictures picked up at Lepkes. The group I
am sure you will enjoy, though I like better the por-
trait by Van Dyck. There is a haunting sort of look
about it, reminding me of someone I have known
somewhere. I wonder if you will discern it? Probably it was only a passing fancy, one of such as have
filled my brain all day long.

Again love and good-by.   ELLEN.

From the Baroness Von Eulaw to Mrs. Perces Thornton.

MENTONE, Italy, August 10, 1893.

DEAREST MOTHER: How rebellious my heart and impatient my pen as I take it up to write words which only your mother's ear should catch from my lips!

Where shall I begin to tell you the history of the past month? Really, my memory seems too surcharged with a sense of bitterness and wrong to do me service. But I must lead you step by step, reluctant as I know you are to follow me behind the gilded arras.

After his return from St. Petersburg, the baron developed more pronounced signs of jealousy than had ever appeared hitherto. Perhaps this feeling was stimulated by my last letter to you, which I inadvertently left unmailed, and which he opened and read. Suspicious husbands you know are as jealous of moods as of men, and not to be miserable "when the Sultan goes to Ispahan" is indeed a crime. I believe there are few jealous husbands who are themselves guiltless. I do not think, however, that this test applies to my own sex, albeit I do not take refuge in the exception—Heaven save the mark!

But the baron came home, as I said, quite confirmed in many unpleasant ways I had remarked before. Without any apparent cause he stole about my room in unslippered feet, and listened furtively at the keyholes. He locked the doors whenever he passed through, and spoke to the servants through a crevice. Instead of his usual violence he whined his complaints of my demeanor toward him in the weakest and most

supine fashion.   But that which exasperated me most
was, and is still, his unaccountable pertinacity.   He
would place his chair close by me and hold his knee
against mine, or his elbow, or his foot, while, with pur-
pling face and hanging mouth, he entreated me not to
leave him, until, in half insane protest, I would break
clear of him and throw open a window, or bathe my
hands and face in utter exhaustion, or—I had almost
said—sense of contamination.   In his fits of rage there
is something genuine from an animal, if not from a
manly, point of view.   But how shall I deal with this
new phase?   Ah, well! let me get on with my letter,
for I have much to say, and that is why I am dallying.

I consented to come to Mentone on account of my
health.   Finding myself growing weak and failing, the
physicians ordered an immediate change, and recom-
mended the old cure virtually—to take myself out of
their hands.   The baron loves to play, and I suspect
is a little too well known in gaming circles in Berlin.

Therefore when he proposed Mentone so early in
the season, or, indeed, altogether out of season, I—
quite knowing that it meant Monte Carlo—accepted,
and with valet and maid and dear old Boston we came.

Result, financial ruin!   The baron played recklessly.   Each time when I saw him he was feverish
and abstracted.   I did not ask the cause, whether he
were winner or loser, for, like most women, I believe
that everybody finally loses, but I was not prepared
for the dénouement, for he has absolutely lost not only
all his ready money, but is heavily in debt, and will
need to resort to further mortgage of his landed estates.

Weak and foolhardy as he was, I pity him, for what must have been his feelings as, driving down the Corniche road overhanging the old sea, he reflected how many men had sought forgetfulness for just such acts of folly in the tideless waters. Only that the baron has other ideas about reparation, for he came home and first proposed that I write my father for money to make good his losses. Taking courage from my silence, he suggested that I cable my message at once.

This latter I proposed not to do, as I informed him in very few words. He has left the hotel in a terrible fit of rage, vowing revenge with his last accents. And I am writing this letter while I wait, meanwhile wondering how much I ought to blame myself for my unhappy life, or if I ought not to lock the secret in my own breast, even from you, my mother. But a secret is a dumb devil, and so long as there is another hand to glance the dart, it rarely wounds to death. I will mail this at once in order that it shall not fall into his hands.

Dearest mamma, are these letters never to cease? I think I notice that your replies are more reserved, and I have thought full of pain and discouragement. But do not feel discouraged. I realize the resources within me, and I have a fund of reserved power which I may summon in an exigency. I have not fairly contemplated anything in the future; to deal with the present has been my purpose. Each joy and each sorrow in its turn, so shall no preconceived action operate to the ends of injustice or unfairness. I close this in haste but lasting love.

As always your daughter,   ELLEN.

From the Baroness Von Eulaw to Mrs. Perces Thornton.

MENTONE, Italy, September 1, 1893.

O MY BELOVED MOTHER: While I feel always sure of your earnest sympathies, how shall I expect you to appreciate the sentiment of horror which this new and fiendish device for torturing my feelings visits upon me! How can I write it?—my poor little Boston is dead.

That fact, with a few silent tears, and a day or two of depression, I could have borne as the end of all things mortal. But he was as foully murdered as ever was the victim of the most infernal plot, for he was given no poorest or most unequal chance to fight for his life, which was as dear to him as mine to me—and that is the least possible to be said. I am in no condition of mind to discuss ethics, or to philosophize upon the events which led to this tragical termination of differences, of which poor little Boston's life paid the forfeit.

It may be that I was wrong, certainly I would have made any terms to have saved my poor terrier from his terrible fate, few as were the years he would have lived at most.

I am not unaware that there are certain concessions, and certain acts of graciousness, which, in a limited sense, may properly be expected of every wife toward a reasonable husband. Not his boasted superiority by any means, but the fact that she is measurably relieved from financial stress or responsibility, constitutes an unwritten law among well-thinking wives everywhere, I believe, and makes the demand upon her. But I considered nothing but the enormity of my husband's exactions, and erred in my estimate of the possibility of my husband's brutality. I wish there were a stronger word which I might politely use.

Shall I give you briefly the harrowing details of this ruffianly act of cowardice? I think I told you in my last how the baron had left the house, filled with vindinctive rage at my refusal to demand of my father large sums of money for his gambling losses. In about an hour he returned and renewed his proposition with increased violence, at the same time seizing a pen and writing a cablegram, which he commanded me to sign.

Remembering that I had given him considerable sums of money from time to time, amounting to many thousands of dollars, I entreated him to wait for a day, while he should make me understand the condition of his financial affairs. This proposition he received with the most frightful oaths. He declared that he would take my life, and would begin by killing my pet dog. No sooner said than done. He rushed to the veranda, where poor little Boston lay stretched upon his cushion asleep in the sun, and, seizing him by the neck, he dashed him violently to the ground below. A few minutes later my little friend was brought to me still feebly conscious, but mangled, bleeding, dying.

How can I ever forget, who ever did who has ever witnessed it forget that last questioning, beseeching look of affection and dumb fright which a dying animal turns upon the face of someone he has loved? Is it less than human or more? Not till the mists gathered across his pretty brown eyes was that last eloquent appeal swept away. "What have I done?" "What have I done?" was the question he was asking of me. Who shall say whether he received his answer in some later and easier translatable speech than mine, in some new and disenthralled state of being? Who shall say that he did not carry away with him a love which was all love, with no taint of selfishness or ulterior thought, quickened by no new speculation, or tradition, or sanction, or human edict? Who shall say that the attributes of faith, and self-surrender, and charity, and forgiveness, and loyalty are lost because in one incarnation they were tongue-tied? For myself I want to see my dogs again. They were my loved companions, as are my books or my works of art. And if the fire destroy them, are their contents naught or worthless because an unlettered man could not read them? At best an after life is a problem, but let us put the problems together and one may help to solve the other, for half a truth is oftenest a lie.

I have sought distraction in these comments, but my sorrow returns to me, dear mother, and my eyes are too full of tears to be able to see the lines. *Vale*, poor Boston, and a grateful throb of gladness that I have a dear mother to whom I can tell my grief.

Your loving but unhappy   ELLEN.

CHAPTER X.

IMPERFECT definition and classification, followed by hasty, inaccurate, and unwarranted generalization, are fruitful sources of popular error. To the misinformed or uninformed mind the Indian is a noble savage, whose hunting-grounds and corn-fields have been taken from him by the ruthless paleface, and who passes his time pensively leaning upon his rifle, with his face to the setting sun, the while he makes touching appeals to the Great Spirit, and mourns the disappearance of his race.

In the country west of the Rocky Mountains and south of Green River, the sentimental Indian with whom Cooper doped American literature, has absolutely no existence. Uncas and Chingacook never journeyed so far westward as the Rio Grande, and prosy old Leather Stocking, with his Sunday-school soliloquies, and his alleged marvelous marksmanship on knife blades at three hundred yards, would have been elected president of the Arizona Lying Club by acclamation.

Many tribes of Indians in that section of the country have scarcely any belief in a future state of existence, and no words in their jargons to represent the ideas of gratitude, of female chastity, or of hospitality.

Their opportunities of obtaining food have been in nowise lessened by white occupation of the land. There never were any buffalo there, they never hunted bears or any combative animal, the fish and small game and pine-nuts are nearly as plentiful as ever, and the bacon-rinds and decayed vegetables to be found near every mining camp furnish the noble reds with a food supply more agreeable to their indolent habits than the hard-won trophies of the chase.

Yet there are Indians and Indians, as there are Christian bank presidents and unsanctified bank robbers, and it is as incorrect to class the devilish Chiricua Apache with the dirty but gentle Yuma as it would be to similarly couple a hook-nosed vender of Louisiana lottery tickets with a blonde-haired solicitor for a church raffle.

In the mountains of Eastern Arizona and Western New Mexico, occupying a country hundreds of miles in area, a country which, for their benefit, has been reserved from miner, settler, and grazier, live the White Mountain Apaches during the winter months, when they are not "on the war path," as their pillaging and murdering expeditions are somewhat bombastically designated.

Whatever may be said of other savages in other localities, the Arizona Apaches are without a single just cause of complaint against the government, or against any of the Caucasian race. No cruel white men have ever invaded their hunting-grounds, or given them high-priced whisky in exchange for low-priced peltry. Red-handed and tangle-haired have these marauders and their ancestors lived for centuries in their mountain lair.

Since the United States of America became, forty years ago, the nominal suzerain of the territory occupied by these peripatetic "vermin ranches," they have been unprovoked invaders, thieves, and assassins, and their summer raids upon the miners, teamsters, and cattle ranchers of Arizona and New Mexico, have been as regular as their winter acceptance of the bacon and blankets with which a generous but mistaken policy feeds and warms them, at a cost equal to that of providing each savage with a suite of rooms at a fashionable hotel.

It is but a few years since a small party of the most vicious and untamable of these bandits, who were captured with the scalps of their victims at their belts, were declared by the authorities at Washington to be not answerable to trial or punishment by the courts of the Territory whose people they have robbed and murdered with impunity for many years. But, partly in deference to outraged public sentiment, and partly in apprehension of the acts of a possible committee of vigilance, these Indians were condemned for their crimes to imprisonment in a government fortress in Florida.

Unlike white prisoners who were condemned to labor and isolation, these tawny murderers were allowed to be accompanied in their journey across the country by their wives and concubines, who were transported, fed, clothed, and made comfortable, at government cost. Arrived at their destination, it was found, after a few months' sojourn, that the humid air, lower altitude, and uncongenial surroundings of Florida, and, later, of North Carolina, disagreed with the digestion and disgruntled the disposition of the noble reds, and, upon a proper showing that their health demanded a return to their former homes, lest confirmed nostalgia should set in, and possibly remove them permanently from the scene of human activities, they were surreptitiously returned by the government to their old reservation, where they promptly expressed their appreciation of the clemency accorded them by breaking out once more and heading for the Mexican Sierras, marking their track with burning ranch houses and murdered settlers.

In the summer of 1893 a party of about forty of these Apaches, headed by the most cruel, malignant, and treacherous of savages—the thrice-pardoned and faith-breaking Geronimo—left the reservation for their annual raid. The military post at Fort Lowell having been abandoned and the troops removed in the interest of government parsimony, the savages found it convenient to make a detour by the valley of the Santa Cruz, so as to cross the railroad track in the vicinity of Tucson, and reach their mountain fastnesses in Sonora by the Arivaca Pass.

It chanced that David Morning, on his departure from Waterspout for New York, while riding from the Rillito station into Tucson, and riding by night, to avoid the heat of an Arizona sun, was seen by the Indians, who, having emerged from a defile in which they had been concealed during the day, were now stealthily and swiftly journeying in the same direction. The opportunity to murder a white man was one not to be neglected, but the report of a rifle might attract attention and instigate speedy pursuit, so two of Ge-

ronimo's followers were detailed, armed only with bows
and arrows, to follow the wayfarer through the dusk,
and bring back a scalp, that might be obtained without
danger and without noise.

If Morning had been riding a horse, this tale might
have had sudden ending, but he had found for his necessarily frequent journeys between the mine and Tucson no such convenient and comfortable mode of transportation as a seat upon the back of Julia. The
equine in question was a large jet black saddle mule
bred at the ranch of Señor Don Pedro Gonzales,
which was situated at the foot of the mountain, on the
opposite side of the Rillito Valley, about three miles
from the road.

The mule, as an animal, is often both misrepre-
sented and misunderstood. No creature tamed by
man has keener instincts or greater sagacity, or is
governed to so great an extent by intelligent self-inter-
est. A mule is always logical. His ordinary reason-
ing is a syllogism without a flaw. A horse impelled
by high spirit, and patient even unto death, will travel
until he drops from exhaustion, and will pull or carry
without complaint a load that causes his every muscle
to pulse with the pain of weariness.

But where lives the man who was ever able to impose upon a mule? Strap an unaccustomed or unjust
load upon the back of this animal of unillustrious pa-
ternity, and he will not move except in the direction of
lying down. Attempt to ride or drive him past his
rightful and usual resting-place, and there may be
retrogression, and there may be a circus, but there
will be no advance.

In addition to his other virtues a mule has an exceedingly keen scent. He seeks no close acquaintance with either grizzly bears or Indians. He will get the wind of either of his aversions as quickly as a hound will whiff a deer, and, like the hound, he will give his knowledge to the world, in a voice that is resonant, magnetic, and—on the whole—musical. The bray of an earnest mule is not after the Italian but the Wagnerian school. It is not the sweet, tender tenor of Manrico, it is Lohengrin sounding his note of power. It is not, perhaps, equal to an orchestra of nightingales, but it has a rhythm, and passion, and power, and sweetness, nevertheless.

The quick instinct of Julia caught the scent of the Apache assassins, and as they crept up she was engaged in a struggle with her rider, who, with voice and spur, was vainly endeavoring to induce and compel her to proceed along the usual road.

"Why, Julia," soliloquized Morning, "you must have been browsing on rattle-weed! What is the matter with you?"—and he tugged vainly at her bridle.

Whizz! whizz! went the arrows. With one shaft quivering in her flank, the mule fairly sprang into the air, while the other transfixed the left arm of David Morning, and pinned it to his side.

And then his question was answered, and he knew what was the matter with Julia.

The frenzied animal leaped the Rillito at a bound, and swept across the valley to the corral adjoining the Gonzales ranch house. Once within the inclosure, she stopped and uttered her most melodious notes of delight. With a crescendo of welcome a dozen of her kindred greeted Julia, and the swarthy major-domo of the ranch, accompanied by half a dozen vaqueros with lights, rushed out, and Morning, weak from pain and loss of blood, was half-led and half-carried into the ranch house.

The Señor Don Pedro Gonzales a year before had journeyed into Paradise, from the effects of an attack of mountain fever, aggravated by too copious use of mescal, and left his ranch houses and corral, his two hundred mules and horses, his two thousand cattle, his brand of G on a triangle, and his rancho Santa Ysbel to his señora, the Donna Maria, who, with her family, continued to occupy the place.

Messengers dispatched to Tucson returned with physicians, who cut out the arrow and found that the wound was severe, and its result might be fatal. They agreed that for Morning to endeavor to travel with such a wound would be simply suicide, and that he must not attempt to leave the shelter and care which the hospitable Gonzales family were glad to accord him.

CHAPTER XI.

"It is only mirage."

A LONG, low, adobe building, roofed with tiles of pottery clay, situated near the banks of the river Santa Cruz. Long rows of cottonwood-trees spread their branches nearly over the little stream, and the graceful masses of pepper, combed to a fringe, drop their courtesied obeisance to every passing breeze, and throw their uneasy shadows well over the walls, neatly stuccoed with cobblestones.

The air curdles with the heat rising from the arid plain, and hangs, a shimmering sheet of translucent vapor, between the eye and the ever-lengthening distance, which softly melts into the Santa Rita Mountains.

Is that a lake out of which rises the well-outlined range of nearer hills? or a sea, throwing up billows of foam and shadow, with islands of green glimpsing their shapes in the placid waters that encircle their feet? And ships, with well-fashioned hulls and wide-spreading sails, and pictured rocks, and beating breakers, and lifeboats with men tugging at the oars. No! it is only mirage, a pretty picture written with the electric pen of nature upon the parchment hot from the press of her untongued fancies. In her luring tale strong men have trusted themselves to fatal

(130)

deception, and beasts, with lapping tongues, and knotted with water greed, have gnashed their teeth at her beautiful garments of fateful film, and lain down to die. Art has been outvied in pictorial effects, for she filters her shadows from daintiest clouds, and borrows her bath of oscurial glints from the unfathomed deeps of heaven. Even austere science hides his forged shackles shamedly away, and turns with unsatisfied scorn from the flitting gleam of her mocking brow.

"It is only mirage, one of nature's cleverest tricks; and what more is life?" comes once and again from parched lips and longing eyes. For, although water, sweet and cool, drips from an *olla* near at hand, yet, stretched upon a bed carefully prepared of finely-stripped rawhide, placed upon the well-beaten and smooth earth, under the sheltering roof of a *ramada* connecting two sections of the Gonzales *casa*, lies David Morning, hot with fever, and still unable to leave his couch.

A little apart, and softly swaying in her hammock of scarlet and gold, one foot lightly touching the ground, half reclines the small, undulating figure of Murella Gonzales.

The ancient blood of Castile had never been suffered by the Gonzales family to mingle, with the sanction of the church, with ignobler currents. The late Señor Don Pedro, although only possessed of the estate of a prosperous Mexican cattle rancher, was yet a Hidalgo of Hidalgoes, who could have covered the walls of his *casa* with his quarterings. As for his wife, was she not an Alvarado? and—Santa Maria!—

what more would you have in the way of blood? Certainly, from her arched instep to her wealth of blue-black hair, the Señorita Murella was a wondrously beautiful maiden.

"Murella," spoke the sick man, turning his emaciated face toward the girl, "during the early days of my illness, I gave you a letter to mail, do you remember?"

"Si, señor."

"Do you remember how many days ago, Murella?"

"Si, señor, seventeen day," and the small ears deepened red behind the creamy oval face.

"Did you give Jose the letter to post?"

"Si, señor."

"You are very kind, señorita, and I thank you."

The girl glanced swiftly across the court at an open door wherein stood the madrona, the customary shawl of black Spanish lace drawn tightly across her mouth, leaving two shining black eyes fixed steadily upon her.

"A few days more, and I shall be leaving your hospitable roof," continued Morning.

"Why will you not take a me with you?" said Murella, with imperturbable gravity, and with no change of expression.

The man illy concealed his look of surprise, as he tucked the richly embroidered pillow more firmly beneath his head, and replied kindly:—

"Such a thing could not possibly be, little girl, for more reasons than your pretty head could contain."

"Then you do not a lof me, and you told a me a lie," and the dark eyes lit with a flame of Vesuvian fires like the red light in those of a tiger.

"What do you mean, señorita?" and a faint flush overspread his own pale face.

"I mean you call me your beloved Ella, such name as Americans give a me, and you hold me close in your arms, and say you will never part from me, not for one hour—only ten day ago—and now you leave a me!"

This was an awkward situation, and Mr. Morning recognized its full significance upon the moment. In his delirium he had used the too familiar name, and had coupled with its use endearments which had been compromisingly misappropriated. He reflected a moment. There was nothing left but to tell the truth and accept the consequences. Another girl would laugh. What would Murella do?

"Señorita," he began slowly, "I have, as you know, been very ill, and on several occasions have lost my way in delirium, and have been wandering over scenes belonging to other days. Can you not forgive me if I have called you by a name which you mistook for your own prettier one? Can you not pardon me if in my fevered imagination I gave you for the moment a place long ago sanctified and dedicated to forgetfulness?"

"Then why cannot you lof a me? Am I not as lofely as she?"

"You are very beautiful, Murella."

"Machacha!" shrieked the duenna from the entrance to the *ramada*, "what are you saying?" and then followed invective in every key, and words of scorn in every cadence, until, pale with anger and chagrin, the girl sprang from her hammock and ran swiftly away.

For a long time our hero lay lost in speculation. After all, it was only a misunderstanding, and not liable to be remembered overnight.   In any event, he had not compromised the maiden, and finally he concluded—as was indeed the truth—that the cunning señorita was all the while cognizant of the situation, and not at all deceived, and so he dismissed the subject from his mind.

And what was the first move of the panic-stricken maiden?   Speeding swiftly over the ground, she sank in the shadow of the ocotilla hedge inclosure, which formed the corral, and drew cautiously from her pocket the letter committed to her care by Morning. Reopening it, for the envelope, sealed only with mucilage, had been carefully broken, she drew forth a picture of the Baroness Von Eulaw, older by many years than the name she now bore, and much thumbed and worn beside.

This unconscious incendiary Murella first regarded disdainfully for an instant, and then deliberately spat upon it.   She then proceeded to possess herself of the contents of the letter, which was brief, and, regarded as a wholesome irritant for a recent wound, rather ineffectual.   She spelled it out laboriously, and it read as follows:—

To the Baroness Von Eulaw, Berlin.

You may have forgotten that several years ago, and through wholly legitimate means, let me say in self-defense, a specimen of art, of inestimable value to me, came into my possession.   I have hitherto deemed it no breach of honor to retain it.   Finding myself very ill, however, and warned by my physicians of the probable fatal termination of my malady, I esteem it prudent and not less just to return to you the last token of a mutual recognition which I have the faith to believe is among the things that are undying.

It is, perhaps, unwillingness to pass the veil which enshrouds the great mystery, without first vindicating myself in your esteem, that impels me to tell you that which I have heretofore thought to keep secret—that your letter, written in February, 1883, was accidentally mislaid in an old desk, and was never opened or perused by me until the day after you became the Baroness Von Eulaw.   Always yours sincerely,

DAVID MORNING.

Murella spread the letter upon the ground and pondered.   Plainly it was not a love letter, as she had expected—almost hoped! for she missed the ecstasy and exhilaration of that desire for vengeance which is the stimulus to passion in the breast of any true scion of the Spanish race, and devoid of which life has little zest.

It might have been written to his grandmother for all she could gather from its contents, and the thought suggested the duenna, with her cruel eyes and hard, wrinkled mouth, whose duty it was to watch her from all points of the compass.   So she folded the letter, and, taking up the picture, again scrutinized it.   "Devil! devil! devil!" she broke out, as she smote the pasteboard with her tiny soft fist.   Then, folding it away with the letter, she slipped them into her pocket, and, gliding around the ocotilla palings, she entered her apartment through an outer door, where she resealed the missive, and, summoning the messenger Jose, bade him forthwith journey to Tucson, and deposit it in the post office there.

The sun was sinking behind Tehachape Mountains, and its parting rays, full of the color of leaf and bough, fell brightly upon the prostrate form of the invalid, and as Murella dropped softly to the ground before a low window, which opened upon the *ramada*, she parted her muslin curtains and gazed devouringly upon the well-knit, shapely form, and the broad-browed, tinted face, while the light faded, and soft voices grew higher as the family supper hour approached, and tinkling sounds from mandolin and guitar filled the night with music. Then, taking a last look, she arose, and, stamping her foot upon the ground, impatiently she ejaculated:—

"Oh, bah! He too good for anyting."

She joined the family group at supper with a look of high disdain on her beautiful face, but otherwise undismayed, and ate her *frijoles* and *tortillas*, and scrambled for the whitest *tomales* among her younger brothers, very much as if David Morning had overruled his physicians, and departed for Tucson in an ambulance the day after he was wounded, as he had once determined to do, instead of having lain there for a month, drawing first upon her pity, and then upon her fancy, and stirring things in her imagination generally.

Late in the moon-lit night, the soft summer winds still busy among the boughs, a sweet girlish voice, melodiously attuned to the notes of the mandolin, ran through the dreams of David Morning, carrying the passionful refrain, "Oh, illustrissimo mia," and he awoke, and still the sweet refrain, "Oh, illustrissimo mia."

Several days went by, summer days full of work and growth and promise outside, and still Morning was unable to leave the Gonzales ranch. His pulse, which the doctors declared had never regained its normal beat, was low and intermittent, and the hectic flush never left his cheek. At length typhoid fever was developed, and for weeks he lay at the verge of death, and for as many weeks Murella Gonzales sat at his head by day, and made her bed at the foot of his couch by night. The señora, the madroña, even the cocoanut brown *machacha* of all work, each brought fruit and drink and delicacies to dissuade him from his delirium and tempt him back to health, but Murella sat always with her graceful head resting lightly against his pillow, silent, languid, and lovely.

Sometimes the doctors remonstrated and begged her to leave him, but she only said, "*Mañana, mañana*," and to-morrow never came. But it proved to be only a question of time, and before the gray linings of the poplar had slid into umber, or the pomegranate had gained its full meed of sweet juices, David Morning was brought a picturesque basket of Indian workmanship, quite filled with letters which had found him out, calling him back with the imperative voices of business demands, to take his place again with the rank and file of affairs.

So the last day came, and Murella, abandoning her customary hammock, sat all the morning upon a thick rug spread upon the ground, exhibiting her irritable feeling by nervously tossing the clinging folds of her lace mantilla back over her shoulder, or tracing the figures of the rug absently. Morning seemed lost in reverie for a long time; finally he spoke, evidently a little doubtful where to begin.

"I do not need to tell you, señorita," said he, "that I feel the greatest gratitude toward the inmates of this household, and I ask you to tell me, not what you would wish me to do for you, but what is the wish most dear to you if I were not in the world?"

"Oh, if Señor Morning die, I shall die too."

"Oh, no! if some fairy should wave its wand, or some Fortunatus should drop uncounted gold at your feet, what would you do first?"

The soft eyes of Señorita Gonzales flamed as never eyes of Saxon maiden burned, and she quickly replied, rising and drawing nearer:—

"I would have a *casa grande*."

"And where would you have a grand *casa*, here?"

"No, no!" giving her hand a truly Delsarte sweep of motion. "Long time ago my mother take a me to Yuma, and there I hear much talk about Castle Dome; it is twenty, thirty miles up the great river Colorado. One time we sail up there in steam a boat, and such a rancheria—beautiful! Great trees, and rocks, and the Indians have been show how by the padres long time ago, and they have beautiful trees of figs, and oranges, and lemon, and great vines. And I have tink about it always. When I am rich a I shall drive the Indians away, and give money for make a them not hungry, and make a *casa* all like a same in picture."

"We all have our castles in Spain. Why not you,

Murella?" and he drew forth a pencil, and, spreading paper upon the table, asked her to sit down.

"Now," said he, "we will build this fine house upon paper. What shall we do first?"

"We shall have a dance-house."

Morning smiled grimly; the mining camps enjoy a monopoly of literary phrasing, and the compound word was familiar, so he only said, "All right, a salon for dancing."

"Si, señor, saloon," repeated Murella gravely, "and a grande saloon for beautiful flowers."

"A conservatory, of course, though that will be superfluous," he added, "in a country itself a hotbed for tropic bloom. Why not hanging gardens like those of Babylon?"

"Oh, beautiful!" clasping her little fingers in ecstasy.

"Very well," looking into her face, pencil suspended.

"And a beautiful room for a you," and she paused for a moment, "with, with what you call, wall like the sky before the sun a come, and morning glory flower go all around the top," pointing to the frieze, "a like a your name, Señor Mia."

Morning suddenly discovered something upon the toe of his boot, and the girl struggled on in very bad English, but with charming enthusiasm. She planned and he interpreted. They first laid out the grounds, availing themselves of the groves already planted by the Indians. They covered acres of ground with rare exotics, studding them with statuary in creamiest marble, chiseled from designs of their own, with a

Psyche and Cupid to guard the main entrance to the park.

"What is that ting she a hold in her hand?"

"That is a torch," explained Morning. "Psyche is the soul, and Cupid is love, and she is going in search of him."

"And did she find a him?" archly questioned the girl.

"I think not," said Morning, gloomily drawing forth a fresh sheet of paper.

"And about the *casa grande*," continued Morning, "of what shall it be built?"

The señorita rested her pretty chin between her two palms and meditated. Finally she decided it should be like the cupids, of shining marble, with agate or onyx for columns, and garnets—found in quantities in Arizona—for smaller decorations. This most elaborate plan having been at length crudely completed, Mr. Morning folded it, quietly saying he would submit it to an architect.

"Not truly?" said the girl, springing to her feet with shining eyes and hands crossed upon her breast.

"Yes, really and truly, for your own sweet self, and for your hospitable family; and with my kindest regards and deepest gratitude."

Murella turned very pale. Dreams were not dreamed to be so realized. Was he teasing her?

Hitherto her self-love had made her the central figure in her own mind. All things about her had been dwarfed and become inconsequent in her egotistic life, because she was wholly ignorant of any possibilities outside of the power she wielded through her beauty and her grace.

But a new element had been added to her limited experience, and it had developed into a magician, or had it done so really? The doubt took momentary possession of her, and she arose in an attitude of defiance, her flashing eyes resting upon the amused but open countenance of David Morning.

Then she knew that she looked into the face of her god, and she fled to her room, and, sinking upon the floor, she covered her face with her mantilla, and sobbed convulsively.

CHAPTER XII.

It was October when Morning arrived in New York City. Steel had been prompt in shipping the gold not covered with copper, and Morning's bank accounts in New York now amounted to sixteen millions of dollars, while the fame of the Morning mine as a producer of four millions of gold bars per month had already created a marked sensation in financial and business circles, and in the newspaper world, but none suspected the immense actual production.

Morning visited Washington, and bought a stone warehouse near the foot of Sixth Street. He purchased a similar building in Philadelphia, near the Pennsylvania Railroad freight depot, and he bought a third warehouse alongside the track of the New Jersey Central at Hoboken. He caused switches to be constructed into each of these warehouses, and provided each of them with heavy iron shutters and doors. He employed four watchmen for each building, divided into day and night-watches of six hours each. He arranged that the copper-pigs containing gold should be loaded on the cars at Tucson by his own men, who were themselves unaware that they were handling anything but copper, and the cars locked and sent in train-load lots through, without change or rehandling,

(142)

to New York, Philadelphia, and Washington, where they were run into his warehouses and there unloaded. It was given out that he was at the head of a copper syndicate, and was storing the surplus product of the mines for higher prices. His plans worked with perfect smoothness, and his wealth accumulated openly at the rate of four millions per month, and secretly at the rate of one hundred millions per month, with a vast amount of newspaper comment concerning the four millions, and no suspicion anywhere as to the real sum.

The advocates of free coinage of silver, who were defeated in the Congress of 1889–90, renewed their contest in the Congress of 1891–92, and in February, 1892, a free coinage law passed, but it was vetoed by President Harrison. The silver men carried the fight into the presidential election of 1892, and were so far successful that Congress, in February, 1894, enacted a law the text of which was as follows:—

"From and after July 1, 1894, any person may deposit at the treasury of the United States in Washington, or at either of the sub treasuries in Boston, New York, Philadelphia, Chicago, St Louis, New Orleans, Denver, or San Francisco, gold or silver bars of standard fineness, and receive the coined value thereof in United States treasury notes. The secretary of the treasury is authorized and directed to prepare and keep on hand a sufficient amount of treasury notes to comply with the provisions of this act."

The influence of Morning as the largest single producer of gold in the world, as the owner already of thirty millions of dollars, and, if his mine should hold out for five years, of a sum that would cause him to outrank any millionaire in the world, was very great, and that influence, legitimately exercised in behalf of free coinage, proved very potent with senators and representatives, and did much to reconcile the adherents of a single gold standard to the overthrow of their system.

It was argued that if the gold supply of the world was to be increased forty per cent per annum by the yield of the Morning mine, that would diminish relatively the production of silver, and the ancient parity of the metals might be restored "without danger to our financial interests, Mr. Speaker."

Thus reasoned the Honorable Senile Jumbo, who represented a New England district in the House. Jumbo was a banker at home, and because he was a banker was supposed to know something about finance, and was, in consequence, accorded a leading position on the House Committee on Banking and Currency.

In fact, Jumbo only knew a good discount from a poor one. His definition of a banker would have been that of the Indiana editor, who described such a functionary as "a gentleman who takes the money of one man without interest, and loans it to another upon interest, and places both depositor and borrower under obligations."

By his small shrewdness Jumbo had gained a large fortune, and secured a seat in Congress; but of the laws which govern finance in its politico-economic relations he had no more knowledge than has a locomotive fireman about the law of dynamics, or a dry-goods clerk about the culture of the silkworm.   Yet the Honorable Senile Jumbo looked wise, and talked from the pit of his stomach, and respected the views of other rich men, and as a congressman he averaged with his colleagues.

What strange distortion of brain is it that causes men conspicuously unfit for public life, to seek elevations which can only expose their intellectual poverty? One who does not comprehend the French tongue or know anything about science, would be laughed at for seeking to be elected a member of the French Academy of Sciences, yet senatorial togas and congressional seats are constantly sought by gentlemen whose previous pursuits have unfitted them to "shine in the halls of high debate," and who, indeed, would be puzzled to put together, while on their feet, ten sentences of grammatical English.

The great and growing wealth of Morning caused his society to be courted, and many a managing mamma was not unmindful of the fact that the "Arizona Gold King," as he began to be called, was a bachelor.   This man did not "wear his heart upon his sleeve," and did not proclaim that his bachelorhood was confirmed, or had any special reason for its existence, but all plotting against him was in vain, for the Ellen lost to him was the constant companion of his thoughts, and to all movements and plans and purposes of life he applied instinctively the test, " What would she think of it?"

CHAPTER XIII.

IT was the anniversary of one of the great victories achieved by Germany in the war of 1870, and Berlin had scarcely known a day so filled with noise, and glitter, and color, and esprit as this day had been.

The Baroness Von Eulaw, the beautiful American, was more sought for than ever, and the too arduous round of social duties and engagements were beginning to tell upon her delicate constitution. Cards had been received by the baron and his wife for a reception at the palace, and such an invitation could scarcely be overlooked, especially as no entertainment seemed acknowledged by her friends to be complete without the presence of the baroness. Therefore, retiring a little earlier this evening than was usual from her own drawing rooms, the baroness was well advanced with her toilette when she discovered letters which the footman had left upon her table during her absence, and among them one bearing the postmark of Tucson, Arizona, and addressed in a well-known hand.

She felt too excited to trust herself farther, and, before tearing the envelope, she sent her maid with a message of her sudden indisposition, which she begged the baron to deliver in person to the emperor, and asked, furthermore, not to be disturbed.

(146)

It was all one to the baron at this hour, and though he speedily departed for the imperial palace, it is doubtful whether the high officials in waiting deemed it advisable to admit him to the imperial presence.

Dismissing her servants, the baroness was left alone for the night. Then she turned to her dressing-table and stood while opening the letters, glancing hurriedly at their contents, all but one, and this she turned over many times. What was the burden of its mission, and what did it contain? Finally her trembling fingers picked absently at the envelope, as if she had forgotten how to proceed. She might be unafraid, for there was his own handwriting before her.

With this thought a thrill went through her heart, and with a sudden motion she tore the envelope quite apart, and her own photograph fell to the floor. She did not stoop for it, for her eyes were fixed upon the page. Slowly she read word by word, lingering over the last, and cutting it away from its context, as if fearful that another word should overwhelm her reason.

She finished, and an awful silence fell upon her. She could hear her heart beat against her rich corsage, and her breath crackled as it came through her dry lips. What was the purport of that letter? She had already forgotten. Something surely had left a heavy pain at her heart. Just as slowly she read it through again.

Then he was not dead—or, stay, he might be, for did he not say "probably," not "possibly"? Then, still standing before the dressing-table, she leaned forward, and, putting her face close to the mirror, she muttered, looking into her own deep eyes the while, "Great God! what did I do?" For a full moment she stood thus, then, lifting the powder-puff from the jeweled case, she mechanically swept her cheeks and brow and sat down. Then she caught the letter and read it again, this time more clearly and calmly, "the probable fatal termination," and again, "until the day after you became the Baroness Von Eulaw."

She looked at her toilette. What was she doing bejeweled and brocaded that night? Where were the sackcloth and ashes she had earned? She arose and pulled the diamonds from their places, and the beautiful robe from her lovely shoulders, and put on a gown of creamy plush, bordered with some dark, rich fur, and, slowly tying the cords, her eyes fell upon the picture at her feet.

She took it between her fingers as if it were a dead thing, and thought at the moment that it weighed a pound at the least. And this was Ellen Thornton! Then she thought how old-fashioned her dress looked, and for a moment she felt glad that she had gotten the picture back. Another revulsion of feeling as she looked upon the torn envelope. What would she not suffer for the hope, the uncertainty, she had clung to when she tore that paper half an hour ago?

If only the doctors could have said " possibly," not " probably;" perhaps that was what they meant, and not " probably," she repeated. Doctors are so clumsy —especially some—and they do so exaggerate in order to magnify the importance of their case, and for a moment she took unction in such logic.

Suddenly a new thought took possession. The

baron—"where did he come in?" as he himself would have expressed it, and she half smiled at the grotesqueness of the thought. Was she not married? and did she not owe him allegiance as a woman of honor? If she had told him all that her soul held in keeping for another, would he have made her the Baroness Von Eulaw?—Very likely, but she was not prepared to believe it. She had no right to hold him responsible for offenses against her while she was holding perfidy to her heart, and she marveled that she had failed to make this argument a shield against the shafts of her great sorrow and her almost greater chagrin.

She would destroy both the letter and the picture, and put away all thought of the unhappy occurrence. But, examining the picture again, she discovered two little punctures just through the pupils of the shadowy eyes, and she thought and queried for the cause of such an accident.

Finally she concluded that her old lover had made them inadvertently in fastening the picture to his wall or mirror frame, and so, pressing her lips warmly to the tiny wounds on the unconscious paper, where she fancied his fingers had rested, she locked both the photo and letter in her desk, and, just as daylight broke, long after the clanging of the locks had ceased and the brightness was withdrawn, she braided her hair as she had worn it so many years ago when the image was made, and, with a long look in the mirror to find a trace of her old self, she turned away to her couch, and disposed herself for an hour of sleep.

But the last among her sea of speculations was this: "I wonder who made those pin-holes in my eyes!"

CHAPTER XIV.

THE Hod-Carriers' Union and Mortar-Mixers' Protective Association, of San Francisco, adopted a resolution in February, 1894, to fix the rate of wages of its members at $3.00 per day, and admitting no new members for a period of one year. The immediate cause of this resolution was the letting, by certain capitalists, of contracts for the construction of several blocks of buildings on Market Street, including the new post-office building.

Phelim Rafferty, in proposing the resolution, said:

"The owners and the contractors, Mr. Prisident and gentlemen, are min of large means, sor, yit they propose to pay us, the sons of honest toil, sor, widout whose brawny muscles they could not build at all, sor, they propose to pay us a beggarly $2.00 a day, sor. Why, the min in the public schools who taich the pianny to our gurls, sor, recaive more nor that ! Now, sor, if we pass this risolution we put our wages to $3.00 a day, and hould them there. We have the mortal cinch on the contractors, sor, for if any mimber of our union works for less than $3.00 we'll expel him; and by passin' this risolution we'll keep min from the East away, and keep the mimbership in San Francisco shmall, and we'll be sure of a job.

(150)

"Faith! the bosses will have to be mighty civil to us to git us at all, sor. And if they thry to put to work min who are not mimbers of the union, their buildings will niver rise out of their cellars, sor, for the other thrades are compilled to sthand by us, sor."

Mr. Lorin French, the millionaire contractor and owner of the great San Francisco Iron Works, read in the journal next morning an account of the action taken by the Hod-Carriers Union and Mortar-Mixers' Protective Association, and he smiled a grim smile. That day he sent invitations to a number of capitalists and contractors to attend a meeting at his offices, and the result of the conference was the formation of a Manufacturers' and Builders' League, of which Mr. Lorin French was chosen permanent president.

The daily papers the next morning contained the following advertisement:—

WANTED.

On the first day of next month, two hundred hod-carriers and mortar-mixers to work on the new post-office block. Three dollars per day will be paid until further notice. Men who have applied for and been refused admittance to membership in the Hod-Carriers' Union will be preferred.

LORIN FRENCH.

1099 Market Street.

This base attempt of capital to coerce or bribe the worker into allowing another worker an equal chance of obtaining employment, was denounced by Rafferty the next night in a ringing speech at a special meeting of the Hod-Carriers' Union, which meeting resulted in a convention of the Federated Trades being ordered.

At this convention it was resolved by a three-fourths majority, after a hot debate, that no member of any trade organization would, on penalty of expulsion, be permitted to work in or upon or in aid of the construction of any building, or in any shop, mill, foundry, or factory, or in or upon any work where any person not a member of some trade-organization was employed, or where any material was used which had been manufactured by non-union labor.

"My frent from the Plumbers' Association speaks of this resolution, Mr. President, as a poomerang," said Gustave Blather, a labor lecturer, who on this occasion represented the Dishwashers' Lagerbund. "I don't know as such languitch is quite broper coming from him, for a goot many beople haf their doubts whether plumbing is really a trate or only a larceny.   But, my fellow pret-winners, if the resolution is a poomerang, it is one that will knock the arrogance out of the ploated wealth-owners, and teach them that in this republic—established by the ploot of our fathers [Blather's great-grandfather was a Hessian soldier in the British army, and returned to Darmstadt after the surrender of Cornwallis]—in this republic the time is close at hand when suppliant wealth will be compelt to enture the colt and hunger it has gifen to labor for many years."   And, amid a storm of applause, Blather sank to his seat.

The post office block was begun on the day appointed, with a force of men, all of whom were members of the trade organizations, and the work progressed steadily for a week.   At the Saturday-night meetings of the several trade organizations, the members congratulated themselves that "old French" had concluded not to carry out his programme, and in several lodges it was proposed to signalize the magnificent victory of labor over capital by demanding a general advance of twenty per cent in the wages of all mechanics; but some of the wiser heads discouraged the movement as premature, and one pessimistic house carpenter observed, amid expressions of dissent from his colleagues, that if all the mechanics followed the example of the hod carriers, it would "bust wide open every builder and contractor in Frisco, or else put a stop to all building."

On the next Monday morning there appeared on the scene ten men clad in blouses and overalls. Three of them worked at mixing mortar, three of them carried hods, three of them commenced laying brick, while the tenth man directed the labors of the other nine. Each had buckled about his waist in plain sight a cartridge belt from which hung a dragoon revolver.

As soon as their presence and labors became known, word was sent to labor headquarters, and Delegate Brown was deputed to interview the strangers and ascertain the situation.

Pap Brown was a journeyman stone cutter on the other side of the sixties, who did not often work at his trade. The salary he received from the trade unions was sufficient for his support, and he fully earned his salary. He was shrewd, suave, and persistent, and his fatherly way with "the boys," and deferential manner to employers, often secured to the former favorable adjustments of contests that would have been denied to the "silver-tongued" Raffertys and Blathers.

Pap Brown approached one of the men who was engaged in mixing mortar, and inquired whom he was working for. The man addressed made no reply, but signaled the foreman, who came forward and curtly answered:—

"We are all working for Mr. Lorin French."

"What wages do you get?" asked Brown.

"Well," replied the foreman after a pause, "strictly speaking, I don't know as that concerns you, but I have no objection to telling you. The mortar-mixers and hod-carriers get $3.00 a day, the bricklayers $4.00, and I get $5.00."

"Them's union wages," said Brown, approvingly. "You are strangers in Frisco, I jedge?"

"We arrived last Friday night from Milwaukee," replied the foreman.

"Have you got your cards as members of the union?" said Brown.

"No," replied the party addressed, "we belong to no union."

"Hum! I suppose you are calkilatin' to jine the unions here?" inquired Brown in a persuasive accent.

"I am told," replied the foreman, " that so far as the Hod-Carriers' Union is concerned, we cannot join if we wish to; that they have resolved to admit no new members."

Pap Brown slowly revolved his tobacco quid in his mouth, and rapidly revolved the situation in his wise old brain. "Hum!" said he at length, "I reckon that can be arranged for ye, so that ye can all jine."

"Well," replied the man from Milwaukee, "I may as well tell ye that we don't calculate to jine anyhow. We don't much believe in unions nohow—too many fellers a settin' around drinkin' beer, which the fellers that work have to pay for."

"Mebbe you don't know," said Pap Brown, "that only union men will be allowed to work here."

"Who will stop us?" said the stranger.

"There are a good many thousand of the brotherhood in this city," said Delegate Brown, still persuasively, "and there are only ten of you."

"Well, we ten are fixed to stay," said the foreman, glancing significantly at his cartridge belt.

"Hum!" remarked Pap Brown, as he walked away.

That night there was a conference at the labor headquarters of the Executive Committee of the Federated Trades, and Delegate Brown was called upon to report.

"I find," said he, "that these ten men have all worked at their trades somewhere, and our watchers say that they are good workmen; but clearly they have been hired more as fighters than as hod carriers or masons. I jedge, from what I hear, that there is an organized force behind them. They sleep and take their meals in old French's building on Market Street, and don't go out to the saloons, and we can't very well get at them. Old French is as cunning as Satan, and he has fixed the job upon us, and put these men to work to bring things to a point. There is a big force of Pinkerton's men in the city all ready to be sworn in as deputy sheriffs in case of a row, and I reckon it is put up to call in the soldiers at the Presidio and from Alcatraz in case of trouble, for the post-office building, where the men are working, is government property."

"What action do you suggest we should take, Mr. Brown?" said the chairman.

Pap Brown rolled his quid from one cheek to the other, and then solemnly deposited it in the cuspidor.

"It won't do," he replied, "to monkey with Uncle Sam; my jedgment is to jist let them ten men alone."

"But," interposed a member of the committee, "old French will never stop there. Those ten men are merely the small end of a wedge with which he intends to split our labor unions to pieces. He will not give us the sympathy of the people by lowering wages, but he will put on scabs, a dozen at a time, and discharge our members, until the city is filled with new workmen, the unions broken up, and we can all emigrate to Massachusetts or China."

"I shouldn't wonder," said Pap Brown, "but violence to them ten men would simply be playin' into old French's hand. He has figgered for a fight, but we mustn't give it to him."

"We will carry out," said the Chairman, "in a peaceful way, the resolution adopted by the Congress of Federated Trades."

"That," said Pap Brown, "means a gineral strike and an all-around tie-up, that's what it means, jest at the beginnin' of the buildin' season, with our union treasuries mostly empty, and our brethren East in no fix to help us, for the coke strikes and the shettin' down of the cotton factories and iron foundries this winter have dreened them all. I was agin that resolution of the Federated Trades at the time, and I'm mighty doubtful about it's workin' any good to us now. It was well enough for a bluff, but if we are called down we haven't got a thing in our hands, that's a fact."

"Well, what can we do, Mr. Brown?"

"I believe that the best thing all around would be to give in to old French now, repeal that fool resolution, and wait for a better time to strike."

"What! surrender without a blow? That, Mr. Brown, we can never do."

"Well, then," rejoined Pap Brown, "I reckon we've got a long siege ahead."

The Executive Committee appointed a delegation to wait on Mr. Lorin French and inform him that unless the employment of the ten non-union men was discontinued, the resolution of the Federated Trades would be enforced, and all Trade Union members working for him, or for any member of the Manufacturers' and Builders' Union, would quit work.

Mr. French received the committee very curtly.

"Those ten men," said he, "will continue their labors though they shall be the only ten men at work in the city of San Francisco. If one, or one thousand, or ten thousand of you are fools enough to quit work at the high wages you have yourselves fixed, simply because I have given work at the same wages to men who don't choose to join one of your bullying unions, why, you can quit. You can't hurt me by quitting as much as you will hurt yourselves. My money will keep and your work won't. But take notice that every man who does quit work will be blacklisted,

and he can never get another job in this city from me,
or any of the gentlemen who are members of the association of which I am president, and we include
about all the large employers of labor in this city."

"You know, Mr. French," said the Chairman of
the committee, that if you insist on keeping these ten
non-union men at work we can order a general strike."

"Yes, I know it," replied French. "I know that
you can bite off your own noses to spite your own
faces. I feel sorry for you workingmen at times, you
are such unreasoning and unreasonable and everlast-
ing fools. When you order a strike, you order the
absolute destruction of the only property you have—
your labor—and you do this in order to prevent a few
men from selling their labor; a few men whose only
offense is that they don't believe with you in the wisdom of harassing and plundering capitalists."

"Well, I suppose we have a right to strike, haven't
we?" said the Chairman angrily.

"No," said French, "you have not. The worker
who joins a strike faces at least the possibility of capital closing its works and retiring from the field, and
the men who have been extravagant, idle, unthrifty,
or unfortunate, and most of you have been one or the
other, have no moral right to bring upon themselves
or those dependent upon them, either suffering or
mendicancy."

"Mr. French," said the Chairman, "you know a
good many things, but you don't know the power of
the labor organizations of the land. If we willed it,
we could in one day stop production and transportation all over the United States."

"You would do well to think three or four times," replied French, "before exercising any such power as that. You workingmen are overstepping the bounds not only of moderation, but of common justice and common sense. Suppose you should do what you threaten, what do you suppose the capitalists would do in turn? You don't know? Well, I can tell you. We would say that we were weary of your exactions, your interference, and your airs. We would say to you: 'You have stopped the wheels; very well, we will not start them. You have extinguished the furnace fires, we will not rekindle them. You have disabled the engines, we will not repair them. With the downward stab of your vicious knife you have cut our surface veins, but you have received the force of the blow in your own vitals—bleed to death at your leisure. We will retire for a while and nurse our scratches.'

"You don't know what you are talking about," continued the old man. "You don't conceive the misery and ruin that would result from sixty days' stoppage of labor in the fields and foundries and factories and furnaces, and sixty days' suspension of traffic over the railroads of our land. With the disabled engines in the roundhouses, and the cars covered with dust in the deserted yards; with ships and steamers lying idle at the wharves or sailed away to trade between the ports of other lands, whose governments, wiser or more powerful than ours, would not suffer the moral law to be violated by either individuals or societies; with moss gathered upon the turbines; with chimneys towering smokeless to the skies; with the music of forge and anvil hushed; with almshouses crowded, asylums filled, and jails overflowing; with men suffering and women growing gaunt from hunger, and little children sobbing themselves to the fevered sleep of famine; with the furniture in the auction room, trinkets and clothing in the pawn shop, and families once comfortable wandering shelterless under the stars; with even disease welcomed as a friend who should pilot the sufferer to the deliverance of death, would you find consolation for it all in the reflection that you had, maybe, carried your point and prevented non-union men, who are as good as yourselves in every way, from working alongside you at the same wages you demanded for yourselves?"

"Mr. French," said the Chairman, "what do you wish us to do?"

"I don't care what you do," was the response, "but if you have any sense, you will go home and repeal your fool resolution to strike if non-union workers are employed."

"That, Mr. French," said the spokesman, "we cannot and will not do."

"No?" replied the millionaire. "Well, you must go to destruction then in your own way. Good-morning."

At noon the next day the hod-carriers dropped their hods, not only at the post-office block, but at all buildings in process of construction by any capitalist or contractor belonging to the Builders' and Manufacturers' Union. The brick-masons stopped work because they would not lay brick with mortar mixed or carried by a non-union laborer. The house carpenters declined to drive a nail in aid of the erection of any building in which a brick should be laid by one not belonging to the Bricklayers' Union. No plumber or gasfitter would carry his tools to a building whose timbers had been put in place by a scab carpenter. The teamsters would not haul sand, brick, lime, or lumber for use in any building to be erected by any member of the association of which Lorin French was president. The iron-moulders abandoned in a body the great shops, rather than work on columns or fronts which had been ordered for the tabooed buildings. Engineers and firemen struck, rather than attend to the running of machinery in factories where non-union men were employed, and all workers engaged in any factory, foundry, mill, shop, or business owned, in whole or in part, by any member of the Builders' and Manufacturers' Union, joined the general strike, while the railroads were compelled, in self-protection, to refuse freight offered by any member of the organization of which Lorin French was president.

No attempt was made by French or his colleagues to supply the places of the strikers with non-union workers, although every mail from the East brought hundreds of applications for employment, but each factory, foundry, and shop was closed, one after the other, as the workers joined the strike. The ten men whose labors on the post-office building had begotten all this commotion, continued steadily at work. They were surrounded each day, while at their labors, by hooting thousands, who gathered in the vicinity, but any near approach to them was prevented by a company of Pinkerton's men, armed with Winchesters, who had been sworn in as deputy sheriffs, and who escorted them to and from their labors, to French's building, No. 1099 Market Street, where they, as well as their guards, were accorded quarters, and in the upper story of which Mr. Lorin French had, under existing circumstances, deemed it expedient to establish his residence as well as his offices.

After a fortnight had elapsed these ten men were withdrawn from their labors, in deference to the request of the Mayor of San Francisco and the governor of California.

A committee from the Federated Trades then waited upon Lorin French, and informed him that, as the *causa belli* had been removed by the withdrawal of the ten obnoxious non-union laborers, the strikers were willing to resume work. His reply was that whenever work should be resumed generally, the ten "obnoxious" men, as well as all other non-union men he might see fit to employ, would resume work; and so negotiations came suddenly to an end.

At the close of the third week of the strike the Congress of Federated Trades assembled and declared a boycott against all members of the Builders' and Manufacturers' Union, and against all who should violate the boycott; the boycott to run also against any railway or steamship line that should accord them or their families transportation out of San Francisco.

It was expected that this last and most drastic measure would bring the capitalists to terms, for its enforcement would deprive them and their families of the necessities of life. Their employés left them under the pressure, and their offices and places of business were closed. Their house servants departed, and

they were unable to obtain substitutes even among
the Chinese, for the Celestial who should labor for a
boycotted household was given his choice between
exile and death. Hotel proprietors were compelled
to refuse a boycotted person as a guest, or lose their
own waiters, cooks, and chambermaids. The restaurant proprietor who should serve one of them with
a meal would be compelled to close his doors for the
want of help; and the grocer, fruiterer, butcher, baker,
or provision dealer who sold supplies for. their use,
would be posted, and lose his other customers, for the
boycott was declared against all who violated the
boycott.

Mr. French was equal to the exigency. He caused
representations to be made, and influence exerted at
Washington, and the United States steamer *Charleston* was detailed for special service. The members of
the Builders' and Manufacturers' Association, with
their families, were taken on board of the war-ship,
guarded by the Pinkerton men, and carried to Vancouver, where they were dispatched East over the Ca-
nadian Pacific Railroad. Lorin French, with a few of
his fellow-members, refused to go, but, establishing
themselves comfortably on the upper floor of the
building No. 1099 Market Street, they managed to
provision themselves and their guards, despite the
boycott, and announced their determination to see
the contest out.

It was the last week in April, 1894, and the tenth
week of the great strike. Business was almost suspended in San Francisco. Thousands of the strikers
had wandered out into the country, and every farm-

house within a hundred miles of San Francisco was besieged by men glad to work for food and shelter, while the highways were crowded with tramps. In the city the streets were filled with idle thousands, and at the daily meeting at the sand lots twenty or thirty thousand auditors were addressed by favorite speakers.

The orators made no appeals which were calculated to incite violence, and there was no police interference with the meetings. Indeed, there seemed logically no place or opportunity for violence. The offending employers had done absolutely nothing that the workers could even denounce. They had discharged nobody, and they had not attempted to fill the places of those who reluctantly left. They had simply suspended operations. They had accepted the refusal of the workers to work, apparently, as final. They had locked up their factories and places of business, and, with their families, had left the State.

The strikers generally regarded Lorin French as the prime mover against them, but his property they could not reach for the purposes of destruction if they had been so inclined. It consisted of mines in Nevada and Utah and Montana, of sheep and cattle in New Mexico and Arizona, of vineyards and orchards and grain-fields in California, of mortgages and bonds, and of unimproved real estate in San Francisco. On this latter he was now preparing to erect business blocks. But the buildings were in embryo. The mob could neither burn nor dynamite an unbuilded structure, and there was no visible property upon which to wreak vengeance.

Yet the most ample provisions had been made against

any mob uprising. Two batteries of artillery, with guns shotted with grape and canister, two companies of cavalry, and four companies of infantry of the California National Guard, were in readiness, a portion being under arms, and signals were arranged for calling the entire force together at the armories, ready for action, on less than half an hour's notice.

On Saturday night, late in April, 1894, the Congress of Federated Trades again met, and, after a short debate, it was sullenly resolved to accept the situation. The strike was declared at an end, and all the resolutions adopted since the preceding February, including the original resolution of indorsement of the action of the Hod-Carriers' Union, were rescinded, and it was enacted that hereafter the employment of non-union workers should not be a cause of strike except by workers associated in the same work, and against the same employer.

A committee of three, to consist of the President of the Congress of Federated Trades, the Mayor of San Francisco, and the Chief of Police, was appointed to wait, early next morning, upon Mr. Lorin French, communicate to him the action taken by the Federated Trades, and receive his reply.

It was surrender on the part of the workers—absolute and unconditional. It was a blow to their pride, and a relinquishment of that which, with many of them, was a cherished principle; it was brought about by hunger and suffering, and they gave up the contest utterly, and placed themselves at the mercy of the conqueror. Only a brute could have misused the vanquished, but Lorin French had worked himself into a relentless fury during the progress of the strike, and, unfortunately, he had been left in full charge and invested with plenary power by the departed members of the Builders' and Manufacturers' Association.

At nine o'clock the next morning, in the sunshine of an April Sabbath, the committee appointed by the Federated Trades was permitted to pass the Pinkerton guard, and mount the five flights of stairs—for the elevator service had long been discontinued—which led to the top story of the building No. 1099 Market Street, where they were received by Lorin French, who arose from his breakfast table to greet them. He listened without changing his countenance while the Mayor, as Chairman of the committee, communicated to him the substance of the resolution adopted the night before by the Congress of Federated Trades.

"I expected exactly such a result," said French; "it would have saved a great deal of money and a great deal of suffering to these Federated fools if they had adopted a similar course two months ago." ·

"Well, Mr. French," said the Mayor, "these misguided men, with their families, have been the greatest losers and the severest sufferers by it all. I will not discuss the rights and wrongs of it with you. There is more than one side to it, and we might not agree. I am rejoiced, for their sake and yours, and for the sake of the city and State, that it is all over, and that the workers can now return to their work, and business resume its usual channels."

"These misguided men, as you call them, Mr. Mayor," said French, "will be compelled to transfer

their opportunities for future misguidance to some
other locality. They are all blacklisted here. Their
own signatures to receipts for wages when they quit,
constitute the blacklist. Not one of them shall ever
earn another day's wages in this city in any enterprise owned, controlled, or influenced by me.''

''But, Mr. French,'' remonstrated the Mayor, ''this
is unworthy of you. These men have homes here;
they have families to support; the long strike has
left many of them utterly without resources, either to
go away with or to establish themselves elsewhere.
The industries of San Francisco need them. Why
bring in others to take their places? They have abandoned their strike. They have already been sufficiently punished for that which was, after all, only an
error of judgment. If work be refused them, they will
starve.''

''Let them starve,'' savagely replied the millionaire;
''not one of them shall ever get a job of work from
me.''

The President of the Congress of Federated Trades,
who was one of the committee, had hitherto been
silent. He was an iron worker by trade, who, in
twenty years of residence in San Francisco, had almost
lost the Scotch burr which, as a lad, he had brought
with him from Glasgow. In moments of feeling or
excitement it returned to him. He addressed himself
to French:—

''Oh mon,'' said he, ''but thou art hard; and thou
art a fool as well! 'Tis a mad wolf that cooms oot of
the mountain shingle to make a trail through the
heather for the hoonds. Gin ye hae no mercy for

God's poor, hae ye no fear frae the divil's dogs that your words may loosen on ye? Dinna ye ken there be ten, aye, twenty thousand men on the sand lots this blessed Sabbath morn, who love ye not, and who, if they get your words just spoken, and get them they maun, unless ye recall them, would, if they but reach ye, and reach ye they will, for a' your guards and guns, would send ye to God's throne wi' your bad heart a' reekin'?"

"Go and tell the loafers and brawlers of the sand lots exactly what I have said," shrieked French. "It is what I mean to say, and mean for them to hear. If you don't take the message I will send it through the press. Let them do their worst. I do not fear the blackguards, and I am ready for any who choose to visit me," and the old man snapped his fingers as the members of the committee sorrowfully departed.

Half an hour later a speaker who was addressing an audience of thirty thousand people from the central stand at the sand lots, paused as he saw the President of the Congress of Federated Trades making his way through the crowd. The orator had been commenting on the resolutions adopted by the Workers' Congress the previous night, and had been congratulating the people upon the approaching end of the distress occasioned by the long strike, and on the days of peace and plenty which were in store for them, and it was with beaming faces and glad shouts that the multitude welcomed the man who was to announce to them a resumption of their labors in factory and shop.

"My friends," said the tall Scotchman, "I have

just come from an interview with Lorin French, and I am vara vara sorry to bear you the message with which I am charged. He bids me tell you that the notice he gave to us all before the strike begun shall be carried out, and that no man who quit work then shall ever again have work in this city, if he can help it."

The temper of the vast multitude changed in an instant. Shrieks and yells of anger filled the air, and for many minutes the crowd gave way to demonstrations of rage and indignation. All at once there walked to the front of the central platform a tall, angular woman dressed in a gown of plain black stuff. Her features were unprepossessing, to the verge of ugliness, but a wealth of white hair crowned a low brow, surmounting eyes of fierce blue. As she stretched forth a long arm, the multitude hushed to silence, for they recognized the renowned female agitator, Lucy Passmore.

"Friends, brethren, men," said she, in a voice whose magnetic quality vibrated to the farthest edges of the crowd, "it seems that it is the malignant will of one man which savagely condemns thousands to suffering and starvation. If the rattlesnake is coiled for ye, will ye strike first or wait for him to strike? If the wolf is waiting upon your doorstep, will you feed to him the babe he is seeking or will ye give him the knife to the hilt in his hot throat? The death of Lorin French would end this struggle, and your wives would cease to weep and your children to cry with hunger. Men, since God has so far forgotten you as to suffer this devil to live so long, why do you not remedy God's forgetfulness? Are you ready to march now or do you want an old woman to lead you?"

A yell arose from the surging crowd, as, with one mind, thousands comprehended and were ready to act upon the suggestions of Lucy Passmore.

Most of the men had long before furnished themselves with arms of some sort, and their lodge organizations had provided them with elected leaders, who usually attended the sand-lot meetings. As if by magic they formed themselves into companies and battalions and marched, an orderly and almost an organized army, forth from the sand lots, and down to the building No. 1099 Market Street, which they speedily surrounded.

The iron shutters of the upper story were at once closed, and the muzzles of rifles pushed through loop-holes previously prepared for such purpose. An attempt was made from the inside to close the iron gate in front of the main staircase, but the mob surged past the guard, took possession of the lower hall, and started up the stairs. They were met at the top, just below the first landing, by twenty Pinkerton men standing upon the top five steps—four on each step— who, after vainly warning the ascending crowd to desist, at last lowered the muzzles of their Winchesters, and opened a murderous fusillade, which covered the stairs with dead and dying.

The mob hesitated for an instant, but only for an instant, for those below pushed forward those who were above. A hundred revolvers were fired at the Pinkerton men, half of whom fell, and the other half were borne down, shot, clubbed, and stabbed as the mob rushed past and over them, and gained the first landing. The crowd continued to push from below, and in the same way, with great loss of life on each side, they gained successively the third and fourth stories. By this time, however, the forces on the fifth floor had opened fire on the mob outside. Two riflemen at each of the eighteen windows commanded the main entrance to the building, and such a rapid and accurate fire was maintained that Market Street for a hundred feet on each side of the entrance was piled with bodies, and further re-inforcements prevented from reaching those within the building.

At this juncture Battery X came galloping into Market Street from Fourth. Two guns were placed in position, and one, loaded with grapeshot, was fired just above the heads of the crowd. The whistling of the shot in the air above them gave notice to the mob of what was coming, and, with cries of terror, they fled, panic-stricken, into the adjacent streets. The assailants inside the building, hearing the noise of the cannon, followed by the triumphant shouts of the Pinkerton men in the upper story, and finding no further pressure or re-inforcements from below, desisted from further assault, and, turning from the fourth landing, fled down the stairs.

Lorin French, from a loophole in an iron shutter, watched the firing, and the dispersion of the mob outside, and in a few minutes he was informed by a Pinkerton sergeant that the contest was over.

"It's a sorry day's work, sir, said the officer; "we have lost over thirty of our best men, and there must be two hundred rioters dead and wounded on the stairs and in the halls, beside those killed in the street."

"I will help you with the wounded," said French, starting for the passage.

"Better remain here, sir," said the officer. "It may not be quite safe for you yet in the lower halls."

"Nonsense," replied French, "the fight is over," and so saying, he walked out into the hall, and descended the stairs to the fourth story. He paused in horror at the sight which met his eyes. The floor was wet and slippery with blood, and the cries of the wounded pierced his ears. He stood for a moment as if dazed, and then, turning his back upon the scene, prepared to ascend the staircase and gain his room.

And as he turned, a man who was sitting propped up against the wall twenty feet away, raised a revolver which had been lying in his lap, and, clearing with his left hand the blood which obscured his eyes, took rapid yet careful aim and fired.

The bullet struck Lorin French in his backbone, which it shattered, and, with a cry of agony and fear, the owner of $20,000,000 fell forward upon his face on the stairway.

CHAPTER XV.

"In the matter of the estate of Lorin French deceased, the application of Louis Browning for letters executory is before the court. Who represents the applicant?"

"The firm of Bruff & Baldwin, your honor," replied a tall gentleman with spectacled nose and a beardless face.

"Are there contestants?" said the Court.

Then from their seats within the bar of the court room there arose a decorous multitude of lawyers, short and tall, old and young, fat and lean, the white-bearded Nestors, and the complacent, chirping chipmunks of the bar, and in various forms of expression it clearly appeared that there were contestants.

"I think," said his Honor with a weary smile, "that my associates might have sent this case to another department, for I have had a surfeit of contested will cases. Proceed, Mr. Bruff."

"In behalf of the Society of Bug Hunters, who are legatees under a former will," said a sepulchral voice, proceeding from the rotund diaphragm of a bald-headed and full-bearded gentleman, " I have twenty-three objections to offer to the admission to probate of the alleged will of Lorin French, and—"

" Will my learned brother Lester permit me to in-

(173)

terrupt him for a moment," twanged a catarrhal tone, "while I state that I wish my appearance entered here on behalf of the recognized natural son of the deceased, and I protest—"

"On the part of the Australian cousins of Lorin French," shrieked a lean man with red hair, "I have a preliminary objection to offer to the will being read in court at all, and—"

"I object!"

"I except!"

"Will your honor please note the exception of the Nevada heirs?"

"I demand to be heard!"

Then from the entire front of the bar came cries of excited counsel, learned in all law save that of decorum, while the Court rapped for order.

"Gentlemen," said he, "you will all please be seated. The Court itself would like to be heard. The will of our deceased fellow-citizen, Lorin French, who was never more regretted by me than at this moment, or"—and the Court smiled deprecatingly— "the paper which purports to be his will, is presented here by our Brother Bruff. Now, unless some gentleman denies the death of Lorin French, it occurs to me that the reading of the paper offered as his will can but tend to our common enlightenment—"

The deep-voiced Lester, with his twenty-three objections, sustained by a "brief" which covered ninety pages of manuscript, arose.

"I have not yet finished," said the Court. "It is apparent that many of the objections urged will be against the reading of the will. Such objections may be discussed more intelligently if the Court can be suffered to gain some knowledge of the contents of the paper offered, and I shall ask, gentlemen, that you suspend argument or motions while the clerk reads the will. It will then delight the Court to devote the remainder of the term to hearing arguments why the will ought never to have been read. Mr. Clerk, proceed, and I will send to jail for contempt any member of this bar who shall interrupt you until the reading shall be completed."

There was silence in the crowded court room as the clerk opened and read the document:—

In the name of God, Amen, I, Lorin French, of San Francisco, California, being of sound and disposing mind and memory, but being assured by my physicians that the wound received by me must within a few days prove fatal, do make, publish, and declare this my last will and testament, revoking all wills previously made by me.

The free use of my hand enables me to make this will holographic, and this labor I undertake in order to more completely demonstrate to the court where it may be offered for probate, that it is altogether my own act, and that I am sane, clear of mind, and fully possessed of my own memory and judgment.

The near approach of the world into which my spirit is about to journey, brings, possibly, a clearer judgment, and I think now that if my decision to employ no strikers had not been communicated to the mob, I should have reconsidered such decision. However, my approaching death, which will incidentally result from that decision, afflicts me less than the fate of those who fell in the affray, for my own life was drawing to a close.

If the example I shall offer in attempting to adjust the relations of capital and labor shall be followed by others, it will result in advantage to the workers of this land, and great permanent good may thus grow from the bitter struggle which ended with the wound which will terminate my life on earth.

I am unmarried and childless, and my nearest living relatives are cousins of remote degrees, with whose names and places of residence I am scarcely acquainted. No relation of mine has any moral or rightful claim upon my estate, and the disposition I am about to make of my property will work injustice to no living creature.

I appoint as executor of this my last will and testament, my friend Louis Browning, to serve without bonds, and I direct that for his services as executor, and in lieu of all commissions, he receive the sum of $50,000 out of my estate.

I direct my said executor to forthwith pay to the widows, or next of kin, of each man slain in the late riot, the sum of $10,000, to each man permanently disabled by wounds received therein, the sum of $5,-000, and to each man wounded but not permanently disabled, the sum of $1,000.

I direct my said executor to proceed as speedily as possible to prudently dispose of all my estate, and convert the same into money, to be paid over by him to the corporation hereinafter named.

I request that my said executor, Louis Browning, shall, in co-operation with the Governor of California,

the Mayor of San Francisco, and my friends David
Shelburn, Lawrence Slayter, George Morrow, and
Francis Dalton, proceed forthwith to form a corporation under the laws of this State, to be entitled the
'Lorin French Labor Aid Company,' to which corporation, when organized, I direct that the proceeds
of my estate be transferred, to be used by it in providing capital for the use of such co-operative and profit-
sharing corporations as may, from time to time, be organized to avail themselves of its aid.

The Lorin French Labor Aid Company will not
itself engage in any industrial enterprise, but will con-
fine itself strictly to loaning money at three per cent
per annum to such organizations of mechanics as may
seek its assistance and comply with its rules. Those
rules must require that one-fourth of the wages and
all the profits of the members of the borrowing corporation shall be paid to the Lorin French Labor Aid
Company, until the debt due the latter is discharged,
and that the borrowing corporation shall be organized
and conducted in accordance with certain conditions
and rules.

My meaning may be made more clear by the following illustration:—

Suppose that five hundred men shall desire to establish a co-operative foundry. They will make a
preliminary organization and apply to the officers of
the Lorin French Labor Aid Company for the capital
necessary to conduct the enterprise. Those officers
will—after careful inquiry—ascertain that the buildings,
land, machinery, and plant of such a foundry will
cost $900,000, and that it will require a cash capital of

$100,000 to carry the current business. They will purchase such a foundry, taking title in the Lorin French Labor Aid Company in trust, and will select a general manager, who will employ and discharge men, fix the rate of wages and hours of labor, and have full charge of the works. After the indebtedness of the Foundry Company to the Aid Company shall have been fully paid with interest, the members of the Foundry Company may elect their own general manager, but, until then, that officer shall be chosen by, and be subject to the control of, the directors of the Aid Company.

Each man employed in the works, from the general manager to the lowest-paid helper in the yard, must be a shareholder, the number of shares to be held by each being regulated by his wages. If a workman should die, or leave employment, either on his own motion or because of his being discharged, his shares would be turned over to his successor, who would be required to make good to the outgoing man or his widow or heirs whatever amount had been paid upon the shares, and the money for such payment might be advanced when necessary out of a fund for such purpose provided by the Foundry Company, the shares standing as security for the advance. No shares could be transferred except to a successor— employed in the foundry.

A portion, say one-fourth, of the shares of the corporation should be reserved for allotment to workmen whose employment might be required by the growth of the works, though it will be the object of the directors of the Lorin French Labor Aid Company to encourage the continued organization of new co-operative labor corporations rather than the enlargement of old ones. Yet such encouragement must be prudently granted, having reference to the natural growth of business and the demands of a healthy trade, and over-production must not be stimulated, for it is my main purpose to help the laborer to rid himself of the payment of high interest and large commissions, to bring him as nearly as possible in direct communication with the consumer, to save him the waste of strikes, and the salaries of the brawlers who foment difficulties between laborers and their employers, to make him his own employer and his own capitalist, to encourage him in sobriety and thrift and the possession of such high manhood as of right belongs to citizenship of our republic.

The capital stock of such an iron-workers' co-operation might be fixed at the sum borrowed from the Lorin French Labor Aid Company, say $1,000,000, divided into shares of the par value of $10 each.

Thus, five hundred men properly managed, working industriously, and allowing one-fourth of their wages and their entire profits to accumulate, might be able in five years to own a plant of the actual value of $1,000,000, with the good-will of a business worth as much more, and thereafter the worker might receive full wages and an additional income from dividends, which, if placed in endowment insurance, or in similar safe investments, would enable him to retire, if he wish, in fifteen years with an assured competence.

The $20,000,000 which will be received from the sale of my property, all of which I hereby give, devise, and bequeath to the Lorin French Labor Aid Company, ought to, and I doubt not will, be sufficient to establish co-operative iron foundries, sawmills, woolen factories, glass works, brick yards, and other industrial enterprises, in San Francisco, sufficient to provide remunerative employment for fifteen thousand men. The fund will be invested safely, for it will be based upon the security which is the creator and conservator of all property and property rights, industrious and intelligent labor. The accretions to the fund, even at the moderate rate of interest of three per cent per annum, will add, probably, a thousand workers each year to the number of its beneficiaries, while the re-payment and re-investment in similar ways of the original fund, will add several thousand more each year.

The practical operation of the plans I have endeavored to outline will work no injustice to the owners of existing manufacturing establishments, for it will be in the interest of the workmen to purchase such plants and business at their value, rather than to build up new and rival establishments. It is true that some persons now making a profit off the labors of others will be compelled to enlist their capital and energies in other lines; but this, if a hardship, will not be an injustice, and individual convenience must be subservient to the general good.

"I think I have made clear the purposes to which I hereby devote the fortune I have accumulated by fifty years of toil and care—yet in the accumulation of which I have found great enjoyment. The details of my plans I must leave to those who now are, or who hereafter may be, charged with the execution of this trust. In the life upon which I am about to enter—for

I have never so questioned the wisdom of the Originating and Ultimate Force of the Universe as to suppose that the death of this body of flesh will be the end of all conscious individual existence—in the life upon which I am about to enter, I hope to derive satisfaction from the fulfillment of the objects of this my last will and testament, to which I hereby affix my signature and seal, this thirtieth day of April, eighteen hundred and ninety-four.   LORIN FRENCH [SEAL].

We, William Jelly and Thompson Blakesly, declare that Lorin French, in our presence and on the thirtieth day of April, eighteen hundred and ninety-four, in the city of San Francisco, California, signed the foregoing document, which he then declared to each of us was his last will and testament, and we then, at his request and in his presence, and in the presence of each other, sign our names hereto as witnesses.

WILLIAM JELLY,
THOMPSON BLAKESLY.

The voice of the clerk ceased, and for a few seconds there was a hush in the court room, which was broken by the harsh, cold tones of Counselor John Lyman.

"I submit to your Honor," said he, "in behalf of the Public Administrator for whom I appear, and who asks that he be accorded administration of the estate of Lorin French. I submit that this so-called will, although rhetorically and otherwise a very interesting attempt at unpractical philanthropy, is—as a will—simply waste paper. In spirit and in letter it is an utter violation of two sections of the civil code of California. Section 1275 of that code provides that 'corporations—except those formed for scientific, literary, or educational purposes—cannot take under a will, unless expressly authorized by statute.' The proposed Lorin French Labor Aid Company is, in its plan, a corporation, neither scientific, literary, nor educational. Considered as a benevolent corporation, it is not now in existence, and is, of course, not authorized by statute to receive this, or any bequest—"

"How is it," interrupted Mr. Bruff, "that the Society for the Prevention of Cruelty to Animals, the Sisters' Hospital, and other corporations, have received bequests?"

"Simply because they have been expressly authorized by act of the Legislature to do so," was the reply.

"Then if I wish to leave a sum of money to found and support an asylum for one-lunged lawyers, or one-eyed baseball umpires, I am unable to do so, am I?" said Bruff.

"You can go to Sacramento and have a law passed to enable your one-eyed and one-lunged corporations to take your bequest," said Lyman.

"How much," said Bruff, sarcastically, "would I probably be obliged to pay the statesmen for passing such a law?"

"My party is not in power," rejoined Lyman. "I do not know the latest market quotations for votes in your caucus."

"Order, gentlemen, order," said his Honor, grimly.

"And suppose," said Bruff, "the Legislature were not in session, would it be necessary that I wait a year or two before I could make a valid will, with the chance of dying in the meantime?"

"Possibly," replied Lyman, "you might make a bequest to a corporation not empowered at the time of such bequest, to receive it, but which might subsequently be expressly authorized by statute to do so."

"I have led my learned friend to the very point desired," said Bruff. "Why, then, I ask him, can the corporation which the will of Lorin French proposes shall be created, not be authorized by the California Legislature, at its next session, to receive his bequest? I do not apprehend that the most docile Democratic lamb, or the most fearless Republican boodle hunter, would dare to refuse his vote for such a law."

"But the corporation proposed by the late Lorin French," said Lyman, "is not only unempowered to receive, it is not yet in existence as a corporation. It may never be created, and a bequest to either a natural or an artificial being, not even quickened with incipient life, not even conceived at the time of the bequest, may be questioned as of doubtful validity. But it is profitless to discuss these questions, because there is another section of the civil code which disposes completely of this so-called will. I refer to section number 1313. Thirteen is certainly an unlucky number for the workers of San Francisco. By that section it is provided that no will devising property for charitable or benevolent uses, shall be valid unless made at least thirty days before the death of the testator, and that in no event can a man bequeath more than one-third of his estate for such purpose, if he have natural heirs. It is also provided that all dispositions of property made contrary to the statute shall be void, and the property go to the residuary legatee, next of kin, or heir, according to law."

"That was one of the wise laws that the sand-lot statesmen gave us," said Bruff, sarcastically.

"Deed, and it wasn't a sand-lot law at all," interrupted a stalwart, red-bearded attorney with a slight Milesian accent. "It was passed away back in the seventies. Old Moriarty was down with typhoid fever, and Father Gallagher was pressin' him every day to save his soul by lavin' his millions to the Jesuit College and Hospital. But before the priest could get the old man in condition, Mike Moriarty slipped Nat Bronton—the king of the lobby—up to Sacramento with $20,-000 rint money that Mike collected while his father was ill, and the bill was rushed through under suspinsion of the rules. Two days after the bill became a law, Father Gallagher coaxed and dhrove old Moriarty into signing a will that cut Mike off wid $50,000, and left $3,000,000 to the church, and the next week they buried the old man, with masses enough to put him through purgatory in an express train. They say that there was a scrappin' match between Father Gallagher and Mike when the priest found that he had been outgeneraled, and Mike lost the top of his left ear, but he saved his father's estate. Sure, the whole case is reported in the fortieth California, under the title of the Society of Jesus against Moriarty, and it decides this will of French's sure enough."

When the ripple of laughter which this interruption provoked had subsided, Mr. Lyman resumed:—

"My learned friend Casey is right, your Honor; the case he quoted does decide this one. If this will had been made more than thirty days before the death of Mr. French, it could at most have disposed of but one-third of his property. But it was made only two days before his death, and, under section 1313 of the code, is utterly void," and the speaker resumed his seat.

The Court turned to the attorney who had offered the will for probate.

"What have you to say to this, Mr. Bruff?" he inquired. "All the claimants for the estate will doubtless agree with the position taken by the attorney for the public administrator. They are joined in interest in overturning the will. You alone defend the beneficent purposes of the dead man. What have you to say?"

"What can I say, your Honor?" said Bruff, bitterly. "It is another instance of a man conceited and obstinate enough to attempt making his own will. If my old friend French had called me in, I would have told him that courts aud juries in California seldom allow a man to dispose of his own estate, if it be a large one, and he must give his savings away in his lifetime if he wishes to prevent his sixth cousins from rioting on them. I would have had Lorin French convey his vast property to trustees to carry out his plans, and have affected the transfer completely while he was yet alive. But he, great and simple soul, supposed, naturally enough, that he had a right to do as he pleased with his own, and that, being without near kindred, and no person having any claim upon him, he could help the poor with the money it had taken him half a century to accumulate. He was originally educated to the law, and, although he had been out of practice for thirty years, he knew how to formulate a will. But he was not aware of the ravages committed by a California Legislature among the time-honored principles of the common law. Mark the result of legislative folly and individual inadvertence. Twenty millions of dollars, which their owner proposed to devote to a grand and comprehensive experiment for adjusting the vexed relations of labor and capital, will now be consumed in court costs and witness fees, divided among a horde of attorneys, and finally scattered in selfish enjoyment, and in ways unuseful to man, all over the world from Australia to Elko. It's the law, I suppose, and neither your Honor nor I can help it, but it's an accursed shame, nevertheless."

And Mr. Bruff, pale with excitement, resumed his seat.

"The Court can not only pardon your emphatic language, Brother Bruff," said his Honor, "but indorses it. If I could discover any loophole which might be crawled through, or any way by which I could break down or climb over the legislative barrier, and validate the bequest of Lorin French, I would certainly do so. I will reserve for further consideration the question of the validity of the legacies to the wounded, and the families of those killed in the riot. I am inclined to think that portion of the will may be good, and so carry with it the right of Louis Browning to letters testamentary. For the present, however, I am reluctantly compelled to sustain the objection of the attorney for the public administrator, and refuse the will admission to probate. It is ordered accordingly. Mr. Clerk, note the exception of Mr. Bruff to my ruling. I will take my summer vacation now, and go fishing. I shall adjourn court for one month, and the further hearing of this case for two months. In the meantime, if the gentlemen who represent the various applicants for letters of administration, will leave their papers with the clerk, I will, upon my return, give them careful attention.''

''Does your Honor desire that I leave all my papers?'' queried the sepulchral-voiced Lester.

''All,'' replied his Honor, and he paused for a moment, and glanced at the ninety pages of manuscript lying in front of counsel learned in the law, '' all except your brief, Mr. Lester.''

The proceedings of the day in the superior court were reported fully, and commented upon freely, by the newspapers throughout the country, and a fortnight afterwards the proposed executor of the rejected will received the following letter:—

OFFICES OF DAVID MORNING, 39 Broadway, }
New York City, June 10, 1894. }

MR. LOUIS BROWNING, San Francisco, Cal.—*My Dear Sir:* Such a wise and noble plan as that of the late Lorin French ought not to lack accomplishment for want of money to execute it. If you, and the gentlemen named by him as your associates in the trust which he vainly endeavored to create, will organize such a corporation as he proposed, I will devote to it a sum equal to the value of his estate, which I understand to be, in round numbers, twenty millions of dollars. Very truly yours, DAVID MORNING.

CHAPTER XVI.

MANHATTAN ISLAND, west of Broadway and south of
Trinity Church, was, during the last century, occupied
by the substantial mansions of the ancient Knicker-
bockers, and as late as the first third of the present
century was not relinquished as a place of residence
by people of aristocratic pretensions.   Before the civil
war, the annual fairs of the American Institute were
held in Castle Garden, within whose walls Grisi and
Mario and Jenny Lind sang, and on summer after-
noons children, accompanied by nursemaids, romped
upon the grass under the grand old trees on the Battery.   Then the Bowling Green Fountain, with its
picturesque pile of rocks, was still an ancient land-
mark; and the goat pastures above Fifty-ninth Street
were being cleared for the planting of Central Park.

After the war the few remaining occupants of pre-
tentious residences fled to the northward of Madison
Square, and the sightliest and most picturesque portion of New York City was abandoned to saloons,
emigrant boarding houses, warehouses, and shops, for,
unlike the down-town section east of Broadway, it
was not invaded and colonized by bankers, brokers,
and importing houses.

(188)

Mr. David Morning, now widely known as the Arizona Gold King, selected this portion of New York City for the experiment of organizing pleasant and economical home lives for a class of dwellers in cities not ordinarily the subject of elemosynary effort.

The poverty of the very poor, who sometimes lack even for food or shelter, is hardly more distressing to the sufferers than the poverty of men who struggle to maintain a respectable position upon incomes inadequate, even with the most economical management, to meet their expenses. How is a married man, having an income of one, two, or even three thousand dollars per annum, derived from work which must be performed by him, as clerk, journalist, physician, or lawyer, upon Manhattan Island, to live there with such surroundings as are befitting his education and position?

He will be compelled to pay one-third or one-half of his income for a flat; an entire house is out of the question, unless he betake himself to such a locality in the city as will exile his family from social consideration. If he live in the suburbs, he must arise at daylight and stumble along unlighted lanes to the railroad station, and pass two or three hours of his time each day standing in a crowded ferryboat, or hanging to the straps of a jammed car, alternately frozen and roasted, and always stifled with the reeking perfume of unventilated vehicles and unsavory fellow-travelers, for while it may be true that all men are politically equal, they are not always equally well washed.

The alternative is to bring up his family in the

brawl and small scandal of a boarding house. His wife requires always a certain amount of dresses and bonnets to maintain herself in a respectable position in the estimation of her friends, and dresses and bonnets entail an uncertain amount of expenditure. A man's tailor will inform him in advance exactly how much his garment will cost, and one can contract for a bridge across the Mississippi at an agreed sum, but there is no force known in nature that will induce or drive a dressmaker into foregoing an opportunity for advantage taking, or persuade her to fix in advance a price for the making and trimming of a gown.

The married bookkeeper or salesman on a salary in New York City, is forever upon the ragged edge of embarrassment, unable to save the amount of the payments necessary for adequate life insurance, or to provide a fund for a rainy day. The laborer or mechanic who earns six hundred to nine hundred dollars per annum is, in comparatively easy circumstances, for he can live in a tenement house in a cheap neighborhood without loss of caste, and caste is of almost as much consequence in free America as in the Punjaub.

After some thought, Mr. David Morning devised a trial scheme for the relief of married men of small incomes, whose duties required their daily presence in New York City, below Canal Street, and in the autumn of 1894 his agents began to quietly purchase the real estate between Rector Street and the Battery, and bounded by Greenwich Street and the Hudson River. Some months were consumed in the acquisition of title to the realty, and in a few instances long prices were exacted by sagacious and selfish owners, who held out until the others had sold, but the bulk of the property was purchased at about its value, and the brokers were finally instructed to close with all persons willing to sell, without haggling as to price.

It required about $15,000,000 to complete the purchase, and for this sum sixteen hundred lots were secured of the orthodox dimensions of twenty-five by one hundred feet each. Electric lights turned night into day, and several thousands of men and hundreds of vehicles, divided into three armies of eight-hour workers, were at once employed in the work of demolition. Temporary railroad tracks were laid from the land to the North River piers, and the material and débris not needed to fill cellars and vaults was carried on cars to barges, which were towed to the Jersey flats, where their contents were dumped upon ground previously acquired by Mr. Morning for that purpose, and by the first of February, 1895, the lower part of Manhattan Island west of Greenwich Street was as bare as a picked bird.

The work, although generally prosaic, was not without its romantic and interesting incidents. In a stone house on Greenwich Street, which was once the colonial mansion of Diedrich Von Wallendorf, a walled chamber was opened. The rugs and hangings it had contained were fallen to shreds, but the Queen Anne cabinets, tables, and bedstead were in as good condition as when the room was closed with solid stone masonry, two centuries ago, without any reason now apparent for the strange proceeding.

Under the cellar floor of another house an earthern

"crock" was found filled with sovereigns, coined in the
last century, and through the destruction of an old
wall cabinet, there came to light a package of letters
from Lord North to Sir Henry Clinton, letters which
indicated that the British Ministry of that day had
been in negotiation with other patriot leaders than
Benedict Arnold for a surrender of the revolutionary
cause.

The consent of the city authorities to a resurvey
and remodeling of the streets and avenues of the destroyed section of New York, was obtained without
difficulty since Mr. Morning was now the sole owner
of the land affected thereby, and the rearrangements
proposed by him were made at his own cost, and in-
sured greater uniformity and greater convenience to
the public than those which were superseded.

The land was platted into blocks four hundred feet
in length and eighty feet in width, running north
and south, thus giving to the occupants of the new
buildings either the morning or the afternoon sun.
These blocks are divided by streets of a uniform width
of one hundred feet, having a park thirty feet wide in
the center of each street, with lawn, shrubs, orna-
mental trees, and a fountain in the center of each
block. Gas, water, and sewer pipes, and electric
light and pneumatic tubes, have been laid in the new
streets, and by means of a powerful pumping engine,
erected on the Battery, the sewers are flushed every
day with sea water. The new streets are paved with
asphalt, with sidewalks of cement. The city received
from Morning land at the foot of Canal Street purchased by him, in exchange for Castle Garden and

vicinage, and the Battery—filled with fountains, statues, and increased acreage of lawn and garden—is restored to its ancient functions, and more than its ancient glory.

The buildings erected upon each of the one hundred blocks thus created, are of uniform size and style. Each building—occupying an entire block—is four hundred feet long, eighty feet wide, and seventeen stories high. The roofs are covered with glass, making the structures eighteen stories aboveground. One-half of the area of the eighteenth story in each block is laid out in plots filled with ten feet of rich soil in beds of perforated cement, the other half in broad walks of plate glass—guarded by copper netting—so as to admit light to the seventeenth story and to the large air shafts.

In each of the buildings are one hundred and fifty suites of five rooms, each suite having a floor area of sixteen hundred square feet, and every room having an outlook upon the street. A broad hall runs through the center of the building on every floor, lighted by means of plate-glass windows at each end, and also by three shafts, one hundred feet apart, running from cellar to roof. Every room is provided with steam, dry, and gas heat, and with gas and incandescent lights. Each suite has a household pneumatic tube service connecting with the store rooms in the basement, and with the kitchen and dining rooms in the seventeenth story. Each suite has also a cooking closet, with gas range, hot water, and steam pipes, porcelain-lined sinks, and pneumatic tubes for carrying away garbage.

Six hydraulic elevators furnish ample accommodations for reaching every floor at any hour of the day or night. A network of perforated steel pipes is concealed in the walls and floors, with separate connections for each room with the great tanks on the roof, which are in turn connected both with the Croton water system, and with the great steel water main bringing water from Rockland Lake. In case of fire the walls and floors of one room, or of any number of rooms, can instantly be saturated with water, and twice in each week, at an appointed hour, a warm, gentle rain is made to descend for a sufficient length of time upon the trees and shrubs in the roof garden.

Each suite has separate sewer connections, and each room is provided with registers in the wall, from which either hot air or cold air can be turned on or off at will, the hot air ascending from the furnaces, and the cold air being forced by a pumping engine from the refrigerating room in the basement. Those whose fate it has been to swelter on Manhattan Island in the dog days can appreciate the latter luxury. The fortunate occupant of a room in one of the Morning Blocks commands his temperature. Whether the thermometer registers thirty degrees below or one hundred degrees above zero outside, he can arrange the climate in his own room to suit himself, and *pater familias* can connect a wire with the register in the parlor, and, if "Cholly" protracts his visits to Gladys to an improper hour, he can shut off the hot air, turn on a current from the refrigerator, and in ten minutes make the young man choose between departure and congealment.

These buildings were planned for the relief of women. The great source of waste and care in our American domestic life is in the kitchen, and it is impossible to organize a more advantageous trust for both producer and consumer than a "kitchen trust." The daily history of every American family is one of almost unavoidable waste. In food, in fuel, in the labor of cooking, and in many other details of housekeeping, there is uneconomic use of both labor and materials. Probably one-fourth of the expenditure of every American householder who is able to keep one or more servants is unnecessary and wasteful, and where only one servant, or none at all, is employed, the health and beauty and life of the wife are expended in kitchen drudgery, and her opportunities of growth and culture are lost.

The Morning Blocks were designed as theaters of experiment, which, if successful, will be copied elsewhere, for freeing the household from the waste and vexation and tyranny of the kitchen. Mr. Morning's plan for bringing about this beneficent result is both simple and effective. The kitchen, or general cooking room for the block, is situated in the seventeenth story, where there is one large, and one hundred and fifty small dining rooms. Each dining room is lighted either from the street or the roof, is perfectly ventilated, and has an electric bell and pneumatic tube service connecting it with the kitchen, with the market house in the basement, and with the suite of apartments below, of which it is an adjunct.

The happy householder in one of the Morning Blocks will have his choice of methods. He and family may take their meals at the restaurant or general dining room in the seventeenth story, either by the carte, meal, or week. He may use the general dining room, or his private dining room, or dine in his apartments below—the pneumatic tube service extending to all, and a private waiter will be furnished at a fixed price per hour. He can purchase cooked provisions by weight, delivered at either place, or purchase his own supplies at the market house in the basement and have them cooked in the general kitchen, or use his own cooking closet, where, without waste of fuel—gas being used—his selections may be prepared for the table and served either there or sent by pneumatic tube to his dining room above.

Prices for everything furnished, whether of materials or labor, are fixed from time to time by the manager, and all bills are required to be paid every Monday, on penalty of the tenant losing his privilege of occupancy. The prices charged are less than those demanded for similar service or material elsewhere. An account will be kept of each householder's disbursements, and his proportion of the profits made will be returned to him at the end of the year, according to the usual co-operative process, the object being to furnish each occupant of the block with whatever he needs of food or service at actual cost.

The rent asked for the apartments in the Morning Blocks has been adjusted upon the basis of paying taxes, insurance, repairs, and three per cent per annum upon the capital invested in the enterprise.

Mr. Morning has conveyed the one hundred blocks to the governor of New York, the mayor of New

York City, and the president of the New York Chamber of Commerce, who, with their official successors, are made perpetual trustees of this munificent gift. In the trust deed it is provided that the three per cent interest on cost, received from tenants, shall be invested in an endowment fund, payable, with its accumulations, to the tenant whenever he leaves the building, or to his widow or legal representative in the event of his death while a tenant.

The tenant in a Morning Block will be supplied with hot and cold air, hot and cold water, steam, gas, electric light, food, and service at actual cost. His rooms will be provided him at the cost of taxes, insurance, and repairs, and he and his family will be made the beneficiaries of a fund, which he will be required to create for the contingency of his death or departure from the building. To guard against overcrowding, no one suite of apartments will be rented to any family of more than five adults, and no subletting or hiring of apartments will be permitted.

The cost of the land is estimated at $16,000,000, and of clearing it and erecting the new buildings at $30,000,000. The taxes, with insurance, repairs, employes, and such other expenses as are in their nature incapable of apportionment among the tenants, will amount to $810,000 per annum. This sum divided by fifteen thousand, the number of suites of apartments in the one hundred Morning Blocks, will give $54 as the annual sum to be paid by each tenant for his apartments, and he will pay $108 additional annually toward a fund for his own benefit. In all he will pay about $14 a month for accommodations that it would be difficult to obtain elsewhere for five times the amount.

The manager of each block will receive a salary of $3,000 per annum, and will, in the first instance, be selected by the Board of Trustees, but on the first Monday of January, 1897, and each year thereafter, the occupants of each block, by a majority vote, can elect a manager, who will, however, in the discharge of his duties, and in the employment of assistants, be subject to the direction and supervision of the trustees.

Mr. Morning in the trust deed conveying the Morning Blocks has named the qualifications of tenants as follows: The applicant must be of good moral character, married, over the age of twenty-five and under sixty. He must have been at the time of his application for more than one year previously in the employment of some person, firm, or corporation engaged in a reputable business in the city of New York south of Canal Street, and be in receipt of a salary of not less than $1,000 or more than $3,000 per annum. If a lawyer, physician, dentist, architect, or civil engineer, author, clergyman, or journalist, his net income must be of a similar amount.

Applicants for suites of apartments must file their applications and references at the office of the Morning Blocks prior to 12 o'clock noon on the fifteenth day of August, 1895. The credentials of all applicants will be examined and careful inquiry made as to their habits, characters, and antecedents, and only those will be accepted as eligible for tenancy who can strictly comply with the requirements.

Should there be, as is most likely, approved applications in excess of the suites to be rented, the fifteen thousand who can be accommodated will be selected by lot, and the others registered, and whenever vacancies occur a tenant to fill such vacancy will be selected by lot from the list. Apartments will be apportioned by lot among the successful applicants. Tenants will be permitted to exchange apartments by amicable arrangement, but no transfer of apartments from a tenant to one who is not a tenant will be permitted. The tenant can surrender his right to occupy his apartments at pleasure, but he cannot assign it, or sublet the whole or any part of the premises accorded him.

Should six tenants who are heads of families on any floor make complaint against one of the other four tenants on that floor that he is obnoxious, and that in the general interest his tenancy ought to be terminated, a jury of fifteen tenants of that building, selected by lot, one from each of the other floors, shall be made up to try the accused, who shall have opportunity to cross-examine the witnesses against him, and to present his defense. The manager shall preside and preserve order, and if twelve of the fifteen jurors shall concur in finding that the tenancy of the accused ought to terminate, he may appeal to the Board of Trustees, and unless they unanimously exonerate him, his tenancy must cease.

Our reporter interviewed Mr. Morning, who was found at his offices in lower Broadway, and inquired of that gentleman if it were true, as rumored, that he intended to erect similar buildings on another part of Manhattan Island.

" I have secured," replied that gentleman, "all the land for a hundred blocks in and about the locality known as 'the Hook,' and I propose the erection of buildings there that will accommodate forty thousand families of mechanics and laborers. There will, of course, be less room for each occupant than in the blocks just completed, and less expensive arrangements in many particulars, but the rent and cost of living will be less, and the premises will be rented and conducted substantially on the same plan, with only such difference in rules as may be necessary."

"What will be the cost of these latter buildings, Mr. Morning?" said our reporter.

"With the land, about $30,000,000," was the reply.

"It is a pity," commented our reporter, "that every city in the land cannot count a David Morning among its citizens, with a gold mine at his command."

"The mine is not necessary," said Morning. "There are a dozen men in every large city of our land who, without any gold mine, could do what I have done. I hope," continued the speaker, "not to be alone in the work of helping the people both to employment and homes."

"None of our millionaires," said the reporter, "have thus used their money."

"It must be remembered," rejoined Morning, "that the very great fortunes of this country have mainly been created during the last twenty-five years, and in the eager and necessarily selfish strife incident to their acquisition, their owners have not always considered that their possession is a great trust which brings with it duties as well as rights."

"But I see the dawn of a better day and a better feeling," continued Mr. Morning. "I hear of many gentlemen in different parts of the country who are proposing to use millions for the erection of homes, and the secure establishment of co-operative industries for the benefit of the workers of the land. My idea is that no man should be accorded an unearned dinner who has refused a chance to earn it, but that it is the duty of society to provide every man with an opportunity of earning. Of what value at last is wealth unless one can use it for the benefit of his fellow-men? Charon will not transport gold across the Styx at any rate of ferriage. Of what use is money here except in one form and another to give it away? No man can expend on his own legitimate and proper comforts and pleasures the interest on $1,000,000 at five per cent per annum."

"There are many men, Mr. Morning, who expend a good deal more than $50,000 a year."

"Not in the sense of personal expenditures. Mansions, laces, diamonds, furniture, horses, carriages, and the like are investments rather than expenditures. Receptions and banquets may be classed with gifts. He must be an industrious man who can, with his family, eat, drink, and wear out $50,000 worth each year."

"But is there not the pleasure of accumulation itself, Mr. Morning?"

"I suppose so," replied that gentleman, "or men would not pursue it; but it is a cultivated and not a natural taste. Every man for instance, requires a pair of trousers and a hat, but after he has acquired

enough of such articles for the use of himself and his
family for life, and a generous supply for his descendants, why work the balance of his days to fill warehouses with trousers and hats?   I do not know," continued Mr. Morning—and our reporter thought that
there was a deeper shade in his sea-gray eyes—"I do
not know that I shall ever marry, but if I had boys I
would leave them no fortunes larger than would suffice
for a generous support."

"Will you, then," queried our reporter, " expend
in your own lifetime all the great revenues of the
Morning mine?"

"All that I can find time, strength, and opportunity to expend in ways that will help the world," rejoined the Arizona Gold King.

[From the New York Times, July 17, 1895.]

Mr. David Morning is engaged in works of apparent charity, which to many thoughtful men will seem
an injury rather than a benefit to the world.   Capitalists are entitled to receive interest upon their investments, and if inducement to accumulation be taken
away by the competition of such Utopians as Mr.
Morning, then frugality may cease to be accounted a
virtue.

On the whole, wouldn't it be better for the business
world, and the stability of property and property
rights, if the tenants of the Morning Blocks were compelled to pay the full rental value of their apartments?

[From the New York Socialist, July 19, 1895.]

Dave Morning is endeavoring to throw dust in the
eyes of the working masses of the country, by erect-

ing seventeen-story palaces for boodle bookkeepers, and twenty-story tenement houses for mechanics. He has filled San Francisco, Chicago, and several other cities with his humbug Co-operative Labor Aid Societies. He is evidently plotting for the presidency in 1896, and expects to reach the White House by a golden path.

"The poor of this country should accept no employ-ment as a boon, nor consent to engage in any wage-saving and profit-sharing corporation that will force them to accumulate, and they should take no such favors from the rich as cheap rents or free homes. Let the unnatural accumulations of rich scoundrels be distributed among the people. No man is honestly entitled to have or hold anything except the fruits of his own labor. It would be better for the world, and for the great cause of socialism which the pseudo philanthropy of Morning delays and obstructs, if this Arizona Gold King could be tumbled head first down one of his own shafts, and his seventeen-story marble-paved Edens be dynamited out of existence.

CHAPTER XVII.

"Plans of mice and men gang aft aglee."

Morning's business offices were on the west side
of Broadway, below Trinity Church, but he gave attention to his large and increasing correspondence in
his rooms at the Hoffman House, where he had a suite
of apartments fronting on Broadway.

The largest room of the suite had always been reserved by the proprietors for a private dining room,
but Morning insisted upon its constituting a part of
his suite, and as he permitted the hotel keepers to
name their own price, it was reluctantly surrendered
to him. In this room Morning had a large-sized
phonograph receiver fitted into the wall opposite his
desk, the instrument itself being placed upon a long
table against the partition in the adjacent room. A
cord which swung over the desk was fastened to a
lever connected with an electric motor, also in the
next room.

It was Morning's habit each day after breakfast to
seat himself at his desk, open his letters, pull the cord
which started the electric motor, and "talk" his replies to the phonograph receiver. The instrument
in the next room was arranged to hold a cylinder of
sufficient length to receive a communication an hour
in length. After Morning had completed this portion

(204)

of his daily labors, it was the duty of his secretary to remove the cylinders, and place them in other phonographs, where two and sometimes three clerks received their contents, and reduced the same to typewriter manuscript.

This simple contrivance had still another use. Morning knew that there was no such fruitful source of business difficulties and consequent litigation as that which emanated from misunderstanding or misrepresentation of verbal communications. He endeavored, therefore, to conduct all important business conversations in this room, and all the utterances of either party were recorded by the faithful and unerring phonograph, and the cylinders upon which they were reported were properly labeled, dated, and stored away. He did not fail in any instance to inform the person with whom he was conversing that all their words were thus finding accurate record.

One day in October, 1895, while Morning was in Chicago—where he had gone to perfect the organization of a Labor Aid Corporation—the great financier, Mr. Arnold Claybank, stopped at the Hoffman House on his way down town, and ordered a choice dinner for three to be served at seven o'clock that day.

"And have it served in the room fronting upon Broadway, where we always dine," said the millionaire.

"Very sorry, Mr. Claybank," answered the clerk, "but that room is at present rented to Mr. David Morning, as a part of his suite, and when he is in town he uses it as a room in which to receive and answer his correspondence; at present he is in Chicago."

"If he is in Chicago," replied the Wall Street magnate, "you can have our dinner served in the room as usual. It will not disturb him, certainly, even if he should know of it, and he is not likely to know of it unless you tell him. I have dined in that room with my friends at least once a week during the last twenty years, and, not supposing you would ever rent it for other purposes, I have already invited them to meet me there this evening. I don't like to change, in fact, I won't change, and if you will not accommodate me I will take my patronage elsewhere."

After some hesitation, the clerk agreed to have dinner served in the room desired, and at seven o'clock that evening Mr. Arnold Claybank, with his guests, Mr. Isaiah Wolf and Mr. John Gray, assembled to discuss both the menu and the subject of their gathering.

Not until the last course was removed, the Burgundy on the table, the cigars lighted, and the waiter excused from further attendance, did the great capitalists approach the real object of their meeting. Mr. Claybank observed that they might need writing materials, and, stepping to Morning's desk, he seated himself thereat, and pulled what he supposed to be a bell cord that would summon a waiter. No waiter appeared in answer to the supposed summons, and Claybank, taking a notebook and pencil from his pocket, remarked that they would serve his purpose.

These three gentlemen had dined well, and should have been in a pleasant frame of mind toward the world, for good dinners are, or ought to be, humanizing in their tendencies. Yet there are natures which will remain unaffected even by terrapins, Maryland style, and roasted canvas-back duck, assimilated with the aid of Lafitte and Pommery Sec., and no tigers crouching in the jungle were ever more merciless and conscienceless in their rapacity than these three black-coated capitalists.

Mr. Arnold Claybank was the leading spirit of the conclave. His wealth was popularly estimated at $100,000,000. He had inherited none of it. At thirty-five years of age he was a dry goods merchant in an interior city in Ohio, possessed of less than $100,000. During his frequent visits to New York to purchase goods he was in the habit of "taking a flyer" in the stock market. These flyers proved so continuously successful, and added so largely to his capital, that in a few years he closed out his dry goods business, removed permanently to the metropolis, bought a seat in the stock board, and soon became known as one of the boldest and shrewdest operators in the street.

He was rapid and usually accurate in judgment, and always possessed of the courage of his convictions. He was as cunning as the gray fox, to which he was often likened. He was suave in manner but merciless in the execution of his plans. He was identified in the public mind with several of the boldest and most unscrupulous operations in the history of Wall Street, and his millions had steadily and rapidly increased, until now, at sixty years of age, he was one of the acknowledged kings of New York finance.

Isaiah Wolf was, as his name indicated, of Hebrew origin. He was about the same age as Claybank, and had many of the qualities of that gentleman, lacking, however, his courage and his quickness of comprehension and movement. He was a gambler by birth, education, and instinct, and a gambler who never failed to use all advantages possible.

Thirty years before he had been a clothing merchant and dealer in city, county, and legislative warrants at Portland, Oregon. He furnished the impecunious legislators, when they came down from the mountain counties, with an outfit of clothing; he discounted their salaries at three per cent per month; he was usually the custodian of the lobby funds, and he could always introduce senator or assemblyman to a quiet game of "draw," where, whenever a huge "pot" was in dispute, Isaiah could usually be found safely entrenched behind the winning hand.

When the Comstock mines began to yield their great output of silver in 1875–77, the Wolf Brothers located in San Francisco, made their homes on Pine and California Streets, and gambled in mining stocks from the vantage-ground of secret knowledge, for in every mine were one or more miners under pay, not only from the mining company, but from Isaiah Wolf. In 1879, when the transactions in the stock board of San Francisco had dwindled to a tithe of their former magnitude, and when the sand-lot agitators succeeded in grafting their ideas of finance and taxation upon the organic law of California, Isaiah Wolf and his brother Emanuel gathered their assets together and joined the exodus of millionaires. In New York City they opened a bankers' and brokers' office, and were now accounted as jointly the possessors of $80,000,000, the management of which was left almost exclusively to Isaiah.

John Gray was an insignificant-looking old man of seventy. From his unkempt beard, watery eyes, shrinking manner, and small stature, he might have been taken for a congressional doorkeeper who had seen better days. In truth, there was, under his ignoble exterior, one of the broadest, wiliest, and best-informed minds in America. He was the acknowledged leader of Wall Street in ability and resources. His wealth was estimated at quite $150,000,000, and it had been created by himself in about forty-five years.

He began life as a Vermont peddler, but at the age of twenty-five carried his New England education, his capacity for calculation, his retentive memory, his frugal habits, and his tireless energy into New York City, where he began as porter and messenger in the office of a broker. He soon learned the history and methods of the principal operators of the Wall Street of that day, and his savings were shrewdly, quietly, and boldly invested on "points" which he picked up while delivering messages or awaiting replies. He soon accumulated a large sum of money, yet he kept his humble place, and his employer never suspected when he paid the faithful porter his $40 at the end of each month, that the quiet and deferential young man could have purchased not only his employer's business, but the building in which it was conducted.

Gray remained as porter and messenger for five years, declining all offers which were made to him of promotion to a desk and a higher salary. The place he held gave him opportunities which could be obtained

14

in no other way.   None suspected the quiet and stolid-looking man, who seemed so dull of comprehension when any verbal message was intrusted to him; and words were dropped and conversations held in his presence which, when fitted by his quick and comprehensive brain into other words and conversations held in other offices, often enabled him to forecast events.   The man who by any means is accurately advised of the real intentions of the leaders of Wall Street a day or even an hour before their execution, has a key to wealth, and Gray used this key, conducting all his operations through one broker, who was pledged to secrecy.

At the time of the great deal in Harlem, so successfully engineered before the war by Commodore Vanderbilt, Gray was still occupying his place as messenger.   He overheard a conversation held in the commodore's private office between that gentleman and his confidential clerk, and, comprehending the magnitude of the opportunity, he directed that all his resources, which then amounted to nearly $200,000, be placed in Harlem stock.   He was enabled, under the system of margins which prevailed in Wall Street, to purchase $2,000,000 worth of the stock, which he sold at an average advance of fifty per cent, clearing $1,000,000 by the operation.

The old commodore, who had himself made $6,-000,000 by the deal, found that somebody had been sharing profits with him to the extent of $1,000,000, and, not supposing that this was the result of guess-work, he used means to discover who was the cunning operator and what were the sources of his information.

Without much difficulty he traced the transactions to John Gray, and, remembering the presence of that young man in the anteroom at the time of giving directions to his confidential clerk, he was not at a loss to determine how it came about.

The commodore considered that Gray had gained $1,000,000 which should have come to his own coffers, and he determined to "give the young fellow a lesson, sir," as he said to his confidential clerk. That morning Gray's employer received—to his great surprise—a call from Vanderbilt, who, to his greater surprise, informed him of the true status of his messenger, who had become a millionaire. Gray's employer readily promised to assist in the scheme which Vanderbilt formed for punishing Gray and "stripping him of his ill-gotten gains, sir." Vanderbilt required only that Gray's employer should next day send Gray to Vanderbilt's office, with a verbal message, inquiring, "What is to be done about Erie?"

The next day Gray called and delivered his message to the commodore in his private office.

"Take a seat, young man, until I can write a reply," was the direction, and Gray deferentially seated himself upon the edge of a chair, and gazed at the carpet stolidly, while the commodore penned the following: "Buy all the Erie offered at market rates up to fifty-three. C. V." This note the commodore placed in an envelope, which he directed, but apparently forgot to seal, and handed it to Gray, who thereupon departed. As the door closed behind the messenger, the veteran bull smote himself upon the sides, and threw his head back and laughed.

Gray noticed that the envelope was not sealed, and before he reached the bottom of the stairs, he possessed himself of its contents.

Then he fell into a train of thought. Erie was selling at $37, and Gray was thoroughly posted as to the resources, liabilities, and business of the road, and knew very nearly who were the principal stockholders. He knew that the commodore held fully one-third of the capital stock of Erie, which had cost him not more than $30 a share, and he also knew that the old gentleman had been for some time selling his stock at $37 as fast as he could do so without breaking the market. Thirty-seven was really a nursed price for the stock; it was more than the condition and prospects of the road warranted, and Gray did not believe that Vanderbilt intended to purchase any great quantity, even at $37, or that it would be possible for him to run the stock to $53 without purchasing the entire amount.

Gray delivered the note to his employer, and asked that gentleman if he might be excused for half an hour to attend to some matters of business of his own. Leave of absence was graciously granted, and Gray was watched to the door of the office of the broker who had bought and sold his Harlem stock. Then Gray's employer walked to the office of the expectant commodore and informed him that the young man had swallowed the bait, for he had gone to the office of his broker, probably to order large purchases of Erie.

Vanderbilt thanked the broker, assured him that in the division of the spoils he should not be forgotten, and authorized him in furtherance of their project to purchase all the Erie offered up to $42, to which figure Vanderbilt proposed to run the stock before letting it drop.

Gray directed his broker to purchase Erie in one-hundred-share lots, beginning at $37, and to follow the market up to $53 if it reached that figure, but not to purchase more than five thousand shares in all. Having given this direction, he walked into the back office of a firm of brokers, who, although leaders in the market, had never succeeded in obtaining any business from Vanderbilt, and between them and that gentleman there was a business feud of long standing. The quiet messenger was well known to the head of the firm, who greeted him pleasantly.

"What can I do for you, Gray," said he.

"I would like to take your time for not more than five minutes," said Gray.

"I am pretty busy," said the gentleman, "but I will try and oblige you," and he led the way to an inner office.

The broker's eyes distended with astonishment as Gray rapidly told how he had made such use of his opportunities as porter and messenger as to accumulate, by speculation, a large sum of money, and that he desired now to employ their firm in an operation which, for reasons of his own, he did not care to intrust to his regular broker.

The gentleman smilingly agreed to accept Mr. Gray's business, and opened his eyes still wider when Gray took from his pockets large packages containing bonds and securities to the amount of half a million dollars, and, depositing them as collateral, directed the broker to sell all the Erie for which he could find buyers at forty and over, and to buy it whenever it went below thirty-three.

That day Erie mounted, under the pressure of Vanderbilt's purchases, and the flurry created thereby, to $43, at which figure an immense quantity changed hands.   Then it fell rapidly, point by point, back to $37, and, under the influence of a temporary panic, went down to $32, at which figure it rallied and mounted to $35, where it stood at the close of the day.

Mr. Gray's regular broker reported to him purchases of five thousand shares Erie at prices ranging from $37 to $42, and averaging about $39.   He regretted that Mr. Gray had not authorized a sale at $43.25, which was the highest point reached, and at closing figures Mr. Gray must lose about $20,000.

And Mr. Gray's new brokers reported to him sales of eighty thousand shares of Erie, at an average of $41.50, which had been repurchased at an average of $34.50, with a profit to Mr. Gray of $540,000, which they held, subject to his check.

And when the returns were all in at the office of the old commodore, and that white-whiskered, choleric, kind-hearted, and courageous old bull found that he owned more Erie than ever, at higher prices than those for which he had sold a small part of his holdings, and that the rattan which he had prepared for Gray had fallen upon his own shoulders, he stormed for a while and clothed himself with cursing as with a garment, and then he cooled off and laughed.   Then he sent a note, this time not to John Gray's employer, but to John Gray himself, which read as follows: "Young fellow, you are a genius. Come and dine with me at six o'clock to-day, at Delmonico's. C. V."

The friendship cemented at that dinner, between the great capitalist and the ex-messenger—for Gray returned no more to his duties as a porter—continued until the day of the commodore's death.

Gray continued to operate in Wall Street, both in small and large ways, and seldom made a loss. When the first loud mutterings of the civil conflict began to shake the land, he became a heavy purchaser of tar, resin, and cotton, and, later, of gold. When the Union armies were defeated and the day looked darkest, and gold mounted to two hundred and eighty premium, he never faltered in his belief in the ultimate triumph of the nation, and he sold gold and bought government bonds, and margined one against the other, and risked little and gained much.

A year after the sun went down upon Appomattox, the Yankee peddler was worth $20,000,000, and ten years later he was worth $50,000,000. He abandoned such stock operations as were dependent for their success upon other men's movements and plans, and only engaged in such as he could absolutely control. He gambled only with marked cards and loaded dice. He bought a control of the stocks and bonds of badly-managed and bankrupt railroads. He consolidated them, re-equipped them, built feeders, opened new sources of traffic, and so doubled, trebled, and quadrupled his investments. He sold short the stock of a prosperous railroad, and obtained, by purchase of proxies, the control of its management. He cut rates, diminished traffic, enlarged expenses, and passed dividends until he depreciated the value of the stock to a point where he could gain millions by covering his shorts, and other millions by again restoring the road to prosperity. In one instance, by his paid emissaries, he promoted a general strike, until, through riot and fires and suspension of traffic, the stock of the afflicted corporation was depreciated to the price at which he desired to purchase a controlling interest.

John Gray was an exemplary father and husband, a good neighbor, and, in a small way, generous and charitable; but in his larger dealings with mankind he was a moral idiot, without conscience or perception. The world is no better for his life; the youth of the land are the worse for his example of successful scoundrelism, and those who wish well to their country and their kind, will have a right to stand beside his coffin and thank God that he is dead.

"I suppose," said Mr. Arnold Claybank, "that we all understand the general outlines of our project, and that this meeting is for the purpose of talking over details."

"Our purpose," said Mr. Wolf, "of I gomprehent it, is to use the bower dot we haf in our hants, to make for ourselves about fifty millions of tollars apiece. Is not dot apout vot it vas, eh?"

"We need not, I think, discuss that question," said Gray suavely.

"Exactly," said Claybank. "Now I propose that we list the securities which we shall place in our pool, at the closing quotations of the Stock Exchange to-

day, each one of us being credited with his contributions. The stocks contributed will aggregate in value
about $150,000,000, at present market prices, and, as
nearly as possible, will be contributed by us equally.
It is also understood that the stocks and bonds placed
in the pool will constitute the entire holdings of each
and all of us, in that class of property. Am I correct?"

"Quite so," said Mr. Gray.

"Dot is also my unterstanting," said Wolf.

"Very well," resumed Claybank, "these securities
are to be placed in the offices of different brokers, and
turned into cash as rapidly as possible without breaking the market. The public will, I think, take them
easily in a week, for the market is rising, and permanent as well as speculative investment is in order."

"Ont then we lock up the gash for which we sells
the stock, ain't it?" said Wolf.

"Not immediately," rejoined Claybank, "it must
be left in the banks in the usual channels for a time, or
there will be no money for them to loan to the buyers
of stocks. Having sold our own securities, we will next
proceed to sell short at ruling prices to as large an extent as possible."

"Your plan is admirable," said Mr. Gray. "We
will next arrange at the banks for borrowing all the
money that they can spare without suspending payment, and we will compel them to withdraw all loans
now out. Through our joint and separate control of,
and influence with, the officers and directors, we ought
to be able to borrow in this city, and in Boston and
Philadelphia, as much as $150,000,000, which, added

to $150,000,000 received from sale of our stocks, will give us control of $350,000,000 in cash.''

"Will dey loan so much as $150,000,000 even upon the personal security of such men as we?'' said Wolf.

"They will not be asked to do so," said Gray. "The money borrowed can be sealed up and left as special deposits in their vaults as security for itself, with a small margin of one or two per cent to cover interest.''

"Dot inderest, of we borrow for thirty days at six per cent, on $150,000,000 will amount to three kevawters of a million of tollars; ont that amount we lose out of our bockets; ont the interest on our own $150,000,-000 which will be itle for a month will be another three kevawters of a million.   It makes us $500,000 each to lose.   It is a great teal of money to lose,'' said Wolf.

"That," said Claybank, "is all we lose, and is practically all we risk.   It is essential to the success of our plans that for a brief period we shall withdraw from the channels of commerce a large portion of the money of the country.   We cannot withdraw it unless we control it; we cannot control it unless we borrow it; and we cannot borrow it without paying bank rates of interest upon it.''

"How," said Gray, "do you propose to supply the necessary margins for the stock which we sell short?   When you borrow stock on a rapidly-falling market, the loaner expects at some time a reaction, and an equally rapid advance, and you will have to give him a pretty big margin beyond the money which you receive from a sale of the borrowed stock.''

"We shall have for that purpose," replied Claybank, "the $150,000,000 received from the sale of our own stock. This, at fifty per cent fall in prices, will margin borrowings of three hundred millions of stock, and this money we can arrange to have locked up in special deposits as well as the money we borrow."

"Ont to how low a point shall we put brices before we commence to cover?" said Wolf.

"That," replied Claybank, "will be a matter for future consideration. My present impression is that we can by thus locking up the currency bear the market one-half. We must not proceed so far as we might go, or we will ruin everybody, so that there will be no investors to purchase stocks when we wish to sell them again after we have loaded up for a rise."

"Ont how much we makes by bearing fifty per cent?" asked Wolf.

"It is easily calculated," replied Claybank. "If our plans succeed, we sell one hundred and fifty millions of our own holdings at present prices. In order to bear the market fifty per cent below present prices, we must continue to sell down, diminishing the quantity we sell as prices recede, and when we begin to cover, we must buy all we can at the lowest point, diminishing our purchases as prices advance. Those not familiar with such things would be surprised to know that the ebb and flow of values in the stock market is almost as regular, and can be almost as certainly predicted, as the movement of the tides. Such a movement as we propose is artificial, yet, to an extent, it will be similarly controlled by the influences of human nature.   If we sell one hundred and fifty millions of stock at an average of say one hundred, and three hundred millions at an average say of eighty, and buy it all back at an average of sixty, we will gain one hundred and twenty millions, and that, I think, is about all we can calculate upon."

"But have you considered, gentlemen, the other side of the question?" said Gray.   "Have you fully considered whether there may not exist influences that will defeat us?   Depend upon it, once we inaugurate this raid, our rivals in business will plot to overthrow us.   Such great newspapers as are not in our control will denounce us.   The Treasury Department at Washington, which is under the control of the Farmers' Alliance party, will use every effort to break down our combination, and we shall be howled at generally as ghouls and villains.   I do not care much about the public or the newspapers, but we must take every possible precaution against failure."

"That is right," said Claybank.   "I have considered all these things and I do not see how our plan can be defeated.   The newspapers may denounce us but cannot overthrow our plan, which, at last, is very simple.   We produce a panic and depression of prices by locking up the circulating medium, and prices can only be advanced by unlocking the money and restoring it, or other money in its place, to the channels of commerce.   The money which we lock up in special deposits must remain in the bank vaults until we release it.   No bank officer would for any reason or under any pressure dare to touch a special deposit. It would be a penitentiary offense to tamper with it."

"Are you sure," said Gray, "that other capitalists may not combine, and provide other money to take the place of that which we lock up?"

"The only other very large sum of money in the country within the control of anybody," replied Claybank, " is $300,000,000 in the treasury vaults at Washington. The laws authorizing government deposits in banks, as well as the law authorizing bond purchases in the discretion of the secretary of the treasury, have, as you know, been repealed. There are absolutely but two ways to get that $300,000,000 out of the treasury vaults. One is by the ordinary disbursements of government, which would take a year or more, and the other is by somebody depositing, under the law of 1894, gold or silver bars to that amount, and nobody in the world is able to command three hundred, or one hundred. or even fifty millions of dollars in gold or silver bullion."

"The new mining capitalist, David Morning, might supply the bars from his mine in Arizona if we gave him a few years' time," said Gray.

"Yes, and if we gave him time he would be crank enough to do it," replied Claybank. "But we won't give him time. How much does his mine yield, any-how?"

"Four millions a month in solit golt," said Wolf. "It has yieltet that sum now for teventy months. I hear that it is nearly worked out, but nopoty can get into it, and you can't tell anything apout it. If it continues to yielt at that rate for a few years, dot fellow is going to make us all some trupple. He is crazy as a loon, though he has taken out of his mine over eighty millons of tollars."

"Even his $80,000,000, if he has them in money, might disarrange our plans," said Gray.

"He has plown them all in, puilding plocks for glerks ont poor people, ont he disgriminates against Hebrews, or his trustees do. A Jew knows a goot thing when he fints it, ont there were eighteen thousant applications from Jew glerks for the prifilege of renting apartments in the Morning Blocks, ont the committee made up a mean drick to get rit of them. They requiret every man who applied for rooms to answer whether it was easier to fill to a bob-tail flush or a sequence, ont those who answered the question they refused to pass, on the grount that they knew too much apout draw poker to haf goot moral characters."

"I do not see," said Claybank, after the laughter at Wolf's indignation had subsided, "that we need take Mr. Morning into consideration as a disturbing element in our present plans. If the present output of his mine shall continue, it must, by and by, greatly advance prices of stocks and all other property, but that is in the future."

"Have we anything further to consider?" said Gray.

"I think," replied Claybank, rising, "that we understand each other perfectly. I will have triplicate memorandums made of our agreement, which we can execute in my office to-morrow morning at nine o'clock, where we will have our stocks brought at the same time. This Burgundy is the genuine article, Clos Voguet, vintage of 1875. I propose as a parting toast, ' Success to our enterprise.' "

And the phonograph needle in the adjoining room wrote in mystic scratches upon the wax, "Success to our enterprise." Then came the shuffling of feet, the sound of a closing door, and the faint buzz of the electric motor until it ceased, and silence reigned.

CHAPTER XVIII.

" Uncle Sam to the rescue!"

DAVID MORNING returned to New York three days after the dinner party described in the last chapter. His typewriters were in attendance as usual, and he began opening his accumulated correspondance, when his secretary knocked at the door communicating with the next room, and, entering, said to his employer:—

"Mr. Morning, pardon me for disturbing you, but will you please step into the phonograph room. There is a good deal of matter on the cylinders which has been placed there by others in your absence, and, I judge, placed there inadvertently. I think you had better hear it yourself before it is transcribed."

Morning walked into the other room and was for half an hour an interested auditor of the revelations of the wonderful phonograph. He directed his secretary to remove, label, and lock up the cylinders containing the dinner-party conversation, and said in conclusion:—

" Mr. Stephens, somebody has evidently been having a dinner party in this room during my absence. It was not a nice thing for the proprietors to do, but I shall not notice it. Try to find out who dined here, without disclosing that I am aware that the room

(224)

was occupied. I think I recognize the voices of the occupants, but I wish to be sure."

By inquiring among the waiters, the secretary ascertained, and reported to Mr. Morning, that the guests were Claybank, Wolf, and Gray.

That night our hero departed for Washington, and early next morning he was closeted with the secretary of the treasury, to whom he revealed the knowledge gathered from the phonograph cylinders.

"It is an infamous piece of business," said the secretary warmly, "but what, Mr. Morning, can I do about it?"

"Mr. Secretary," said Morning, "will you pardon me for saying frankly that it is your duty to baffle these conspirators and restore values to their normal condition. It is the business of the government to provide a supply of money for the needs and uses of commerce. These scoundrels will bring about a panic by locking up in the vaults of New York, Philadelphia, and Boston banks, $300,000,000, which ought to be in circulation among the people. You have three hundred millions of coin and paper money in the treasury. Why not pour this money into Wall Street, break the back of this conspiracy, and relieve the people?"

"But I have no authority, Mr. Morning, as you must know, to use one dollar of this money for any other purposes than those designated by law. If I had the power, believe me, I would be only too glad to exercise it as you desire."

"Does not the Act of Congress of February, 1894, known as the free coinage law, permit you, Mr. Secre-

15

tary, to substitute gold or silver bars of standard fineness, for the coined money and paper money in the treasury vaults?"

"Yes," replied the secretary, "but I do not see how that law can be invoked to relieve the situation. There are not three hundred millions of gold and silver ingots in private ownership in the country, or, probably, in the world. The very large output of $1,000,000 in gold per week from the Morning mine will not serve us in this exigency. It would require six years' yield of your mine, Mr. Morning, to furnish enough gold to release the money now in the treasury, and baffle Messrs. Gray, Claybank, and Wolf. Three hundred millions of dollars is a good deal of money, Mr. Morning—a good deal of money."

"Relatively it is, Mr. Secretary, but I have five times that sum in gold bars here, in Philadelphia, and New York."

The secretary glanced at the Arizona Gold King, and looked uneasily at the bell cord which hung above his desk.

"No, I am not crazy," said Morning with a laugh, "though I do not blame you for thinking so. The time has come somewhat sooner than I expected for intrusting you with my secret. The Morning mine is a phenomenal deposit of gold. It is so large that, fearing any general knowledge of its extent might cause demonetization of gold by the nations, I took measures to conceal its true yield, and for every ounce of gold which I shipped to New York or London as the ostensible product of the mine, I shipped twenty-five other ounces disguised as pig-copper to this city, or New York, or Philadelphia, or Liverpool. In the latter place $1,000,000,000 are stored, and there are $500,000,000 in each of the American cities I have named. A month ago I sent four of my trusted men from the mine to this city, where they have since been busy with cold chisels, releasing the gold bars from their copper moulds. They will go from here to Philadelphia and New York, and thence to Liverpool, for similar labors. I did not intend, Mr. Secretary, to offer any of this gold for coinage or sale until able to present it simultaneously at European and American mints. But the present exigency induces me to turn over to the United States for coinage, the five hundred millions of gold bars now ready for delivery in this city. I may add, Mr. Secretary, to quiet the apprehensions which your deep interest in the commercial prosperity of the country might lead you to entertain, that I have not intended, and do not now intend, to throw $2,500,000,000 of new money immediately into the channels of commerce. I shall change the gold bars into money at once, in order that the present value may not, by demonetization, be taken away from gold; but, once transformed into money, it will be fed gradually to the world, and not precipitated upon it."

"But, Mr. Morning, it will require the constant labor for a long time of the mint and all its branches to coin this large sum, and you require the money at once."

"I propose, Mr. Secretary, to avail myself of the law of February, 1894, and claim treasury notes for my ingots. That Act of Congress will enable you to print in two or three days enough bills of large denomination to cover the whole sum."

"You astound me, Mr. Morning, but I suppose I must believe you."

"If you will ride with me to the foot of Sixth Street, Mr. Secretary, I will exhibit to you $500,000,000 in gold bars."

"But, Mr. Morning, even $500,000,000 suddenly poured into Wall Street will create a wilder panic and precipitate worse results, than those which may come from the pending conspiracy."

"I do not think so," said Morning quietly. "It is contraction and not inflation that hurts. A flood may be disastrous to the crops in places, but a general drought will surely kill them all."

"If Congress were in session, Mr. Morning, it would be likely to demonetize gold. It would never suffer fifteen hundred millions of money. to be thus added to the present currency. Why, such an amount will double at once the entire paper and metallic money of the country!"

"But Congress is not in session, Mr. Secretary, and you will pardon me for saying that, whatever may be your individual opinion as to consequences, you have no power to refuse to issue gold notes as fast as you can cause them to be engraved, for any amount of gold bars that I may offer."

"True," replied the secretary.

"But I repeat, Mr. Secretary, that I hope to guard against the evils you apprehend. I should be an unworthy custodian of the great trust which has come into my hands, if I could misuse it to harm either my country or my fellow-men."

"I believe you, Mr. Morning."

"For the present I can only use the ingots which are here in Washington. The New York and Philadelphia hoards will be ready in about a month, when I shall require treasury notes for them, but before I offer them to you, and before their existence shall be known generally, I shall endeavor to place in the mints at London, Paris, Berlin, Madrid, Milan, Vienna, and St. Petersburg, and in the banks of the principal cities of Europe simultaneously, in exchange for metallic and paper money of those countries, the one thousand millions now in Liverpool."

The secretary bowed.

"Will you order three hundred millions of gold notes, of the denomination of $1,000 each, printed at once, and arrange to weigh, test, and receive the five hundred millions of bars in my warehouse at the foot of Sixth Street? If it be not irregular, you might receive the ingots where they are, deliver to me at once the two hundred millions of paper money now in the treasury vaults, and the remaining three hundred millions when printed. The gold bars can be removed to the treasury vaults at your convenience. I ask that this method be followed because, if I am to relieve the situation in New York, I must be on hand there with the actual currency. Ordinarily treasury drafts would answer the purpose, but, under present circumstances, they would be useless, as no bank could cash them, and they are not a legal tender. These bandits will have locked up all the money in special deposits, and their well-devised scheme can only be baffled by one who has—outside of any chan-

nel within their control, and outside of their knowledge—a vast sum in actual money."

"How, may I ask, do you propose to defeat their
plans, Mr. Morning?"

"My brokers will purchase for cash all the stocks
they offer, and, on deposit of sufficient margin, loan
them the stocks back again, to be again sold to me.
In brief, I will take all their 'shorts,' and all the
stocks sold by others which their conspiracy will force
upon the market. When they have forced prices
down to a point where they are ready to cover their
shorts and buy for an advance, I will suddenly jump
prices to the level they occupied before the conspirators commenced their operations, and thus commend
to their own lips the bitter draught they have prepared for others. I shall know—for I have many
sources of information, Mr. Secretary—I shall know
what portion of my purchases of stock will come from
the conspirators, and what portion from men who
will be forced by the panic to part with their holdings.
I shall subsequently make good to those others all
their losses.   The one or two hundred millions which
I may by this process extract from Mr. Gray, Mr.
Claybank, and Mr. Wolf, I shall not "—and Morning smiled—"restore to them.   I shall devote it to
founding and maintaining industrial schools."

"Your plan, Mr. Morning, is a brave and gigantic
one.   Is there no chance of its failure?"

"Not if I can have your co-operation, Mr. Secretary, in keeping secret for a week or ten days the fact
that you have, under the law of February, 1894, received five hundred millions of ingot gold, and issued

treasury notes therefor. These scoundrels will have locked up all the available money in the great financial centers. They know that, under the present law, the three hundred millions of paper and coin money in the government vaults cannot be released so as to flow into the channels of commerce except by deposits of gold or silver bullion to take its place. My secret has been carefully kept, and they do not dream of the existence in private ownership of five hundred millions, or even fifty millions, in gold bars. If I can keep this secret from them until the hour to strike arrives, I will give them a lesson that will cure them for the future of any disposition to lock up money and constrict the arterial blood of commerce for the purposes of private gain."

"But will not their losses be largely on paper, Mr. Morning? What if they refuse to pay?"

"I shall not go into court with them, Mr. Secretary, and it will not be necessary. Let me further illustrate. They sell one thousand shares say of Northwestern at $110, and I buy it. They take the $110,000 received by them from my broker and add to it ten or twenty thousand dollars for margin, and borrow from me the one thousand shares of Northwestern just sold me, depositing the one hundred and twenty or one hundred and thirty thousand dollars as security for the return of the borrowed stock. When Northwestern, under the pressure of their sales, descends to $100, they put up additional margin for the stock borrowed, and borrow more stock on the same terms. If they continue this process until they have forced Northwestern down to $80 or $70, and could then buy enough to replace the borrowed stock and call in the money they had deposited as 'margin,' they would make as profit the difference between the low price at which they purchased and the average of their sales. But if Northwestern should suddenly jump in price to a point higher than the value to which they had margined it, then my brokers would purchase, at this high rate, enough Northwestern to make good the stock loaned to them, using for that purpose the money deposited by the conspirators as 'margin.' I propose to let these gentlemen have all the rope they want, and when they attempt to turn and become buyers, I will spring stocks at once to their original price, and confiscate all their margins.''

''I will aid you, Mr. Morning, as you request, by keeping our transactions secret as far as possible, though I can't promise you success in that. At least a dozen men will be required to print the gold notes in the Bureau of Engraving and Printing, and those men will know of the issuance of so vast a sum as $300,-000,000. Half a dozen more must know of the removal of the two hundred millions of paper money now in the treasury vaults, and at least a dozen men will be needed to weigh and remove the gold bars from your warehouse. What is known to thirty men will soon, I fear, be known to the world. I will detail only discreet men, who shall work under pledges of secrecy, the violation of which shall cost them their places, but, after every precaution shall have been taken, who shall baffle the ubiquitous newspaper reporter in search of a 'scoop'? He will crawl through the coal hole or the area railings. He will walk with

the cats on the top of spikes and broken bottles. He
will act as a car-driver, a barber, or a purchaser of old
clothing. I verily believe that if he had lived in the
olden days he would have coaxed Cæsar to reveal
the plan of his next campaign, and wrested from the
Egyptian Sphinx her secret. I fear, Mr. Morning,
that the reporters will prove too much for us."

"I have had some experience in keeping secrets,
Mr. Secretary, and if you will permit me to direct the
details of the movement, I will undertake that no ink-
ling of it shall reach the ears of the reporters."

"How will you avoid it, Mr. Morning?"

"Anticipating your consent and co-operation, Mr.
Secretary, I directed the captain of my steam yacht,
the *Oro*, to come here from New York without
delay, and by to-night she will be moored in the
Potomac, opposite the warehouse at the foot of Sixth
Street. I propose that, with the officials and men
whose duty it will be to test and weigh the gold bars,
you shall examine them where they are in the warehouse. You will take the keys and take possession,
and, if you desire, will detail guards for the warehouse
who will not know what they are guarding. As soon
as satisfied of the quality and quantity of the gold, you
will direct the printing of three hundred millions of
treasury notes, and will deliver me the two hundred millions of paper money now in the treasury
vaults. The three hundred millions can be printed
in bills of the denomination of $1,000, and may be
packed in five good-sized trunks. The $200,000,000
now in the treasury, being in bills of smaller denominations, will require fifteen trunks for their accommo-

dation. My four trusted men, who have been busy here for the past month cutting the gold bars out of their copper jackets, will procure fifteen trunks of different makes and marks, and after they have been filled with currency at the treasury vaults, will carry them in an express wagon, which I will purchase, to the railroad depot, and check them for New York in four different lots, purchasing two or three passage tickets for New York for each lot of trunks. They will go as ordinary baggage to New York, and there be taken to my office on Broadway, without exciting suspicion or comment. Two of the men will return from New York here, and a similar plan can be pursued with the $300,000,000, which will be printed in the meantime.''

"I do not yet see, Mr. Morning, how you propose to close the mouths of the treasury officials engaged in the business here.''

"I ask, Mr. Secretary, that for all this work you will select reliable men, unmarried, and who can be absent from their places of abode for a fortnight without comment. Inform each man selected that he will be employed in a matter requiring secrecy, and that it will involve an ocean trip. I propose that every man connected with the transaction, except yourself, Mr. Secretary, every man, from the official who tests the gold, to the official who packs the currency into the trunks, shall, from the time he enters upon the performance of his duty, until it is completed, remain in place. I will have food, and, if need be, cots for sleeping at the warehouse, and the placing of the currency in the trunks will not require more than an hour or two of time. Each man, as he completes his duty, will go on board the *Oro*, and when all are on board, the steamer will put to sea, with orders to cruise for two weeks and then return here. Each of the gentlemen taking this voyage will be presented by me with the sum of $1,000 for his services. The examination and weighing of the gold bars in the warehouse, and the packing and shipment of the two hundred millions of paper money now in the treasury, can, I think, be completed by to-morrow, and the *Oro* steam out to-morrow night, with a passenger list including the names of all those who have any knowledge of the fact that two hundred millions of treasury notes are on their way to New York, and that the government has $500,000,000 worth of gold bars in its vaults."

"And how about the three hundred millions of notes ordered printed?"

"Those engaged in the printing can be similarly detailed, similarly instructed, and similarly dealt with. I have chartered the *New Dominion*, now lying at Norfolk, for a voyage to Port au Prince, on the island of Santa Domingo. She has steam up, awaiting orders. She will be here in time, and all those who have knowledge of the printing or shipment of the other three hundred millions, will, on the completion of their duties, go on board of her for a trip to Hayti, and, on their return a fortnight afterwards, receive the same gift of $1,000 each for his services."

"Your plan is ingenious, yet simple, Mr. Morning, and seems likely to be effective. So far as this department is concerned, its execution will involve a departure from all rules and precedents, and I shall not escape hot criticism if I order it, especially from th: New York papers controlled by the conspirators But I see nothing really wrong or objectionable in it, and ' nice customs courtesy to great kings,' and you are a great king, Mr. Morning."

' Say rather that the exigency is a great king, Mr. Secretary. You will then aid me as I ask you."

"Yes."

"Thank you, Mr. Secretary. In the future any favor you may ask of me, personal or official, will not be denied."

CHAPTER XIX.

"The arms are fair when borne with just intent.

It was blue Monday in Wall Street. It was the beginning of the second week of the most disastrous panic ever known in the history of finance. Capital fled, affrighted, to its strong boxes, and refused to come forth at any rate of interest, or upon any security. Values had been going downward without reaction for six days. The yellings and shoutings in the stock board were such as might have been indulged in by escapes from an asylum for violent lunatics. Fortune after fortune had been swept into the vortex in a vain attempt to stay the current. Stocks which had ranked for years as among the most reliable of investments, descended the grade as rapidly as the "fancies." Northwestern had fallen from $112 to $60; Western Union from $80 to $45, and Lackawana from $138 to $70, and even at these prices more stock was apparently offered than found purchasers.

The conspirators were, apparently, successful. Three men whose combined wealth already aggregated $300,000,000, had produced this storm of disaster merely to increase their millions, regardless of ruined homes. They sold their own stock as they had plotted, seventy-five millions of it at full rates, and seventy-five millions at an average reduction of fifteen per cent, early the preceding week, and before Morning had perfected his arrangements, or appeared upon the scene.   Their subsequent short sales were made at lower prices than they had estimated, for others came in competition with them, as vendors. They locked up both the currency received from their sales, and the currency they had borrowed, so effectually that merchants, brokers, and others, who were unable to obtain the usual banking accommodations, were compelled to throw upon the market their holdings of bank, railroad, and telegraph stock.

Wolf, who personally led the bear raid in the board, followed prices down with fresh lines of shorts, to an amount beyond that originally intended, and at the close of the previous week, the short sales of the conspirators amounted to $400,000,000.   In one particular they had miscalculated, for, after stocks had fallen twenty per cent, the brokers who purchased them refused to loan them again for resale on the customary margin, but believing, or affecting to believe, that prices would advance with greater celerity than they had receded, they demanded an amount of money as margin equal to the difference between the existing market price of the stock loaned and the market price that ruled before the break.

This demand was made under the direction of Morning, who did not appear in public, but, from his private office on Broadway, sent orders to a dozen different brokers whose services had not been engaged by the Gray-Claybank-Wolf syndicate.   After the first break, Morning was the purchaser of nine-tenths of the stock sold, and after each purchase the money paid for the stock, with the margin added, was locked up in the vaults of one of his brokers, or in banks not under the control of the conspirators. In this way the syndicate had been compelled to add $60,-000,000 to the $140,000,000 they had received from the sale of their own stock.

On the morning of the second Monday of November, 1895, the "Gold King" was the owner, by purchase, of stocks which had cost him $400,000,000, but which were worth, at the prices which prevailed before the raid, $600,000,000.

These stocks had been loaned to the conspirators by Morning, repurchased by him, loaned and repurchased again, until he now held in his control two hundred millions of money, put up by the syndicate as margin, or security, for the delivery to him of stocks which needed only to be restored to their former value to cause the conspirators to lose $200,000,000, and Morning to gain that sum. If, however, prices could be kept at panic figures until the conspirators could turn buyers, and cover their shorts, they would gain $200,000,000, which would be filched from whomsoever had been compelled to sell.

There were $400,000,000 at stake on the game. The bear syndicate thought they were playing with loaded dice, and so they were, but the load was against them, instead of being in their favor.

On Sunday night a private conference was held at Mr. Claybank's residence, on Fifth Avenue.

"To-morrow," said Gray, "let us stop selling and begin buying, and cover as rapidly as possible. There are some features of the situation which fill me with uneasiness."

"Ont so I thinks, Misder Gray," said Wolf. "I don't gomprehent where the money comes from on Fritay and Saturtay with which our sales were met. As I figure it, we hat every tollar locked up on Thurstay that was anywhere available, but so much as a huntret, or, maby, a huntret and fifty millions of new money came into the street on yesterday and Fritay."

"It probably came from Chicago," said Claybank.

"No," replied Wolf. "Chicago sent only fifty millions, ont it vas all here by Wednesday. It buzzles me, ont I ton't like it, ont I believe it is full time to commence closing the deal."

It was, accordingly, agreed to close it, and on Monday morning these three worthies appeared in their seats in the Stock Exchange, for they were all members of that body, although they seldom or never participated in its proceedings, preferring to transact their business through other brokers.

Morning was also a member of the Stock Exchange, having purchased a seat a year previously, but he did not often appear there, and had never bought or sold a share of stock himself in open board. Even amid the excitement of the panic, his presence gave interest to the occasion, for his sobriquet of the "Gold King" attached legitimately to his ownership of a mine that was yielding $4,000,000 per month, with the probability of making its owner in a few years the greatest billionaire in the world.

There were probably few among the active members of the Stock Exchange who did not, at this time, know nearly as much about the causes of the panic as even the three men who produced it, and among all the brokers, except those in the employment of the syndicate, only indignation was expressed at the operations of Wolf, Claybank, and Gray. The New York stockbroker is neither a Shylock nor a miser. He is usually a genial, generous sort of fellow, who prefers a bull market to a bear raid. He likes to make money himself and have everybody else make it. A boom is his delight, and a panic his abhorrence. If a majority of the board of brokers could have had their way, they would have hung the members of the syndicate to the gallery railings, and the question of reaching them in some lawful way, and relieving the board from the effects of their conspiracy, had been informally discussed.

But nothing was attempted, because nothing seemed really practicable. It was well known that the existing condition of things had been produced by locking up the currency. So long as it remained locked up, prices must remain at whatever figures the conspirators might choose to place them. Only the power that withdrew the money from circulation, could restore it to the channels of commerce. There was absolutely nothing for those not already ruined to do except to hide in the jungle until the three tigers should have fully gorged themselves. When Claybank, Gray, and Wolf should graciously permit the money to be unlocked, then stocks would advance to their real value, business would resume its proper channels, and the panic would be over—and not until then.

In the Exchange, stocks were called alphabetically, and the first upon the list of railroad securities was

the Atchison, Topeka, and Santa Fe. This was not
a dividend-paying or favorite investment stock, and,
probably, three-fourths of it had been held in the street
for years, in speculative and marginal holdings. Morning had special reasons for securing control of this road
in addition to his general purpose of thwarting the
conspirators. Prior to the panic, Atchison, Topeka,
and Santa Fe had vibrated for months between $27
and $33, and on the Saturday previous to the Mon-
day which saw the beginning of the bear raid, it had
closed at $30. Under the operations of the conspira-
tors, it had been hammered down to $15, at which
figure it closed on the previous Saturday.

One of the syndicate brokers who sat by Wolf,
opened the ball by offering two hundred shares of
Atchison at $15.

"Taken," cried Morning, from his seat.

"Five hundred Atchison at $15½," said the broker.

"Taken," replied Morning.

A shade of uneasiness covered the features of the
broker, but, in response to a gesture from Wolf, he
called again:—

"One thousand Atchison offered at $16."

"Taken," said Morning.

The broker dropped into his seat and mopped his
face with his handkerchief.

"Any further offers of Atchison for sale?" cried
the caller.

And there was no reply.

"Two hundred Atchison, Brown to Morning, at
$15: five hundred Atchison, Brown to Morning, at
$15½; one thousand Atchison, Brown to Morning, at

$16. Are there further bids for Atchison?" said the caller.

Wolf arose and cried, "Fifteen dollars is offered for one thousand Atchison."

There was no higher offer, but the caller did not proceed to cry the next stock on the list. Somehow everybody seemed to feel that a crisis had been reached; it was in the air, and, amidst a hushed and expectant silence unprecedented in the history of the New York Stock and Exchange Board, the voice of David Morning rang out like a trumpet.

"I will give," said he, "$30 per share for the whole or any portion of the capital stock of the Atchison, Topeka, and Santa Fe Railroad Company."

Then pandemonium reigned. The quick wit of the stockbrokers comprehended the situation in an instant. It was all as clear to them as if it had been written and printed. They knew that Claybank, Wolf, and Gray had joined forces, locked up the currency, brought about a panic, broken down the market, and ruined half the street. They knew that the country was prosperous, the mines prolific, and the crops good. They knew that the depression in prices was wholly artificial, and that it must, sooner or later, be followed by a reaction and restoration of values, and they had so advised their customers, but they supposed that the period of such reaction was wholly within the control of Gray, Claybank, and Wolf.

They had no reason to expect that relief would come from any other source, and the appearance and action of Morning burst upon them like a revelation. Here was a man who was a new-comer to fortune and to finance, a man who had devoted the immense revenues of his mine to beneficent rather than business purposes, and who was above the necessity or the temptation of increasing his wealth by speculation. His presence in the Board, and his bid of $30 a share for Atchison, demonstrated that he knew of the Claybank-Gray-Wolf conspiracy, and that he proposed to baffle it. He must have measured the forces of the members of the syndicate and be advised as to the amount of money necessary to meet them. Possibly he had found a way to unlock the federal treasury, or had from some source obtained the necessary millions. Certainly he had obtained them or he would never have thus challenged the magnates of Wall Street to combat. Clearly, the panic was at an end, the man from Arizona was about to lead them out of the wilderness.

And they shouted, and roared, and cried, and hugged each other, and mashed each others' hats, and marched up and down and around the floor, and joined hands and danced around Morning, and disregarded all calls to order, and were finally quieted only when Morning, escorted by the President of the Stock Exchange, ascended the stand.

The President, as soon as silence was secured, said:—

"Gentlemen, it seems to be the general wish that the regular call shall be temporarily suspended, and that we shall hear from Mr. David Morning."

That gentleman, after the roar of greeting had subsided, said:—

"Gentlemen: I think you will agree with me in

believing that the prices of securities listed on this exchange have, during the past week, ruled altogether too low. I propose to put an end to this condition of things, which ought never to have been brought about, and I have authorized my brokers here to offer, during to-day and to-morrow, and for the rest of this week, to purchase, to the extent of $700,000,000, any and all railroad stocks listed on this Exchange, at the prices which ruled at the close of the board on Saturday week, before the panic began.''

A great cheer went up from the throats of the multitude, and, after it subsided, Isaiah Wolf, livid with rage and excitement, arose and exclaimed:—

''Does this lunatic then expect to make fools of us all? Is it to be beliefed dot this crazy man has got seven huntret millions of tollars in cash to buy stocks mit? His golt mine has turned his prain. It vos better dot we don't all pe too fresh apout this pizness.''

Morning quietly continued:—

'' Anticipating that my purchases of stock might possibly be large to-day and during the week, I have made arrangements to dispense with the customary methods, and so will avoid the usual delays in receiving and paying for stock. I have quadrupled my usual force of clerks, and my offices on Broadway will be open every day this week from nine o'clock in the morning until nine o'clock at night. No checks, certified or otherwise, will be issued by me, but the stocks bought by my brokers will be paid for on delivery at my offices at any time during the hours named, and paid for in treasury and national bank notes.''

"Where," roared Wolf, "did you get such a sum of money as seven huntret millions of tollars? You are either a liar, a lunatic, or a counterfeiter."

"Two hundred millions of dollars of the money which I hold," replied Morning, "was deposited by you and your colleagues in the conspiracy, as security for the return of stocks which I bought of you, and then loaned to you to sell to me again and again. Under the rules of the stock board these $200,000,000 will be forfeited to me unless you restore the borrowed stocks on the usual notice. The notices will be served on you to-day, and when you begin to buy in to cover your shorts, you will be compelled to pay full value. I think I can count upon your $200,000,000 to aid in paying for to-day's purchases, Mr. Wolf." And, amid continued cheers and laughter, Morning descended from the caller's stand, and started for his seat.

Claybank and Gray had left the hall, but Wolf remained, and as Morning passed along the aisle, the Jew, with face white and twitching, and with foam on his mustache, stepped out and confronted him.

"You have made a beggar of me," said he with a curse, "but I will have your heart's blood for this," and he reached for Morning's throat.

But the man from Arizona stepped backward and then forward, and at the same moment his right arm went swiftly forth from his shoulder.

"Smack! smack! smack!" and the nose of Wolf was spread over his face, and the crazed man was hustled and hurried by the crowd, and greeted with oaths and blows as he went, until, with torn clothing and battered face, he was literally kicked into the street.

CHAPTER XX.

[From the *New York Times*, November 20, 1895.]

FINANCIAL.

HOLDERS of stock and bonds in the Atchison, Topeka, and Santa Fe, Denver and Gulf, Kansas City and Chicago, Lakeshore and Michigan Southern, New York and Erie, and New York and New England Railroads, who desire to dispose of their holdings, will find a purchaser in me at the rates prevailing at the close of the Stock Exchange yesterday. I already own a majority of the capital stock of the roads named, and intend to consolidate them in one company without any bonded indebtedness, with the intention of providing the public with a double-track road between Portland, Maine, ·and San Francisco, California, *via* Boston, New York, Buffalo, Detroit, Chicago, Kansas City, and Denver, with a branch to Galveston. This consolidated road will not be run with a view to profit beyond four or five per cent per annum above operating expenses. In making this experiment I deem it only right to relieve the present holders of stock and bonds from loss, and this offer of purchase will remain open for one month.

DAVID MORNING,
39 Broadway, N. Y. City.

2 sq. 1 m., November 19.

We copy from our advertising column the foregoing, which presages the most important event of the

century. Whatever may be thought of the wisdom
of Mr. Morning's plans in any direction, there can now
be no question as to his ability to carry them forward. The brilliant strategetical movement by which
he bagged two hundred millions of piratical money
from Gray, Claybank, and Wolf, and, while defeating
them, restored values and prosperity, is still fresh in
the public mind, and his subsequent course in searching out all other persons who lost by the panic, and
reimbursing them the amount of their losses, will not
soon be forgotten.

The brave and sagacious action of the Secretary of
the Treasury in going outside of the channels marked
by red tape in order to promote Mr. Morning's plans,
is generally commended by the public, and meets
with no criticism except from the baffled syndicate of
scoundrels.

Whatever action, if any, Congress may take next
month when it assembles with regard to the demonetization of gold, and whatever may be the course pursued by the German Reichstag, the French Chamber
of Deputies, and the British Parliament, all of which
are now wrestling with the great economic problem
which the vast gold yield of the Morning mine pre-
sents, yet one thing is certain, David Morning has
quietly and shrewdly placed two thousand five hundred millions of gold in the mints and treasuries of
Europe and America, and obtained therefor money,
the legal tender quality and value of which, no future
legislation can impair.

It is fortunate for the world that this vast sum is in
the hands of a man who seems to comprehend the na-

ture of the problems which its existence, its introduction to circulation, and its subsequent use, will create, and who also seems disposed to treat his great treasure-trove as a public trust rather than a personal possession. It is a curious fact that some statesmen who have, without much reflection, been characterized as visionary, urged vainly for years upon the public attention the wisdom and feasibility of creating vast sums of fiat money, which were to be loaned upon land and crop values. It will not escape notice that the Congress of the United States might, at any time within the past few years, by passing a land and property loan law, have created the same conditions, whether they prove to be conditions of prosperity or disaster, which are now upon the world by reason of Mr. Morning's gold discovery. But it is not our purpose to attempt discussion of the situation generally. We intend only to give to the public a reliable account of the railroad projects of Mr. Morning. On reading his advertisement, we dispatched a reporter, who found him, as usual, frank and communicative. No comment of ours would add force or importance to the utterances of the Arizona Gold King, and we will let him tell his story in his own way.

"My plan," said Morning, "is not complicated, and not original with me. I only supply the means to try an experiment which it has often been suggested should be tried by the United States Government. If successful it will be of incalculable benefit to the people of this country. It will require not more than $250,000,000 to carry it out, and its failure would not involve a loss of more than $50,000,000.

"I marvel," continued the gentleman, "that public opinion did not years ago act upon Congress so as to cause it to deal with the transportation question in the interest of the people.   I marvel that some of our great capitalists have not joined efforts, and devoted a portion of their possessions to providing the people with cheap transportation.   Suppose that a dozen of them should have together made a pool of $200,000,-000, and undertaken a work—not of charity, but of helping the toilers to help themselves.   It would not have taken one-third of their possessions; it would have deprived neither them nor their children of a single luxury, and yet it would have allayed the disquiet and antagonism of multitudes, and, more than bronzes or marble shafts, it would have linked their names to immortality."

"Will not Messrs. Gray, Claybank, and Wolf have supplied the funds for your experiment?" queried the reporter.

Morning laughed as he answered: "Well, in a way, yes; and if I had not already devoted their contributions to founding and maintaining industrial schools, there would be a sort of poetical justice in making such application of that fund."

"Will you give me, for the *Times*, the details of your plans, Mr. Morning?"

"Certainly," replied that gentlemen. "I have nothing to conceal.   The railroad lines of this country, especially the transcontinental lines, were built when material and labor were much higher than now, and some of them when gold was at a high premium. Stock and bonds of many roads have been watered, and in paying present market prices for them I shall probably pay much more than the sum for which the roads could be duplicated if constructed honestly and economically at present cost of labor and materials, and allowing nothing for subsidies, bounties, stealings, and profits of speculators, contractors, and legislators.   But it would not, I think, be right to punish present holders of stocks and bonds for the sins of their predecessors in interest, and I therefore propose to pay the present inflated value of these securities. I shall not, however, attempt to make the reorganized road carry the burden of paying interest and dividends upon the sums which I shall pay."

"What do you estimate to be the present market value of the roads you propose to purchase, Mr. Morning?"

"At present market rates, and I shall pay no more, the total amount that will be required to buy in both stocks and bonds, will be, in round numbers, $150,-000,000.   I am advised by experts that the cost of widening roadbed and bridges, and laying additional iron, so as to make four tracks from New York to Kansas City, and a double track from the Missouri River to the Pacific, will, with the necessary buildings and shops, be about $70,000,000."

"Then the proposed line, when completed, will have cost you about $220,000,000?"

"Exactly, less the sum which may be received for rolling stock, which I propose to sell.   But I am informed by my engineers that a similar line might be built now for $150,000,000, and I therefore take $150,000,000 as the actual value of the roadbed, station buildings, and shops for repairs, and I estimate traffic charges upon that basis."

"Why do you sell the rolling stock? How can a road be used without locomotives or cars?"

"I propose that the company I will cause to be organized shall, except in certain contingencies, run no trains whatever on the road except repair trains. The roadbed will be open at uniform tolls to any person, firm, or corporation who may wish to run trains upon it. The tolls will be fixed upon such a basis as will provide means sufficient to keep the road-bed up to the highest standard, and pay five per cent per annum upon the actual value of the road, which, in the first instance, will be fixed at $150,000,000."

"Will not the value of the road advance, Mr. Morning?"

"I expect so," was the reply. "All values will advance with the increase of standard money, caused by the yield of the Morning mine, and there will be a re-valuation of the roadbed each year, by disinterested and competent engineers. If the amount received for tolls in any one year shall exceed the sum of five per cent on the valuation of the previous year, the tolls will be reduced for the next year. If it shall fall short of that sum, the tolls will be increased for the next year."

"Will not the ownership of the roadbed by one company, and the ownership and management of rolling stock by a dozen or a hundred other companies, be productive of confusion and accidents?"

"Not at all. On the contrary, accidents will be almost impossible. Switches and side tracks, capable of accommodating from one to a dozen trains or more, will be provided every five miles, with buildings for receiving freight and passengers, at every station. Between Boston and Kansas City two tracks will be devoted to passenger trains and two to freight trains, and a uniform rate of speed be established, of thirty-five miles per hour, including stoppages on the main track, for passenger trains, and fifteen miles an hour for freight trains. Between Kansas City and San Francisco, so long as there shall be only one double track, on which both freight and passenger trains must run, a uniform rate of speed of twenty miles an hour for both freight and passenger trains will be established, except on mountain grades, where the speed must be lessened. There will be an interval of not less than fifteen minutes between trains east of the Missouri, and half an hour west of it, and whenever a train leaves or passes by a station, its passage over the rails at that station will, through an electric wire, be made to ring a bell, set a signal, and close a switch at the next station behind it, and no train will be allowed to leave or pass by a station until a signal shall be received that the preceding train has passed by the station ahead."

"Suppose a train conductor or engineer should proceed without receiving the signal, and in defiance of orders from the station master?"

"His train would be automatically shunted off upon a side track, where it would run up against elastic buffers of rubber, filled with air. The main track would not be clear until the train passed the station ahead. Until then the switch leading to the side track would be open."

"And how would that switch be again opened, after being closed?"

"Automatically, by the passage of the train over the rails ahead of it."

"That is a very ingenious and original idea, Mr. Morning."

"Ingenious and simple, but it is not my own. A similar contrivance was in use on the Italian roads twenty years ago, although the idea was suggested to me by an Arizona rancher, who was averse to having cattle straying in his alfalfa fields, through which several public roads ran. In order to avoid the cost of fencing the roads, he put up automatic gates. The weight of the horses and vehicle upon a platform a few yards from the gate, on either side, operated upon a lever, and swung open the gate, which was released automatically by the passage of the wagon, and so swung shut."

"You seem, by these arrangements, to have secured the safety of passengers and train hands, but how about the speed? Will the traveling public be content with twenty miles an hour between Kansas City and San Francisco?"

"I do not know. If they shall not be, still the speed would be satisfactory to the freighters. My own belief is that the greater safety and lower rates of passage that will prevail on this road will attract to it a large share of the passenger traffic. Those who are in haste can travel over one of the other lines."

"Your object seems to be to give to the public cheaper railroad service."

"It is partly that and partly to give the railroad employes better pay and greater regularity and permanency of employment. I will try to divide the benefits equitably."

"Will not those who run trains upon your road defeat your object by combinations among themselves, to put up the price of freight and passage, and put down the wages of railroad hands?"

"It will be practicable, I think, to guard against both these things. If the Brotherhoods of Locomotive Firemen, and Locomotive Engineers, and Train Hands, will establish and maintain reasonable rates of compensation and hours of labor, and will enable all qualified workers to become members at will, then the directors of the company owning the roadbed will only allow its use to trains managed by Brotherhood members. If persons or companies owning rolling stock shall advance freight or passenger rates beyond maximum, or reduce them below minimum, rates, fixed by the directors of the Railway Company, they will lose their right to run trains, and if a combination should be made to diminish facilities to shippers or travelers, then the Roadbed Company will itself place a freight and passenger service on the track."

"Will you expect to personally superintend this great work, Mr. Morning?"

"No, I must leave it to others. Once it shall be well started I have other projects which will require my attention."

"Who will run it, Mr. Morning?"

"The Board of Directors will, in the first instance, consist of the governor of each State through which the roadbed shall be constructed, from Maine to California.   To these fifteen or sixteen governors will be added thirty experienced railway managers, who will be selected by me.   Each governor will serve as director only during his term as governor, and will be succeeded as director by his official successor as governor.   The thirty directors appointed by me will receive liberal salaries, will not be permitted to be interested in any other railroad, and will serve until they resign, or die, or are removed for cause by a two-thirds vote of the other directors.   Vacancies thus occurring will be filled by a similar vote.   Subject to the principles of management I have endeavored to outline, the control of the affairs of the company will be with the Board of Directors.''

"Will not the vast sums of money which the yield of the Morning mine must add to the standard currency of the world so inflate values as to make difficult any equitable adjustment of freight or passenger rates, or of the wages of railroad workers?''

"Freight and passenger rates, and wages, will necessarily advance with the increase of all values. It will be like the tide at the Dardanelles, which never ebbs.   No man who has any knowledge, or exercises any care, need be overwhelmed or hurt by it, and all men who try can guide their barks to prosperity upon its swell.''

"Would you consider it really a healthful state of affairs if, by an inflated currency, prices were so increased that a dinner which one can now buy for fifty cents should cost $5.00, and a $20 coat sell for $200?''

"Why not if prices were similarly advanced over all the world? People indulge in a good deal of loose talk about inflated currency, debased currency, and fiat money. In truth, all money is fiat money, for a bar of gold is not a legal tender, and inflation of values is the law of commercial growth. In the middle ages a penny was the price of a day's wages or of a bushel of wheat. Money which has for its basis either precious metals or substantial property in lands or merchandise is good money, while money lacking such basis is bad money. Clipped shillings, French assignats, and Continental and Confederate currency, were no more fiat money than are American double eagles or five-pound Bank of England notes. It is the stamp of the government, the fiat of its power, that turns the metal or the paper into money."

"But do not all financiers consider inflation a disaster, Mr. Morning?"

"Inflation," replied the gentleman, "whether of metallic or paper currency that is accepted by the world or by a great commercial nation as a legal tender, can do no harm except to those who loan money. A dollar is a mere term. You pay now five dimes, or fifty cents, or five hundred mills, for your dinner. Suppose by large continued increase in the production of gold and silver, the money of all countries shall be inflated so that you must pay fifty dollars instead of fifty cents, or five hundred dimes in place of five hundred mills, for your dinner. What of it? You could carry as much paper money as now. It would need only to increase the denomination of the bills. All property and services would advance proportion-

17

ately. Only the loaners of money would be left, and they would soon find it to their interest to put their money into property, which would necessarily advance in value, rather than in loans, which would, in their relation to property, necessarily decrease in value. Under such conditions interest would not compensate the money owner for the depreciation of his principal, and the loaning of money, except for brief periods, would cease, while property of all kinds would always be saleable for cash, because always sure to increase in value, while idle money would not so increase.''

''What will be the effect of your project on the other railroads, Mr. Morning?''

''My hope and expectation is that the successful working of my project will induce large aggregations of capital to acquire and conduct all the railroads in the country under one management, which should itself be under the direction and control of the Federal Government. Four thousand millions of dollars would purchase and free from bonded indebtedness all the interstate railroad and telegraph lines in the United States, and $1,000,000,000 more would improve such property to the highest point of efficiency. A company with a capital of $5,000,000,000, having no bonded debt and economically and honestly managed, could pay dividends of five per cent per annum on its stock, which stock might be increased in amount as other values increased. Present railroad bondholders would be transformed into railroad stockholders, and the stock of the United States Consolidated Railroad Company, guaranteed by the United States Government to pay five per cent per annum, and so conducted as to earn that dividend, above cost of repairs and construction of new lines, would be a favorite investment. Such stock might be made the basis of currency issued thereon to national banks. It could be held by benevolent and educational institutions, and trust funds could be invested in it. It would take the place of the present United States bonds as a lazy fund, and it would not be a lazy fund, for it would be an investment in earning property. It would substitute the earned increment of labor for the unearned increment of interest. Interest on money at best belongs to conditions which are passing away. It is an attribute of a former civilization, and I predict that during the next century it will come to an end altogether."

"How would the United States Consolidated Railroad Company affect railway patrons and railroad employes?"

"By adjusting freight and passenger charges, and wages of employes, so as to produce an income of five per cent on the investment, and by discontinuing non-paying lines, building new ones, and developing profitable connections—in brief, by running all the railroads in the land as one company under one management, in such manner as to produce from earnings a net income of five per cent, on a capitalization of all existing stocks and bonds at their market value to-day—the prices of freight and passage would be reduced, and the wages of railroad workers increased."

"I think," continued the Arizona Gold King, "that the entire system should be under government supervision, or even under government direction, and, depend upon it, nobody would be harmed, except about forty thousand people, who now own sixty per cent of all the real property in America, and even the damage to them would be slight, for they could purchase stock in the Consolidated Company, and learn to be satisfied with five per cent and no stealings."

"You spoke of a provision being made in your company for the future of railroad employes. How would that be done?"

"In the company which I propose each employe will be required to agree that not less than fifteen per cent of his wages shall be withheld from him and annually invested in the stock of the company, which stock shall be non-transferable. It will be delivered with its dividends, likewise invested, at his death to whomsoever he may designate, or, if he live to the age of sixty, it will be paid to him."

"Do you think that the worker needs this sort of compulsory guardianship, Mr. Morning?"

"I certainly do. For one of them who lays up for a rainy day, nine are possessed by the very genius of unthrift. I have known miners to work for months, and mining is the hardest work in the world, and then draw their wages and expend hundreds of dollars in one spree. Where the worker uses liquor—as most of them do—he lives from hand to mouth, and even among the temperate, it will be the rare exception to find one who has enough savings to support his family for six months."

"Is it only the workers who are imprudent, Mr. Morning?"

"No, the habit of careless unthrift is common to all

men. It is not confined to the worker. It appears more frequently in him only because his necessities are more urgent and apparent, and, in this respect, he lives more in public. But extravagance is a part of the original savage man, the leaven which has survived all civilization. I have known lawyers, and doctors, and divines, and journalists who, with their families, might have been saved from embarrassment and suffering if there had been some power every month to seize a portion of their earnings or income and make a compulsory investment of it for their future benefit."

"But," said the speaker, "to return to my subject. There is yet another advantage to be considered. If the United States operated, or even supervised, all the railroads, it would not be difficult—by requiring each railroad hand to report for drill and practice one day in each month—it would not be difficult to provide the nucleus and material for a great army, if such should ever again be necessary."

"Will the time ever come when armies can be dispensed with, Mr. Morning?"

"I think it has come. I am about to have made some experiments with the new explosive 'potentite,' which, if successful, will, I think, demonstrate to the world that hereafter war will mean simply mutual annihilation, and that in conflict there will be small odds between the weakest and the most powerful of nations. But I wander into the domain of speculation, and you newspaper men require only facts."

"Do you propose any reform or changes in the present methods of railroad management, Mr. Morning?"

"Several."

"For instance?"

"There will be a uniform rate per mile for passage, all tickets will be transferable, no inducements will be offered to travelers to perpetrate falsehood and forgery, and freighters will not be required to expose their business secrets to the officers of the railroad company.

"Do you know," said Mr. Morning, "that a demand has actually been made upon me by the railroad companies for freight at regular express gold bullion rates on $2,500,000,000 worth of gold bars which they carried from Arizona to the East disguised as copper? For freight on the supposed copper I paid their regular rates of charges, amounting to about $200,000. They say that if I had shipped it as gold their charges would have been six and one-quarter millions, and they claim the difference."

"But you shipped it as copper at your own risk, did you not, Mr. Morning?"

"Of course I shipped it as copper at my own risk, and on ten bars, worth really $400,000, which were lost from the ferryboat in transporting freight during the flood at Yuma, I collected from the company only their supposed copper value of $320, and I had no end of trouble and delay in making the collection. But they assert that in covering the gold bars with copper sheaths, I worked a 'gold brick swindle' on them, and they want the difference."

"Will you pay the $6,000,000 claimed, Mr. Morning?"

"Not if I can help it," smiled the gentleman. "I

have other uses for the money. I have in view several other reforms in railroad management. Railroad employers who, through no fault of their own, are hurt in railroad accidents caused by the negligence of a fellow employe, shall have the same right of recovery at law against the company as an injured passenger would have. Train men, in stopping at country stations, shall consult the convenience of passengers rather than their own, and shall not halt the baggage car in a sheltered spot, while they compel disembarking passengers to wade through the mud. Brass-mounted conductors shall not glower at question-asking passengers, and, to all requests for information, answer flippantly, ' Damfino,' and small dogs shall not be torn from their friends and suffered to wail their strength away in mute despair in a strange and comfortless baggage car, without bones to beguile or friendly faces to encourage them; but every reputable lapdog who pays his fare, and abides noiseless and contented in the same seat with his mistress, shall be left in peace.''

CHAPTER XXI.

"Their country's wealth, our mightier misers drain."

It was a bright, warm day in December, 1895, when a tall man, with iron gray hair surmounting a wrinkled and careworn face, paused for a moment before the plate-glass front of the Tenth National Bank of Birmingham, Alabama.

Making his way into the building, he walked to the cashier's office in the rear, which he entered without knocking. A short, stout gentleman of forty years looked up from the desk at which he was writing, and inquired of the stranger who it was that he wished to see?

"I kem in, suh, to see the Kashyea," was the reply.

"I am the cashier of this bank, sir. What can I do for you?"

"Well, I allowed to bowwow some money foh to stock my fahm foh a cotton crap, and to cahy me ovah the season, suh, and I heard as how the money might be had heah."

"Take a seat, sir. What is the name?"

"John Turpin is my name, suh."

"And what amount do you wish to obtain, Mr. Turpin?"

"I reckon about $3,000 would answer the puppus, suh."

"Where is your property, Mr. Turpin, and what does it consist of?"

"It is on the White Creek, in Madison County. There are foh hundred acres of cotton land. There is a house, bahn, and outbuildings in faih condition, suh, but I don't count them as much, in a money way."

"What do you estimate to be the value of the land?"

"Befo the wah it sold for fohty dollahs an acre. Land went very low aftahwuds, but the land has not been crapped, and of late yeahs, business has picked up mightily in old Alabama, and it ought to be wuth as much now as it ever wor."

"How long have you been farming it there?"

"Well, not at all, suh. The place was owned by my uncle, and he jest lived there since the wah, and never tried to make a crap. He was Captain of Company K of the Ninety-third Alabama. He was wounded at Chickamauga. Both of his sons were killed at the second battle of the Wilderness; his wife died while they were all away, and when he kem back he seemed to lose all interest like. He couldn't abide free niggahs ever, and there were no othahs, and foh twenty-seven yeahs he jest moped around the old place, raisin' only a little cohn, and a few hogs and some geyahden truck. Last spring he died, and the place has fallen to me. There is no debt on it, and it's prime cotton land, but it will take right smaht of money to clean off the land and put in a crap."

"Are you farming elsewhere, Mr. Turpin?"

"No, suh, I have been wuking for several yeahs for

the Louisville and Nashville Railroad Company, as their station agent at Coosa, but I was raised on a cotton plantation, and I know all about the wuk. I have two likely boys; one is twenty and the othah eighteen. My wife is a wohkah, and so is our daughtah. We all want to go on the old plantation and live thar.''

''Will $3,000 clear the land and stock it?''

''Yes, suh. It will buy us mules and fahm implements, and seed, and supply us with provisions and foddah, and pay the wages of such niggahs as we will hiah to help us.''

''How soon could you repay the $3,000.''

''Well, in the old times we could moh than pay it with one crap, but thar ain't the money in cotton that thar used to be. Cotton is powerful low, I do allow.''

''And it costs more to raise it now than it did when you had slaves to work for you, does it not, Mr. Turpin?''

''Well, I allow that don't make much diffahence, suh. I can hiah niggahs now for $16 a month, and they find their own keep, while befoh the wah we had to pay that much and moah, and feed them beside. The interest on the value of a good niggah then was nigh onto as much as we pay him now foh wages. The niggah don't get much moah now than he did when he was in slavery. He just gets his keep and a few clothes: No, suh, I can raise cotton now cheaper than I could befoh the wah, but cotton kain't be sold foh no such prices. Still, thar is some money in cotton, and my boys and I can pay off the $3,000 with interest, out of the profits on the craps, in three yeahs, and if we live powerful close mebbe we can do it in two yeahs."

"Why do you not get the money you want from the bank at Huntsville?"

"Well, suh, I went thar before I kem yeah, and the kashyea thar tole me that they wah not fixed to make any but shote loans. He said as how they wah a nayshunal bank, and couldn't loan money on land nohow, and he advised me to come heah, suh."

"But this is also a national bank, and subject to the same restriction, Mr. Turpin."

"Yes, suh, I know; so he tole me, suh. But he said as how you wah also loan agents for Northern capitalists, who had money to invest in long loans, on good security."

"We are such agents, but our instructions do not permit us to loan on anything but improved city property. Our clients do not like to put their money in plantations."

"But, suh, what will become of the cities if the people do not help those in the country? My place is wuth easily foh times the money I want to bowwow, and every dollah of the money bowwowed will go into the place."

"It does look, Mr. Turpin, as if money ought to be had for such purposes. But all of our local capitalists have their money tied up in the city, and outsiders won't loan on farms."

"Then I kain't bowwow the money, suh?"

"I am afraid not, Mr. Turpin. You might try elsewhere, but, to be candid with you, I do not believe you will succeed."

"' Well, suh, then I will have to go back to my wuk at the railroad station, and let the land lie idle. Why kain't the govuhment loan us on our fahms the money needed to cultivate them? 'Pears like I hearn tell thar was a man out in Calafohnea what wanted the govuhment to do that likes."

"Yes," replied the cashier, "there is such a scheme, but it is totally impracticable. Of course the government cannot embark in the business of loaning money on landed security."

"But ain't the govuhment in the loanin' business now, suh? Whar do you get the circulatin' notes of youah bank? Don't you bowwow them of the govuhment, without interest, by puttin' up United States bonds as security?"

"Oh, that, you know, is quite a different thing," answered the cashier, smilingly.

"Whar's the difference in principle?" persisted the man from Coosa. "If a govuhment bond foh $1,000 air good secuhity foh $900, what is the reason that a piece of land wuth $1,000 kain't be good secuhity foh $500?"

"The bond," said the cashier, "could always be sold at par. It is not so easy to find a purchaser for land, even at half its value; it might be worthless, you know."

"I am not supposin', suh, that the govuhment would loan money on wuthless land any moah than on counterfeit bonds. I'm talkin' about sich land as ain't wuthless, and kain't evah be wuthless. I'm talkin' about land that has an airnin' capacity, when human labor is applied to it. I allow that sich land, when valooed honestly, and not countin' any buildings or improvements, or anything that can be burned up or carried away—I allow that sich land is just as good security foh a loan of half its value, as any govuhment bond is security foh a loan of nine-tenths its valoo.   If the land ain't wuth nothin', I'd like to know what the bond is wuth?   As I argefy, all the valoo's on the yearth, suh, bonds and banks and govuhments theyselves rest upon the land and the labah that tills it."

"But the amount of national bank notes that can be issued on government bonds is limited by law," remonstrated the cashier.

"Suppose they be.   Kain't the govuhment limit the amount of greenbacks it would loan on the fahms? Kain't it allot jest so much to each State or to each county, or to each numbah of folks?   I don't see no use of a limit nohow.   Govuhment don't limit the bales of cotton or bushels of cohn, or numbah of hogs a man can raise, noh the tons of ihon he shall smelt, noh the numbah of days' wuk he shall do in a yeah.   What foh do they want to limit the numbah of dollahs that shall be made?   Why not leave that to be settled outside of papah laws?   If you raise cohn for which there is no demand you kain't sell it, and if you print dollahs for which there is no demand you kain't lend them.   A dollah ain't got no nateral valoo nohow. Ye kain't eat it, noh drink it, noh weah it.   Ye kain't sleep on it, noh ride it, noh drive it around.   A dollah is just a yahdstick foh the cloth, a scale foh the sugah, a quart measure foh the vinegah.   Suppose govuhment went to limitin' the numbah of weighin' scales and yahdsticks and gallon cans thar should be in the land, and then didn't allow enough to be made foh to go around!—A nice fix the country stohs would be in wouldn't they? You city folks would corral all the yahdsticks, and all the scales, and all the pint pots that the govuhment allowed to be made. You'd organize measurin' companies and bowwow all the scales that the govuhment made, and pay nothin' to the govuhment for the use of them; and then you'd hiah them out to folks at a big rent, and make the folks as hiad them leave half the measures on deposit with you, and you'd hiah that half again to other folks, and you'd squeeze the people, and squeeze 'em, and squeeze 'em, until you turned every man who wasn't an ownah of measurin' tools into a puffeck slave to them as was ownahs. That's what you hev been a doin' with us right along. I mean no disrespeck to you, suh, puhsonally, for you have treated me moh politely than a bankah usually treats his bowwowin' customahs; but you bankahs and capitalists have jest been a monkeyin' with the currency until you have got every fahmah, and wukin' man, and stoahkeepah in the country tied hand and foot, with no chance to wuk at all unless they wuk foh you. We have been a lot of everlastin' fools, suh, to stand it, and we aint a goin' to stand it much longah."

"What will you do about it, Mr. Turpin?" said the cashier, quietly, but with a shade of satire in his tone.

"I allow, suh, that we'll tell the yawpers who run political conventions to get along without our votes, and we'll elect men to the Legislatoor and to Congress, and mebbe a President, who'll take their ideahs from the fahmas and wukahs of the Sooth and West, and who won't go to Wall Street foh ohdahs; and we'll give all the old questions a rest, and we'll make it lonesome for the politicians who fight us, and we'll kind o' resolute that so long as this govuhment won't let any State or any puhson go into the business of manufacturing money to supply the necessary wants of the people, it is likely that the govuhment itself ought to do it, and we'll fix it so that no man who is willin' to wuk as I am, and knows how to wuk as I do, and has land to plow as I have, will have to see his land lie fallow, and his boys loafin' around, just bekase he kaint bowwow from nobody, even at ten per cent a yeah, one-fifth of the valoo of his land, to buy a few mules, and a plow or two, and some seed cohn.''

''You will compel the government to go into the business of printing and loaning all the money that anybody wants, will you?'' said the cashier.

''Well, suh, I'm no bankah, and no lawyah, but I take it that it is the business of govuhment to provide all the money necessary foh the use of the people, and if the govuhment itself won't do it, then let it untie the cohds it has put around States and people, and suffah them to do it foh theyselves.''

''You would go back to the days of State banks and unlimited currency, Mr. Turpin, with a wild-cat bank at every crossroads, when the man who traveled never knew whether the bank bill he got in change, when purchasing his breakfast in Alabama, would buy him a supper in Tennessee,'' said the cashier.

''Well, suh, I remembah those days, and while they may not have been so agreeable foh those that traveled, they war a heap better foh folks as stayed at home. A wild-cat bank at the crossroads on White Creek, that would let me have $3,000 of its missuble money, which my neighbors would take in exchange foh mules, and the stohkeepah would take for goods, so that I could put in a crap on foh hundred akahs of the puttiest cotton land in Noth Alabama, would be a heap bettah foh me just now, suh, than a national bank with a plate-glass front, in Buhmingham, that won't even look at the security I offah foh a loan. Good-day, suh."

And Mr. John Turpin, of White Creek, arose, and, with a heavy and sorrowful step, walked out of the Tenth National Bank of Birmingham, Alabama, and the rotund cashier smiled at the episode, and adjusted his gold-rimmed eyeglasses, and resumed his interrupted labors.

Yet relief was in store for Mr. John Turpin, for on that very day the mail from New York to Washington carried the following communication:—

OFFICES OF DAVID MORNING,
39 Broadway, N. Y., Dec. 15, 1895.

To the President of the United States—

SIR: Under certain conditions I will donate to the Government of the United States the sum of $2,400,-000,000 in gold bars, which I will deliver to the treasury department at the rate of $100,000,000 per month, during the ensuing two years.

The money coined from, or issued upon, these gold bars, shall constitute a perpetual fund, to be loaned at two per cent per annum to the farmers of the country, the fund never to be diminished or appropriated for any other purpose, although the interest received from it may be used to aid in defraying the ordinary expenses of government.

The amounts to be loaned may be apportioned among the several States and Territories, according to their populations as given by the last census, but the loaning must proceed from, and be under the control of a department of the Federal government, to be created by Congress for that purpose. Loans may be made payable at any time, at the option of the borrower, and may remain indefinitely, so long as the interest is paid, and must be secured by pledge of productive land.

Not more than one-half the actual cash value of the land, without estimating improvements, must be loaned, or more than $10,000 to any one borrower, or more than $20 per acre in any case.

The celerity with which Congress, during the War of the Rebellion, created an effective system of revenue and finance, leads me to the conclusion that it will be equally apt - in the creation of the necessary legal machinery to speedily effectuate a permanent and safe system for making loans to the people. I shall trust implicitly to the wisdom and patriotism of Congress to carry out details if my gift is accepted, as I think I may assume it will be, and I shall attempt no interference with its action, even by suggestion, beyond stating the conditions upon which the fund of $2,400,000,000 will be provided.

It will, possibly, not be out of place for me to assign here a few of the reasons why I require that loans be limited to the owners of productive land, and why I

18

do not permit dwellers in towns and cities, and those engaged in commerce and manufactures, to share in the opportunity for procuring cheap money.

To this very natural inquiry I might answer that I have already arranged in San Francisco, in Chicago, and in New York, for aiding co-operative labor corporations to procure, at a low rate of interest, the money necessary for their use; that I design extending similar aid in other localities, and that I hear of several instances of other gentlemen conveying large sums in trust for such purposes.

But the duty of aiding the farmers to cheap money is so great, and so pressing, and extends to so many persons, and over so large an area, that any concerted effort in such direction is not only beyond the capacity of individual wealth owners, but requires the machinery and power of government for its adequate discharge.

The farmers, of all men, most need the aid of capital, and of all men they find it most difficult to secure such aid. For years before the accidental, or, rather, providential, discovery of an immense deposit of gold-bearing quartz in the Santa Catalina Mountains in Arizona enabled me to attempt alleviation of some of the evils under which the world suffers, I had observed that even when the manufacturing and commercial interests of the land were in a fairly prosperous condition, the farmers did not share in the general bounty, and I observed that usually the produce of the farmers' land could only be sold at such low prices as left them, at the close of the season, a little more in debt, and much more discouraged.

The official report of the Illinois State Board of Agriculture for 1889 exhibited the distressing fact that the corn crop of that State for that year actually sold for $10,000,000 less than it cost to produce it, and conditions since then have only slightly improved. Even as I write, there are thousands of families all over the land, not merely in a few localities where the crops have failed, but on the virgin prairies of Dakota, on the rich soil of the Mississippi bottoms, and in the fertile valleys of Virginia, who are in distress, not because they have been idle or dissolute, but because their last crops did not sell for enough to pay the cost of their production and transportation to market, including interest at six, eight, and ten per cent per annum on the value of the land.

Low prices, according to all standard writers on political economy, are the direct results of a contracting currency, and a consequent increasing scarcity of money, and the cost of production is not only greatly increased by inability of the producer to obtain money except at high rates of interest, but the terms upon which money can be had at all are often so exacting as to discourage permanent improvement. The farmer will not cultivate except for immediate crops if he sees no hopeful outlook for the future, and not only fears but expects that the mortgage he has given will, in the end, cause his home to be transferred to a purchaser at sheriff's sale.

The yield of the Morning mine has already largely increased the volume of standard money all over the world, and this may do much toward removing some of the unfortunate conditions to which I have referred; but such yield may also have a tendency to discourage the loaning of money on long loans, for men who have means to invest may prefer to place them in property, the value of which must advance with the increase of the volume of money, rather than in loans, the value of which must remain stationary absolutely, and cannot but diminish relatively.

It has been and will continue to be my purpose to use the gold produced at the Morning mine, either in the purchase of existing loans, or the making of new loans, so that whatever of loss may come from diminution of the purchasing power of a dollar may fall not altogether upon those who have loaned money, but in part upon those who have deliberately or accidentally caused such increase. I suggest that if such increase in the currency be caused by the government, a similar moral obligation would rest upon it.

The addition of $2,400,000,000 to the currency of the country will unquestionably largely increase all values. It will at the same time encourage—nay, almost compel—capital to seek investment in active industries rather than in dormant funds. For the present it will supply those who can use money to advantage with a sure and convenient method of obtaining it at a cheap rate of interest, while its ultimate tendency must be to eliminate interest on money from the world's transactions, and bring money to what I conceive to be its true function—a measurer of values only.

When no interest can be obtained for the use of money, then money will cease to be the most valuable and become the least valuable form of property, and the investor will be required to share the risk, if not the labor, of producing values, instead of leaving this to others, while he absorbs the profits to himself.

I believe that civilization is ready for this forward step. The discovery of gold enough to compel it may have precipitated the movement, but the movement would have come all the same if the Morning mine had never been discovered.

There is not a single benefit which the donation of twenty-four hundred millions of gold will confer upon the people of the United States that might not equally be conferred by an act of Congress providing for the issuance and loaning of the same number of paper dollars, not based upon gold at all.

The credit of this great government used for the purpose of accommodating the business, increasing the resources, and stimulating the industrial activity of this great people, and, supported by the indestructible and undepreciable security of land, would be quite as solid a basis for twenty hundred millions of paper dollars as five thousand tons of yellow metal.

I am, Mr. President, your obedient servant,

DAVID MORNING.

CHAPTER XXII.

"The product of ill-mated marriages."

From the Baroness Von Eulaw to Mrs. Perces Thornton.

BERLIN, November 1, 1895.

DEAREST MOTHER: What an insufferable egotist I must appear to you. A life made up of local coloring—a central figure with no accessories—a record of ways and means unwisely, perhaps, submitted to you, since they may only pain you. Better a gray and monotonous sea, without sail or sound, if so I could spare you the burden of apprehension which every anxious mother must feel for a destiny she has helped to direct. Following the train of argument, think you the loving Father acquits himself of responsibility when a helpless soul is launched for eternity? Truly no! and this conviction sustains my courage, and makes me unafraid to do my heart's bidding.

It has been an observation that the thing we most condemn in others, we shall find in ourselves. Many years ago I conceived a prejudice against the popular cry concerning the wrongs of woman, a movement affirmatively named "woman's rights," for while it undoubtedly aided some women in obtaining justice, its aim was largely the gratification of some hysterical ambition or some love of conspicuousness.

Thus I am brought to question if, in my individual case, I am not exaggerating evils and magnifying wrongs by placing them under the strong light, if not of worldly criticism, at least of self-love and secret pride; if, instead of dealing soberly and wisely with flesh and blood, I am not following an ideal, or whether my matrimonial point of view is not interrupted by such inappreciable angles as seldom vex the eye of faith and perfect love.

All these questions, and many more, I wish to make clear to my own conscience and your mind, that you may be able to advise me when, if ever, the time shall come for me to ask your loving counsel.

To speak more personally, I conclude, after mentally reviewing the characteristics peculiar to my husband, the baron, that his faults are less of malice than of temperament, and that he would not really sacrifice any actual interest of his wife, not even her permanent peace of mind, any more than I would compromise those of the baron. If it were not so, I could less well afford the many hours of thought I give toward the fashioning of apologies for him, lest in my own mind I do him an injustice.

But, so believing, I must take many things on trust, and, after all, I am full of faults myself, no doubt of it. You know it is a popular theory over here that American girls must be broken like bronco horses before they are fit for wives, and I must say that my own mouth is a little tender to the foreign bit already.

We have invitations to a grand ball, although I have not yet seen them. Kindest love to papa, and a heart full of devotion for you, as always. When will

you write to tell me you are coming to your affectionate daughter   ELLEN.

*From Mrs. Perces Thornton to the Baroness Von
   Eulaw.*

BOSTON, November 10. 1895.

To my daughter, the Baroness Von Eulaw.

DEARLY BELOVED CHILD: In these revolutionary
times, the air thick with maledictions and curses, "the
putrid breath of poverty, and the beetling brow of labor," to quote the press, hot with greed for the
ground they are slowly but surely losing—in these
times I say, I am thankful that you, my child, are
resting in the security of strong and wise rule.

There seems to be no end to the vindictiveness
of the common people here. Your father, as you
are aware, is president of the new Aerial Navigation
Company, and, although, as he says, his policy is un-
aggressive, and his weight of counsel unswervingly
in the direction of the interests of the poor and the
laboring classes, they seem determined to make the
breach as wide as possible, and go so far as even to demand a division of the proceeds of every enterprise,
based upon the labor of either brawn or brain, and
insolently propose to tax the companies to the extent
of what they call their "labor investment."

What nonsense! It makes me so mad I don't
know what to do. Papa says—he is always so conservative, you know—that the poor fellow who effected
the invention of air navigation, really ought to have
been paid better for it, but that he was a genius, with
no common sense—none of them have, you know—

and nearly starved, at that; that there is a man out West, whose name I have not heard, who is going to make it very warm for men concerned in such transactions as this, which he denounces as highway robbery, and in a short speech, wherein he maintained that labor was as much a factor and an investment as capital, in all successful enterprise, he called one Jack Spratt, and the other Jack Spratt's wife, which simile pleased me immensely. We don't know where it is going to end, but hope for the best.

Now, my darling, I want to say how gratified I am at the contents of your last letter. In it I discern a spirit of what Christians call humility, very consistent and very encouraging, considering the noble personage whom you are so lucky as to have captured by your charms and graces alone, for of course your fortune had nothing whatever to do with it.

If your husband were an American, I would advise you to stand up for your rights. American husbands, uxorious though they are, and they have earned the name, bring you no title, have no legitimate entrée to foreign courts, and even the most stupendous fortunes only inoculate and leave a scar. Really, the only clean business is an out and out marriage, love or no love, though, for the matter of that, one must feel toward the dear baron as the hero-worshiping woman said concerning the wife of Henry Ward Beecher, that she ought to be proud to bow her head and allow the great divine to pluck every individual hair out by the roots. "A most touching test of devotion," I hear you say.

Do write, my dear, and tell me all the court gossip. Since the California practice of shooting obnoxious editors has been introduced in Boston, there has grown up a virtual censorship of the press hereabouts, and the newspapers are as dull as death. Every woman's character is kept in a glass case, and one would suppose the men graduated from a meeting-house. In fact, the reading public who lived upon scandals are dying of *ennui*, hence, I have no news to write you to-day. Present me with continued assurance of high respect to the baron, and receive, yourself, my undying love.   As ever,

PERCES THORNTON.

From the Baroness Von Eulaw to Mrs. Perces Thornton.

BERLIN, November 20, 1895.

MY DEAR MOTHER: The grand ball, the mention of which seems to catch your fancy, is to be given at the Chateau d' Or, a magnificent edifice on the heights overlooking the river. Its turrets, and domes, and roofs, and arches, and balustrades, glitter against the background of bluest skies like shining gold—hence its name. Indeed, its architectural device is so cunningly conceived as to catch and fill the eye with radiant color like the fasces of a diamond, while its proportions suggest all the beauties of form to be found in the scale of harmonized effects.

It is just completed, and is a wonder. Its occupants are not much talked about; indeed, I do not even know who they are, though I fancy the baron does, for I recall that he replied curtly to my question concerning them, that I should not wish to know them, by which I fancied they might be Americans.

Neither can I give you any idea of the bidden guests, although, of course, it promises to be a magnificent affair. As you know, in compliance with custom, I could, in no event, make excuse for non-appearance with my husband. Such women as accept their titles and position from their lords, are expected to follow, unquestioning, his leadership through all social labyrinths, and I am no exception to the rule.

Dear mother, forgive me, if I say I feel very disinclined to these gayeties. Since our experiences at Mentone, I decided to give over all control of the exchequer into the hands of the baron, accepting only a regular stipend. I find this the only means of securing harmony, and altercations weary and depress me overmuch. Wherefore it is I have lost interest in handsome toilets, and therefor it is I shall have nothing new for the occasion.

Did papa receive my letter acknowledging and thanking him for his munificent gift? and does it occur to you that it is a good deal of money to invest in methods of pacification? But what is the remedy? This is a question I am puzzling my head about to a much larger extent, let me say, than about what I shall wear to the ball.

The baron dines at home to-day, so I will close, in order not to be a moment late. You see I am growing to be a model wife, if not a heroic woman. I see the baron from my window beating a poor dwarf, at the entrance of the alley. He has lost at play. In haste and love, dear ones, adieu.

Faithfully your own,   ELLEN.

*From the Baroness Von Eulaw to Mrs. Perces Thorn-
ton.*

BERLIN, December 2, 1895.

DEAR MOTHER: Is there but one depth for a creature like him I call husband? What mockery in a name! What have I suffered for him, and what concealed in my pride! And this is my reward!—To have been made the dupe of a dastardly plot to ensnare cowardly victims! to have sullied my skirts with the dust of a usurer's and gambler's den! to have my name blazoned side by side with the modern Cora Pearls in every court journal in Europe! to have been led into the lair blindly, by one who is sworn to be my protector! to have followed in faith the man who could load the dice of his self-imposed despair, with a wife's dishonor!

But I must remember that all this is a riddle to you, and must read like the ravings of a maddened brain, so I will give you the story of my shame and rage, albeit it has probably already been telegraphed over two continents. Verily, it is too sweet a morsel to escape the newspapers.

As I believe I mentioned to you, invitations were issued for a ball, to be given at the Chateau d'Or. I noticed that the occurrence was making rather a stir, and especially that the baron was unwontedly nervous over the event, insomuch that when I proposed sending regrets, he fell into a violent rage, and declared that I would ruin him, past and future. Naturally, I did not comprehend his meaning, but, seeming to take it so much to heart, I readily consented to accompany him, asking no further questions.

Arrived at the place of what later proved to be a scene of the most disgraceful orgies, we entered the salon, and instantly my heart misgave me. There was present a mixed assemblage of people, among them a few whom I had met in the best circles—a few who seemed equally out of place with myself—and many of that nondescript quality found in every society, who defy comment. But not until we were presented to the receiving party, was my amazement at its climax. I am not yet sufficiently in possession of myself, to describe the magnificent apartments of the interior of this most superb mansion. All that wealth could bring from the uttermost ends of the earth, contributed to the sumptuousness of these most artistic apartments. No smallest detail had been forgotten in the programme for this entertainment, even to the grottoes with singing birds, and floes of ice in seas of wine.

But the recollection is hateful, and I hurry on. The host was a tall, sinewy, middle-aged man, with a strongly-marked Hebraic cast of face, and an oily, obsequious manner, quite at variance with his prominent features. He greeted us with an air of the most profuse cordiality, and passed us along to a bevy of much-painted and overdressed, or, rather, underdressed women, who vied with each other in chattering society phrases.

From the first moment, an undeniable air of dissoluteness pervaded the entire place, and I looked to the baron for an explanation. He pressed my arm nervously, and politely warned me to hold my tongue. There was no mistaking the animus of this party. It was revelry, riot, unrestraint. Answering a sign from the host, the baron soon left my side, and joined the convivialists, I being politely led to the main salon, where there was dancing.

Pleading indisposition, I declined to take part, and remained aside observing the dancers. I noticed that many of the women were singularly lovely and exquisitely attired, but generally lacking in grace of movement and aplomb. I observed, also, groups of women, some of them deathly pale, others flushed with indignation, evidently discussing the situation, and the truth slowly dawned upon me that these were women of the demi-monde, and that I had been tricked into an attendance upon this reception.

After two or three attempts I succeeded in bringing the baron to my side, much the worse for wine but quite docile. I demanded to be led to my dressing-room, and at first he temporized. Finding me insistent, he begged me to remain, promising to be among the first to depart at the proper hour. His conduct was unusually conciliatory, and when I referred to the character of the entertainment, his manner was full of conscious guilt, while he assured me that he would explain everything later, but that he dared not precipitate a scene by taking me home.

At this juncture Count Volenfeldt, whom we knew, accompained by the Prince of Waldeck, came our way, and, saluting, faced us, and, remarking somewhat satirically upon the unexpected numbers in attendance, gave me an opportunity to ask if his wife were present.

"The countess is not here to-night," replied the count, a little dryly. "She is not well."

"And my wife *is* here," put in the prince bluffly, "but she will not be longer than till I shall have made my way through this crush."

"Let us join the prince's party and leave this place at once," said I.

Meanwhile the music had for the moment ceased, and loud laughing and shrill voices, mingled with smoother tones and words of entreaty, were heard, and there was a simultaneous movement toward the dressing-rooms and places of exit. Suddenly word came back that the doors were locked, and the frightened lackeys had fled from their posts, with orders that no one should be allowed to leave the house. Then followed a scene of consternation and confusion,—wives demanding redress from their husbands, and husbands denouncing the violation of hospitality by their host, and through all the din the gutteral tones and the piping taunts of the unsainted.

Presently the tall form of Herr Rosenblatt showed, a head above the crowd, adding to his length the height of a fauteuil, upon which he balanced, with a drunken man's nicety of poise, for he was drunk but coherent.

"Gentlemen," said he, "we have met together, as we have met before, for the purpose of proving which man among us has the staying qualities, and who is willing to risk his money in this little game. You come to me and say, 'Open your doors, my lady wishes to go,' but how many of you dare to go when I say to those who will go, 'To-morrow I shall expose you, to-morrow you will sign over your estates to me, to-morrow you shall be ruined and I shall be winner.' I did not make this party for your money—nor that you shall play, at my tables and lose, for that you have already done, but one thing I want which money will not buy,—social recognition,—and that you shall give me. You will not leave my house, gentlemen, till morning. The ladies will not talk about this entertainment. It is too beautiful; they will not attempt to describe it. Now, gentlemen, I bid you to stay and I shall make myself sure that you enjoy yourself. These remarks make it long for the champagne to wait, and the ladies, poor things, will be wanting refreshments. And such refreshments! Oh, *mon Dieu*, that the gods could sup with us," and the speaker was helped caressingly to the floor.

My dear scandalized mother, what did I do? I, an American girl, with the blood of heroes in my veins? Why, I remained and supped and smiled with the others, for not a man even tried the doors. Thereafter there was no restraint. It was, as I have said, a night of orgies. Each man felt that he was no more deeply involved than his neighbor, and that Herr Rosenblatt had told the truth when he said to all, that he held their fates in his fist, otherwise they would not have been there.

He was right, the affair was not talked about except among themselves. But some mischievous astral — some ubiquitous spirit of a reporter,—was floating about, and before twenty-four hours had elapsed, the court journals had published an account of the whole affair, comments included.

Dearest mother, this letter is long, and I can write no more to-night. I have decided upon nothing so far.   So soon as I have done so, I will write, but I must have time for reflection.   In tears and love adieu.

As ever yours,   ELLEN.

From the Baroness Von Eulaw to Professor John Thornton.

BERLIN, December 5, 1895.

MY DEAR, DARLING PAPA: I have your telegram telling me to come home without delay, also message for the American Minister in case I should need it, as well as that to my banker.   Wise and loving provisions all, for my fortune is squandered, my home dishonored, and my heart more than broken, in that I perfidiously assumed to give a love which was not mine to give, and if I had obeyed my first impulse I should have been on the way to your arms, and to the dear old hearth I so thoughtlessly deserted.   But can you understand me when I say that all this I have brought upon myself?   I was not a child; I had a fitting experience and was of sound judgment.   I knew I did not love this man as it was in me to love, indeed, I felt for him neither the admiration nor esteem which must form the basis of genuine passion.   I respected, aye, coveted his position, his title, and I brought myself feebly to hope that some day I should be a devoted wife.   I staked my future, as he staked my fortune, and lost.   If the money was not his own to lose, neither was my heart mine to lose.

One other test I have applied, and the result is in his favor.   If I did love the baron as I ~~have~~ might love another, would I be so ready with my revenge? —Verily, no; I would wear my life out in the effort

19

to cancel or correct the wrong against myself. Sacrifice is the residue found in love's crucible; passion is the flux which passes off in the process of retorting. In my crucible, alas! I find nothing but dross—the more the pity.

And so I have decided to remain in Berlin for the present. I am sketching out my plans for the future, but they are crude and unformed, and are of a sort of lighthouse quality, meant to warn people of the rocky places. But more of this anon. Tell my mother, dearest papa, how condemned I feel to give her so much agony on my account. Don't worry; I will be quite happy now that my mind is settled. Possibly we shall come over in a few weeks, but only possibly. I am sorry I wrote my last to mamma with so much feeling. Good-night, and good-by.

Your devoted,   ELLEN.

CHAPTER XXIII.

"Shut that door!" thundered the baron from over the washbowl in a Pullman car, as he stood half-dressed in a small apartment, taking his morning bath.

"Who are you addressin'?" answered a pale-faced young man—who was passing—from under a broad, stiff-brimmed hat, the crown of which was encircled with the skin of a huge rattlesnake. "I reckon you want your nose set back about an inch anyhow, and I'm the man that can perform that little blacksmithin' job right here."

The baron glanced at the gray-clad figure, with its gleaming silk 'kerchief knotted carelessly, and arms akimbo, then down at the high boots with their fair-leather tops, behind which gleamed the ebony and silver handle of a bowie knife, and then, meeting the steady, mild blue eyes of the Arizona cowboy, said apologetically:—

"Beg pardon. I thought it was the madam. She just left the compartment."

"You did, did you?" said the youth. "That's what I allowed, en that's why I tuk an interest in ye. Look a yer. That woman ain't no slouch, and Gila monsters like you ain't popular nohow, yearabouts, so you jest keep a civil tongue in your mutton head, an' it'll be all right." And with the movement of a leopard, he glided quietly away, while the baron, after softly closing the door, sank into the nearest sofa, and awaited the return of his wife.

"Benson," shouted the keen-eyed brakeman. "Change cars for Tombstone, Nogales, Hermosillo, Guaymas, and all points on the Gulf of California. Passengers for Tucson, Phœnix, Yuma, San Diego, Los Angeles, and San Francisco remain in the car."

The baron's party consisted of the baroness and her maid, Professor and Mrs. Thornton, Doctor Eustace, who had accompanied the Von Eulaws from Europe, and Miss Winters, an old friend of the baroness and a graduate of a woman's law school, who had left a thriving practice in Denver rather than sacrifice her life in the pursuit of a profession for which no woman is really fitted either mentally or physically. The party was *en route* to Coronado Beach—the baron as one of a score of representatives selected by the emperor of Germany to attend the "dynamic exposition," as it was generally designated.

Six weeks or less before the Prime Minister of every recognized civilized power had received a letter couched in the following phrase.

Offices of David Morning,
39 Broadway, N. Y., January 1, 1896.

To ....

I respectfully invite your government to appoint so many representatives, not exceeding twenty in number, as it may desire, to be present in San Diego, California, during the first week of April *proximo*, to observe and report upon experiments which will then be made in aerial and submarine navigation, and use of the new explosive "potentite."   It is my hope to demonstrate that hereafter international differences should be submitted for adjustment to a Congress or Court of Nations, and that land and naval warfare —as at present conducted—must come to an end.

The gentlemen who may be credentialed by you will be my guests upon their arrival in San Diego—if they will so honor me—and I beg to be informed at your early convenience, by cable, of the names of those who may be expected.

I take the liberty of inclosing exchange on London for twenty thousand pounds, to defray such expenses as your government may incur in complying with my request.

I have the honor to be, very respectfully, your obedient servant,

DAVID MORNING.

The fame of Morning, as the greatest wealth owner in the world, was now coextensive with civilization, and his invitation had been promptly and generally accepted.   The Emperor Wilhelm II. chose for the German delegation, five of his most distinguished field marshals, five high officials of the German navy, five great civil engineers, and five members of the diplomatic corps.   Among the latter was the Baron Von Eulaw, who was indebted for his appointment— although he did not know it—to an urgent unofficial representation made by the American envoy to the German Chancellor, to the effect that, for certain personal reasons, Mr. David Morning greatly desired the attendance of the Baron and Baroness Von Eulaw.

Such a request from such a source was favorably considered, and the baron—greatly to his astonishment,
for he had not been in favor at court since the affair
at the Chateau d'Or—received the appointment.

Professor Thornton and Doctor Eustace had received invitations to attend, and the baron, finding it
convenient to leave Berlin in advance of the other
members of the German delegation, sailed from Ham-
burg late in January, and, after a brief visit with his
wife's parents at Roxbury, the party journeyed to the
Pacific Coast, to enjoy its climate and scenery for a
month or more in advance of the "dynamic exposition."

"I feel," said the baroness, as the train rolled out
of Benson, "as if I had a renewed lease of life; these
delicious airs stir the blood like wine, and, entranced
with the perfume of almond and oleander and jasmine
bloom, I forget that it is still midwinter in the East."

"You are drugged, madame," said the doctor,
slowly passing his finger scrutinizingly over the soft
flesh upon his hand. "You could be lured to your
death in a few hours by—I wonder what ails my
hand?" he broke off meditatively, still feeling for
the insidious and evasive little hair.

"Cactus, sir," put in an "old-timer" across the
car, "and you ain't got no use to look for it, if it
does feel like an oxgad. I could hev tole you when
I see you foolin' around them fine flowers at the
station, but you fellers hev all got to try it once;
another time you'll know better."

"This is Mr. Morning's state, I believe," observed
the doctor, after the laugh at his expense had sub-

sided, and all sat dreamily looking away to the dimly-outlined mountains in the distance, "and we must be nearing the place of the wonderful gold deposit, with the results of which he is rapidly revolutionizing the world."

"You are right, sir," said a bright-eyed, smooth-shaven, portly gentleman, of forty years of age, who occupied an adjoining seat. "It is Morning's state in every sense of the word. He has made it—industrially, politically, and socially. His enterprise and money have constructed great reservoirs, and laced the land with irrigating canals, and changed its wastes into orchards, and its deserts into lawns. He is the idol of its people, as he ought to be, and his ideas are embodied in our constitution and laws. They are all the product of his thought, from marriage contract-laws to abolition of trial by jury."

"Abolition of trial by jury," said Doctor Eustace.

"Yes, sir; at least the jury is composed of judges, instead of men who don't know the plaintiff from the defendant, and we have no Supreme Court."

"No jury, and no Supreme Court!" observed Miss Winters. "What a capital idea. I shall come here to practice."

"Well, miss, if you practice law here, and wish to patronize the twelve men in a box, or enjoy the luxury of an appeal, you must bring your case in the United States Court, or take it there. In our State courts we have dispensed with all that ancient rubbish."

"Rubbish!" exclaimed the doctor.

"Even so," rejoined the stranger. The judicial

system in vogue elsewhere than in Arizona is as much
a relic of barbarism as slavery or polygamy. It is no
more fitted to the wants and enlightenment of the age
than the canal boat for traveling, or the flint lock
musket for shooting pigeons. Suppose you wish to
recover a piece of land from a jumper in California or
Maine, and one side or the other demands a jury trial.
Every good citizen who is busy shirks duty as a jury-
man. Every intelligent citizen who reads the newspapers forms an opinion and is excused. From the
residue—which is sure to contain both fools and
knaves—you get twelve clerks, mechanics, laborers,
merchants, farmers, and idlers—none of whom have
any training in untangling complicated propositions,
weighing evidence, remembering principles of law
and logic, and according to each fact its just and relative importance.

After these twelve men have listened to a muddle
of testimony, objections, law papers, and speeches,
concluding with bewildering instructions, which half of
them fail to remember, and the other half fail to understand, they retire to the jury room and guess out
a verdict. The losing party appeals, and, after weari-
some delay, the Supreme Court decides that 'someone has blundered,' and, without attempting to correct
the error by a proper judgment, sends the case back
for another trial, another batch of blunders, and
another appeal.''

" And how does your Arizona system correct the
evils you depict?'' queried the doctor.

"We commence at the other end of the puzzle,''
said the stranger. '' We place the Supreme Court in

the jury box. We have a preliminary court of three judges in each judicial district. Every plaintiff must first present his case informally to this court. He states on oath the facts he expects to prove, and gives the names of his witnesses. Any willful mis-statement of a material fact, is perjury. If the evidence would, if uncontradicted, entitle him to recover, an order is issued giving him leave to sue. In practice, not one-half of the proposed suits survive the ordeal. The saving of time and money is great. Under the old system, after a jury had been impaneled, and days consumed, the plaintiff might, after all, be non-suited. Now it is all disposed of in an hour or two. The preliminary court practically puts an end to all blackmailing litigation."

"And when leave to sue is granted, what is the next step?" inquired the doctor.

"The case is brought under the same rules of procedure as of old," replied the stranger, "with only such changes as were necessary to adapt litigation to the new conditions. We have three judicial districts in the State, and nine judges for each district. Upon questions of law arising during the trial, the judges pass by a majority vote, and in making the final decision, from which there is no appeal, seven judges must concur."

"Does this system satisfy litigants?" asked the doctor.

"Much better than the old method," replied the stranger. "What honest litigant would not prefer to have his rights determined by nine men, who were trained to sift truth from error, who were honest and

just, and without other duties to distract them, rather
·than by twelve men such as ordinarily find their way
into the jury box? The judgment of seven out of
nine judges will be as nearly right as human conclusions can well be, and people affected by it are
better satisfied—even when they lose—than by the
guess of a stupid and sleepy jury.''

''Can the courts you have organized attend to all
the business?'' asked the doctor.

''Easily,'' was the rejoinder. ''No time is consumed
in procuring juries, and much less in objections to
testimony. Arguments are abbreviated, and instructions eliminated. In practice, four cases out of five
are decided from the bench.''

'' Are not the salaries of so many judges a heavy
tax upon you?'' asked the doctor.

'' The system costs the public treasury less than the
old one,'' was the reply. '' Many court expenses are
dispensed with, and the expense to litigants is reduced, although the loser is now compelled to pay
the fee of his opponent's attorney, which is fixed by
the court.''

'' As you have no court of appeals, I suppose no
record is made of court proceedings,'' remarked the
doctor.

''Oh, yes, each court room is provided with one of
the new automatic noiseless receiving and printing
phonographs.''

'' And how about lawyers who have bad cases?''

'' They endeavor to take them into the United
States Court, where the old practice prevails.''

'' Beg pardon, ma'am,'' said the Pullman conductor, approaching Mrs. Thornton, "but we are passing over the new line, which runs north of Gila River, and a view may be had of the sleeping Montezuma now, and the passengers generally like to see it."

"The sleeping Montezuma! What is that?" asked the lady addressed.

"It is the giant figure of an Indian resting on his back on the top of the mountain. You can see it now quite plainly from the right-hand windows of the car."

And across the plain—in centuries gone densely peopled by some prehistoric race, and then for centuries a waste, and, since the completion of the Gila Canal, a checker-board of orchard, vineyard, and meadow, the eye looked upon the lavender-tinted mountains to the northward, and it required no aid from the imagination to behold, upon the summits of those mountains, the profile of a stately figure and majestic face, with a crown of feathers upon the brow, lying upon its back.

Once there lived, in the shadow of this giant, a race, of which traces may still be found in mounds containing pottery, and in the ruins of great aqueducts, and in stone houses seven stories in height, a portion of the walls of which are still standing.

"The Indians hereabouts have a story," said the conductor, "to the effect that Montezuma went to sleep, when the sun dried up the waters, and his people died, and they say now that Morning's canal is making the country green again, the old chief will awaken."

"You were saying," said Doctor Eustace, by way

of suggestion to the stranger, "that there are some peculiar marriage contract laws here."

"It is all expressed, sir, in the preamble to the law, and in the law itself, a copy of which I happen to have with me, as I am on the way to attend court at Yuma. Here it is." and he offered the book to Professor Thornton.

"Read it aloud, professor," said the doctor, and the professor read:—

"The Senate and Assembly of the State of Arizona recognizes the truth that not easy divorce laws, but easy marriage laws, are at the root of the conjugal evil; that men and women have been accustomed to marry, disagree, and divorce in less time than should have been allowed for a proper peried of betrothal; that the loose system now prevailing often results in children destitute of the inherent virility of virtue and affection; that no adequate defenses have hitherto been builded for the protection of young females too unthoughtful and too trusting; that the laws underlying the physical as well as the mental constitution, with their multiple of subtile, gravitating, and repellant forces, have hitherto been wholly unstudied, or disregarded; that the arbitrary conditions of society compel woman to accept marriage, in violation of her higher aims; that in certain human organizations the conditions created by propinquity are altogether false and ephemeral; that certain other human organizations are, by nature, filled with inordinate vanity and self-love, which qualities, beguiling the judgment, constitute fickleness and instability of purpose, and that the true solution of the great social problem is likely to be found in preventive rather than in remedial laws.   Therefore, be it enacted"—

"Hold up, John," said Dr. Eustace.   "That is all my mentality can assimilate without a rest.   Are you not reading from an essay by Mona Caird, or a novel by Tolstoi? Is that really and truly the preamble of a law enacted by a Western Legislature?   Have all the cranks, and all the theorists, and all the moonstruck, long-haired, green-goggled reformers on earth, been turned loose in Arizona?"

"Doctor," said the professor solemnly, "the truth is a persistent fly, that cannot be brushed away with the wisps of ridicule.   The Arizona legislators have fearlessly attempted to deal with conditions which every close observer of our social life knows to be existent."

"Papa," said the baroness, interestedly, "in what way is it proposed to deal with the problem?   Please read further."

"The law is too lengthy," said the professor, after glancing over a few pages, "to be read in detail, but I will summarize it for you.   Marriages are declared void unless the parties procure a license, which can only be issued by an examining board of men and women, composed in part of physicians, and in part of graduates of some reputable school, dedicated to physiological observations and esoteric thought and investigation."

"Anything about ability to boil a potato or sew on a button?" interrupted the doctor.

"Peace, scoffer," said the professor.   "It seems to be required that all applicants for license shall have had an acquaintance of at least one year, and be under marriage engagement for six months, and shall pass examination by the board upon their mutual eligibility, as expressed through temperament, complexion, tastes, education, traits of character, and general conditions of fitness."

"Is red hair, or a habit of snoring, or a fondness for raw onions, considered a disqualification?" queried the doctor.

The professor, ignoring the interruption, continued: "It is required that one or both of the applicants shall possess property of sufficient value, to support both of them for one year, in the manner of life to which the proposed wife has been accustomed."

"A gleam of common sense at last in a glamour of moonshine," said the doctor. "But how can such a marriage law be enforced?"

"The act provides," said the professor, "that children born to parties who have no license, shall be deemed born out of wedlock, and all such children, as well as all children born to extreme poverty or degrading influences, may be taken from their parents and educated at the public expense."

"How does this experiment of turning the State into a moral kindergarten for adults, and wet-nursery for infants, succeed?" said Doctor Eustace to the stranger.

"The law was enacted only a few weeks since," replied the gentleman, "and it is too soon to answer your question."

"Humph! have you any more of such revolutionary legislation?"

"Nothing so important as the marriage contract act, but on page 72 you will find some provisions of law which may interest you."

The doctor read:—

"Women who perform equal service with men shall be entitled to recover an equal sum for their labor, and all contracts made in derogation of this right shall be void."

"Good!" applauded Miss Winters.

Again the doctor read:—

"The men who represent the State of Arizona in the United States Senate shall be chosen by a majority of the voters, and not by the Legislature, as in other States of the Union, and no man, however favored, shall be eligible for the position whose property interests, justly estimated, exceed in value the sum of $100,000."

"That will exclude Mr. Morning from the millionaires' club, will it not?" queried Dr. Eustace.

"Yes, sir," answered the stranger, "but he favored the law. Of course, under the United States Constitution, this section is not legally operative; but it is morally binding, and the Legislature has always elected to the Senate gentlemen who were previously designated by the people at the polls, and thus far no man suspected of solvency has ventured to be a candidate. Arizona is friendly to progressive legislation. You will find our law for the prevention of cruelty to animals on page 56; it may interest you."

The professor read:—

"Any person or persons convicted of having beaten, abused, underfed, overworked, or otherwise maltreated any horse, mule, dog, or other animal of whatever kind, may thereafter be assaulted and beaten by any person who may desire to undertake such task, without the assailant being responsible civilly or criminally for such assault."

"That," said the doctor, "to quote a Boston girl on Niagara Falls, 'is neat, simple, and sufficient.' Have you any further novelties in the way of legislation to offer?"

"Our law of libel is in advance of all other states," said the stranger; "you will find it on page 163."

The professor read:—

"Any man or woman or newspaper firm lending themselves to the dissemination of scandal, or defamation of private character, to the moral detriment of innocent parties, shall, on conviction, be adjudged outlaws, and may be lawfully beaten or killed at the pleasure of the party injured."

"Lord," said the doctor, piously raising his eyes, "now lettest thou thy servant depart in peace, for mine eyes have beheld thy glory."

"We take a great deal of pride in that libel law," said the stranger. "It has inspired a degree of courtesy on the part of Arizona editors that would have made Lord Chesterfield ashamed of himself. The Yuma *Sentinel*, which was accustomed to personal journalism, lately alluded to a convicted highwayman as 'a gentleman whose ideas on the subject of property differ from those of a majority of his fellow-citizens;' and the Tucson *Star*, which used to be the chief of slangwhangers, reviewed a sermon and spoke of Judas Iscariot as 'that disciple whose conduct in receiving compensation in money from the Romans for his services as a guide, has caused his memory to be visited by all religious denominations with great, and probably not altogether undeserved, criticism.' But we are at Yuma, sir, and I must bid you good-by. Boats run up the river from here to Castle Dome. There is an excellent hotel here. Tourists usually stop over to visit the Gonzales place, and I suppose you will not neglect the opportunity. The house is a marvel of beauty. It was built by direction of Mr. Morning."

"Does he live there when at home?" queried the baroness.

"Oh, no, madame! The Gonzales family nursed Morning through an attack of fever, after he was shot by the Apaches near the old Gonzales hacienda several years ago. The Señorita Murella never left his bedside for weeks. Really, the doctors say the girl saved his life. He was, naturally, very grateful, and, when he recovered, he bought the Castle Dome rancheria from the Indians, and had a rock tunnel run into the Colorado River, and took out the water and carried it in irrigating canals over a thousand acres of land, which he had planted in oranges, lemons, vines, olives, and other fruit. It will pay a princely revenue to the Gonzales people in a few years.

"Morning ordered built upon the dome overlooking the river the most beautiful marble palace on the coast, and they say it is not surpassed anywhere on earth. The whole business must have cost him several millions, but money is nothing to him. The place is kept up in princely style by the Señora Gon-

20

zales and her daughter. They entertain a great deal of company, and are always delighted to welcome strangers who may visit the place."

"And I suppose that Aladdin is a constant visitor at his palace?" sneered the baron.

"Morning? Oh, no; strangely enough, he has never been near the place since its completion, two years ago! Too busy, I suppose, helping the world out of the mud. But he is on the coast now, preparing for his 'dynamite exposition,' and may put in an appearance here."

CHAPTER XXIV.

" A hospitable gate unbarred to all."

"ALL aboard for Castle Dome," and the baron's party filed up the carpeted gang plank, and looked smilingly about them.

"I have often heard of the sumptuousness of the Mississippi steamers, now grown traditional, but this exceeds even their reputation," commented Miss Winters.

"This is the Morning line, madame," answered the gaudily-dressed steward boastfully, "and they do nothing by halves, you know," and he pompously led the way to the ladies' saloon.

"Except by half millions," returned the doctor jocosely.

"These steamers were built for the accommodation of the people who came to the World's Fair at Chicago," explained the steward. "Morning's a queer sort of fellow"—and he grew confidential. "He could have brought his air ships and new-fangled things, such as he had on exhibition at the fair, but he wouldn't. He said it was kind o' throwing off on nature, that God never made but one Colorado River, and he for one hadn't the brass to discount it."

"Do you have many visitors belonging to the nobility?" asked Mrs. Thornton, evidently inclined to change the conversation from its personal trend.

"Oh, lots of 'em! There's a Spanish count and an Italian prince stopping up at the Gonzales place now. The Italian has been there some time, making himself solid with the señorita, I reckon. And we are expecting a party this week, Baron Von Boodle, or some such name, with his friends"—here the baron rose abruptly and walked out of the saloon—"at least Mr. Morning telegraphed the captain from San Diego that when this party arrived he meant to run over here and make his first visit to Castle Dome, which will be an event, for, after all the millions of money he has spent on the place, he has never been near it, and everybody is wondering at it."

After a night's rest at the great Rio Colorado Hotel, built upon the bluff at Yuma, the party had made an early start, and had been on board the *Undine* for some time before the line was thrown in and the steamer began to move.

The steward bustled away, and the baroness rose, with a deep breath of relief, and walked to the mirror. It may have been observed of many women that any new or sudden sensation or condition or emotion suggests a looking-glass. Not that they see or are thinking of themselves, but they seem thus best able to collect their thoughts. So it was with this woman, only that now she did observe two very bright eyes and a radiant face, with the swift blood coursing back from her cheeks, across the smooth white surface of her neck, to the closely-defined growth of hair—that oracle of beauty which no ugly woman ever wore, whatever her features. She turned quickly away, and, following the doctor and her father, the three ladies went out to view the scenery.

"You observe this bend in the river," a voice was saying, "where many a poor fellow has gone to his death, for there swoops the most fatal pool of eddies, perhaps, to be found in the whole channel of these whimsical waters."

The baroness turned to look for the speaker, whose voice seemed familiar, and there, under the shade of the awning, in full silhouette, looking in the face of her husband, with whom he was pleasantly conversing, stood David Morning.

Her first thought was to retreat to the saloon and wait for him to present himself, but as his swift eye swept the deck, he caught sight of her face, and came quickly over, followed by the baron, saying, as he cordially took her hand, and held it closely for a long time, "I enjoy one advantage over you, baron, my acquaintance with the baroness dates back of yours. I hope she has not forgotten me."

The woman made no reply to this remark; she simply said, "How do you do, Mr. Morning," and presented him to her friends.

The brief trip up the river among the cliffs and cascades and whirlpools and caves and cañons and towering cathedral rocks, furnished prolific and auspicious topics for conversation, but it need not be said that neither the baroness nor Mr. Morning knew altogether what they were talking about. She could not fail to see the pupils of his sea-grey eyes grow very large when he looked at her, and he in turn observed that she scarcely looked at him at all.

The professor talked a little dryly at first, and Mrs. Thornton sat apart, evidently nursing her chagrin,

for Mr. Morning was at this moment not only the
wealthiest but the most famous and powerful man in
all the world, and, had he sought it, could have obtained orders of high nobility from every crowned
head in Europe. The baron, who would have seen
"Helen's beauty in a brow of Egypt," if that brow
possessed the attribute of Midas, looked at the situation from an altogether different standpoint, and was
thinking at what period of the new-formed acquaintance it would be prudent to ask the loan of a few,
or, possibly, more than a few, thousand pounds.

Presently the boat rounded into a little cove and
stopped. The brief but eventful journey was over,
and the party stepped from the boat to a flight of
marble-flagged steps, leading up to shining floors, out
of which arose columns supporting a light roof in
Pagoda style. Easy swinging seats, with hammocks
and tables, with a few racks and stands, completed
the pretty "Rest" for the landing, and the party began to look about for the path of ascent.

Suddenly a tinkling sound was heard, and, softly as
if it fell from the clouds, a car, sumptuously carpeted,
cushioned, and canopied, appeared before them. It
was, evidently, meant for the accommodation of the
party, and one by one they stepped in. Morning
was the last to follow, and as he came aboard and
closed the plate-glass door, it shut with a tinkle, and
the car arose, moving proportionately aslant as the
grade of the terrace—which had been fashioned and
grown in the short space of two years—inclined.

"My invention works like a charm," Morning was
heard to mutter to the outer air, as they neared the

summit and surveyed the height. The awe-filling overhanging crags, thousands of centuries old, had been blasted and chiseled and coaxed into shelves, and steps, and nooks, and resting-places, softly carpeted with moss, and decorated with growing ferns and lichens. The wind came down the river and shook the leaves above their heads, and stirred the birds into a flood of song, and larks sat upon the twigs and warbled with joy.

"Only two years," said Miss Winters, as they stepped from the car; "'tis not so long in which to make a beautiful world."

"It is much more difficult to people it with the right sort," mused Morning.

"The first builders had to try that two or three times, if my memory serves me," remarked the doctor.

"Are these people of the right sort?" asked Mrs. Thornton significantly.

The baroness shot a quick glance at Morning, and looked over at her rather too loquacious maternal.

"I am too much of an ingrate to answer for them," said Morning, undismayed. "I only know that I owe them my life, and that I have never had the grace to come and thank them."

They had now arrived at the main entrance to the grounds, and the scene presented was one of indescribable beauty and splendor. The dazzling proportions of the structure rose into the air with such exceeding lightness and grace of outline, melting away against the silvery softness of the clouds, that it seemed swinging in the ambient air, and only for the cornices and columns and spires and turrets of onyx and agate which defined the outlines against the sky, one would look to see it float away like dissolving views of the Celestial City. The magnificent dome was rounded with bent and many-colored glasses, the eloquent figures storying events of history both classic and local, in pigments not known since the days of Donatello, who went mad because his figure could not speak. And there, upon its pedestal of purest alabaster, stood the chaste statue of Psyche, just as Morning had hewn it out of his captious fancy so long ago, and Cupid opposite, half eager, half evasive, and restless. Ah, well! and he looked into the deep, appreciative eyes of the woman by his side, and said not a word.

Having selected the most thoroughly skilled architects, artists, and artisans, and no limit having been placed to expenditure, it was evident that every detail of Morning's plan had been faithfully executed. But beyond this his power, or, rather, his supervision or direction, had ceased. At last it was the estate and home of the Gonzales family and not his own, and concerning its management, or the manner in which they should enjoy it, he did not offer even a suggestion. Morning's instructions, left with the Bank of California more than two years before, were to pay all checks signed by the Señora or the Señorita Gonzales, no matter what amount, and charge them to his account.

The Gonzales family had taken their good fortune with great equanimity. Their inclinations led them to a generous and exceedingly promiscuous hospitality, and they had not hesitated to arrange the ménage of their household without regard to conventionalities. Instead of the solemn and ubiquitous functionary at the open door, there was vacancy, while the party stood upon the tessellated floor of the broad vestibule for several minutes.

Presently a young Spaniard in boots and clanking spurs, with silver-laced sombrero and flaming tie, threw wide the door, and simultaneously Morning caught a glimpse through an open court of a female figure leaning upon the rosewood balustrade, mounted with a cable of silver, which surrounded a corridor, and idly tossing with her fan the light, half-curling locks of a man who sat upon a low seat, resting his head against her knee.

It was only a glance as the sun strikes against the steel, sharply cutting its way upon the eye, or like the incisive impress of some exceptional face in passing, whereby one seizes every detail of color and form, void of conscious effort.   It was easy to recognize the graceful outline of the swaying figure as she sat poised under the sunlight, and swift and unbidden even as the *coup dœil* was, the senses of David Morning thrilled with gladness.   Was it the sight of Murella again that sent that shaft of ecstasy through his soul? or was it the all up-building, all-leveling lesson that the Señorita Gonzales was being amused?

The arrival of the party had been manifestly unexpected, and no formal announcement was made, but no sooner had they entered the magnificent reception hall at one extremity than Señorita Gonzales appeared at the other   She entered with a movement of the most exquisite grace, robed, rather than dressed, in a gown of acanthus green satin, flowing in the back from the half-bared neck to the gold-embroidered border of the demi-train. The front was gathered at the shoulder and fell with lengths of creamy lisse to the perfect foot, with its slippers of gold. A corselet of rich embroideries rounded the waist. The sleeves were loosely puffed and draped with softest lace to the white and flexible wrist, while the web-like lace of her mantilla rested lightly upon the shining coils of her abundant hair.

As Mr. Morning advanced toward the center of the room to greet his beautiful hostess, she drew an audible breath, and lifted her finely-arched brows, but no sign betrayed other emotion. Mr. Morning presented his friends in the most casual and easy manner, but when the Baroness Von Eulaw came forward, taller by some inches than the Senorita Gonzales, and with an exquisite manner was about to speak, the little hostess, with an air of special affability and simplicity, asked, showing her small white teeth the while:—

"To who owe I a the honor of this visite of a noble baroness?"

It was a bombshell in satin and lace which fell at the feet of Morning, and for an instant he saw no way to the rescue of the baroness. Then, rallying, he quickly replied:—

"To the reputation for hospitality of the fair owner of this house, and that of her charming family."

"I no know if my name travel so long time a," she rejoined, looking at Morning.

The baron then came forward, and, politely holding her fingers, said in Spanish, "I hope that the Señorita and Señora Gonzales are quite well, as who should not be in this Italy of rare delights?"

"Oh, Italy! that is the home of my parteekler friend. He paint Italia, he sing Italia, and he make me promise for go many times."

"That settles it," Morning muttered sententiously, but no one heard.

Then the conversation became general, the baroness commenting kindly upon the encroachments upon the time of the señorita in receiving curious visitors.

"Oh," retorted Murella with pretty nonchalance, "I no care! I lofe amuse myself," leading the way to the main saloon. "I haf always parteekler frent, same as baroness, ess it not?" and she sank indolently into the cushioned depths of a primrose sofa, waving the baroness to a place beside her, and leaving the party to make choice of seats.

A glance at the original design and superb appointments of this interior suggested the incongruity of hammocks and *ollas*, yet here they were many times repeated, for "ice is the devil's nectar," runs a Spanish proverb, and the *olla* has no rival save the mescal jug.

Every well-to-do Mexican family keeps beneath its roof a corps of female retainers, who are neither servants nor guests, but something between the two. They dine—except on occasions—at the family board, and mingle always at the family gathering, but they assist in the household labors, and sometimes, though not often, receive a stated money compensation. They are usually relatives, more or less distant, of the mistress of the household. The beautiful *casa* and great wealth of the Gonzales family had nearly depopulated the neighboring Mexican State of Sonora of all the needy Alvarados who could claim kinship with the Donna Maria, and a dozen of these señoritas now appeared shyly at the doors, their mantillas closely drawn, though the day was warm, and many voices and excellent music were heard from all quarters of the house and grounds.

After a few moments the Señora Gonzales, with her brother, Don Manuel Alvarado, who acted as major-domo of the estate, were presented, but the señora soon glided away unobserved, leaving her brother to the honors of guide over the mansion.

"You are very beautiful," spoke Murella with apparent naiveté, as they arose to follow the party who had preceded them.

The smile of the baroness was tinged with bitterness as she turned to look into the Madonna face beside her, and ventured to reply.

"And Señor Morning lofes you like heaven and the angels," she continued unctuously.

"Señorita, you forget that I have a husband."

"Is he jealous?"

"Surely no," replied the baroness sincerely.

"Then I no know what you mean a."

"I mean that I owe a wife's duty to the baron," slowly, with rising color.

"And what you owe a to the other fellow?" meaning Morning.

The baroness was too much confused to speak.

"You know him a long time?"

"Before I married the baron and went abroad."

"And you lofe him all these a year? Oh thunner!"

Murella's English must be taken with many grains of allowance. The strongest words in a foreign or unfamiliar tongue seem ineffectual and weak.

"I must plead the indulgence of a guest," laughed the baroness, "and withdraw myself from the searching operations of your cunning catechism, or turn the lights upon you. How long have you known —"

But the señorita had softly glided away, standing apart and giving hurried orders for luncheon.

Morning was in a dilemma. It will have been observed that, after the first moment of greeting, Murella had given him no farther thought. Gratitude is not with the Spaniard one of the cardinal virtues, as he was aware, so that was an unvexed question. If his name had not been so prominently before the world, doubtless they would—the entire family included—have forgotten it ere this. But was it pique, was it pride, or was it embarrassment, that led Murella to thus overlook him?

Certainly she had recognized the baroness at the first glance, to his amazement and bewilderment, for the episode of her examination and temporary custody of the photograph was unknown to him, and just so surely her first impulse had been to render that lady as uncomfortable as possible. But, with her usual swift sagacity, she had, with an eye single to her own cunning tactics, quite changed her base of action, and, with admirable finesse, proceeded at once to make a friend of the baroness, through her charming frankness and unsophisticated confidences. The steady, unflinching eye of Morning, therefore, while trained as the eagle's to catch the fiercest rays of the noonday sun, could no more follow the erratic and elusive movements of the elfish fancy of this fascinating woman than the eye of his horse could follow the flash of a meteor.

"Come, señora," said Murella to the baroness a moment later, "I know the ting you was ask a me, how long time I know Señor Morning lofe a you."

The baroness knew that she had not meant to ask any such question, but rather how long the señorita had known Mr. Morning. But she had scarcely opened her lips when Murella talked on.

"You tink I no know lof when a I see a? Eh! what that on his face when he a tak a your hand for make a me know you Baroness Von Eulaw? Eh? what you call proud, courage, lof, beautiful life!" and her flashing eyes burned like stars in heaven's night.

Strange caprice! the track was cold over which she had set out to run the race for a life, and many a prize had been won and thrown away since then, and now she was burning with the wish that her rival should gain that which she had lost. Was it magnanimity, or was it a natural-born desire to defraud some man of his marital rights, and give some woman a victory?

"Now we will go to the Morning room so I call a;" and together they walked over the exquisite mosaic floors, and halls of parquetry, and stairway glittering as the sun, and figures of classic art looked down, and fold on fold of hues of soft-blent shadows dropped from tinted panes and fell around them. In apparently the most casual way they passed a studio filled with light and color, where, in violet velvet blouse, and cap upon his poetic locks, worked and smoked the master of Italian art.

"This is my parteekler fren—the Baroness Von Eulaw, Señor Fillipo," and they hurried on.

Arrived at the suite, they first entered the dressing room. It was plainly finished in French gray, with gold and blue enamel, the same colors repeated in drapery and cushions. But one piece attracted particular attention. It was an alabaster fountain, the elaborate accessories half concealing a full-sized bust of Morning, the identity of which could not be mistaken. It was exquisitely chiseled, and falling jets, and icy foam, and cascades like cobwebs, built up masses of soft, misty whiteness, shutting back all save an incidental glimpse of outline, and thickening by contrast the boldness of the water plants at the base.

"A very pretty conceit," said the baroness, approvingly. "Who is the designer?"

"Me," said the señorita, coldly, leading the way to the main chamber, to which apartment Murella carried the key. Unlocking the door, the baroness had scarcely time to take in the mute, indescribable effects of the auroral tints on the walls, stippled and faded into thinnest ether, with its golden sky overspread with winged cherubs in high relief, laid in tints such as are only painted on angels, when the baron's party were heard approaching. One thing, however, had struck the baroness, even at a cursory glance. The dust lay thick and undisturbed over all the furniture of the room. A superb curtain of corn-colored brocade hung over one end of the apartment, which also showed signs of not having been disturbed at least for a term of many months. A gesture of impatience was made by Murella as she spoke, in an irascible tone of voice, " What for a he bring a they here?"

However, the party, following their guide, entered, expressing surprise at finding the ladies had preceded them.

The baron at once walked over and engaged their pretty hostess in conversation, laughing genuinely at her piquant expressions and unworldly-wise ways, while Morning talked about some irrelevant thing with Miss Winters, and the rest of the company sauntered to the remoter quarters of the apartments. Mrs. Thornton, however, coveted a view behind the maize curtain, and to this end plied the major-domo with such blandishments as were at her command, and using vigorously the little Spanish she possessed. The Spaniard turned to look for the señorita—she had momentarily disappeared with the baron—and he flung aside the fatal curtain.

There, in a regal frame, in a painting by the famous hand of Prince Fillipo Colonna, master of arts in the Royal Academy at Rome, appeared two full-sized figures. They were those of David Morning and Señorita Gonzales. It was an interior of an adobe house. The saints upon the mud walls, with rosaries suspended beneath them, and the crude decorations about the fireplace, with the hammocks in the shadow were dimly visible. Light came in through a low window, and fell upon the white face of Morning, just tinged with returning health. One hand held suspended a pencil, while with the other, just discernible from out the shadows, he clasped the girlish figure of Murella Gonzales.

It was a master work of art, and more than condoned all malicious or vain intent on the part of the author. The expression upon Morning's face was one of placid amusement, while that upon the girl's was anxious and arch, questioning and trusting, open, yet elusive, like the mimosa growing sturdily from the potted earth in the rude casement, which receded at a sound of the human voice. The noble artist had evidently caught an inspiration from the local color— filtrated through the hot brain of the lovely señorita— and had touched the face of Morning with the light of his lovely companion.

Mr. Morning had just crossed over to catch a word with the baroness when the tableau was unveiled. Her whitening face frightened him, and he looked quickly over her shoulder at the picture. At the same moment a piercing shriek, and Señorita Murella rushed wildly down the room.

"*Madre de Dios!*" she yelled. "What a you do that a for?" and she menaced the poor Spaniard with her small fist.

"It was I, it was I," pleaded Mrs. Thornton. "Don't blame him." But Murella turned from her with high scorn.

"Fool, I will kill a him," she shrieked, again turning to the place where the man had stood.

But Señor Don Manuel Jose Maria Ignacio Cervantes Alvarado, knowing something of the temper of

his niece, had attended not upon the order of his going, but slipped away, and in his place stood Morning.   For one brief moment Murella looked at him,
then, drawing a pearl-handled stiletto from beneath
her girdle, she gashed and stabbed the unconscious
canvas in twice a dozen places, crying all the time,
"Take a that, and a that, and a that!"

Morning thought that his time had come, but he
manfully stood his ground, secretly smiling at the
bloodless assassination, until, exhausted, Murella fell
upon the carpet in a genuine hysterical rage.   After
a moment he lifted her to her feet, placed her hand
within his arm, and led her unresistingly from the
room.

An hour later she stood at the boathouse, leaning
upon the arm of Prince Fillipo, and gayly waving an
adieu to the party, Morning among them; then, with
the artist's arm about her waist, they slowly returned
up the terrace steps, while the decorated steamer
went out of sight around the cove.

And the Baroness Von Eulaw guessed now who it
was that had made the pin holes in her eyes.

CHAPTER XXV.

" No more shall nation against nation rise."

THE Congress of 1892 builded even better than it knew, when it dropped partisan prejudices, and arose superior to local fetterings, and, in a truly national spirit, secured for the United States of America dominion of the seas and control of the commerce of the world.

The Act of Congress which guaranteed the payment of five per cent bonds of the Nicaragua Canal Company to the extent of $100,000,000, and which provided that the canal tolls upon American ships should never be more than two-thirds the amount charged the vessels of other nations, enabled the company to construct the canal with unexpected rapidity, without calling upon the United States for a dollar of the guaranty, while, more than any subsidy or favorable mail contract, it aided to place the Stars and Stripes at the mastheads of the vast fleet of ships and steamers which, upon the completion of the canal in the autumn of 1895, began to pass between the Atlantic and the Pacific.

The local traffic developed by the canal proved something phenomenal. Early in the history of its construction it became generally known that the country, for hundreds of miles about Lake Nicaragua, was not an unhealthy tropical jungle, but an elevated, breezy table-land, environed and divided by snow-clad mountains, with an average temperature only a few degrees warmer than that of California, and with a much more even distribution of rainfall.

A knowledge of these advantages was followed by a large incursion of American settlers. There is perhaps no product of field or forest more profitable than the coffee plant. Steadily the demand for the fragrant berry is upon the increase, while, beside having few enemies in the insect world, the area within which coffee can be advantageously grown is very limited. While the coffee plant does not require an exceptionally hot climate, it will not thrive where frost is a possibility. The hill slopes,and table-lands of Nicaragua were found to be peculiarly adapted for its growth, and thousands of acres of young plantations were already thriving where for centuries only wild grasses had waved. Short lines of railroad, centering on Lake Nicaragua, and running in every.direction, had made accessible a large extent of country. The scream of the gang saw was heard amid forests of dyewoods, rosewood, and mahogany. Mines of gold, silver, copper, iron. and coal were opened. Cotton, sugar, and indigo plantations were developed, and Millerville, on Lake Nicaragua, when the war ships passed through the canal to attend David Morning's dynamic exposition, was already a city of fifty thousand people, provided with electric lights and cable roads.

The advantages to the people of the United States of the completed Nicaragua Ship Canal were almost incalculable. The freight-carrying business of the world between the east coast of Asia and Europe was rapidly transferred to American bottoms. The iron manufacturers of Tennessee, Alabama, and Georgia were given an opportunity, previously denied them, of marketing the product of their furnaces and foundries on the Pacific Coast of North America. The dwellers in the Mississippi Valley could now send their cotton, meats, and manufactures to trans-Pacific and Antipodean markets, and California redwood and Puget Sound fir and cedar lumber could be sent over all the Northwest.

On the Pacific Coast the canal added twenty-five per cent to the productive value of every acre of grain and timber land. The cost of sacking, and half the cost of transporting wheat was saved to the farmer, and the freight upon all machinery and heavy goods brought from the East was greatly lessened.

On Puget Sound the construction of a ship canal, costing less than $2,000,000, connecting the fresh waters of Lake Washington with the salt water in Elliott Bay, gave to Seattle such facilities for warehousing, loading, and dry-docking, and such independence of tides and teredos, that a commercial rival of San Francisco was spreading over the hills of the fir-fringed Queen of the New Mediterranean, while at the extreme southwestern corner of the republic, the city of bay and climate—San Diego—was rapidly regaining the population and prestige which temporarily slipped from her grasp at the subsiding of the boom which, during 1886 and 1887, enkindled the imagination, and beguiled the judgment, and encrazed with the fever of speculation, the people of Southern California.

Even during the dull times which annihilated so many promising fortunes in Southern California, the attractions of Coronado Beach were sufficient to secure for it exemption from the dire distress which overtook other localities.

The company owning this enterprise successfully defied not only a bursted boom but the very forces of nature, for they riprapped the beach in front of their hotel, and baffled the Pacific Ocean, which, after gnawing up the lawn and shrubbery which fronted its restless waters, had set its foam-capped legions at work to undermine the foundations of the great ballroom.

Parks, avenues, and streets were improved, museums and gardens developed, and races and hops and fishing and boating parties encouraged. Excursions from neighboring cities were organized, the East was flooded with pamphlets praising Coronado, and the pleasure-loving and health-seeking world was in every way reminded that in this land of rare delights it could pick ripe oranges and enjoy surf bathing in midwinter, while Boston was shivering and New York swept with blizzards.

The band at the hotel was kept playing every day at luncheon and dinner, and it discoursed sweet music in the ballroom regularly upon hop nights to auditors, who found—as all people can find—more of the physical comforts and delights of life at Coronado Beach than anywhere else in the world, for nowhere else is there such music in the sea, such balm in the air, such sunshine, and fragrance, and healing, and rest.

The faith and patience of the owner of the great hotel were, in the end, rewarded. Month by month and year by year did the numbers of his guests increase, until, in 1895, the capacity of the house was more than doubled, by the addition of a building something over a quarter of a mile in length, and the great hotel could now accommodate quite two thousand guests.

David Morning selected Coronado Beach for his dynamic experiments, and, with some difficulty, chartered the entire hotel for one month, during which time it was reserved exclusively for his guests. He also leased the northerly end of the Coronado Beach peninsula for the construction and equipment of his air ship, and for a laboratory for the manufacture of potentite.

The real Coronado Islands are within the territorial jurisdiction of Mexico, situated about sixteen miles south and west from San Diego Bay, and were, except in cloudy weather, distinctly visible from Coronado Beach. Irregular and ragged masses of red sandstone a few thousand acres in extent towered to a height of several hundred feet above the ocean, faintly staining the horizon with patches of blue, resembling an unfinished sky in water color.

These islands were destitute of water and vegetation, and never inhabited save by a few laborers who were engaged in quarrying rock there, and Morning found no difficulty in purchasing them from their owners, and removing all the occupants.

On the northern end of the Coronado Beach peninsula, Morning caused to be erected a laboratory for the manufacture of potentite, with which to load the steel shells to be carried by the air ship. This new dynamic force, or, rather, storehouse of force, consisted of a combination of explosive gelatine with fulminate of mercury, and possessed a power equal to thirteen hundred tons to the square inch, or sixty times that of common blasting gunpowder, and nine times that of dynamite, and fifty pounds of it properly directed would sink any ironclad afloat. It is quite safe for manipulation, because it is unexplosive, except when brought in contact with a chemical substance—also non-explosive except by contact—which is only added immediately before using.

The *Petrel*, the air ship used at the dynamic exposition, was built by the Mount Carmel Aeronautic Company at their works in Chicago, and sent by rail in sections to Coronado Beach, where she was put together. She was cigar-shaped, one hundred feet in length and twenty feet in diameter, and was built of butternut—the toughest of the light woods. Her engines, with their fans and propellers, as well as the gas generator and tank for benzine, were all constructed of tempered aluminum, made by the new Kentucky process, at a cost of only eight cents per pound. Being stronger and tougher than the finest steel, and only one-third the weight of that metal, aluminum was especially adapted for the construction of air ships.

The machinery of the *Petrel* was propelled by a gas generated from benzine. The fluid was carried in an air-tight aluminum tank, from which it passed, drop by drop, to the generator. This gas, almost as powerful as the vibratory ether discovered by Mr.

Keely, was much safer because more certainly controlled.

The *Petrel*, with all her machinery in place, with two tons of benzine in her tanks, and ten men on board of her supplied with sufficient water and food for use for fifteen days, weighed but ten tons, and the force generated from two tons of benzine was sufficient to lift her, with a freight of ten tons more, to a height of five thousand or even ten thousand feet, and, without any aid from her folding aluminum parachute, was able to maintain her there for a fortnight, at a speed—in a still atmosphere—of fifty miles per hour. No balloon was attached to the *Petrel*, as she relied entirely upon her paddles and wings both for propulsion and as a means of maintaining herself in the air.

She was constructed upon the principle of aerial navigation furnished by the wild goose. That bird maintains himself in the ether during a flight of hundreds of miles without a rest, simply because his strength, or muscular power, is greater, in proportion to his weight, than that of creatures who walk upon the ground. Man could always have constructed wings of silk and bamboo which would have enabled him to fly if he had only possessed the strength to flap his wings.

Aerial navigation never presented any other problem than that of procuring power without weight. Once able to obtain the power of a ten-horse engine, with a weight, including machinery, of less than one ton, one might fly all over the world, and, by taking advantage of the air currents, a knowledge of which will soon be gained, fly at a speed of fifty or even one hundred miles an hour. The recent discovery of the immense power of a gas which it is possible to generate from benzine without the use of fuel, has made the air as available for the purposes of rapid transit by man as the ocean or the land. The great cost of locomotion by this means will doubtless prevent its use for the transportation of freight, or, indeed, of passengers, except for those who can afford the luxury, and for them it will supplant all other methods.

The *Petrel* was provided with the new patent condensed fuel, one pound of which for cooking and heating purposes is equal to ten pounds of coal. She was furnished with parachutes made of thin sheets of aluminum closely folded one above the other. These, when not in use, formed an awning or canopy over her deck, while, in case of accident, they could, by pulling a convenient lever, be instantly spread over an area large enough to insure her a gradual and safe descent, and should such descent be into the water, she was so constructed as to float as buoyantly as a cork upon its surface, while, by lessening the number of revolutions per minute of her aluminum propellers, they could be used as paddles for her propulsion through the water.

The freight of the *Petrel* consisted of two hundred shells of potentite, weighing one hundred pounds each, and the result to the Coronodo Islands of their falling upon it from a height of a mile or more, was predicted long in advance of the experiment. "If," it was said, "fifty pounds of this explosive will destroy an ironclad, what will twenty thousand pounds of it

do to an island of rock?   What would a dozen *Petrels*
accomplish, hurling two hundred and forty thousand
pounds of it upon an army, a city. or an enemy's
fortress?"

They could level Gibraltar with the sea; they could
extirpate an army of a million men; they could oblit-
erate London or Berlin or New York from the face of
the earth.   A fleet of a hundred *Petrels* could ascend
from New York, cross the Atlantic in three days, destroy every city in the United Kingdom in six hours,
and, leaving England a mass of ruins, with two-thirds
of her people slain, return in three days to New York,
with unused power enough to go to San Francisco
and back without descending.

England, or any other nation, could likewise destroy America, for neither aerial navigation nor the
manufacture of potentite are secrets locked in any
one man's brain.

"If Mr. Morning's dynamic exposition," it was
said, "shall fulfill its promise, he can, if he chooses,
as the possessor of so complete an air ship and so
powerful an explosive, be the ruler of the world.
Emperors and Parliaments must, for the time, be the
subjects of the man who can destroy cities and camps,
and who can make such changes in the map of the
world as he may choose."

"If the experiment this day to be made at Coronado," said the President of the United States, "shall
be successful, armies may as well be disbanded, for
there can be no more war, and governments all over
the world must, henceforth, rest upon the consent of
the governed."

Before sending the *Petrel* upon her mission, an examination of the territory to be devastated was in order, and the Hotel del Coronado was nearly emptied of its guests, for the *Charleston*, the *Warspite*, and the *Wilhelm II.*, steamed away to the Coronado Islands, where the American, British, German, French, Russian, Italian, Mexican, and Brazilian engineers, with their assistants, landed, took measurements and altitudes, and a number of photographic views, and examined the islands thoroughly, verifying the accuracy of the topographical maps and profile models in clay previously made by engineers employed by Morning. It was projected to make another survey and set of maps after the potentite had done its work, so as to preserve an accurate and unimpeachable record of the result of what our hero modestly called his "experiment."

The vessels returned to their moorings about three o'clock in the afternoon of the first day of the exposition, in ample time for their passengers and officers to attend the dinner given by Morning that evening to his royal and imperial majesty Edward the Seventh, king of Great Britain and emperor of India. This sagacious prince, rightly conceiving that the dynamic exposition of citizen David Morning was likely to be the preliminary of an entire change in the methods of government, if not in the governments themselves, of the civilized world, determined to head in person the British delegation, which was brought on the *Warspite* from Vancouver to San Diego.

The manner in which King Edward has impressed the American people may be deduced from a remark made at the dinner by a shrewd observer and leading citizen of San Diego.

"That king," said he, "is a dandy. He is credited with being the cleverest and most adroit politician in England, and I believe it, or he could never have steered his canoe out of that baccarat whirlpool. If Dave Morning's dynamics should sort of blow him out of a job at home, let him come over here, and in one year I will back him at long odds to get the nomination for the best office in the county from either the Democratic or Republican convention, and, maybe, from both. What a roaring team he and Jack Dodge and Sam Davis would make for a county canvass! Jack to do the fiddling and dancing, Sam the all-around lying, and Edward the hand shaking and the setting 'em up for the boys!"

The ample gardens of San Diego, San Bernardino, Los Angeles, and Santa Barbara were stripped for the decoration of the banquet hall. All day flowers were arriving by the train load, and several hundred floral artists were at work in the great dining room. The effect was surpassingly beautiful. Suspended from the great dome by ropes of smilax was a gigantic figure of Peace, wrought in white calla lilies, bearing in her right hand a branch from an olive tree, while her left held to her lips a trumpet of yellow jasmine. On the walls the arms of all nations were wrought in camellias, carnations, fleur-de-lis, and roses of every hue. The music and the menu were both incomparable, and, in accordance with the later and better practice of great dinners, formal speech making was altogether dispensed with.

The next morning the shores of Coronado Beach were black with people, and in the great hotel every piazza and window facing southward or westward was occupied. There was a light breeze blowing from the north as the *Petrel* left her berth and rapidly mounted in the air to a height of seven thousand feet, which altitude she achieved with her fans in seven minutes' time. She then put her propellers in motion and was soon a mere speck against the cloudless sky, scarcely discernible by the most powerful glasses.

But though out of sight she soon made her existence and her work known to the multitude. In thirty-five minutes from the time she left her berth, she had compassed a mile and a half in height and sixteen miles of distance and was hovering over Coronado Islands. In twenty minutes more six men on board of her had thrown over the two hundred potentite shells, and in half an hour thereafter the aerial wonder was again resting quietly on the peninsula.

It was a clear day, and the islands were distinctly visible. Sight travels more swiftly than sound, and before any noise was heard, the immense mass of rock, crown shaped, from which the islands take their name, was seen by the gazers on the beach to leap from its place and fall into the sea. Other masses in swift succession followed; then came roars of sound, as if heaven and earth were coming together; roars of sound which rattled the doors and casements of the hotel as if shaken with a high wind. For twenty minutes this awe-inspiring exhibition continued, and when the tremendous cannonading ceased, the Coronada Islands—in the form in which they had previously existed—were no more.

The work of resurveying and making new topographical maps was subsequently performed, as a part of the duty of those connected with the dynamic exposition, but it needed no measurements to demonstrate the awful power of the potentite. An area of solid rock a mile square was rent into fragments for a depth of one hundred feet.

Many improvements in machinery and management were suggested to the officers of the *Petrel*, but the experiment was conceded by all the great engineers who witnessed it, to be so completely successful as to practically eliminate land warfare from the future of nations.

"It is fortunate," said the Marquis of Salisbury, who was one of the British delegation—"it is fortunate that the manufacture of even a small quantity of potentite requires months of time, great skill, and a costly and extensive laboratory, so that it will be not impracticable to prevent its preparation by private persons. But given a piece of land anywhere in the civilized world large enough to permit of the building of air ships and the manufacture of potentite, and sufficiently defended to afford to its garrison three months' time in which to perfect the making of that explosive, and any power, however insignificant, could, with a hundred air ships, destroy in three days all the great cities in Europe."

"As it now appears," continued the Marquis, "this method of warfare would not be so available against a moving object on the sea, such as a war ship. But if the submarine torpedo boat, whose operations we are to witness to-morrow, shall be anything nearly as effective as Mr. Morning's air ship, it seems to me that a convention of civilized powers to adjust international relations and provide for a Congress and Court of Nations, to which all international differences must be submitted, will be an absolute necessity in the future."

"And how would the decrees of such a court be enforced, your lordship," inquired Prince Bismarck, who was listening.

"By the only aerial war vessels equipped with potentite which the allied nations would suffer to exist, your highness, and which vessels would be subject to the orders of the Court of Nations. If any nation refused to obey such decree, it could be disciplined, and if any nation attempted to put a potentite air ship under way, it would be necessary, in self-defense, for the allied powers, after adequate warning, to extirpate the offending parties."

"Might not a potentite air ship be secretly fitted out, your lordship?" asked the prince.

"Hardly," replied the Marquis, "for, with the aid of a corps of observation air ships, and of international detectives in every center of population, the world, both savage and civilized, could be adequately policed at a very small cost."

"And what, in your lordship's opinion, will be the condition in or before the Congress of Nations, of a people who desire separate government and who have been unable to obtain it?" said Mr. Michael Davitt, who was standing by.

The Marquis looked the Irishman squarely in the eye and replied slowly: "I think it will be quite out of the power of any government to retain by force under its rule any considerable number of people, who, with or without a grievance, are practically unanimous for a separate government. The Congress of Nations will, or at least ought to, require that any people seeking separation shall be nearly unanimous. But do you think, Mr. Davitt, to be candid, that the people of Ulster and the people of Galway would ever be brought to agree to any proposition on earth?"

"Begorra, your lordship, if you don't mind me takin' the answer to your question out of the mouth of Misther Davitt," said the Honorable Bellew McCafferty, Home Rule member from Mayo—"begorra, there's one great principle upon which Oireland is, and ever will be, united.   Catholic and Protestant, Far-downer and Corkonian, Priest and Peeler are all heart and soul agreed"—

"To do what?" queried his lordship.

"Never," replied the McCafferty, "never to pay any rint."

CHAPTER XXVI.

"'Tis less to conquer than to make wars cease."

THE *Siva* steamed out of San Diego harbor at nine o'clock on an April morning in the year 1896, carrying as passengers the naval and ordnance officers commissioned by the various European and American governments to examine and report upon the result of the dynamic exposition. The civil and diplomatic representatives were apportioned among the different members of the fleet, which had gathered from the Pacific squadrons of every naval power in the world, and was now lying in San Diego Bay. The success of the air ship the day before in almost obliterating the Coronado Islands, filled every mind with eager anticipation of the results likely to be achieved by the torpedo boats, and there was an especial pressure for places on board the *Siva*, which carried the novel engines of destruction.

The *Siva* had been built at the Union Iron Works in San Francisco, from plans and models furnished by engineers employed by Morning, and no expense had been spared to make her the largest, swiftest, and best-appointed war vessel afloat. Indeed, every other consideration had been sacrificed to speed, and, as a result, a ship was constructed of ten thousand tons' burden, drawing but twenty-one feet of water when fully

(338)

loaded, and able, when under a full head of steam, to make twenty-six knots an hour. Relying upon her speed to keep out of range of the guns of an enemy, and intended rather for a carrier of torpedo boats than a war vessel, she was, for her size, neither heavily armed nor heavily armored, yet she was covered with steel plates of sufficient thickness to resist the largest ordnance, and she was equipped with rifled cannon and pneumatic dynamite guns, equal in size and range to any constructed. Her cost was $8,000,000, and it was Morning's avowed intention to present her to the alliance of nations which he expected would result from the dynamic exposition. The *Siva* rode the seas like a gull, and was as graceful and beautiful as a swan.

Forward of her engines the hull of the vessel was devoted to accommodations for housing, launching, and rehousing the two torpedo boats, the *Etna* and *Stromboli*. Each of these was cigar-shaped, one hundred feet in length and twenty feet in diameter. They were built of steel, with an inner and outer shell. The admission of water between these shells would cause the submersion of the boat to any depth required for the purposes of destroying an enemy, while by the expulsion of water they were enabled to ascend to the surface. In the inner shell was an electric engine, with sufficient power stored in its dynamos to propel the boat under water at a speed of twenty-five miles an hour for a period of five hours. Enough compressed air was stored in steel tanks to supply the needs of ten men for eight hours, and the *Etna* had, on several occasions, as a test, remained submerged with her crew for four hours without coming to the surface.

The construction of torpedo boats for harbor defense was no longer a novelty, but this was the first attempt made to demonstrate that a submarine torpedo vessel could be used on the high seas to overtake and destroy a flying enemy. The *Etna* and the *Stromboli* each carried one hundred shells, each shell being loaded with five hundred pounds of potentite. Chain cradles for holding these shells were suspended to huge fans of finely-tempered steel, shaped like pincers, and the machinery for fastening one or more of these cradles to the bottom of the vessel it was intended to destroy was both simple and ingenious, as were the arrangements for exploding them when fastened. A fuse or wire attached to a steamer running away at the rate of a mile in three minutes would have been impracticable, and the inventor had therefore arranged a time or clockwork cap, which could be set to explode at any given number of minutes from the time the shell should be fastened.

The *Siva*, containing Mr. Morning, the foreign engineers, and the ordnance officers of the American Navy detailed for the service, left her moorings at nine o'clock and steamed down the bay, followed by the *Warspite*, flying the British flag, the French corvette *Garronne*, the Russian frigate *Tsar*, the Italian ironclad *Victor Emanuel*, the Spanish ship *Pizarro*, the Chilean man-of-war *Cero del Pasco*, the Swedish sloop-of-war *Berdanotte*, the American iron batteries *Charleston* and *San Francisco*, and the great German steel war ship *Wilhelm II.* It was intended that this latter vessel should follow the *Warspite*, but there was some delay in getting her under way, and she was the last in the naval procession, being followed only by the *Esmeralda*—the vessel to be destroyed.

At the termination of the Chilean insurrection it was found that the *Esmeralda*—the war ship controlled by the insurgents—was, though not unseaworthy, yet too badly damaged by a contest with gunboats to be serviceable for the purposes for which she was constructed, and she was, therefore, sold by the Chilean Government to Mr. Morning for $1,000,000—something less than one-third her cost.

He purchased her for use as a transport in connection with the construction of the Nicaragua Canal, in which he was interested, and he now devoted her to destruction, as a test of the power of the new explosive, and the efficiency of the submarine torpedo boats.

The *Esmeralda* was an ironclad steamer of the largest size, capable of a speed of twenty miles an hour. She was armored with steel plates, and in every way staunch. On this occasion she carried only sufficient force to navigate her, and she towed a large steam launch, into which her crew would be transferred and conveyed to a place of safety so soon as the torpedoes should be fastened to her. Two life-boats were also swung, ready for launching in case of accident.

Baron Von Eulaw had been indulging the previous night in deep potations, and was, consequently, so belated that the carriage containing the baroness and himself did not reach the Coronado wharf until the

Siva had steamed away, and was being followed by the other vessels in the order described. The launches and small steamers, with the guests apportioned among the different vessels of the fleet, had also left the wharf, and two-thirds of the vessels which were to accompany the *Siva*, with their steam up and whistles blowing, were impatiently awaiting the signal to move, and were uneasily churning into a foam the placid waters of the harbor.

Hastily summoning a boat lying at the wharf, the baron escorted the baroness on board, and, seating himself beside her, directed the crew to row for "that ship," pointing to the *Esmeralda*. It will never be known whether this direction was the result of accident or design, for the *Esmeralda*, in size and general appearance, strongly resembled the *Wilhelm II.*, which was anchored just ahead of her in the stream, and it was the *Wilhelm II.* to which the Baron Von Eulaw, as one of the representatives of the German Empire, had been assigned.

Arrived at the *Esmeralda*, however, the anchor of which was then being hoisted, the baron was politely informed by the officer in charge of the deck that no arrangements had been made to receive guests on board the vessel, as she was destined to destruction. The baron, with real or affected dismay, remarked that the *Wilhelm II.* was already under way; that it would be impossible for him now to gain her deck, and, unless permitted to board the *Esmeralda*, and remain upon her, they would lose altogether the great spectacle they had, by designation of his imperial majesty Wilhelm II., come all the way from Berlin to San Diego to attend.

He would be in lasting disgrace at home if compelled to admit that, through his own negligence and error, he had not witnessed the destruction of the *Esmeralda* at all. Might not the baroness and himself, under the circumstances, be suffered to trespass upon the hospitalities of the officers of the *Esmeralda* until the time came for abandoning the vessel, when they could join the officers and crew on the steam launch, and be placed on board the *Wilhelm II.*, or one of the other vessels of the fleet, or return on the launch to San Diego, as might be most convenient?

With some hesitation, the deck officer of the *Esmeralda*, after brief consultation with his superior, consented to the request of Von Eulaw, and, apologizing for the condition of the cabin, which, in anticipation of the destruction of the vessel, had been stripped of everything save the standing furniture and a few chairs, he invited them to make themselves as comfortable as circumstances would permit.

With salvos of cannon and music of bands, the gaily-decked fleet sped out to sea. Through the narrow channel they steamed, past Point Loma, with brow of purple and feet of foam. When they reached the open sea, they spread out in line abreast, the *Siva* taking a position on the extreme north, and slackening her speed a little so as to accommodate it to that of her companions.

Arrived at the scene of the proposed experiment, sixteen miles west of San Diego bar, the speed of all the vessels was slackened so as to afford only steerage way, and the *Esmeralda* was signaled to leave her position next the *Siva*, and steam away at full speed to the north. Simultaneously with this order, the hatches on the *Siva* were opened, chains and ropes tightened, the vast power of the engines applied, and the *Stromboli*, with her crew and cargo in place, was lifted from the hold of the *Siva*, swung over the side, and launched in the ocean.

It was four minutes from the time the whistle sounded until the launch of the *Stromboli*, and in the meantime the *Esmeralda* steamed quite one mile away. The *Siva* was a few hundred yards ahead of the other vessels, and the *Stromboli* was launched form her port side, so that the launch was witnessed by those who thronged the starboard side of the other vessels. The entire fleet then resumed its former rate of speed, and the distance between it and the *Esmeralda* was soon placed at one mile, at which it was subsequently maintained.

The *Stromboli* glided away for a minute on the surface of the sea, and then, admitting water to the space between her steel shells, rapidly sank to a depth of forty feet. The *Esmeralda* was still at full speed, and making twenty knots an hour, but the *Stromboli* was pushing her way under the sea, propelled by her powerful electric engines, at the rate of twenty-five knots an hour, and in fifteen minutes had overtaken the doomed vessel, and was preparing to make fast the torpedo which should destroy her.

One pair of great steel claws, holding a chain basket containing five hundred pounds of potentite set by clockwork to explode in sixty minutes, was, by the power of the electric engine, raised above the cigar-shaped steel monster gliding through the cool, quiet waters, and driven through the plates of the *Esmeralda*, just forward of the stern of that vessel. A second was placed amidship, and a third near the bow.

The upper deck of the *Stromboli* had a dozen plate-glass openings, through which a number of powerful electric lights illuminated the depths of the ocean, and enabled the men in charge of the machinery to direct with accuracy the work of fastening the torpedoes. If it had been necessary, men in submarine armor, fastened to steel arms projected from the *Stromboli*, and supplied with air through rubber tubes, could have been placed at work on the bottom of the *Esmeralda*, and maintained there for hours, even while she was coursing through the seas. But it was not necessary to invoke this process, for, by the aid of the ordinary machinery of the *Stromboli*, the three great shells were fastened in twenty minutes' time, and the *Esmeralda* was proceeding on her journey with fifteen hundred pounds of potentite fastened to her keel. The officers and crew of the *Esmeralda* all subsequently testified that this work was performed noiselessly and without jar, or any evidence that it was going forward.

But had they possessed all knowledge, they could not have prevented it. No rate of speed possible to the doomed vessel would have enabled her to outrun the speedier submarine torpedo boat, and no machinery or appliance could have reached her under the keel of the *Esmeralda*, or prevented her work, and once the potentite shells were in place, it was beyond the power of man to remove them, and no human skill could prevent the explosion taking place at the appointed time.

The introduction of this deadly force into naval warfare was not intended to be unaccompanied with some merciful provisions for preventing unnecessary destruction of human life, and a code of signals had been prepared for all naval powers, to be used whenever a vessel was to be destroyed.

The *Stromboli*, having performed her duty, glided from under the keel of the *Esmeralda*, and, at a distance of a few hundred yards, shot up a signal pipe above the surface of the ocean, and with her electric whistle shrieked through it a succession of signals that were heard by the multitude upon the fleet a mile away.

"Submarine torpedo boat has been underneath your keel," said one short shriek, and one more prolonged.

"Fifteen hundred pounds of the most powerful explosive known to science are fastened to you," said fifteen short shrieks.

"Make ready to count your minutes of life," said one long and two short shrieks.

"In thirty-six minutes your ship will be hurled in fragments into the air," said thirty-six short shrieks.

"Leave your ship to her inevitable fate. Launch your boats and save your lives. Your enemy will pick you up and receive your honorable surrender," said one shriek, continued for five minutes.

Standing on the deck of the *Warspite*, King Edward the Seventh looked at his watch. If in thirty-six minutes the *Esmeralda* should sink beneath the waves, the navies of England, with those of all other powers, would be as obsolete for the purposes of attack or defense upon the high seas as the galleys of Cæsar, or the barge of Cleopatra. Another Trafalgar would be as impossible as another Actium. The little *Stromboli* and *Etna*, carried in the hold of the *Siva*, could destroy every ironclad afloat. The latter vessel, with her immense speed, could keep out of range of the enemy's guns, and she could send forth the torpedo boats and destroy ship after ship. She could pick up the torpedo boats, recharge their storage batteries, refit their magazines with potentite shells, and their tanks with compressed air, and send them forth again and proceed with such work of destruction until not a ship should live on any sea, except by license of the *Siva*, and subject to her rule.

What revolutions and what changes would this dynamic exposition not precipitate upon the mistress of the seas? India would give her new emperor the choice between walking out and being potentited out, and Canada, and Australia, and every other colony, would be taking leave. And Ireland—well, here was a state of things! Ireland would have whatever Davitt, and McCarthy, and Dillon should agree upon asking, or else every British war ship would be blown up, and every Irishman who could raise the money, would try the effect of a balloon loaded with potentite, upon his friends across the channel. Of course, it was a game in which one could give blows as well as take them, but that is a very unequal game between an anarchist and a king. It looked as if King Edward might be compelled to "rustle" to keep the

British crown on his royal brow. It might be well to look up a good cattle range in Colorado where he and nephew William, with the Hapsburgs, the Bourbons, and the Romanoffs might retire, should it be necessary.

Among the stores of the *Esmeralda* which had not been sent ashore was a decanter of brandy, which the baron found in the cabin, and to which he devoted himself so assiduously that when the whistles sounded, announcing that the torpedoes were fastened to the ship, he was, from the combined effects of past and present potations, in a condition closely bordering upon delirium tremens.

The first officer proceeded to the cabin, where Von Eulaw and the baroness had withdrawn, and, attempting to open the door, found it locked. The voice of the baroness in a pleading tone was heard, followed by oaths and maniacal laughter from the baron.

"The torpedoes are fastened to us, and in thirty-four minutes this ship will be in the air," said the officer through the closed door. "Our orders are to leave the vessel ten minutes before the explosion. You had better go on board of the launch at once."

"Is that so?" yelled the baron. "Well, we will go into the air along with the ship, my American wife and myself. My estates are all gone. The Queen of Diamonds has seized them and given them to the Jack of Spades. This earth has nothing more for me, and we will take now a trip to the stars above."

The officer comprehended the situation in an instant. "He has the jimjams, sure enough," he muttered. "Best way is to humor him. "All right, baron," said he, in a conciliatory tone. "But you don't want your wife to go with you, you know. Open the door and let her come with us."

"Ah, no!" said the maniac. "The Baroness Von Eulaw will go to heaven along with her dear husband, that she loves so much, so much!"

"Madam," said the officer, "can you not unlock the door? If not, I will have it broken down."

"No," shrieked the baron, "she cannot unlock the door, for I have thrown the key into the sea through the window, and if anybody makes any trouble with the door, I have a little pistol, and I will shoot first my beloved American wife, and then the man at the door, and at last myself, and we will all go to the skies in one trip."

"Madame," said the officer, "is he armed?"

"He is, and will, I fear, do as he threatens," replied Ellen, with trembling voice.

"The situation is serious," said the officer. "The torpedoes won't wait for us, and the crew will be getting nervous. In fact, I am nervous myself," added the officer, *sotto voce*. "Suppose one of those infernal machines should go off ahead of time?"

"Leave us, sir," said the baroness. "If I can get the pistol from him by persuasion, I will discharge it as a signal, and you can then break down the door. If I cannot do this, you must save yourselves without us. It would be useless for you to jeopardize your lives for us, for he will surely kill me, and will probably shoot you if you attempt to force the door now."

"What is the matter there aft, Mr. Morton?" shouted the captain.

"Dutch baron crazy drunk, sir. Has locked the door, and swears he will be blown up with the ship. Has a pistol, and will kill his wife if we try to force the door, sir."

"Get a rifle, Mr. Morton, and stand ready to shoot him through the skylight. But I will first signal the *Siva* for orders."

"*Aye*, aye, sir," said the first officer cheerily.

"Something wrong on board the *Esmeralda*, sir; she is signaling us," said the first officer of the *Siva* to the captain.

Morning, who was conversing with a Russian admiral, overheard the speaker and came forward to where the signal officer—the code spread before him—had just answered, "Ready to receive signal."

The little scarlet flag in the hand of the signal officer on the foretop gallant yard of the *Esmeralda* rapidly spelled out the message.

"Baron Von Eulaw and wife came on board as we were starting. He has delirium tremens, and is locked in cabin with her. Refuses to board launch, and threatens to shoot her if we break down door. We can kill him with a rifle through the skylight. We wait orders."

The face of David Morning was white with the whiteness of death, but, with a voice in which there was scarcely a tremor, he addressed himself to the commander of the *Siva*.

"Captain, how far are we from the *Esmeralda?*"

"About a mile, sir."

"How long will it be before the explosion?"

"Twenty-two minutes, sir."

"Is there any way by which the torpedoes now fastened to her can be removed, or their explosion prevented, captain?"

"None whatever, sir."

"Captain, signal the *Esmeralda* to have riflemen in place, but not to shoot the baron unless he offers violence to his wife. Signal her also to slacken speed while we run down to her. Signal the fleet to slacken speed, and fall behind. Get out a boat with crew to put me on board the *Esmeralda*."

There was a rapid fluttering of scarlet flags from main and foretops, and the orders were obeyed.

"I will go with you, Mr. Morning," said the captain of the *Siva*.

"And so will I, and I, and I," came in chorus from a dozen officers and guests who had remained breathless auditors of the conversation.

"No," said Morning quietly, "I will go alone. I do not propose to risk a single one of these valuable lives, or this ship."

Morning picked up a coil of light rope from where it hung on a belaying pin, and descended into the boat, which, with crew in place, was now suspended a few feet from the water. "Captain," said he, "as soon as we are launched you will steam away with the *Siva*, and rejoin the fleet. The steam launch towed by the *Esmeralda* will be sufficient to provide for the safety of all. Run us as close to the *Esmeralda* as you can, captain, before you drop us," and Morning rapidly knotted a slip noose in the rope.

Clang! clang! clang! sounded the signal to reverse the engines; the *Siva* glided alongside and within three hundred feet of the *Esmeralda*, and the boat containing David Morning dropped gently into the foaming water. Clang! again went the gong, and by the time David Morning sprang up the ladder at the companion-way of the *Esmeralda*, the *Siva* was half a mile away.

As the foot of Morning touched the deck of the doomed vessel, it lacked thirteen minutes of the time set for the explosion.

"What is the situation?" said Morning to the captain of the *Esmeralda*.

"Through the skylight we can see that the baroness has evidently abandoned all effort to move the baron, and is on her knees in the corner, apparently in prayer. The baron is walking up and down the cabin floor flourishing a cocked revolver, and muttering to himself. The first officer with three gunners, each with a Winchester rifle, are at the skylight with sites drawn on the baron, anxious to fire as soon as they get the order, and six men with a piece of timber are in place, ready to burst open the cabin door. It is only twelve minutes to the blow-up, sir, and the men are getting uneasy. Shall we shoot and rescue the lady, sir?"

"Not yet, captain. Can you open the skylight from above noiselessly?"

"Yes, sir."

"Do so at once."

With his noosed rope coiled in hand, Morning approached the skylight. Often in Colorado he had, from love of sport, attended rodeos and learned the trick of the lasso. His skill with it was the admiration of the cowboys. "Kin Dave Morning handle a riata?" said one of his enthusiastic admirers to a correspondent of an Eastern newspaper. "Well, stranger, I should smile! Kin he? He kin throw his lariat a matter of forty feet around any part of a jumping steer, hoof or horn. He kin throw a bull buffalo at the head of the herd. He kin make a buckin' broncho turn two somersaults, and land him on head or heels, just as he likes. He kin stop a jacksnipe on the wing if he don't fly too high. Oh, I'm talkin' to ye, stranger! Often I've seen him, when he felt right well, throw his little lasso across the room of the big hotel at Trinidad, and smash a fly on a window pane without breaking the glass. Oh, you can laff, of course! I ain't got nothin' agin your hilarity, but if any gentleman feels inclined to doubt the entire truth of anything I've been a sayin', or has anything to say agin Dave Morning, either as a vaquero or a man, he kin get his gun ready, for my name is Buttermilk Bill from the San Juan Range."

Poising his improvised riata, Morning looked down through the open skylight. The baron, attracted by the shadow, stopped in his nervous walk and looked up. As he did so the noose dropped over his head and shoulders, and pinioned his arms to his side, and he was thrown to the floor, while the cocked pistol he held in his hand was harmlessly discharged. Like a cat, Morning dropped from the skylight upon the floor of the cabin, followed by the first officer and the gunners, all of whom proceeded—none too tenderly— to wrap and tie the rope around the arms and legs of the baron.

"Now, then," sounded the voice of the second officer outside the cabin door: "now, then, my hearties, once, twice, thrice, and away!" and, with a crash, the door flew from its hinges nearly across the cabin.

Morning half supported and half carried the baroness to the launch, which was now lying alongside with steam up, and they descended to the deck, followed by the crew and officers of the *Esmeralda* and the crew of the boat from the *Siva*.

"Where is the baron," said the baroness faintly.

The captain looked at the first officer, who made reply, "He is in the cabin, sir."

"We have still five minutes if anybody chooses to bring him aboard," said the captain.

And after a pause of a few seconds nobody stirred. Ellen looked at Morning.

And Morning leaped upon the deck of the *Esmeralda*, followed by the captain, first officer, and one of the men.

In less than a minute the Baron Von Eulaw, writhing, cursing, and foaming at the mouth, was deposited on the deck of the launch, which steamed away rapidly in a direction opposite to that taken by the doomed vessel.

There were just two minutes to spare. The wheel of the *Esmeralda* had been lashed so as to head her away from the fleet. Her chief engineer was the last man to leave the engine room, and just before he left, he pulled the lever to increase her speed, so that in the two minutes which passed after the steam launch and the *Esmeralda* separated, they were quite a mile apart.

Suddenly a dull sound like the throb of a great muffled drum was heard. An immense arch of water arose in air. Upon its summit was the *Emperor*, broken into a dozen fragments which writhed like a python twisting in the agonies of death. For a moment the broken mass of the giant flashed and scintillated in the sun, and then with a sound of sucking water—the death gurgle of the ship engulfed by the sea —each fragment went out of sight forever, and great billows of foam rolled over the spot where the mighty ship went down.

CHAPTER XXVII.

MORNING accompanied as far as Chicago the special trains containing those of the European guests whose official duties required their immediate departure, but very many, including the Baron Von Eulaw and his party, remained at Coronado.

With a good deal of effort, the episode of the baron's conduct, and the circumstances of the rescue of his wife and himself, were kept out of the press reports, yet the affair was, nevertheless, one of those open secrets with which many people enliven conversation.

Mrs. Thornton was, for once, disinclined to suffer her admiration for a title to induce her to overlook the homicidal freak of her son-in-law, and she urged Ellen in vain to formally separate her life from that of her husband. Possibly her appreciation of the fact that Morning was now more renowed than any European potentate, and outranked any king on earth, and her comprehension of the further fact that he was still deeply in love with her daughter, may have influenced her counsel.

Moved by some impulse, which perhaps she cou'd not have explained to herself, she took occasion when thanking Morning for saving her daughter's life, to confide to him the history of how Ellen's marriage

(356)

had been brought about, to which she added the story of her married life, and concluded by pressing upon him for perusal, a package of her daughter's letters. These Morning carried with him to Chicago, and their reading induced him, after parting with his distinguished guests, to hasten his return to Coronado, where he was advised that the Von Eulaw party would remain for some weeks.

On a delicious afternoon the baroness, with Mrs. Thornton and Miss Winters, sat in the gallery overhanging the old music hall on the sea. Although a new and costlier edifice had been built, with improved acoustics and elaborate design, the little gem at the corner of the hotel, long washed by the waves and threatened by the breakers, seemed still a favorite resort for concert and afternoon recitals, and thither came many who sought for a restful hour under the eloquent discourse of the old white-haired professor's violin.

"It is a pity for the world," said Miss Winters, during a pause in the performance, " that so few are able to look into the soul of Tolstoi's labors. In one of his chapters he expresses the epitome of all musical sensations in half a dozen lines."

"I hope you are not referring to the 'Kreutzer Sonata,' Miss Winters," broke in Mrs. Thornton.

Miss Winters smiled rather than spoke reply. But the baroness took greater liberty and rejoined rather saucily, "The regular thing, dear mother, is to ask for some palliative to remove the taste from your mouth after the mention of the much-abused 'Kreutzer Sonata.'"

Mrs. Thornton replied with a look of high disdain and much fluttering of ribbons.

"I am not punctilious, but I could not sit and listen to a defense of that man."

"I am not defending him, though I might, especially if he were my client," laughed Miss Winters. "I am only deploring that the world will not forgive his truths nor forget his faults in the universal power of his genius."

It was well that the next on the programme was Beethoven's seventh symphony, and that the men strolled in soon afterwards, for nothing is so prolific of enmities as the subject of Tolstoi, unless it be that of tariff.

The enchanting numbers were ended, and the ladies left the hall, the men taking another direction. At the foot of the stairway they were accosted by David Morning, who, after a greeting, turned and joined the baroness.

"When did you return?" said she, looking full into his bronzed face, and again at his traveling clothes.

"Only this moment. And how are you? and has the baron entirely recovered?"

"Completely, I believe, and for me, one could not be so ungrateful as to be ill in this place."

" I trust not," replied Morning absently.

There was silence for a moment, then, turning shortly, and looking into the handsome face of the baroness, he said, without calling her by name, but earnestly, and it may be added a little peremptorily, "I wish to have a few moments' conversation with you after dinner, if you will be good enough to consent."

"For what purpose? When? Alone?"

"Your first question let me answer later. Here, under the palms, on the beach, anywhere, but alone, certainly."

Each question was superfluous, of course, but she was gaining time. At length she answered slowly, "I could wish you had not asked me for this meeting, Mr. Morning."

"But I am going away. Will you, knowing this, still refuse?"

"I will come," she said after a pause. "We will sit here upon the veranda, after eight. The others are going, I believe, to look at the dancers."

And, thanking her, he lifted his hat and withdrew.

The halls were not ablaze on this night, for there is not light enough in the world to coax the sullen shadows from their lurking-places in a modern interior. But the arches of heaven, albeit moonless, were more obedient, and the electric scintillations searched and filled every rood of ground with their unwarm but willing light, or chased with exact pencil the willful outlines of orange and oleander, or the more tender ways of acanthus, pepper, and palm.

Morning had wheeled a luxurious easy-chair alongside of his veranda "shaker," and sat with his hands upon the upholstered back, waiting for the one woman in the world to him, while the promenaders, in full evening toilet, filed in pairs along the thronged corridors, and the soft strains of "La Paloma" floated down from the balcony and mingled with the plash of the sea.

"Engaged," spoke Morning curtly, as a youthful

lord, accompanying the British delegation, attempted to move the fauteuil aside.

"Beg pardon, I wish I were," retorted the scion of a noble house, striding away with the fair one upon his arm.

"There is hope for that fellow," Morning muttered.

"I left the baron to be taken to his room by his valet," explained the baroness approaching. "He is a little tired and nervous," and she loosened the lace about her throat impatiently.

"Yes," dryly, was the only comment.

"He said he might get around here before he retired. I hope you would not mind, he is so very capricious, you don't know."

"Oh, no, I don't mind, but if he comes I am going, for I 'don't mind' saying also I've had enough of that fellow!"

The baroness looked up with surprise, but Morning went on excitedly:—

"Oh, I know I ought not to say this to you, but I must say it, and a great deal more, unless you stop me! I say you are in deadly terror of that man, and you hate him beside, as you ought."

"How can you—who told you this? Surely you are assuming—"

"No, pardon me, I am assuming nothing. I read your letters."

"Who gave you my letters?" asked the baroness in amazement.

"Your mother urged them upon me, and I was disloyal enough to read them, every line," a little triumphantly. He arose hastily and walked away for a few paces, drying and fanning his face with his handkerchief, then, returning, he leaned upon the back of her chair, and, dropping his voice, said huskily, and with quite uncontrollable emotion:—

"Ellen—let me call you so this once, it remains with you whether I ever utter the name again—dear Ellen, answer this from your own sweet lips, have you a spark of love for that beas—man?" correcting himself too late. "I know how capricious the heart of a woman is, and perhaps—but no! take your time to answer, only give me your word," and he walked swiftly away, and looked out on the sea, and saw the waves beat their soft white arms upon the sands, then returned.

The woman had turned to ashen paleness. The ever-repeating and distributing electric light had forgotten the delicate tints of her dainty gown, and the color of her hair and brows, with the roses upon her bosom, and only the waxen face, with its dark eyes filled with glistening tears, uprose whiter than the beams.

"Poor heart!" said he, noting the quiver of the sensitive mouth. "It ought not to be so difficult to speak the truth."

At length the tortured woman found voice:—

"David Morning," she said, in tremulous tones, "I am not meaning to question your right to give challenge to my despair, though, for reasons you can understand, it is from you, more than from all the world, I would have disguised it. You ask me if I love that man? I answer, No, no, a thousand times no! But my sense of obligation as his wife is as much stronger than my hate as misery is stronger than the social bars which contain it, and I deem it neither noble nor just to utter complaints against one who is, whatever may be said, my legal protector before the world. I do not deny that I have suffered untold agonies, but I may as well bear them in one cause as another.''

"I confess," said Morning, with a manner suddenly grown cold, " I do not fully understand you. You speak of ' obligations,' and ' social bars;' you cannot mean that you would deliberately sacrifice your woman's soul, with all its honor and its aims, to a life of dishonor and deceit—for so I dare to name it—for dread of the idle dictum of a malicious social scarecrow?''

The baroness winced, but quickly rallied, and, leaning forward in her chair, so near that he caught the perfume of the roses on her corsage, she replied:—

"No! though I will say in passing that, whatever I might do, no woman, be she termagant or angel, has ever lived long enough to escape the opprobrium arising from the poisonous effluvia of the divorce courts! However, that is not the subject under discussion, and my unhappy feet are placed upon more tenable ground. I confess myself, then, not strong enough to defy the convictions of a life given much—the maturer portion, at least—to an examination of the ethics of the question. And I resolutely affirm that, in my own mind, I am convinced that to seek to evade the results of my own deliberate action, would be sinful, and in violation of my own conscientious perceptions—'a grieving of the Spirit,' in the language of a very old author, and, therefore, a sin against the Holy Ghost.''

Is it possible, thought Morning, forgetful for the moment of the purpose that had brought him there, that in this evening of the nineteenth century a cultivated woman, herself the victim of a system fiendish in its power to forge public opinion, and cruel as the Inquisition, should have the courage thus to look her awful destiny in the face tranquilly, and smilingly set upon it the cold white seal of conscience? And for a brief moment he wondered if she were a saint or a lunatic.

Then he thought of the many shafts of argument that might be let loose to pierce the diseased cuticle of her morbid philosophy, but he had not the heart, or, rather, he lacked entire faith in their efficacy, so he sat silently counting his heart beats. Finally, taking alarm at his protracted silence, she resumed:—

"Do not misunderstand me; I am not narrow enough to convict, or egotist enough to try to convert, others to my way of thinking; I only speak for myself.''

"Your missionary seed would fall upon stony ground if you were so disposed,'' he answered quickly, almost rudely. "Ellen Thornton,'' he continued, ignoring the hateful title that seemed to have engulfed her body and soul for all of him, ''for thirteen years fate has been circumventing our lives. I have heard your name over seas as you have heard mine, familiar to all but each other. I have loved you with hope and without it. Great wealth has been my portion, yet I would be a beggar to-night if you would but share my crust with me, with love like mine.''

Into the eyes of the woman, fierce with resolution and despair, there came tears, half of pity, half of joy—pity for his fate and hers, joy for that the love she had deemed lost and gone from their lives was here, tireless and strong as the sea, immortal and sweet as the morning, and the voice of the man whose head was bent near her own thrilled her with its music.

"During all the years of parting," continued Morning, "I have been neither despairing nor misanthropic, but I knew that the passion of my life had glowed and burned, and—as I thought—died to ashes upon the altar whose goddess was the dark-eyed maiden whom my young manhood adored. When, less than a fortnight ago, I was able to deliver you from the awful death that madman would have inflicted upon you, my exultation had but one sting, that I had saved you for another, and for such a fate; and then, in my insane rage, I cursed myself that I had not let you die under my dizzy eyes, and so have rounded my despair.

"But I have come near to you now, our paths have crossed. O God, how I have waited for the hour! and how can I let you go? If I do, our ways will again diverge, and every remove will bring us farther apart. Do you know what this means to me? It is the dividing of my soul from my body, of my heart from my brain; it means a galvanized life, a career of eviscerated motives, a gibbering, masquerading existence, emasculate of manly and fruitful purpose, a hopeless love"— and his voice trembled and sank—"ashes and dust and nothing more."

The baroness listened with passion tearing at her heart, while her white lips were fashioning words of wise restraint. Could she trust herself to speak? She envied in her soul the women she had known abroad, women of convictions, with uncoddled consciences, charming, virtuous women too, but without the monitor to guide the wayward thought, a sky without a polar star, a ship without a rudder, and then she recalled the burning words of the man beside her.

"I know," said she at length, "that I owe you my life, and, in the logic of natural sequence, I should give back that which you won. But it is love's sophistry, and, in truth, perhaps for no better reason than because I so much desire it, I dare not. One phase of your argument pricks my conscience in turn. You tell me that your usefulness must pay the penalty of my decision. Unsay those words, I entreat you"— and she leaned far toward him. "God has singled you out for a great destiny. Fulfill it. You have the world at your feet; let that suffice you for the present. I do not ask you to forget me!"—and her lips grew tremulous. "I should die if I thought you could. But work on, as you have been doing, for the sake of humanity, and wait heroically, as you have done."

"Wait for what? for somebody to die?" broke in Morning hotly. "For somebody to die, that is the English of it. Most lives are made what they are by some woman. She may be a mother, a sister not likely. Since I received that long-lost letter—anathemas upon that circular desk," and he pounded the "shaker" arm with his fist—"I have had but one inspiration in my projects, one question always ringing in my ears,—'What will she think of it?' Now I have found you only to hear from your own lips that my life is a failure, and yours a moral suicide, which I seem as helpless to prevent as I am to put a stay upon yonder waves that lash themselves to spray upon the rocks.''

''David Morning,'' and her voice was firm now, I think I owe it to you as well as myself to tell you, even with the marriage ring upon my finger, that I wish I were free from the yoke of this fateful marriage; that if I could be delivered from the body of this death, then could I mount with glad wings the great height to which your love would raise me. But I could have no weight of a crying conscience upon my feet, no wail of wounded justice behind me, and so I will bear it to the end.''

''You say, even with that marriage ring upon your finger. What care I,'' said he, rising and standing before her, ''for that circlet of gold upon your beautiful hand? I know it is a mockery, so do you, and but for it that hand might have been mine, and all these years have been saved to love and the heart's gladness. What signifies the sanction of the law if you have not the sanction of your own soul? I shall not seek to dissuade you more, but one question I will ask of you, and if wealth could buy words eloquent enough to couch it in, I would surrender my possessions and delve for it again, if need be, in the depths of the earth. But truth is simple, and so I beg of you to answer from your soul, and thereafter I will do as you bid me. Do you love me, darling? do you?'' and he bent over her chair.

She lifted a face radiant with beautiful light. "Dearest," said she softly, and David Morning thrilled with delight—"dearest, I am glad that this meeting and this understanding have come to us just here, where hundreds of eyes are upon us, for, if it were otherwise, I should forget all else except my desire to comfort you, and should place my arms about your neck, and ask you to seal upon my lips your forgiveness of me for all that I have made you suffer. God help me, I do love you, and I never loved any other. You are my hero, my darling, and my heart's delight. All these years I have loved you, until the hour of death I shall love you, and beyond the gates I shall love you forever, and forever more."

Only a great sob came from the breast of David Morning.

"Noble man," she continued, "you have accomplished a great work in the world. God has selected and armed you for the deliverance of his nations. You have other and greater work to do. In the doing it the luster of your shield shall never be tarnished, as it would be were we to wrong another now. Go forth, my hero, my life, and my darling; go forth panoplied in your high manhood to your duty. In spirit I shall be with you ever. I shall rejoice in your mighty deeds. I shall live in your nobler thoughts. Day and night, my beloved, will my soul dwell with yours. Only in perfect honor and faith can I join you. If the hour for such union shall ever be given to us on earth, come to me and you will find me waiting. If it come only in the other land, I shall still be waiting. But here, my darling, my own, my heart's solace, here we must meet not again."

And she placed her ungloved fingers in his.

The man and the woman sat silently hand in hand. The music floated out from the lighted ballroom, where "the dancers were dancing in tune;" the sea curled its beryl depths to crests of foam, and sounded in musical monotones upon the beach which lay a white line upon the edge of the dusk, and the old, old world, the sorrowful, disappointing world, the weary world, was as sweet and young as when the first dawns were filtrated from chaotic mists.

She broke the silence and withdrew her hand: "Yonder comes the baron."

"Good-by," said he, and he walked away into the night, and as he reached the edge of the balcony overhanging the beach, and felt the sting of the salt spray in his eyes, he muttered something. It might have been a good-night prayer, but it sounded like, "Damn the baron."

[From the San Diego *Union*, May 15, 1896.]

We regret to announce the death yesterday, at the Coronado Hotel, of Baron Frederick Augustus Eulaw Von Eulaw, eleventh Count of Walderberg, eighth Baron of Weinerstrath, and Knight Commander of the order of the Golden Tulip.

The immediate cause of the baron's death was hyperemia of the brain, but he never recovered from the nervous prostration induced by heat and long exposure to the sun, while in the performance of his duty as one of the representatives of the German Empire, on the occasion of the dynamic exposition.

This distinguished nobleman, during his brief sojourn among us, had endeared himself to all with whom he came in contact, by the gentleness and grace of his manner, his kindly sympathies, and unselfish courtesy. The *Wilhelm II.* has been detailed to receive his remains, which will be embalmed for transportation in state to Berlin, where they will be interred with fitting pomp.

The baroness, who to the last was devoted in her attentions to the late baron, will, it is understood, remain in this country in the home of her parents, Professor and Mrs. John Thornton.

CHAPTER XXVIII.

"All's well that ends well."

IT was a lovely morning in June, in the year of our
Lord eighteen hundred and ninety-seven, when a carriage containing a red-headed and red-bearded man
drove rapidly down upon Pier No. 2, North River,
where the occupant emerged from the equipage, and,
elbowing his way through the throng, approached the
gangway of an immense steamer gaily decorated with
flags of all nations.

He was stopped by two officials in uniform, one of
them saying civilly that no strangers were allowed on
board.

"Is not this Mr. Morning's steam yacht the *Patience?*" said the stranger.

"Yes, sir, if the largest and finest vessel in the
world can be called a yacht. Certainly this is Mr.
Morning's ship."

"I was told at the hotel that he would sail to-day for
Europe."

"Your information is quite correct; he goes as one
of the three delegates appointed by the President to
represent the United States at the Congress of Nations,
which will meet in Paris next month."

"Well, I want to see him before he sails," replied
the stranger.

(370)

" It is too late, sir, even if you had a card of admission. His friends are now bidding good-by to the bridal party, and in a few minutes the order will be issued of 'all ashore.' "

" Bridal party? Whose? Not Morning's ?"

" Haven't you heard of it? Why, the papers have been full of it for days. He was married yesterday, in Boston, to the Baroness Von Eulaw."

"Well," said the stranger, "I only arrived this morning from Arizona. I am the superintendent of his mine there, and am here on business of importance. He will be mightily disappointed if I don't see him. Suppose you send word to him that Bob Steel is here and wants to see him before he sails. I reckon he'll give orders to admit me."

The request of Steel was complied with, and directions given for his admittance. After exchanging greetings with Morning and being presented to the bride, Steel stated that he had business of importance to communicate. The whistle had sounded "all ashore," and the guests were rapidly departing. Morning quietly instructed the captain not to have the lines cast off until he should have finished his interview with Steel, and then, summoning the latter to follow him into a private salon, said:—

" Well, Bob, what is it ? "

"Mr. Morning," replied Steel, "the news ain't good, but it is so important I did not dare to trust to mail or wire, so I left the mine in charge of Mr. Fabian, and came on myself. We didn't find no ore last month on the new level at two hundred feet, and I set three shifts to work at every station, and—I'm afraid to tell you the result."

"Out with it, Bob. I was married yesterday, and you can't tell me any news bad enough to hurt me much."

"Well, Mr. Morning, there ain't no ore in the mine below the one hundred and fifty feet level. *The quartz has come to an end.* We are at the bed rock, and the syenite is as solid and close-grained as the basalt wall where we did our first work, you and I, blasting with the Papago Indians."

Morning whistled. "How much do we lack, Bob, of the $2,400,000,000 I donated to the United States?"

"About eight hundred millions, sir; but there is more than enough ore not stoped out in the upper levels to pay that twice over. We have seventeen hundred millions at least."

"That," said Morning, "will finish the payment to the government, complete all the enterprises I have projected, give you ten millions, and all the men who have stood by us from the start half a million each. It will serve also to make some donations I have in mind, and will leave over six hundred millions for the Morning family. It is not so much money now as it was when I made the discovery, but it will keep the wolf from the door. Bob, the whistles are sounding and I shall have to bid you good-by and send you ashore. There is no possibility, I suppose, of this being only a break, or a horse? No chance of the ore coming in again lower down?"

"None in the world, Mr. Morning. In that formation it is impossible. The Morning mine, as a mine, has *petered!*

"Bob," said our hero, extending his hand with a smile, "put it there!"

And Robert Steel and David Morning clasped hands with the clasp of men.

"Bob," said Morning, "on my soul I am glad of it. The problem of overproduction of gold will no longer vex the world, and now I shall have a chance to pass a few hours in quiet with my wife."

9 783743 373440